CHUCK WENDIG

THE HARVEST

THE HEARTLAND
TRILOGY
BOOK III

SKYSCAPE

SKYSCAPE

Published by Skyscape, New York

www.apub.com

Amazon, the Amazon logo, and Skyscape are trademarks of Amazon.com, Inc., or its affiliates.

ISBN-13: 9781477830017 (hardcover)
ISBN-10: 1477830014 (hardcover)
ISBN-13: 9781477830024 (paperback)
ISBN-10: 1477830022 (paperback)

Cover artwork © 2015 by Shane Rebenschied
Book design by Sammy Yuen and Susan Gerber

Printed in the United States of America

To the folks on the ground looking up at the sky

CONTENTS

PROLOGUE

ONE YEAR AGO

CAEL FALLS TO THE HARD EARTH.

And the hard earth catches him.

Wanda stands vigil over the dead corn, and the Blighted stand vigil over her. They hover in the background, a semicircle of shifting, moaning men and women, their flesh given over to leaves and vines and roots.

She knows that she isn't to leave. Nobody's said as much to her, but she understands this. It's okay. She's not going anywhere.

The sun goes up and the sun goes down, and still Wanda remains. Somewhere she's aware of hunger and thirst, but those urges feel like they belong to someone else. She shakes sometimes in the wind, quaking like the stalks of corn do. It occurs to her, almost absurdly, how she must look like just another stalk: thin, reedy, quaking, whispering.

And then, as the sun begins to slide back down behind the Heartland, she hears the cracking of corn.

The Maize Witch is returning.

Wanda's guts tighten the way a noose tightens around a condemned man's neck. The witch, Esther, will be returning with what Wanda knows will be Cael McAvoy's body. The woman told her: *Cael was there. On the flotilla.*

How do you know? Wanda asked her.

I just know.

Is he okay?

No. He's hurt. And he is dying.

Please, I want to go to him—

You stay. I will go to him.

Now the corn shudders and cracks. It turns violently away as a path is drawn through the stalks—as if invisible hands turn the dead spears of Hiram's Golden Prolific into corkscrews and splinters.

The path is made, and the Maize Witch walks.

Behind her walk her two . . . Wanda doesn't even know what they are. Servants. Slaves. Soldiers. The bald woman. The man in the ratty coat. Skin studded with thorns. Tongues of rose petals. Eyes like fruit ready to burst. The witch's Blightborn.

In their arms is Cael.

Wanda breaks and runs toward them. The other Blighted move to stop her, but Esther gives a slight shake of her head and they halt, then recede.

The two Blightborn set Cael down and she drops to her knees. He looks bruised, beaten, run through a laundry wringer. He looks *broken*. Limbs going the wrong way. A gash slashed across his brow—a deep gash, too deep, a gash that shows a glimpse of bone through the blood and hair. Wanda hears the babble rise up out of her—"No, no, no, Cael, I'm sorry, I'm sorry, I'm sorry I hit you, I'm sorry I didn't stand by you—" He's dead. He's just a corpse, a mangled body where the soul has gone into the hands of Jeezum Crow, taken back up to the manse of the Lady and the Lord—

But then Cael coughs. A hard, sharp cough. His lips fleck red with dots of dark blood. His chest rises with a keening wheeze and then he quiets anew.

"He's alive," the Maize Witch says, kneeling by Wanda in a move so swift and so silent that the girl didn't even sense it until it happened. "Your love will not save him, but mine can. Let me save him."

"Please. Anything. *Please.*"

The Blightborn pick Cael up, and they move toward the house.

"Fix him," Wanda says to the witch.

And the witch nods. "I will do what I must."

"Will you go home, or will you remain?"

That question jars Wanda from sleep. She awakens with a gasp, pried forcibly from a dream where something was stuck in her throat, some piece of food, a *good* piece of food, too, like a mouthful of ham hock or a bite of an apple. Her body lurches upright (her stomach growling, that betrayer), and there stands Esther, the Maize Witch.

It was she who asked the question, and she asks it again.

"Will you go home . . . or will you remain?"

"I . . . I can't go home." Her voice is a goaty bleat. She tastes bile. Her eyes feel tired, stinging from crying. They brought Cael in here last night and took him upstairs, and she fell on the couch in this ruined room—the remains of Boyland's yacht pulled out, the gap fixed only by a ragged mesh of vines and roots—and there Wanda wept until she slept.

"You love Cael."

"I do. We're Obligated."

"Then stay. You're welcome to. But staying comes with a cost. You'll need to work."

"Anything."

Esther nods. "Do you want to see him?"

He's alive. "I do."

The witch offers her hand, and Wanda takes it.

They go out to the garden. A crumbling path, stones pushed up by stubborn, shoving roots. Shrubs of red berries, green peppers hanging, the boughs of a tree overhead heavy with pink fruit that she's never even seen—

And then, at the center of the garden, another kind of tree.

A tree that is not a tree.

Thrust up out of the earth, a braid of brown, flaking vine. It spirals up, ten feet, maybe higher. At the top those vines splay out like a cradling hand, and in the center of this tree-that-is-not-a-tree is a gnarled ball of thriving green roots. Bundled like a skein of yarn. It seems to throb and shift.

"That is Cael," the witch says.

"I . . . I don't understand—"

The woman points to the sky. "He fell. From the heavens.

From the Empyrean tower back down to our land of pain and dirt. The city, the Saranyu flotilla, breaking apart around him. Even if one *could* survive that fall, he was battered by debris, pummeled and broken. And yet—he did survive. He fell and the corn reached up to meet him. It reached up like a hand and caught him—that's how I found him. Broken, twisted corn forming a shape that looked much like this one. He willed it to happen. The corn didn't save him because it has a mind of its own—the corn saved him because it had *his* mind."

"But why . . . why this?"

"Because he survived, but he is still broken. His life is not guaranteed. He could still die. His bones are broken. His innards crushed. Even *if* he survives, it remains to be seen the quality of the life that continues."

Wanda chokes back a sob.

"This is a chrysalis. We will see what emerges."

"How long? Wh-when will I know?"

Esther says nothing at first. A pause, as if she's considering how to answer. "It could be ten days. It could be ten years. It may never be."

Wanda wants to close her eyes and go back to sleep, but she can't. She can't even blink. All she can do is stare at the strange shape of the not-tree in front of her, a tangled hand holding her Obligated.

Cael, please.

It's then she decides.

It's then she *knows.*

"The people here . . . you . . ." Wanda says. "You're all Blighted."

"We're all gifted. This is no Blight. We are bound to a life force greater than our own. To the oldest gods of grass and soil, of fig and vine."

Wanda swallows hard, finds the words hard to say—so much so that she can't say them at first; they come out as an awkward croak. But then she stills herself, draws a deep breath, and tries again:

"I want to be like you."

"Do you?"

"I want to be Bl— I want to be gifted."

"Why?"

"Because I want to understand Cael. I want to share this with him. I want to . . . feel him." That last bit makes her blush, and she doesn't mean it that way, so she corrects: "I want to feel *like* him."

Esther nods.

"It won't be easy."

"I don't care."

"It may be painful."

"I *don't* care."

"Good. Then I will accommodate this desire."

The Maize Witch smiles.

PART ONE

OBLIGATED

SEEDLING

CAEL DREAMS NOT OF FALLING, but of having fallen. He dreams of the corn cracking like gunshots. Leaves twirling, stretching, growing. Reaching up as he falls down and catching him. Same way a hand catches a thrown stone.

That dream lingers with him like a smell that won't go away—whenever he had to deal with Nancy the goat, her smell always stuck to him, too, and this is like that. He staggers up onto the Maize Witch's front porch in the middle of the night, but he keeps closing his eyes (tired, so tired), and whenever he does, the dream rises up again: falling, reaching, bleeding, being caught, breaking apart.

Falling, reaching, bleeding, being caught, breaking apart.

Again and again.

He enters through the front of the house. All of it has been repaired—loosely, clumsily, but with boards and not just with plant matter. No new paint, though—just bald, exposed boards,

held there with crooked nails. Everything else looks the same: vines hanging down through holes in the ceiling, shoots growing up through cracks in the floorboards. Water stains on the walls. The heady stink in the air of mulch and compost and life unbidden.

In the middle of the room, a couch. Beyond that, a wall and a mantel and a—a mirror. Old, corroded, streaked with bands of dark stain, but a mirror just the same, and so Cael hurries over to it—

Lord and Lady, no.

The Blight. *The Blight.*

It's taken over. It has *claimed* him.

He tries to cry out, but all he manages is a choked, truncated scream.

His teeth are rose-thorns. His lips, pink petals rolled up like Lane's ditchweed cigarettes. As he weeps, a glossy leaf emerges from the dark hollow of his throat—his tongue, oh, Jeezum Crow, *it's his damn tongue.* Half his face is scaled like tree bark, the other half smooth like the branches of a pricker bush. One eye is a fat, swollen cherry tomato, the other an opalescent seed-pod with little black motes swimming around inside. He reaches up with branch-tip fingers to touch his face, and one scrapes across an eye, poking it, and the cherry tomato splits and ruptures with an audible *pop*—seedy snot runs down his cheek, loosed from inside the eyeball, some of it spattering the mirror—

Cael screams.

"Cael. *Cael.* Cael!"

A hand shaking him. He gasps. The scream cut in half.

It's Wanda.

He gasps again. Sees himself. He's him. Just him. No ruined eye, no thorn-tine teeth, no tongue-of-a-leaf. Still the Blight-vine at the end of his arm, coiled back upon it, but that—and here he almost has to laugh at the absurdity of it—*that* is normal, that is who he was before he came here.

The rest was—what? Just a dream? A nightmare?

A promise of what's to come?

The wind sucks right from his sails, and he almost falls—

But Wanda catches him, helps him over to the couch. She laughs the kind of desperate laugh that comes from somebody who thought it had all been lost, from someone pulled back from the edge—and she holds his hands in her own, and he can see her eyes glistening (though to her credit, she does not cry).

Then she kisses him.

He leans into it. Her lips feel good. Everything about it feels good—the way their faces fit together, the soft intake of breath through their noses, her hands reaching up to cup his jaw, his cheeks. She smells nice—like strawberries. Fresh ones, too.

Her mouth opens, just slightly. So does his. She moans into him.

And then he feels something. A tongue, he thinks—soft, wriggling, just a little bit rough to the touch.

This isn't that.

It's a leaf. Like the one from his . . . dream, promise, hallucination?

It slides across his tongue. Smooth-surfaced and crisply edged.

He pulls away.

She gasps. For a moment, a small string of saliva connects

them, and she laughs. "I've been waiting a long time for this," she says.

"I-I . . . You've . . ." he stammers. Wanda clasps his hands. Two of her fingernails—leaves, also shiny—catch the electric light of the bare bulb overhead. "You're Blighted."

"I'm gifted," she says, her smile small, hesitant. "Like you."

He pulls away. "Wanda, oh no. Aw, King Hell."

She stands suddenly. In another lifetime, he'd know what would happen: She'd cry and run off. But that's not what happens this time. Here, now, all she does is stand, smile again, and nod.

"It's okay" is her response. "You'll understand soon. I'll go get Mother."

Esther sits across from him as he eats. Wanda stands behind her, arms crossed, watching him intently. *Wanda. Blighted. Lord and Lady, why?*

He doesn't want to eat, he wants to hold out and demand answers, but he's famished. It wasn't even something he was aware of until Esther asked him—"Are you hungry?"—and then everything inside him felt like a hungry, sucking bottomless hole that could never fill up no matter how many of these fruits and vegetables and leafy greens he shoves in his dang mouth.

And yet, he doesn't stop.

Blackberry juices running down his chin. Green pepper crunching between molars. Tongue licking leafy bits from the fronts of his teeth.

He sometimes has to pause and grip the sides of the small

table. Not even sure why. Just to hold on to something. To try to tamp it all down.

Finally, he stops. He knows he can't eat anymore—even though, gods, he still wants to. He leans back, gasping.

"I want to know what's going on," he says.

Esther nods. "You've been . . . away from us for some time."

"Away. What? For—what do you mean? Time? How much time?"

But they don't answer. Esther and Wanda just share a look— a conspiratorial connection that, for now, fails to include him. *Shit.* Instead, Esther says, "We'll get there, Cael." Green tendrils curl and uncurl from the tips of her fingers splayed out on the table. Fiddleheads opening, closing.

"I want to know."

"You should rest."

"I don't *want* to rest."

"What do you want to do?" It's like she can sense it.

He says it without thinking: "I want to run."

"So," she says, "go. Run."

The dead corn is thick out here. Thick as the bristles on a boot brush. Cael growls and pushes through, stalks thwacking him across the head and neck and arms, leaves—still sharp, even dead—cutting into him. His feet pound on hard black earth, and somewhere he realizes—

The corn isn't dead. Not really. He can feel something still there. Some mote of life swirling around. Hundreds of motes, thousands, each a fading firefly, each bound to a single stalk of corn—the light dying but not extinguished. He runs through it, feeling these tiny life sources as he passes them, aware of them in a way that goes beyond sight and sound. And still the corn continues to batter him. It pisses him off. A hot fire churns in his gut. A new thread of hunger unspools through him, and he roars and keeps on running—

He makes an ax-blade shape out of his hand, swipes across the corn—

And a wave of corn ahead of him flattens to the ground. Ten feet in a wide arc, crackling and hissing as it mashes to the dirt.

Corn he never touched.

He skids to a halt. It was like a sonic blast, invisible but real.

His own Blight-vine tightens around his arm. As if in anticipation.

As if it's excited.

Is the Blight a life all its own?

Or is it just me?

Is the excitement mine and not the corn's?

He growls, then sweeps his arm out again—and more corn splinter-snaps. Pushed down, matted together like a corn-leaf doormat. Cael does it again and again, roaring and screaming until he's the center of a circular clearing, the corn pushed away from him in every direction.

And then he grits his teeth.

He can still feel it out there. The corn. Living, not dead.

He closes his eyes.

He concentrates, thinking so hard he's afraid he'll piss himself.

The sound greets him—the rustle-hiss of the corn. All around him. That sound rises in volume until it's a deafening roar. . . .

Then it stops. All at once.

When he opens his eyes—

All the corn has stood back up. Battered. Crooked. Shuddering like a shorn sheep in a cold wind. But standing tall once more.

What in King Hell have I become?

The morning sun is up now. And Cael can see how things have changed at Esther's. The Maize Witch has been busy. Her little commune has grown. When Cael left for his run, he didn't stop to look around—he just blasted into the bleak field, feet carrying him into the stalks with no intention but to run, maybe somewhere, maybe nowhere, definitely *away*.

And yet now he returns, and he sees how busy she's been.

Other smaller houses are going up at the edges. Little huts and lean-tos. The garden has grown, too, upward and outward. Other Blighted mill about. A woman with hair like long, knotty tangles of moss. A man with tree-root feet. A pair of young children, not yet teenagers, running around, their fingers intertwined, handfasted with coils of vine and leaf.

As Cael passes, they all, without exception, stop to stare. Not as if he's a freak, but as if he's something special. The look on those faces: What is that?

They're not scared of him.

They *love* him.

He shudders.

On the way back inside the house, he sees a familiar face—

Mole, from Boyland's crew. He chews on a stick. The boy's other arm hangs at his side, limp and crooked. "Hey, McAvoy."

"Mole. I didn't know you were here."

"Well, I am." The boy's lip curls up in a sneer.

Cael struggles to find something to say.

Mole speaks instead. "They all think you're real neat. But I remember you from Boxelder. You were a punk." It's now Cael hears the faint cracking in the boy's voice—his time is almost on him, the time when he'll move from being just a boy to being something close to a man. "And I'd bet all the ace notes that you're still a punk. Wanda thinks you're the rat's right foot, but I know you ain't. You mess with her, I'll getcha."

"All right." Cael almost laughs. "Nice talkin' to you, Mole."

Mole nods and heads past, staring daggers as he does.

What in all the Heartland is going on?

Dinner.

Long table heaped with mounds of food.

And this time, not all fruits and vegetables, either.

Cael smells meat.

Edvard—one of Esther's attendants, now out of his ratty patchwork coat and wearing instead a plain, rumpled white shirt with ivory buttons—pushes a ceramic crock toward him. "Rabbit," he says. "Braised in its own juices. Broth a mirepoix—onion, carrot, celery. And that"—he points to an oval plate with a few chips in the glaze—"is a plate of crispy sweetbreads."

The bald woman with the half-scale face must have seen the confused look that crossed Cael's own, and she adds: "Not actual bread, Cael. Offal. Thymus gland of a fatted calf."

It occurs to him that his lips are slick—Jeezum Crow, he's about to start drooling like a mutt. He quick wipes at his mouth with the back of his hand, but everyone must know what's happening because they all laugh. Politely enough, but he still feels shame rising pink in his cheeks.

Wanda, sitting to his left, reaches out to him, her hand on his. He can feel her—not just the skin on skin, but something deeper. That same kind of firefly mote he felt inside the corn, except with her it's not just a firefly, but a bonfire roaring. Not just a lightning bug, but a sky *filled* with lightning. A million points of light inside her. The Blight. And again he wonders: *Is the Blight separate from her, or a part of her?* Cael doesn't know.

"It's okay," she whispers to him. "I can feel you, too."

He pulls his hand back but tries to smile to cover it up. It feels fake. He knows that. Everything feels off-kilter. Like maybe he's still in a dream. Except he's sure—well, *pretty* sure—that's not true.

He turns toward Esther, sitting at the far end of the long table. He can feel her, too, and if Wanda contains a bonfire, Esther contains ten times the heat and the light. She's a house on fire, a whole cornfield—hell, she's all the world, burning so bright that the dark never settles, that the night becomes a memory, a myth.

And then Esther speaks. When she does, his sense of her closes down, shuts off. The light doesn't go out, but he stops seeing it.

"We should eat," she says.

And so they eat.

Cael goes for the meat.

The rabbit is so tender it falls apart in his mouth. Almost like it becomes one with the broth in which it sits. And the sweet-breads are, as the name advertises, genuinely sweet. An outer crunch gives way to a soft but firm interior, and it's salty, too, and just *off-tasting* enough that it's appealing in some way he can't quite understand. The wildness of it calls to something deep within him.

This is the kind of food he figures sits on the table at the Lord and Lady's manse, ever-replenishing itself.

He has to steady himself. He's almost drunk on the food.

And just as he hits that point, the bald woman—Siobhan—goes to a small wooden sidebar and pulls out a bottle of red wine. She uncorks it with her teeth, follows this with a wink, and begins to pour glasses for everyone. And soon everyone is drinking and eating, and mostly it's Esther, Edvard, and Siobhan talking about simple things: how the new "settlers" are acclimating to life here at the farm, how they've cleared a few more plots and are going to build something called a "longhouse," how they have a lead on a few more calves . . .

"You have cows?" Cael asks suddenly.

Esther nods. "And a goat."

"And a dozen chickens," Siobhan adds.

"Amazing what good food does for the animals," Esther says.

Edvard jumps in: "The rabbit was one I found in our garden. I let him eat for a time. Saw that he had a little . . . wife and a nest of baby rabbits, too."

"Kits," Siobhan interrupts. "A *litter* of rabbit *kits*."

Edvard shrugs it off. "I care not what they're called, I only care that this little Ryukyu left behind a rabbit legacy. Then I felt comfortable putting an arrow through his eye." He mimes pulling back a bowstring.

"Minimal technology," Esther says. "A life predicated on the natural rhythms of living with and for the Heartland. For the whole world."

Cael barely knows what she's saying. The red wine is doing its part, pulling apart his mind like hot, warm monkey-bread. "You said you had a goat. I had a goat. We. My family." His words feel like they're melting in his mouth. Then he says, without thinking: "I want to go home."

He feels dumb for uttering it. It's a childish thing to say. And the way he said it, too: a plea from a mopey little boy. Shit.

But no one laughs this time.

Everyone gets quiet.

"You don't have a home anymore," Esther says.

"Boxelder is gone," Wanda adds. Again, a Wanda different from the one he knows manifests: In an earlier life, Wanda wouldn't even be able to *say* those three words without her voice cracking and tears spilling. But she says them now, chin up, out. Grief is in there, but it's contained. Kept in its cup instead of poured over everything and everyone.

"I don't understand," Cael says.

"The Empyrean took it over," Esther explains. "After the Saranyu fell, the clampdown started with Boxelder. They had advanced notice, so some of the townsfolk escaped. Others stayed and . . ."

"They're not human anymore," Wanda says. There, that time, a hitch in her voice, a grief-struck hiccup. Cael's glad to hear it. Not because he likes her sorrow, but because in it, he still recognizes Wanda. "They've been changed."

"Changed? I don't understand."

"They're mechanicals now," Esther says. "Encased in machine. Humanoid motorvators driven by their former minds but controlled by the Empyrean. A more *effective* worker. They tend the corn without any of that . . ."

"Disagreeable humanity?" Siobhan says.

"Mm." Esther nods. "Metal men do not rebel."

"Godsdamn," Cael says. The wine and the news form a one-two punch. "You're joking, right? Playing a prank on me, the drunk fool?" But the stares around the table tell him differently. He looks to Wanda. "Your family?"

She only says, "I don't know."

"When did this happen? How . . . long ago? How long was I—"

"Just over a year," Esther says.

"A year." His stomach does an internal belly flop. Everything tingles. Sweat beads on his brow like condensation on a glass. He tries to say something else, but his mouth is all cotton, and next thing he knows, he's falling off his chair, hands catching him, knees cracking against the floor. The vine around his arm uncoils, lies slack—

He pukes.

BLOOD MAKES
THE GRASS GROW

HIS MOUTH TASTES of dead rabbit. And stomach acid. His cheeks puff out as he exhales a regretful, embarrassed breath.

The room Esther gave to Cael is upstairs, in the back corner. A small room with wallpaper that once held bold stripes but whose dark lines are now faded and washed out—and peeling anyway. Great strips of it, like sunburned skin curling away from the flesh underneath.

It's Wanda who stops by first. Asks him how he's doing. Sits next to him and pulls his hand to her lap and strokes it. Then dances her fingers on the back of his neck, sending chills in both directions—down to his tailbone and up to the back of his head. His body tingles, skin gone to plucked chicken skin.

Cael sits on the bed.

"You okay?" she asks.

"I seem okay?"

"Point taken."

"*You* seem awful okay with everything."

"I'm a long ways from okay," she says. "A whole Heartland away from it. Everything's different now. Everything's gone all strange and slippery." She shrugs. "But I'm getting there. This is my place now. And I think it's yours, too."

"I dunno, Wanda. I think . . . I think I need to go. Find my friends. Find Pop. I mean, dang, don't you wanna find your family? Maybe they're okay. Hell, maybe that dog of yours is still out there, nosing crotches like a champ."

She laughs, and he does, too—the pressure, vented, if only a little. But then she says: "To what end? What happens if I find them? We run away together. Probably die together—and a whole lot sooner than any of us would've hoped for. Not much use in that. We can be useful here. We can change things with the gifts we've been given." She places his hand on her knee. "Besides, Cael, we're family now."

"We're Obligated, but not yet married."

She leans her head on his shoulder. "No, but we will be soon."

Before he can say anything, she's standing back up. "Mother Esther wants to say some things to you. Talk about . . . what comes next and all."

Mother Esther?

"Oh. Uh. All right."

Wanda stoops and kisses his cheek. Her lips are warm. Her breath smells of grated apples. Then the girl, his Obligated, retreats from the room, and he wonders what happened to her in the time he was asleep. The Blight, obviously, but it's more than that. She's different. Still Wanda, at the heart of it all, but she's tougher, too. More self-assured.

He doesn't know what to make of that. He likes it, though.

Not much time to consider it further, because Esther must've been waiting right outside the door. The woman does not walk in so much as she seems to drift into the room, the way pollen drifts across plasto-sheen after a piss-blizzard—it's effortless and ethereal. Divine, almost, as if she's not even human.

And maybe she's not. He picked up a young man purporting to be her son from the Saranyu, a man who—while only a few years older than Cael—still looks too old to be this woman's child. The Blight isn't just in her or a part of her. She *is* the Blight. Hell, for all Cael knows, it started with her. Maybe she was the first.

The witch sits and reaches back and grabs some of her hair—platinum with streaks of gold and filaments of true green—and begins to idly braid it.

"Time is not kind," she finally says after a long silence.

"I don't follow."

"Everything keeps moving forward, with or without our permission. We can't stop it. Can't slow it down or turn it around. Life continues. Time progresses. Everything alive moves steadily toward death, and everything dead plays host to new life. Time continues, and it's up to us to choose what we do with it. I wish that we had more time together. All of us, here. But that is no longer possible."

"You're still speaking like a . . . like the damn Maize Witch and not like a person who wants to be understood. You wanna say it, get to it."

A perfume rises off her. It's her breath. Before this moment he's never seen or smelled the blooms of a Sweet Alice flower, but he pictures a cluster of little white petals and *somehow* he knows that this is the scent that's crawling up his nose and winding tight around all the switches and levers inside his brain—he can feel it tugging, pulling. But he's aware of it, too, in a way that he wasn't before, and he steadies himself against it, pushing Esther's control away.

His lips curl in a snarl: "Don't. I'm not a poppet doll, so don't try to make me dance. You want something, say what it is or get out."

She recoils. The whites of her eyes shoot through with little tendrils—same size and shape as bloodshot veins, but these are like runner-vines searching dirt for sustenance. Then she blinks and they're gone. She smiles.

"You've changed," she says.

"I'm the same."

She offers no rebuttal, but her smirk tells the story: *Oh no, you're not.* Instead, she says: "You don't want to stay here, do you?"

"No. I sure don't."

"You could do a lot of good here. This could be your home."

"This won't ever be my home, lady. And you won't ever be my mother, no matter what Wanda thinks to call you. I got family and friends. They're my home."

She smiles stiffly. "Then I want your help."

"Can't imagine why."

"You're special. Different."

"C'mon. You're surrounded by . . . special people." *Blightborn.* "You alone have more power in your pinkie finger than I will ever have."

She smiles. "You ever play Checks?"

Checks. Simple enough game board: red and black squares, alternating. Red pieces on the black squares, black pieces on the red. Each a round piece with a different sigil carved into the top of it: crowns, pistols, horses, butterflies. That makes each piece different, each capable of its own move and only that. Goal is to move your pieces, jump them over the enemy's to knock them off the board.

"Pop was a . . . a godsdamn mastermind at that game. He taught me early, and I always thought I had him, you know? But somehow by the end he always managed to jump my damn Queen and knock my ass outta the game."

Pop used to say: *In this game, the Queen is everything.*

A deep ache lances through him. He misses Pop and Mom. Misses them so bad it's like a living absence, a hungry wound.

He wonders if they're even still alive.

"The Queen," she says. "I bet you were aggressive with her."

"Hell yeah I was. Most powerful piece on the board. Can go any direction, jump any poor dummy she comes across. She's a big gun, that one."

"And yet, you always lost her."

"I did."

"What'd your father do with his Queen?"

"Always held her back."

"And he always won."

He shoves his tongue into his cheek. "Yeah. That's right. It's just—I can't wrap my head around it. Why have a weapon like that if you're not gonna use her?"

"She's the most potent, but also the most vulnerable."

"Why?" But then he thinks about it. "Because she's just one piece."

Esther smiles. "Exactly that. She is *just* one piece. That's why you have all the other pieces. To support her. To protect her until that moment when her powers must be used."

He gets it now. "You're saying you're the Queen."

"It feels a bit ego-fed, but the idea is the same, yes."

"So that makes me . . . what? One of your peon pieces?"

"You are no peon, Cael McAvoy. You're more important than that. Though it remains to be seen how important. Are you a Black Rider? Or maybe a Hierophant? Or a Gunfighter? Depends on how tricky you are."

"I'm not tricky at all. If I'm not a peon, then I'm damn sure the Hermit." The Hermit—a piece he never quite understood. It just sits there. Can't move unless to jump an enemy piece that gets near it. But that's who he wants to be now. He wants to just stay away from all this nonsense.

"You're too powerful to be a Hermit." She says it again: "I need your help, Cael. Things are moving fast. The Heartland is on the brink."

"I don't even know what that means."

"It means the Empyrean are going to take all our pieces and knock over the game board. They're taking over whole towns, turning the folks there into metal monsters. It's war, and the Heartlanders are losing."

"And what can I do about that?"

"You can fetch something for me."

"*Fetch.* Like a dumb dog. See? Peon."

"No. Fetch, like a skilled, trained hound."

"You're not making me feel any better comparing me to an animal."

"You're assuming I put *men* above *dogs* in my assessment of animals."

"Okay. Fine. So, whaddya want me to fetch?"

"A . . . case."

"A case. Case of what? Fixy? Micky Finn's gin?"

"The case is a weapon. That we will use against the Empyrean."

He arches an eyebrow so high he's sure that it's floating about three inches above his head. "A weapon? What kinda weapon?"

"A corn-killer."

"I don't follow you. Thought you said this was a weapon against the Empyrean, not a weapon against a bunch of dumb cornstalks."

"Hiram's Golden Prolific is everything to the Empyrean. They use it for food additives, building materials. But most of all, they use it as fuel. To keep their ships aloft. They control the corn, so they control the skies. They control the skies, so they control the Heartland. I want to rob them of that control. I want to kill the corn."

"That's a tall silo to climb."

She smirks. "I created the corn. I might as well be the one to kill it."

That comment from Esther explodes. *I created the corn. I might as well be the one to kill it.* It leaves him reeling, and so she suggests they take a walk. Like on the first day they met, they take a stroll through the back gardens. These, wilder and madder than those in front—gardens without margins or borders, bursting at the seams like a scarecrow stuffed too tight with hay. The effigies of stalk and stick still stand tall but are no longer "naked"—they are dressed as Empyrean. Crude, handmade Pegasus symbols. Some wear helmets like the *evocati augusti*. Others are made to look like what Cael assumes to be specific men and women, given the details—ragged corn silk hair on one, a dark-dyed thatch-worn beard on another.

All around the garden are more structures now. Huts and the construction of what he suspects is the longhouse mentioned at dinner.

Gone is the skiff platform, though.

Cael stops and looks up at one of the effigies. It's three, maybe four times his height. A giant. Its wicker basket head is slumped against its shoulder, arms stretched out in cruciform.

"So," he says, "you're Empyrean."

"Was. But no longer."

It should've been obvious to him. Way she carries herself is . . . what's the word? *Stately*. Like she owns all the world seen and unseen. And her voice has that trim, clipped rhythm.

He asks her: "You created the corn? Just you?"

"I was team leader. But it's my patent. That genetic design afforded me naming privileges. Hiram was my father. I loved him very much—the love I had for him was as strong as the hate I had for my mother. I named the corn after him, because just as he changed everything for me, I knew the corn would change everything for us. I just didn't know how."

"Must be painful to wanna kill it."

"It's not. I've seen the error of my ways. I want to remove its stain from this world. I can free Hiram's name from this poisonous crop."

"And you think I can help you with that."

"I do."

A wind whips through the garden. Flowers nod their heads like agreeable drunks. Leaves hiss and rustle.

He shakes his head. "I appreciate what you wanna do. But I just want to find my family and go home."

"I understand that. I, too, would love to be with my family. And I would love for everything to be wrapped up as nice as a box of Empyrean candy." She offers a small, mirthless chuckle. "My mother was a candymaker. Oh, what treats. Sugar caramels and blood orange truffles and spun lavender floss, light as air, fragrant as a dream. My mother liked everything . . . neat and particular. And when things did not conform to the order that she imagined, she cracked like an egg. What a temper she had. She beat us without mercy, using the flats of her hands. She called it 'spanking,' but my mother wasn't content to bend us over her knee. She knocked my sister's eye out of her head one time. My father found out, and . . . I never saw my mother again."

"I appreciate the family history, I do, but my pop isn't like that. He's a good man and I ought to do my level best to find him. Which is exactly why I can't help you, Esther. I'm sorry."

"Your family has experienced some pain."

"It has. All families have, I guess."

She tuts and shakes her head. "Not most Empyrean families. Mine was an exception, not an example. The Empyrean are creatures of privilege. They don't starve. They don't choke on dust or pollen. They have the luxury of frowning at a day's work as if it's work for the animals." She turns a hard gaze toward Cael. "Their mothers are not saddled with tumors, bedridden and fixed with pain."

"How'd you know that? About my mama?"

"I knew her."

"Horseshit."

"I knew her and your father. Not well. But we met." He's about to follow this trail of bread crumbs, but she keeps talking: "Your father's hip. Your mother's tumors. All the pain of all the families of Boxelder and beyond. It has one source. *One* origin point: the Empyrean. The wealthy monsters above us. They'll do anything to keep what they have, tightening their fists around Heartlander throats. Your life would be different without them. You'd have opportunity. You'd have the food you wanted instead of what was doled out to you." Here, a pause before saying: "You'd have the freedom to marry the one you love instead of the one chosen for you."

He wonders what Wanda would say about that.

Just the same, she's right. A roaring river of anger runs through him like a gush of boiling water. Even just growing a few fruits and vegetables got him and his family and friends labeled as *terrorists*. And now, the Empyrean is doing far worse than that. Turning people into mechanicals?

How is that even possible?

How can that be just?

He tries to imagine a world without the Empyrean telling him and everyone else what to do. A fantasy plays out, fast and loose. Him and Gwennie together. Maybe no kids, maybe a whole litter. Growing a garden. Or tending an orchard. Doing whatever the hell they want, when they wanted. Rigo still with two feet. Lane still with his parents. Pop able to run and jump. Mom up and beautiful without her tumors, helping him milk the goats or butcher a couple of chickens, or teaching him how to talk to girls so they don't think he's some kinda dumb jerk chawbacon asshole—

"I'll do it. Whatever you need, I'll do it."

"That's good. Because I'm afraid if I send anybody else, your friend Lane Moreau will shoot them on sight."

"Lane? What are you taking about?"

"He's mayor of Pegasus City."

PEGASUS CITY

EVERYTHING IS CORN.

That's how the Heartland works. That's how the Empyrean *engineered* it to work. And it's going to be their downfall. Just as Lane is subverting the image of the Pegasus, he and the Sleeping Dogs are going to take over the skies. And that means taking over the corn.

Pegasus City—once the Saranyu—will fly. The engines are mostly intact. Hover-panels undergoing repairs. But they need fuel.

Because this sonofabitch is gonna *fly*.

"I still don't think you should've called it Pegasus City," Killian says. He makes a disgusted sound. "It's a bit . . . on the nose."

"Well," Lane says, pacing, "it's the name I picked, damnit, so it's there and you're just gonna have to like it. And I still think I should've been allowed to go out there. I'm capable, you know. Good with a pistol. Good for morale, too."

Behind him, Killian groans as he leans forward on a broad, round bed. He's pale, sweating. Gone thin, thin as a starved mutt. Beneath his pallor lies various intersections of bony lines. When he grins, it is a skullish one.

"You're no longer a raider captain," Killian says. "You're a *mayor*. Big man now. You don't just . . . flutter out on missions. You lead a city, not a strike force."

The strike force.

Lord and Lady, will it succeed?

Lane's gut clenches. Not far from the wreck of the Saranyu sits the town of Fort Calhoun. Once it was a town bent on doing the one thing that the skybastards always need doing: collecting and processing Hiram's Golden Prolific.

Lane hopes like hell that the Empyrean never expected the raiders to send an attack force, even a small one, to take over some nowheresville corn processing facility. If it were a supply depot? Or a big town? Maybe. But Fort Calhoun was compromised. The people taken. Turned into those . . . *things*.

It's a dead place now.

And hopefully unprotected.

Lane leans forward, looks out the window in the white tower. A tower once used as some kind of prison, it seems: level after level of cages. Ornate, beautiful cages. Brass and iron. It occurs to him only now, at this moment, that they look like birdcages. The Empyrean see themselves as skyborn, and so that is a fitting cell for a creature of the clouds—but why would they jail one another? Not an enlightened idyll, apparently. Here a small voice reminds him that not all the Empyrean are the same, but that is a hangnail he dare not pull unless he wants to unzip the whole thing in a gush of blood and guilt.

"Mayor," Lane says. The word still sounds strange to him.

Killian says as much himself: "Mayors and cities and Pegasus blah blah blah. It doesn't feel right on my tongue, none of it. We're the Sleeping Dogs, my love. Rebels. Revolutionaries. *Beasts with teeth.* Not some poncey, preening, prancey-fancy horse with oh-so-precious wings. It's a ding against morale. You should've called it, I dunno. *Wolfthorn City.* Or, or, ahhh. Hounds . . . ridge. Dog . . . towns . . . ville?" He snorts a laugh.

Lane gives Killian a look and rolls his eyes.

"Well, what the hell," Killian protests. "That's not my job, is it? Naming things. You've got to find a proper *namer* for things like that. You can hire one of those now. Since you're the *mayor* and all."

Past the window, the people of Pegasus City continue their work—breaking things, fixing others, building whole new structures. Industrious like ants. Heartlanders have come from all over to join the Sleeping Dogs (though some folks call the raider group the "Woken Beast" now instead) because they know that this is a safe place. The walls that have gone up around the fallen Saranyu flotilla have yet to fall. The Empyrean have tried to penetrate the defenses and get past those walls.

But they haven't succeeded yet.

And soon, when the raiders get their own corn processing facility, they'll get this city in the air. The ground will no longer be their only home. And the skyborn will piss their very lovely trousers in fear when they see a Heartlander flotilla hunting them.

Lane turns and points. "I told you, I called it Pegasus City because we're . . . we're *subverting* this place. It was theirs. Now it's ours. The Pegasus is their thing. Or was. And now it's *our* thing. Best of all, it's a promise. This baby's gonna take off, and then the Empyrean better worry." Before Killian can say anything else, Lane jumps ahead: "And tell me, my *love*, exactly what *is* your job around here?"

Killian offers a cheeky grin. "Moral support? Sense of humor?" The former captain stands with a wince, clutching his side, then saunters over. He walks a pair of fingers up the opening in Lane's crimson jacket, trailing them across the cleft in the shirt, across the young man's smooth chest. "Midnight kisses? Lusty satisfaction and—"

With a scowl, Lane pushes him back. "No. You're my first mate. That job description does *not* include getting high on Pheen day in and night out."

"I sacrificed," Killian says, his playful demeanor pivoting suddenly to dour and grim. He lifts his shirt, shows the irregular constellation of scars across his chest. "I gave up things. For us. For the Heartland. For *you*. We got out of Tuttle's Church, and I didn't ask to sit and rest. I demanded we *move*. I said we come here and we take this place. And we did. But that . . ." His voice breaks. "That wasn't easy for me."

"It wasn't easy for any of us," Lane says.

Back then, a year ago, the pieces of the Saranyu fell—streaks of bright blue and fire red against the black of the sky. It was, indeed, Killian who said they had to come to this place. They were going to pilfer it—pick over its bones like a skull-vulture, then take off with their bellies full of plunder. But when they got here, Lane felt something—an idea, scratching at the back of his head like a dog wanting to be let in the door. And then the Empyrean showed up.

The battle to hold the wreckage of the Saranyu was long, protracted, an even uglier fight than the one at Tuttle's Church.

It was Rigo who won them that battle.

Rigo, poor Rigo.

Rigo said: "I bet the city's defenses could be activated." He thought if they turned them on, the big sonic cannons could be used to blast the skybastards out of the air. They were up against time. Death was on them like a stink. Back then, Lane was confused, the Sleeping Dogs were down too many, and Killian was already ravaged with an infection, a sickness from his injuries that ran through him like a herd of spooked cattle. But Rigo's idea saved the day. He and Lane together went to those cannons. They got them working.

And sure enough, they shot those Empyrean sons-a-bitches out of the air.

The Empyrean retreated, and as the days and weeks went on, other Sleeping Dogs—and soon other Heartlanders—wended their way to the Saranyu's wreckage. And any time the Empyrean showed their heads, they got smacked on the nose by sonic blasts and sent back to the sky.

Killian's sickness changed him, though. Hard, high doses of Annie pills kept him alive—but for the pain, he began to take Pheen. And drink, too. It saved him. Maybe. But his body has been weak. Ravaged by the teeth of the infection—and the drugs did a number on his mind, too. Now he wanders about like a ghost.

Lane thinks: *I'm too hard on him.* He's always been that way. Hard on his father, on his mother, even on his friends.

Guilt pecks at him like a bird looking for worms.

Shit.

His frustration crumbles, and he moves to Killian and holds the man's hands, then cups his face. "I'm sorry. Okay? I know none of this has been easy. And I know you need . . . to self-medicate. Just try to ease off a little. Because damnit, man, I need you sharp. I'm lost out here. You're my sail, my rudder, my everything. Keep me pointed straight, yeah?"

The former captain grins and kisses Lane just under the jaw. Lane tilts his head back, feels the warmth of lips trailing down his neck.

"Anything, Mayor Moreau. Anything at all."

Killian's hands lace behind Lane's back.

"Mayor Moreau," Killian repeats. "See, now I'm liking it. Are you?"

Lane moans.

Across the room: *ding.*

Lane's visidex. Incoming call.

Killian holds him still. "Don't take that call."

"I need to," Lane says. "You know I need to."

"You need *me*," Killian slurs. His breath is off—something rotten in there somewhere. A foulness, wet and fungal. Like the cure for the infection never took hold, like it's still in there, somewhere, hiding not far out of sight.

Lane pulls away and takes the call.

On the other end: Luna Dorado.

"The facility is ours," she says. "I'm coming home, and I'm bringing friends."

"We gave 'em the kiss-off," Luna says, a mad spark in those green eyes—like lightning flashing in emeralds. "Lost a few of our own, may the Lord and Lady put 'em to work. Lost Pablo Riggins. And Chick Bailey. Dagmar is alive, but she's gonna lose an arm out of this, guaran-damn-teed. But it's done. It's over. The mechanicals are scrap. The place is ours." She bites her lip, pumps a fist.

Luna Dorado is Lane's . . . well, everything's a little rag-tag here, so right now she's called "Captain of the Guard," but that's a bullshit descriptor if ever there was one. Luna is more than that. She's a problem-solver. A fixer. A flare gun you can shoot into the air to bring light to a situation—or straight at your enemies to set them on fire. She's a farking moonbat, wild-eyed and unhinged. And Lane is incredibly glad she's working for the Heartland.

Everything about her is sharp-angled and severe. Jawline like an ax-blade. Cheekbones like bullets. Eyes big and bright, blazing with the craziness of youth (she's only a year older than Lane, after all).

The two of them take the elevator down into the city center—what Lane has named Boxelder Circle—and above them, the reconstructed flotilla rises like broken teeth. It's slapdash, hap-hazard, ugly as a shaved shuck rat, but it'll do. The ships of the

Sleeping Dogs were able to pull the buildings upright. Men and women died anchoring the structures back together with chains thrice as thick as Lane's own (admittedly lanky) body. Most of the city had crumbled or was worthless to them, and some of the Saranyu never fell (or fell too slowly to be of value, buoyed as they were by giant balloons). But from the wreckage remained enough of value. And now those broken teeth composed their city.

The elevator door opens. They ripped out the mechanical man that once controlled it—now it's moved with cables and pulleys, hand-cranked by men, not machines. Been a lot of anti-machine sentiment recently, and anything that even *looked* like a mechanical in the crashed Saranyu was dragged out into the light and crushed with boots, sticks, stones.

Luna and Lane step out of the box.

It's then that Lane sees five men lined up in the circle, kneeling.

Burlap sacks over their heads, bound loosely at the neck with wire.

Luna hoots and cackles. "We took a few prisoners, boss."

Jeezum Crow.

All around stand Sleeping Dogs, many with their wolf and dog masks pushed up over their heads, sweaty faces staring out. Transmitting hatred toward the kneeling men. More are gathering, too, curious to see.

"Wh-what do we do with them?" Lane hisses to Luna so that nobody else can hear.

"We make an example of them," Luna says, then winks.

She pulls out a sonic pistol.

Lane steps in her way. "Luna. *Luna.* Wait. Hold up. What do you mean, make an example of them?"

"C'mon. *C'mon.*" She gives him a look, like, *You're joking, right?* But he presses her with a stare, and so she sighs and says, "The boys and girls of the Dogs like a little justice now and again. We got five traitors to the Heartland here, boss. Two Babysitters. Two facility workers. And the facility boss, man named Hale. These ain't Empyrean. They're Heartland folk who chose a different side. And so they need to be made to understand what happens to folk like that."

The gathering crowd is starting to murmur now. And people are closing in on the five kneeling men. They're not touching them yet, but already Lane can smell the bloodlust in the air. Anger, carried on the wind like a vibration, like a frequency everyone can hear and none can resist.

They're Heartlanders, he thinks.

"You want to hurt them," he says, nodding, starting to accept that.

"We gotta *kill* 'em," she says, smiling.

"Luna—"

"I can do it if you want. But the Dogs wanna follow you, not me. And you don't *want* them following me more than they follow you. You're the top of the pops, the big boss with the red pepper sauce." She spins the sonic pistol around, tilts the grip toward him. "They wanna see *you* do it."

He takes the pistol.

The grip is warm in his hand. And yet it sends chills up his arm.

The men and women gathered—hell, even a few kids hanging around, nestled in between the knees or at the hips of parents or guardians—see him take the pistol. And they start to chant.

May-or.

May-or.

May-or.

MAY-OR!

Grungy, dust-caked faces stare on.

Dark eyes watch.

Mouths open, some in happiness, others in anger. All yelling for him.

Every part of him feels tethered to a cable, and it's trying desperately to yank him back from this. Reel him in. He wants to turn and toss the gun to Luna, or better yet, find a way to give these five clemency. He wishes Killian followed him down. Then he wishes Rigo were here—Rigo, who had to leave the city. Rigo who couldn't, or wouldn't, stay, who felt out of place, who one night just packed his things and left. Gods, it'd be nice to see him now. Rigo would know what was right and what was wrong.

Lane always found the line between those two things blurry.

His mind strays. Looking for justifications. Excuses. *Reasons.* And they aren't far out of reach. The Empyrean has ruined the Heartland. And it has done so with the help of Heartlanders. Men like these who are complicit in the ruination. Who, even when given other options, choose to fight for the bigger side, the meaner dog. Who leaned into the shadow of the bully instead of stepping out into the light.

And that pisses Lane off.

His jaw sets tight, teeth grinding against teeth.

Cael with the Blight. Rigo without his foot. Gwennie gone. Lane's own father dead. His mother on the side of Old Scratch.

He can do this.

Maybe he *wants* to do this.

He steps up. The chants grow loud. Luna is behind him, the small of her hand on his back, urging him to get on with it. He looks at her. The madness dances in her gaze like twisters. That scares him. What do his own eyes look like? It scares him enough to look at the pistol, set the dial back. Reduce the severity just a notch.

Enough to kill. But not enough to knock their brains and hearts out of their bodies. Enough to shock the system, but not enough to spill blood.

He knows the crowd wants blood. But the people will have to settle for just shy.

Should I say something?

He thinks he should, but he can't conjure words. Not sure he could force them past his mouth even if he did manage to figure out what to say.

Lane raises the pistol, fires it into the chest of the first man.

The body tumbles back. The body shuddering, heels juddering against the cracked earth. Crying out from behind the hood. The others begin to wail. Their howls reach Lane's ears, but he can barely hear them beyond the rushing of the blood behind everything, and part of him thinks, *Do it slow, make it count, let them savor it*, but then that strikes him as cruel and needless— and his people are already enjoying it, whooping and hooting, fists pumping in the air. This isn't torture. Right? This is justice and mercy shaking hands.

He shoots the other four in quick succession.

They all drop. Some on their backs. Others on their sides.

Twisting, writhing, dying. Not dying quickly, though, oh no, dying slowly because he didn't set the dial high enough, did he? This isn't mercy. This *is* torture. Lord and Lady, no, no, no. He sets the dial up higher, and the crowd is raging now, bigger, larger, a storm of dust and rage—

He points the pistol at the first man again. Time to end it, really end it, pull the trigger and be a leader—

But then the voice reaches his ears again, a cry that isn't like the others, a cry of a woman, not a man, a cry he recognizes—

No, no, that's not possible. *No.*

Everything seems to go slow, sideways.

The pistol falls from his hand, lands in the dust.

The balls of his feet carry him forward just far enough to drop down onto his own knees, reaching for the hood of the first one to fall. Pulling the hood off. The burlap obscuring the sun for just a moment—a shadow falling, but then light once more.

Lane's own mother stares up at him. Face twisting in pain. Eyes bulging. Mouth ringed with froth. He screams for a doctor. Someone, please, a doctor.

"Mom!"

YOUNG HOBOS IN LOVE

THE HOBO BOY IS IN LOVE.

Or like. Or lust. Something.

It's a crush. The girl is his age, maybe a hair older. She's a sneering, pouty, surly creature. Dirt-cheeked and sharp-teethed. She's got the vibe of an animal trapped in a cage, an animal gone feral—you stick a hand through the metal and you'll pull back four fingers instead of five. And yet, she's a rock in his shoe; he can't quit thinking about her.

He watches her scamper up a building, her short-cropped black hair like a bundle of unkempt grackle feathers. She uses a rust-eaten drainpipe to clamber up, then disappears. Two minutes later, she comes back down again.

Eating a strawberry.

A fat, plump, red-as-arterial-blood strawberry.

She eats it quickly, palming it and biting it in one go, then spitting the green top into her hand. A hand that goes into her pocket before wiping a red smear on the patchwork, moth-eaten denim that covers her legs.

The girl pauses for just a moment.

She turns. And matches eyes with him.

She sees him seeing her.

Panic seizes him in a closing fist. Air out of his lungs. Eyes bulging. He knows he should duck, move, look away, something, *anything*, but he can't. His feet—the good one and the other one—stand fixed to the ground. He knows his mouth is open, catching flies, but he can't quite manage to close it.

She winks at him.

And then she turns and hurries off.

The Fringe, they call it.

The edge of the Heartland. Ringed by the Boundary. The fence posts are gleaming steel spires, each topped with a shining sphere. It looks like you could just walk between them, leaving the corn and entering the thick jungle beyond. But if you did, the wall would activate. A sonic barrier would screech like a hundred thousand crows, shrieking into existence in the same time it takes for lightning to strike—and you would be sheared in half.

Most folks know what will happen. And yet, sometimes, people still walk through that fence anyway. Suicide with a dash of lottery-like uncertainty. *Maybe* this *time I'll walk in and the fence won't get me. And then I'll be free.*

That's what they think.

That's what they *hope*.

Then—the sonic screams. The invisible fence, a fence of sound, rises.

Slice.

The town that sits only a half mile from the Boundary, here in the Fringe, has taken on a senseless, hopeless atmosphere—a feeling that death hangs in the air, an invisible cloud, an unshakable fear. It's a rat's nest of a town, the buildings all leaning up against one another like sluggish Pheen addicts. Tin roofs dented, corroded. Stone walls cracked and crumbling. The plasto-sheen has long been perforated by Hiram's Golden Prolific, and for a while, apparently, folks with sickle knives and Queeny's Quietdown kept the corn culled. They've long given up that fight. The corn intrudes. Pokes up through the street. Through floorboards. Lone stalks serving as advance scouts, bending toward those who walk past, twitching, swiping, thirsty for blood.

The town is Cloverdale, but nobody actually calls it that.

They call it Curtains.

And in the town of Curtains, the people are as ragtag and rotten as the buildings. A sad, rough group of Blighted, hobos, and the infirm. Hollow eyes and black tumors. Missing teeth and missing fingers.

Curtains is the Heartland's gutter. It's where all the slurry runs. Where all the pollen blows, the trash drops, the piss trickles.

The hobo boy saw his first suicide yesterday.

He'd heard that you could go near the fence and find things. Things that people had left behind before they decided to walk through the tall posts. Sometimes, they said, if you were really brave, you could find the halves of the bodies that fell on the Heartland side of the sonic barrier, and sometimes those halves had trinkets or treasures in the pockets that you could trade back at the town Mercado for a bit of food, water, or treats.

The hobo boy is hungry. He misses food.

So he goes into the corn and hobbles the half mile out of town toward the wall. The corn is tall, but soon he sees that the metal posts are taller—they rise high in the sky, tall as ten of him stacked, feet on shoulders.

The corn cuts him in the few places his skin is exposed. The rest of him is bound up with rags. He limps out of the corn— it dies quickly toward the Boundary—and staggers close to the fence. He listens, expecting it to hum or buzz or make some kind of noise, but it's dead silent. Only thing he hears is the wind through the corn. Hissing, as if to hush him.

Then he sees. There, on the ground. Stuck in the leaf-curl of a stunted stalk: a single ace note. Corner bent. A streak of mud across it—

No. Not mud. Blood.

Jeezum Crow in King Hell.

But it'll do. It'll buy him something at the Mercado.

Something he can give to the hobo girl.

He stoops, winces through the pain, and reaches down for the ace note—

Then he stops.

A man stands no more than twenty feet away. Bushy, bird's nest beard. Hollow, haunted eyes set over a nose that looks broken and rebroken.

He's less than a foot from the fence.

He turns to the hobo boy and offers a small wave.

The bottom of his palm—down to the wrist—is fringed with little squirming pea-shoots. Green as wet moss. He realizes what he's done and quickly hides the hand behind his back.

He sniffs.

The hobo boy says: "Wait."

But the man steps through the fence and the sonic wall screams.

Don't think about it. Don't think about it.

But how can he not? He's back in town, and he keeps feeling his face for more flecks of blood. Not his. The man's. He felt the faint mist as the invisible barrier split the Blighted hobo. He's been wiping at his face ever since.

He hides in a small alley, holds up the ace note again to look at it. He wants to think about *this*, not *that*. Think about what he'll buy for the girl. At first he thought food of some kind: somebody's rations. But rations have been cut down or cut off for people. Food isn't easy to come by anymore, though some supplies have trickled out of and away from the wreckage of the Saranyu flotilla. Pegasus City. Besides, the girl has access to strawberries or something, right?

So, maybe something else then. A trinket. A piece of jewelry. That might be nice. Isn't that what boys do for girls? Give them jewelry?

A scuff of a heel behind him.

He turns, expecting to see the girl standing there. Because

how perfect would that be? She'd appear. See him with the ace note. Probably steal it.

But it's not her.

It's another boy. Knotty like rope. Freckled face. Upper lip with a soft, deep cleft that shows yellow teeth.

"Hey, fatfuck," Cleft Lip says. "I see you found my ace note."

"What?" the hobo boy says. "No, no, this is mine—" He moves to try to tuck it back under his shirt, but Cleft Lip catches his wrist.

"Yeah, yeah, I lost it. I can tell you it's mine because I can describe it. It's an ace of hearts. Bent corner."

Of course he can say that because he just saw the damn thing.

"No, I found it—"

"It's mine, ain't that right, Cashew?"

"Right as rain," says a sloppy, lisping voice. The hobo boy turns, sees a girl enter the alley on the other side. She's got broad shoulders. Thick. Fat, even. Built like a dang motorvator. Hands as big as a hog's head. Half her face is a sludgy avalanche of loose skin. It covers one eye, a nostril, part of her mouth. A line of drool slicks her chin before she licks it away.

The hobo boy feels for her—the way she looks, what she must go through. Whatever it was, it lent her a kind of *meanness*, a dark spark ready to catch fire. He stands, tries to step away from the two of them, but the alley is narrow and he doesn't have anywhere to go.

The big girl steps in and—

He staggers against the wall as she clubs him in the face with a fist. He tastes blood and hears a ringing deep in his ear.

"What's that there?" Cleft Lip says. "Lookie at that. Got

something more valuable than an ace note, Cash. Got hisself a fakey foot."

"I need it," the boy says. "Please."

The girl—Cashew—steps in close.

Cleft Lip hems him in on the other side, clucking his tongue.

"That'll go big at the Mercado. Always some poor dirt-farmer needs a new leg." Cleft Lip leers. "You either take it off and give it here, or we're gonna have to knock you sideways and take it ourselves. It's your bag, dumpling."

"You can have the ace note—"

"I know we can have it," Cashew says with her mush-mouth. "We'll have that *and* the leg and anything else we want to take from you."

Cleft Lip grabs his crotch. "Maybe I'll use your mouth as a toilet."

"Please, no, don't."

"Maybe I won't have to use you as a piss-hole if you gimme that leg."

The boy closes his eyes, knows how this is going to go, but he's not like that man at the fence. He won't just step through into oblivion.

He runs.

Or tries to.

Truth is, he can't run for squat. The fake leg strapped to his knee makes him slow like a shovel-struck dog. By the time he's lurching forward, desperately trying not to fall, his two attackers already have their hands on his shoulders and they slam him up against the wall.

Cleft Lip hits him in the cheek. He sees stars. Tries to fall down to the ground, cover himself up, but the big girl won't let him. She props him up as Cleft Lip beats him and kicks at him. The hits land with dull thuds, and each meaty slap sends his brain rattling 'round his skull. Before long his head hangs forward, twin streams of blood pouring from his nose.

The punches have stopped, and the boy's leg jiggle-juggles as Cleft Lip works at the leather straps holding the fake leg to the thigh.

He tries to plead but finds his words caught behind his blood-slick lips. He throws a fist of his own, but Cleft Lip just leans back and avoids it same way you might avoid a tree branch or a buzzing horsefly.

Cashew laughs. This hee-haw jackass laugh. *Haw haw haw*—

Then the laugh cuts short.

Grrrrrk!

The hobo boy looks up. Blinks, trying to make sense of what he's seeing. Cashew's face has gone red as beet juice. Her one visible eye strains at its sockets, ready to pop as a wormy, sluglike tongue licks at the air.

She's choking. Reaching up at the folds of her neck, trying desperately to—to what? The hobo boy stares, sees a long thin wire wrapped around Cashew's neck, and he follows that wire to the roof—

Cleft Lip looks up, too, and yells, "What the—? Beryl, you little bitch!"

It's *her*.

The hobo girl sneers from above, wire held in gloved hands.

The girl—Beryl—lets the wire go. Cashew gasps, then falls.

Then the hobo girl jumps. Both feet collide with Cleft Lip's body—his head smacks back into the crumbling wall and he howls in pain. He scampers away, trying to stand, but she brings a knee against the side of his head.

"Told you to skip town, Eddie," the girl—Beryl?—says. "And Cashew, you human lump of melted candle wax. You ought to go, too."

Cashew writhes on the ground, clawing at her bleeding neck. She chokes out the words: "Old . . . Scratch . . . take you . . ."

Beryl gives her a middle finger. "Far as you're concerned, Old Scratch is my daddy, my boyfriend, and my guardian Saintangel. Now suck piss."

Then she turns and walks to the end of the alley.

She looks over her shoulder before she turns the corner.

"You coming, Rigo?"

And then she's gone.

Rigo thinks: *How in King Hell did she know my name?*

Of course he follows after.

And of course he gives Cleft Lip a kick—with his fake foot, because why not?—right to the crotch before hobbling out of the alley.

Rigo enters the streets of Curtains. It's a town bigger than Boxelder by two, maybe three times the size, and since the Saranyu fell, it's been collecting misfits and castoffs with a far greater frequency. Any walk down the streets of Boxelder, you'd see a dozen people, and that was it. Here, particularly around the mouth of the Mercado warehouse, they gather in crowds. Some have rough dogs or feral tabbies on chains that bark and hiss as Rigo passes.

The girl, Beryl, doesn't stop there. She keeps going. Not running, but keeping enough of a pep in her step that Rigo has to limp along double-time, sending jolts of pain up into his hips.

Ahead, she turns the corner, ducks into an old theater. Not a holo-theater, like the one they found in Martha's Bend, but a proper one—used for plays and the like. THE WHEELHORSE, it says out front on a sign tilted so far it looks like the letters could just spill out like sand.

Rigo looks around to make sure Cleft Lip and Cashew aren't following along and then ducks through the front door.

The smell climbs up his nose and stays there: rot, ruin, mold, pollen. *Pollen.* His head starts to feel pressure behind the eyes. The sensation of a pair of fingers pinching his nose closed. He tries not to sneeze but can't help it—

Sneezing sends a little hurricane of dust up. It blows across shafts of light—columns of sun shining from holes in the roof far above.

Beryl is nowhere to be seen.

"Hello?" he calls out.

Ello, ello.

Echo, echo.

Birds stir in the eaves.

He winds his way through the center aisle—dark seats on each side, long fallen to disuse and disrepair, half collapsed, fabric torn. There's a slight decline here, and Rigo grunts as he navigates even this slight shift—

"Hey, Rigo."

Beryl. Up on the stage. By a red curtain so dark it might as well be black.

"Why did you help me?" he asks.

But she ducks behind the curtain. *Curtains in Curtains*, he thinks. He's about to haul himself up on the stage—no easy task given that he can't see a set of dang steps around here—when he pauses. Last time he was alone in a creepy, half-abandoned building, he ended up finding a fake baby and getting a jaw trap around his leg. An act that lost him his leg once infection set in.

This could be another trap. Maybe all of it is. Maybe Cleft Lip and Cashew are just waiting for him behind that curtain, ready to snatch up his limb and beat him half to death with it. Or all the way to death.

Behind the curtain, he hears Beryl whistling. He recognizes the song, but at first he can't put a name to it. . . .

"The Ballad of Calla and Kade." A love song.

A love song that doesn't end very well, but sounds nice just the same.

Oh, hell with it.

Rigo reaches out and drags himself up onto the stage, bracing himself with the fake leg and throwing the good one up over the edge. It takes him longer than he likes and he feels like Wanda's mutt, Hazelnut, rolling around on her back and showing her belly like a big ol' doofus.

But somehow, he manages. He stands up, takes a deep breath—

And walks behind the curtain.

For a moment, it's all fabric and dust. And again he starts to sneeze, but this time he tamps it down, chokes it back. The curtain seems to go on forever, endless folds that have no end, and a weird thought strikes him: *I wonder if this is what having sex for the first time is like*, lots of pawing and not sure where everything begins or ends, and now he's blushing thinking about how he's never done it and probably never will do it, but if he *did* manage to find someone gracious enough to be his first it sure could be Beryl, but boy howdy, does he think about sex too much these days, he should really quit —

He steps out from behind the curtain, starts to fall as the fabric catches on the heel of his fake foot—

A hand catches him, helps him up.

It's not Beryl.

Rigo gasps.

"Pop," he says.

"It's nice to see you, Rodrigo," Pop says.

Then Cael's father hugs him.

"THE BALLAD OF CAEL AND WANDA"

HEARTLANDERS TELL all kinds of stories about the cycle of day and night. One says that the Lord and Lady take the sun in every night to cook their food and warm their baths. Another says that night is a punishment for Old Scratch—or, in a variant tale, a punishment for the oldest gods of the earth—blinding him so that he cannot find his way into the minds of men and women and children while they sleep. (This is why some speak the common refrain, *Nothing good happens after sundown*.) The most popular story, and the one Cael has heard the most often, says simply that the sun represents the story of Jeezum Crow, for the sun dies every night and is reborn every morning.

He knows all that's a bindle full of horse apples. Pop told him the truth: The Heartland revolves around the sun, along with other worlds, and that revolution means sometimes they face the sun, sometimes they don't. No gods and goddesses, no disagreeable mythologies competing with one another, just a simple arrangement of objects out there, objects given over to what Pop called "scientific principle, the laws of a world and a universe in perpetual action."

He misses Pop.

Right now, he feels like he's not facing the sun or even the moon, but rather a wide-open darkness. A dangerous pit of shadow that will consume him. The Blight-vine around his arm twitches as if—well, as if what, he doesn't know. Maybe the vine fears the darkness, too. Maybe night really is the playground of Old Scratch, and maybe this thing he's got inside him marks him as one of the legions of King Hell: a lord of darkness, not a scion of light.

What the hell is happening to the world?

Things are supposed to get better. But they've always just gotten worse. Like a hill of dirt and scree, where everything slides down, down, down.

He sits there on Esther's porch, looking out over the eventide corn, sun spilling its guts across the horizon, bleeding out as darkness creeps in at the edges.

A bag sits next to him, full of supplies for the journey.

He senses her before he hears her. Seconds before the floorboards of the porch squeak, he can already *feel* Wanda standing behind him. A sense that goes beyond sight, sound, smell. It's that firefly glow again. Like a cloud of them forming a human shape, twinkling like the stars in the sky.

Her hands find his shoulders. He gets chills as she runs them up under the collar of his shirt. It's not just her fingertips. Tendrils tickle.

"I hear you're coming with," he says, repressing the urge to lean into Wanda. The smell of honeysuckle reaches his nose.

"Mother Esther says you'll need help. And that your Obligated might as well be the one to help you."

Mother Esther. He lets that go again, though he knows he'll have to address it sooner than later. He pulls away from her hands and stands up. "For someone so resistant to the Empyrean way of doing things, she's awfully cozy with the idea of us being Obligated."

"Maybe she sees there's something between us. Something real."

He doesn't know how to respond to that. The vine around his arm tightens like a cob-snake choking the life out of a shuck rat. His blood feels hot as a rush of it rises to his cheeks, chest, wrists. Wanda's perfume fills the air.

Instead, he says, "She coming down?" *To say good-bye to the lambs she's leading to slaughter?* The thought strikes him as paranoid, but it is what it is.

"She said we should go."

"So it is, then." He hikes the ratty bag over his shoulder. It's heavy with goods for the journey. Wanda takes her bag, too, and links her arm with his.

They walk out toward the corn.

He expects a quiet exit, thinks they'll just walk through the garden and then step into the stalks, and that'll be that, but things are never that simple.

Soon as they step under the mossy trellis and into the garden, he sees that the Blightborn have gathered there, lining their path. Dozens of them, staring on with the madness of hope in their eyes, arms clasped before them.

"The hell is this?" Cael whispers to Wanda.

"They're saying good-bye. Wishing us well."

"Why?"

"Because everything hangs on us."

He doesn't want that burden. It's an uncomfortable fit, like a pair of hand-me-downs too tight, too rough against the skin. And now all these people watching them go, it's strange—he doesn't matter in his own mind, and yet to them, he sure seems to. Cael offers up an awkward wave that turns into him gesturing for them to back up and go home.

"Thanks, thank you," he says, "but you can all go about your business. We'll be fine, I uhh, we appreciate it—"

But none of them move. They all keep staring and smiling. A young girl with one arm like a tree branch uses the tip of a curling leaf to wipe away a tear rolling down her cheek. Next to her, an older woman with twisting fiddlehead eyes pulls the girl close to give her comfort.

And then, at the end, the Maize Witch steps out. She's in full Blight—a demonstration for those who have gathered. Flowers blooming at the ends of her fingers. Drupe-fruits hanging from the undersides of her arms, dropping to the earth with wet plops. Vines trailing. Waves of scent rolling off her: rose, then fresh peaches, then burning birch.

She says nothing. She merely leans in and gives both Cael and Wanda a kiss on the forehead. Again he senses her, lit up like a cornfield aflame—so much life (or is it so many *lives*?). Her kiss tugs on him, like she's trying one last time to assert control over him. He almost gives in to it, because it feels good. And because it feels *easy*. All too simple to let someone else make decisions for you, to yank the leash and lead you around like a dog.

Still, Cael's got a stubborn fire burning in the well of his belly, and he can't give in even if he wants to. He bolsters his will and pushes her back—not physically, but with a wave of scent all his own. A corpse-flower stink.

Esther seems to notice it. Her brow wrinkles, but her lips twist into a smirk.

"Go with my blessing," she whispers. "Save the Heartland."

Wanda pauses, eyes squeezed shut like she's basking in it.

Cael pulls her along out of the garden. "C'mon," he says.

The corn twists, broken by invisible hands. A path forms ahead of them.

Wanda gasps.

"What?" he asks. "You've seen her do it."

"I didn't know *you* could do it."

"Can't you?"

Her gaze stays with him for a second, almost like she's seeking his permission, or at least trying to read what he's thinking. Then carefully, her stare flicks toward the corn and she reaches out a hand—fingers trembling, thumb tracing circles in the air.

"I can feel it. There's still life here."

She twists her hand suddenly to the left. Then to the right.

Nothing happens. The corn doesn't even shudder.

Her hand drops, and she pouts. "Aw, shucks."

They wait a few moments, then Cael nods and keeps walking, Wanda right alongside him.

"Saranyu's about a week's trip," she says.

"Wouldn't be if we could just go right to it. But we gotta take the long way."

"Mother says—"

Mother says. Ugh.

"—that the Empyrean have been running patrols at the end of the dead corn in that direction. But we go west a ways, we can take cover and maybe find some supplies at that dead town out there."

A ghost town. Heartland's full of them, but now Cael wonders if even more will be drawn on the map—fresh, ragged X's scratched over once-healthy towns. If the Empyrean really are clamping down because of the Saranyu—like they did with Martha's Bend—then that's the likely outcome.

"Fine," he says. He doesn't like it, but he'll trust it. Last thing he wants to do is run afoul of some skybastard patrol and cut this job off at the knees.

He thinks about—but dang sure doesn't wanna talk about—Lane. Lane, still with the Sleeping Dogs. Now ruling the city that's grown up out of the Saranyu's wreckage? Jeezum Crow. Things sure have changed. But Lane must be having a field day.

As they walk, Wanda feels his eyes on her. He tries to sneak these looks, casting his gaze at her like a hunter trying not to spook his prey. But she feels him looking. When he does, they connect in an invisible way—unseen threads winding together.

After hours of walking he finally asks: "Why'd you do it?"

"Do what?"

"Become . . . this." He holds up his Blighted arm, commands the vine to unspool and form shapes in the air, like a twister dancing across the earth. "Did she do this to you? The witch, I mean."

"I chose it. And she's not a witch." *And she made me special.* Not like the other Blightborn. Maybe not even like Cael.

"Uh-huh. Well. A witch is what everyone calls her."

"Because they don't know her."

"*You* don't know her, either. She's Empyrean. Or was, once."

Wanda smiles, then presses a fist to her chest. "Not in here. She has the Heartland in her heart now. Mother Esther has all our best interests—"

"All right, whoa, no. Let's hash this out. She's not your mama, Wanda."

"I know she's not." She pouts. "She's mother to us all."

He stops. Points a finger. "That's cuckoo talk. Crazy as a starveling rat. She's not your mama, she's probably not even your friend. She's got an agenda like everyone else out here in the corn. Maybe, right now, that agenda lines up with what we wanna see happen. And I'm not saying she's evil, only that she's got *her* interests put ahead of *our* interests. Lord and Lady, she compared all of us to game pieces on a godsdamn *Checks* board. She's thinking about ten moves ahead, and I gotta be honest, I'm still trying to figure out all the moves that already happened."

"You'll see," Wanda says. "She cares about you." She hesitates, kicking her feet around the broken stalks. Before, she might've kept this all buttoned up, but she's feeling bold, brazen, ready to jump. The words come tumbling out: "I care about you. You wanna know why I did it? Why I . . . wanted to be like *this*? Yeah, okay, it was scary. Damn scary! At the time I didn't think of it as being special or getting some kind of gift like it was Crow's Day or something. I thought of it as being cursed. I still thought of it as the Blight, but I wanted to be close to you, Cael. I wanted us to share something. I wanted you to *see* how much I loved you and would give up for you—and this isn't just because we're Obligated. I've always loved you. You were strong and cocksure, never wantin' to just roll over and let everyone get their kicks in. When I got your name on Obligation Day, I about fell out of my shoes. I was happy then, and I'm happy now, and I hope one day you'll see that I can make you happy, too."

While she's speaking, Wanda can feel him there—a small firefly glow growing brighter and brighter, all these individual embers swirling together until he's ablaze with it. It washes over her, and she returns the light, returns the heat. And as her excitement grows, her voice gets louder, her words come quicker, and the corn around them quakes and crackles.

Cael crosses the open space between them, stalks snapping underfoot. Wanda catches a burst of scent there in the invisible distance—a mingling of heady, floral odors. The smell of trampled grass, of lush leaves torn in half. Her heart pounds. Cael reaches for her. His hands on her cheeks—she's cold, he's warm.

He leans forward.

Their lights merge—the scents overwhelm.

The kiss is long and deep.

His vine coils around her middle. She grabs one of his hands, and their fingers sprout coils and curls of green—all of it braiding together so that she's starting to lose where she ends and where he begins.

Dry, dead earth splits with the sound of rocks breaking.

Roots reach up, pull them down together. They never break the kiss.

Thought is lost to sensation.

It devours him as they devour each other.

They do this once. Then they do it again, the next night. And the night after that. Days of traveling through the corn. Nights of merging together.

Each time, the act leaves an imprint—

Plumes of fragrance. Meshed fingers, tangled vines. Wet kisses and trailed saliva. Sticky, tacky sap. Dead earth churned fresh, tilled back to life by the movement of the boy and the girl above it and roots crawling through the earth like worms below them. Tongues tasting nectar. The softness of skin together, and the whisper-rasp of green against green. Vines twining, unspooling, twisting, teasing. Pinning wrists. Small grunts. The snap of branches. And then release—like trees losing leaves in a hard wind, shuddering and howling.

Cael feels lost to it all. A part of his mind still wants to do the human thing and think about what is happening. Him and Wanda? What about Gwennie? But it feels good, it feels *right*, and he can't help his attraction to Wanda now. At first he thinks it must be due to the Blight, but then he remembers seeing her back in the corn outside the Empyrean depot—her with the rifle, her *seeing* his Blight and still having love in her eyes—and she seemed strong and confident in a way she hadn't before. . . .

But then all those thoughts get buried underneath a more primal urge. A tide of feeling that isn't human and maybe not even animal. It's all colors and textures. Memory stirred by smells and tastes. The heady floral scent; the spoor of sweat; the taste of that sweat mixed with the sweetness of something else; the feeling of skin too smooth to be skin—

He gives in to that. Reeling. Reveling. Wanda moans against him. She moves to get comfortable, nuzzles into the curve of his outstretched neck, hand draped on his thigh like a resting butterfly.

The ground is soft. Welcoming.

Sleep takes him swiftly.

He dreams of being swallowed up into the earth. Roots pulling him down. Black, churned earth opening up. Teeth of rock and broken stalk. A hellsmouth of the mad, hungry world.

Then: a vibration through it.

A thrumming. He draws a sharp breath through his nose.

A ship.

His eyes snap open.

A shadow moves in front of the light above. Streaks of white go to wincing black. Cael thinks: *Is it morning? Past morning? Already? How did that happen? How did time slip away so dang quick?*

Someone stands over him.

A tall shape. Broad. Blotting out the sky.

He reaches up, starts to protest—

"Hey, who in King Hell—"

Something cracks him hard in the face.

Wanda screams as consciousness threatens to slip away. Blackness bleeds in at the edges of his vision, and he sees his attacker—just some Heartlander, he thinks at first, but then he sees. The skin isn't skin—it's some kind of rubber casing, flesh-colored but not actually flesh. The material bunches up around the joints, and when the thing moves, he hears the servos whine and metal grind on metal. He sees not human eyes but blue glass disks bulging from a peach-pink face.

It raises an arm, and a sonic cannon roars to life.

THE BRUTAL GIRL

SPARKS RAIN DOWN off the mountain like a water-fall made of fire, bright embers leaving streaks through mist.

Enyastasia Ormond, seventeen years old, stares down off a steel grate platform at the sight. From time to time a small black shape emerges from behind the cascade of sparks, coming through it and catching fire—fluttering and jerking about, clearly in pain, trying to rise higher before falling. A burning star.

They're bats. Here the Empyrean is constructing the new flotilla in the mountains of the Workman's Spine, the various peaks serving as assembly sites for the new flying city. And here, where they're constructing the control tower, sits a cave for juniper bats. Little black mousy things. Creatures who love the little pale berries on the everblue trees that grow in the gorges below. If the bats were smart, they'd stay in their bat cave. But they don't. The construction disturbs them. And so about every half hour, one decides to be brave—or perhaps it just can't deal anymore with the anxiety of all this light and sound, all this clamor and brightness—and it flits out into the mountain air, flying like a poppet on a string.

And it flies right through a curtain of fire.

The bat burns, and it dies.

Enyastasia thinks this is very funny.

Not ha-ha-out-loud funny. But quietly, internally hilarious.

It lifts her spirits because, as a metaphor, it works. These bats are an emblem of the Heartlanders. They're animals. Animals who don't know how to remain content and cling to their cave spires like good little beasties. The Heartlanders are trying to escape the cavern. They want to fly. But when they do, they will be met with a shower of sparks and a rain of fire.

They will be met by Enyastasia Ormond.

Wind whips. The cataract of fire is moved by it, embers cast wide.

A few bats flit free and escape, squeaking as they seek freedom.

The girl grunts. Irrational rage rises inside her. But she stills herself and remembers that the bats are fundamentally stupid. Occasionally lucky, but always dumb. The bats will come back to their cave.

And when they do, they will catch fire.

Behind her, a voice.

A girl like her. A year younger. She has a name, or had one. Bettina. Her face is a labyrinth of fresh scar tissue, healed but pink. The puffy ridges sporting delicate black lines cresting each tiny hill of skin. It's a living mask. A reminder of what the girl has lost. A reminder of what the girl can never be again. And in this, she is no longer Bettina.

She is only Harpy. One of many.

"Dirae," the Harpy says. "It's time."

The cylindrical chamber wraps around one of the peaks of the mountain—this peak called Zebulon's Finger for reasons Enyastasia does not know. (Nor, frankly, does she give even a single damn; history is of no interest or value to her. The future, on the other hand, is hers to own.)

Two men sit in chairs the color and shape of blood orange halves. Red cushions, burnt umber exteriors.

The one man is old, long, and livery. Flesh hanging off him like a rag tossed over the peg on a coatrack. He's tall, thin, and knobby as a coatrack, too, and sitting there in the chair he looks kinked-up, given over to discomfort.

The other man is younger. Not as young as she is, certainly—Enyastasia knows that ultimately she is just a girl, and he is no boy. But compared with the ancient spirit sitting across from him, Heron Yong looks fresh-faced and innocent. Naive, even. Mouth pressed to a flat line, hair bound in a small knot behind his head, above the base of his skull. He looks nervous.

The old man speaks. His body appears ancient—shaking like a broom in the hands of a palsied maid—but his voice is strong as a horse's hoof stomping dirt with its iron shoe. Deep, resolute, unwavering.

"Enyastasia Ormond," the old man says. "It seems that we have heaped a great deal of trust—or, rather, faith—upon your shoulders. Looking at you now I question if you have the frame to support this burden."

Fuck you, old man.

She sniffs and forces a stiff smile. "As this burden is not a literal physical one, I don't think my stature or frame hold a great deal of relevance, Master Architect."

Master Architect Berwin Luzerne makes a face like he just took a bite out of a rotten apple. A horse apple, maybe. He stands. She thinks he'll walk the way he shakes, a doddering, juggling step. But his stride is fast and swift—equal more to his voice than to the shudder in his hands.

One of those hands lashes out, grips her jaw tight. She can feel the pinch of his arthritic claw. Her teeth grind and pop.

"Look at you," he says. "Your grandfather would be disappointed in you. Such potential wasted. All that schooling. All that time spent grooming you for great things. And for what?" He runs a thumb over the scars she cut into her own cheek. "You've marked yourself like a savage."

"A savage girl to fight savage people." She thinks but doesn't say: *And my grandfather was a pipe-addled half-wit. Smart in architecture and design. Dumb in everything else.* That old wisp of a man, living by the urges he felt in his pants, discarding wife after wife—as her grandfather got older, his wives got younger. And he still wanted the children to call them "grandmother."

Puke.

"Let us walk back outside," he says, relinquishing his grip on her jaw.

As he turns and points that long stride toward the door, she rubs her jaw, and Heron gives her a look. She scowls, turns away, a red rage rising to her cheeks. Heron hurries after the Master Architect, waving her on.

The Master Architect: overseer of all new flotilla construction and of all the Grand Architects beneath him. He, like they, is master of his own flotilla, too: the Luzerne Garam Ilmatar, built by—who was it? Luzerne's great-grandfather? Great-great? Whatever. That, again, is history and she can no longer peer too deep in the past lest she overlook those events in recent memory. She is the hand of vengeance. She is the one who will reclaim the honor and might of the Empyrean. It is with her spear that she will remind the Heartlanders that their place is either kneeling in the dust or hanging on the end of a godsdamned pike.

She scowls and follows after. Why come inside if they were just going to go back outside?

Wind whips.

The Harpy nods her head as they all pass.

Luzerne walks to the edge, gazes out on the construction spanning miles of mountain peaks, some connected with walkways and cables, others independent. Not far, welding skiffs hover and bob as they approach, firing mooring cables into the mountain rock to hold steady. It's a dangerous job. Fire the anchoring piton into the wrong spot and *boom*:

Avalanche.

"We would usually build this flotilla in the sky," he says, stating something both she and Heron already know. "But the Yong Heron Herfjotur is valuable enough to warrant hiding it from the . . . *raider scum* below."

"I agree," she says.

"It is not your *place* to agree," he chides her. "Agreement from you sounds as if you are also afforded the chance to disagree."

I am. This was all my design. All of this. You think I'm just some dumb little girl and you hold my mooncalf grandfather in the highest regard, but all this is happening because I was smart enough and angry enough to demand that all the Grand Architects listen.

And listen they did.

Over the last year, she's been working tirelessly. Losing sleep training an army of young girls like herself—children orphaned by the fall of the Saranyu, children whose parents were on the flotilla when it fell but who were themselves studying on other flotillas (as is the Empyrean way these days). They scarred their faces and marked them with ash and ink to ensure they will always be seen as the Harpies that they are. Creatures of vengeance.

It was her idea, too, to construct a new flotilla to replace the Saranyu—and not just another floating city. Not some island of pretty buildings and vineyards and scholarly white towers. This would be a warship, a city built to tame those animals scrabbling in the dust bowl below. A flotilla designed with one goal: to punish the terrorists for thinking they could tear down the sky.

Herfjotur. All her idea.

Just a girl.

"The flotilla will fly in a matter of months," he says. "Perhaps sooner?"

"Yes," Heron offers. "Sooner is the goal."

"But," Enyastasia says, jumping in, "the Harpies are ready. It's time to enact Project Raven. The Initiative is in full swing, but the mechanicals can only do so much. Their use as soldiers is valuable but ill-fitting and incapable of the finesse necessary—"

"Project Raven is dead."

"Wh-what?"

"It is over. I have found it unbecoming of a young girl in our care—the granddaughter of one of our own architects, no less—to be carving up her face and the faces of other Empyrean children to serve as assassins. It is ludicrous."

She makes a sound somewhere between a laugh and a howl of rage. "You're kidding. You're seriously godsdamned kidding. I've worked for a *year* to train these girls. We're ready! The . . . the Heartlander menace is spreading. But we can end it. We don't do it by killing them all, we don't do it by going to war, we do it by going down there, finding the ones with their hands on the leashes of all the dust-eating dogs, and cutting off their heads. It's a targeted—"

"We will have the war-city Herfjotur. We will not need you."

"The war-city is a symbol!" she cries. Heron watches the two of them argue, fear flashing in his eyes. "A reminder that we maintain supremacy in the sky. It's a weapon of last resort. The architects voted for this!" *They voted for* me.

He shrugs. "They were bewildered and desperate. The fall of the Saranyu left many reeling. They grabbed the first solution put before them—they were starving children willing to eat filth to satisfy their hunger. Tonight I will be holding a new vote, and they will overwhelmingly agree that your plan is not one of Empyrean favor. I've already canvassed them. They're convinced to let this field go fallow at my urging. All we need is the vote."

It's like a gut-punch. "The Harpies and I . . ." But the words rot in her mouth. All she can say is: "You're an idiot."

Heron gasps.

The Master Architect wheels on her. Again he grabs her face, hard enough this time that she knows bruises will form in the wake of his grip. "You are a strange, vile girl. Likely a psychopath. Certainly deluded. You had opportunity well and beyond what others already had and yet you wasted it. A violent girl. An *ugly* girl." Her teeth grind together. Her eyes begin to water. "I am only glad that I stepped in before your delusions took us all for a—"

His eyes go wide. He continues speaking—or, rather, his lips continue moving, but no sound comes out. Just a squeal like a stuck pig.

He looks down as she draws the knife out of his middle.

Blood drips onto his shoes. *Pat, pat, pat.*

"What's wrong?" Heron asks, stepping toward them before crying out, "Oh, by the gods. Lord and Lady, *Lord and Lady.* Enya, what did you do?"

"Shut up," she hisses. "Shut. Up. I got you this job." She points the bloody knife at him. "I named you to this. You're not a Grand Architect, Heron, not yet. You . . ." But she doesn't know what to say. She's losing the thread. Berwin Luzerne is standing a foot away from her, clutching his middle, face bloodless as a rag wrung of its water.

"You . . ." the old man wheezes.

Mercy of the gods. A knife-hole in his gut is a death sentence for him—*and* for her. That won't do.

But.

But.

She meets his eyes. Hateful embers like the sparks raining down.

Enyastasia tries to transmit her own hate right back at him.

Then she gives him a gentle shove off the platform.

The Master Architect reaches for her, but it's too late. His arms pinwheel, as if he's a bird trying to fly. A bird with clipped, broken wings.

A bat on fire trying not to die.

He falls through the mist to the jagged peaks below.

For a moment, she just stands there, breathing the cold, thin air. Snake-tails of steam leave her mouth with every exhale. *I just killed the Master Architect.* She tells herself it was the right thing. He was a throwback, the last of his breed—a breed whose extinction she hastened but did not create. A little voice reminds her: *You are a strange girl. Other girls your age have taken lovers by now. Other girls, other boys. They've begun their studies. They travel to other flotillas to learn. And what have you done? Scarred your face. Trained other girls to be violent like you.* She was always violent—even when her father didn't keep her in a box. A biter in proto-school. A scrapper after that. Claws out, teeth bared. Her grandmother said something was wrong with her, that she didn't come with the part of the brain that everyone else must've come with. Her father called her a "brutal girl."

Heron bleats like a throat-cut sheep, startling her.

He saw what she did. Did anyone else?

She looks up.

There. The welding skiffs.

Two of them.

Men looking. Pointing. They're too far away to know for sure, but . . .

She turns to the Harpy. The one who was once Bettina.

"You," she barks. The girl, to her credit, snaps right to attention—unlike Heron, she isn't standing there, staring at the space where Berwin Luzerne once stood. She stands tall and stiff, shoulders back, feet together.

"Yes, Dirae."

"Go. Take two of your sisters. Kill the men on those skiffs. Make it look like an accident. Understand?"

A short, clipped nod from the girl, then she's moving inside, to the elevator. To the other Harpies, a few pods below.

Breathe. Breathe. Steady your heartbeat. This is good.

This is what progress looks like.

Heron stammers: "Wh-what are we going to do?"

"We're going to keep going" is her answer. "Nothing changes."

"He's dead! That's a change."

"He *fell*," she corrects. "He was old. And careless. And he fell. The other architects will gather and take control for a time. Eventually they will name a new Master Architect."

"And if that Master Architect disagrees with your plan?"

"He won't," she says. "Or *she* won't. And you won't tell anyone what really happened here, because if you do, then by the gods . . ."

He stiffens, swallowing hard.

Enyastasia says no more than that. Instead, she just stands at the edge of the platform, breathing in, breathing out. Not sure if she should laugh or cry. Eventually, she sees shadowy shapes running along the anchor cables, spears in their hands. Soon after, the screams of men dying. Bodies thrown overboard. Then both skiffs explode, and fire rains down.

THROWING KNIVES

A KNIFE FLIES FAST, embedding in the man's head. It rocks back on its mooring, coming loose, and rolls off onto the ground. The skull breaks apart, and dry corn scatters like a cupful of loose teeth.

The cob man is dispatched.

"Finally learning how to throw those things," Squirrel says in her squeaky voice. She swings her arms and claps her hands. The girl can never seem to stay still. She's a bundle of energy vibrating on a whole other frequency.

"I learned from the best," Gwennie says, walking over and reclaiming the throwing knives from the body of the corncob man: a dummy they built together for target practice, cobs strung together under a ratty burlap shirt. She boots the head into the hungry corn.

Her little brother, Scooter, hops out of the way as it tumbles past. "Nice kick, sis." He doesn't smile, though. He hasn't smiled in a while. And his arm still looks crooked—it works, but it's weaker than his other one. From where it broke.

Still, she thanks him. Walks past and musses his hair. "Where's Mom?"

"Back in her room."

"She okay?"

"She's okay." But the way he says it, Gwennie knows that isn't true. Means her mother is having another one of those days. Her gray days. Never gets outta bed.

Squirrel comes up, snatches one of the knives out of Gwennie's hand. Balances it on a fingertip, then hops it from one digit to the next. "Papa would still say you need to do better."

"I do need to do better."

"I miss Papa."

"I know. I miss mine, too." She chances a glance at Scooter, who looks lost and sad.

Damn.

Squirrel shrugs. "I'm sorry yours is gone. But Papa will be back for me one day soon. You'll see."

A vein of defiance and anger in that statement. Gwennie has not yet had the heart to pinch that vein and close it off. She carries her own grief: the loss of her father, the death of Cael. Hopelessness has settled into her bones like an infection. She can't do the same to Squirrel. The girl wants to believe her father survived the city falling, so be it. Reality will get in its punches soon enough.

• • •

She goes and sits down on her bed. No. Not her bed. *Their* bed. Soon, very soon, to be her wedding bed. A crummy, rickety thing as comfortable as sleeping on a grave-mound. It lists to the right, too, like a boat in a hard wind—Boyland's heavy and gives the bed a drunken lean. Even when he's not in it.

On her pillow is a single apple.

Big as her fist. Skin shined to a gleam.

A note tied to the stem. From Boyland?

She sits at the edge of the bed, ignoring the apple. Her stomach growls. She's hungry. Not starving—they have food here, thanks to Balastair and Cleo living a mile over. Balastair had seeds with him. Always had seeds with him, he said. Turns out, he was the one who gave the seeds to Arthur, Cael's father. They knew each other, though Balastair said not well, and mostly through his mother and . . . oh, King Hell, none of it matters anymore. Gwennie *is* starving, but not for food. She's hungry for something else. *Anything* else.

They live in the shadow of the Workman's Spine mountains. They came here, as per the map—it's in the corner of the Heartland, miles from a small town called Tin Cup and not much else except the sonic Boundary and the mountains past it. With what little money they had and what work they could offer, they all carved out small homes here.

In one week, they're getting married.

Because, really, she thinks, *what choice do I even have?* Every time she lies underneath him, the bed jumping and thumping against the wooden floor, that's the thought that goes through her. *I don't have any choice. This is my best option.* And yet, no matter how many times she thinks it, it never feels true. Some things are true and don't feel that way, she knows that. That's what Gwennie tells herself to help find sleep at night.

Of course, when she sleeps at night, she dreams of Cael and Balastair. She thinks of her time as a raider, a short time among the Sleeping Dogs on the flotilla. She thinks of the map that hung on Balastair's wall, a map that showed a world much greater than just the Heartland, a world with places called the Braided Glades, the Moon Coast, the Atlas Ocean.

An ocean! A coast!

Something. *Anything.*

Anything but this. Living here in the upper corner of the Heartland map, hoping to be like a marble that rolled under a bed or a ring that slides to the back of a drawer, hoping to avoid attention, hoping to never be found. A while back she told Balastair she wanted to be out of here, wanted to leave, but he said they couldn't. He said it was too dangerous. Things were changing out there. The Empyrean was a convocation of eagles protecting its nest and eggs now—vicious, ready to kill without provocation.

Then she kissed him. And he kissed her back. And it was good. She asked him again: *Now will you go away with me?*

But he said no, no, they need to stay safe. Shelter in place.

She cried that night.

The next day she told Boyland they were getting married. They set a date. That date is fast approaching. Nobody talks about it. It's just assumed to be happening, like a train you know will arrive. A train you think might run you over.

She hasn't cried since. Instead, she feels dried up. Like ground gone parched from greedy, thirsty roots. A thought strikes her like a thrown stone:

I need a change or I'm going to die here.

She looks down at one of the throwing knives in her hands.

Die here in forty, fifty years. *Or die here now.*

The knife is heavy. Sharp.

She grabs it, grabs the apple, and cuts into it. The note falls onto her thigh and she turns it over—

A little sweetness —B.

The calligraphy—elegant. Looks like it was written by a human of some taste, not a witless clod with all the brains of a tree stump.

Which means: a gift from Balastair, not from Boyland.

The apple skin pops under the knife as she cuts a few little slices. Chews on them. It is sweet. She barely tastes it.

Footsteps. The rickety shack-house shakes.

In comes Boyland, big dumb grin on his big dumb head. His arms are crossed, and his chest is puffed out like a dog that just killed a chicken.

"I did it," he says.

"Good" is her only response. It's a hollow word, a dead word.

"You don't even know what I did."

"Nope."

"You're still mopey. Okay. I know, I get that. This'll fix it." His mouth spreads into a big flat-toothed grin. "I've set us up. After the wedding, we can get rid of this shack. Build a proper farmhouse. Get a new boat, maybe—"

"What did you do?"

"Whaddya mean, what did I do? Helluva way to ask that question. Lord and Lady, Gwennie. A wife is supposed to have faith in her husband—"

I'm not your wife yet. "Just tell me. Just tell me what you did, Boyland, that's gonna set us up for life out here in the middle of Old Scratch's crap-hole."

He stops for a moment, staring flatly at her, but then seems to find his center again: "I made a deal with Tin Cup's Mercado Maven. Little goblin-lookin' fella named Solow. I promised him fresh fruits and vegetables for a, a, a . . . what's the word, a *premium* payout and—"

She finds herself on her feet, in his face. His logjam arms grab her behind her back and pull her close for a kiss—he must think she's happy about this, which means he really is as dumb as the headless cob man out back—so instead, Gwennie pulls away and punches him in the arm.

"You ass," she says.

"What the hell?"

"Balastair told us those were *our* fruits and vegetables. That we couldn't sell them. Because selling them will draw *attention* to us. Empyrean attention!"

Boyland sneers. "Your *boyfriend* and I don't agree on that point. Nobody's paying attention to Tin Cup, Gwennie. We're at the godsdamn edges of the Lord and Lady's creation—"

The world is much bigger and much smaller than you think, buckethead.

Buckethead. That was Cael's word for him.

Cael.

Shit.

"He's not my boyfriend, you turd."

Boyland keeps on ranting: "—and nobody cares about these fancy-pants fruits and veggies, nobody cares because nobody's looking, and it's not my job as your husband to take care of that snooty Empyrean prick and his bitchy priss ex-wife or wife or whatever it is that they're doing now—"

"Wife," Gwennie growls. "They're back together."

"And I can see that burns you, too. You know what?" Here he thrusts one of those meaty sausage fingers in her face, just an inch from her nose, filling the minimal space between them with an aura of threat and menace. "I've let a lot slide with you. Because you're going to be my wife and because I love you."

"I can *really* feel the love."

"Oh, shut the hell up. You ain't been nice to me since we got engaged. I'm trying to take care of you. Take care of *us*. I gotta do what's best for you and me because if we're gonna try to bring a couple of babies into this world—"

Her laugh is a bitter purge. "You wanna have kids with me? Dream on, buckethead."

"You're mean. Mean as a rat snake." He nods suddenly like he's made some kind of decision. "I've been too nice to you. Lettin' you have your way and all, lettin' you think you're an equal partner in all this. My father didn't just let my mother have a share in the decisions, and she didn't want any, either, because as a woman she knew her place—"

"Your father was a drunk, and your mother was weak."

Bam.

He slaps her. Not hard enough to knock her out or send her backward, but his meaty paw still forces her teeth to clack together and leaves her face stinging. Gwennie roars, and even as he raises his hand again, the knife flashes, cutting the air with a hiss, and he reels his hand back. He holds his right hand with his left, and blood wells up through the fingers.

Boyland looks stunned. Not angry. Just shocked into silence.

"You killed Cael," she says, feeling the poison bubble up out of her—it had been stewing inside her for so long, pooling in her lungs, swimming in her guts, and here it is, spat out all over him as he cradles his knife-slashed palm. "I almost had him. Almost. If you had helped me, maybe we could've gotten him in the skiff. And he wouldn't have died there."

Boyland's voice is soft, not angry—a fraying, raggedy sound. "I had to do it to save you. If you had gone over with him, I dunno what I'd have done."

"No. You had to do it because if he was left alive, *then* I would've gone with him. Would've been me and him, not me and you. He saved my little brother. And that wasn't the first time! When Scooter was about to fall, what did you do? Tell me, Boyland. Tell me how *you* would've saved my little brother."

But Boyland doesn't say anything. Gwennie thinks in that moment that the real knife in her hand has nothing on the invisible one she just stuck in his heart.

"You hit me again," she says, "and next time I take the whole hand."

"Gwennie, wait—"

She pushes past him.

Out through the dingy shack, flinging open the rotten-board door. It falls off its hinges, rattles against the ground.

"I'm sorry," he calls after. "I'm so sorry. I just—I don't want to live like this anymore. In this . . . rat-trap. I'm sorry, I love you, Jeezum Crow, I do."

She marches out toward the skiff.

"I'll be back," she barks.

"Where are you going?"

"To fix your screwup."

Mole watches as a narrow little vine, thin as a rat-tail, trails across the Checks board. It gets to one of the peons, then the end of it blooms into a flower the color of fresh blood. The petals grab the piece like a soft, delicate hand, then use it to jump one of Mole's Gunfighters, knocking that piece out.

"Aw, man," he says. One step away and his Queen will be taken. He can move her. But he knows what happens next: Mother Esther will chase him around the board like he's a toad hopping away from a rumbling motorvator, trying not to get ground up in the threshing bar. Dangit. "I give up."

"Don't," she says, sitting across from him. Watching him, not the board. Her eyes swirl, iridescent colors. Like fly-eyes. Beyond the porch on which they sit—where they play Checks— the Blightborn continue their work at the farm. Work he sometimes helps with, though they never look at him like he belongs. She does, though. Esther never treats him like an out-sider. She smiles at him now and says: "You never know. You might get lucky."

"You said this game is about skill, not luck."

"So is life, and yet, luck matters."

"Uh-huh. Okay, okay." He considers his next move. As he

does, he says: "You seem to be putting a lot on that McAvoy jerk."

"Him and Wanda. The two of them."

"She's special." Mole snorts. "He ain't."

"They're both special. For different reasons."

"It true?"

"Is what true?"

"I heard Edvard saying that you sent them right into the path of danger. Not away from it like you told them. Said they'd run into trouble a couple-few days out."

She nods. "That is true."

"Why? If they're so special, don't you want them to survive?"

Esther smiles. "Only if they deserve to."

"So it's like a test?"

"It's a test."

"But Wanda could get hurt."

Esther nods.

Mole sits up straight. "She gets hurt, I'm blaming you. Which means I'll kill you dead myself."

"You like her."

"I *love* her."

"Good. Now put some of that passion into your game and make a move."

Tin Cup is barely a town. It's more a shanty popping up out of the corn. No plasto-sheen street—just a dirty, gravel-pocked X with a collection of crummy lean-tos and houses clustered together like hobos at a burn barrel.

At the far end sits the tallest building—a three-story hatbox with a rusted sign hanging out front reading BHAGRAM'S BAR.

It's where Solow, the Mercado Maven, will be. Solow doesn't make his wares public, like with most markets. He "curates." (His words.) Curates both who gets to see the collections and what goes into—and out of—the market.

Gwennie parks the skiff out front. No time to do otherwise. She storms into the bar.

It smells like cigarillos and puke in here. The chicha beer is to die for—maybe literally, because any time Bhagram pours a bowl, he first scrapes the mold off the top before handing it to you. It doesn't just smell sour, it smells like a cup of puke soup.

Everyone's gathered around the bar. A bar that is, in fact, just a series of old barrels strung up together, the hoops rusted, the wood stained.

Gwennie sidles up at the far end of the bar, away from the crowd of men hovering over something. They're jostling together, gasping and laughing. She doesn't know many people in this town, but she sees Bhagram there, obviously, and Horgo— that pig-nosed, toothless hobo. Resident drunk. Never *not* here in the bar. She has no idea how he makes the ace notes necessary to pay for drinks, unless Bhagram just serves him that sour mash bile-beer for free.

Thing is, she doesn't see Solow. Maybe Bhagram knows where he is. She raises a hand, tries to get the bartender's attention.

"Hey," she says. "Hello."

He holds up a silencing, impatient finger.

"Play it again," he says. Not to her, but to the crowd. "Turn it up this time, turn it up."

Gwennie looks over, notices that their faces are lit by a faint glow. A visidex, she guesses. Used to be those were a rare find here in the Heartland, but since the Saranyu fell, more have trickled out—so-called jail-broken devices that still connect to the Empyrean network but don't send out signals. Which means they can't be tracked. You get caught with one, the skyborn bring the pain, so most folks keep them hidden. Heartlanders use them mostly to follow news and watch Empyrean sex videos.

Which is probably what they're watching now.

And then, out of nowhere, she hears Cael's voice.

It's like a ghost calling out to her.

Faintly, distantly: *Gwennie, run.*

Her breath, trapped in her chest like a bird caught in a hand.

She looks to the window. Then the door. Expecting him to be standing there, staring in. Waving his arms. Warning her about—what?

But then she realizes. It's coming from the visidex.

With no thought toward rudeness or, frankly, her own safety, she pushes into the men and tries to spy the visidex. But the men push their shoulders together, walling her off. Bhagram's the one who says, "Let her through, let her see, this is wild, *wild*. Replay it. Replay it!"

They grudgingly make room for her. She smells sweat and sour beer and breath that could kill a goat-fly—

All that is lost when the video begins to play.

Grainy video. Static, unmoving. As if mounted on something.

Horseheaded Empyrean soldiers—*evocati augusti*—march out of the corn with two prisoners, each with arms bent behind their backs.

One of them is Cael.

The other she doesn't recognize at first. A girl.

Cael's face is a bloody mess. They shove him toward the camera, and she realizes that it must be mounted on the front end of a skiff or a ketch-boat. He looks dazed. Beaten. When they shove him, he staggers, almost falls.

The two *evocati* flank him, and two more shapes come up on the side.

She recognizes the herky-jerky walk—

Mechanicals. Two of them. Chests like metal barrels, heads shaped like Boyland's bucket skull. Each has an arm that looks like a sonic cannon. These are different from the ones she's seen. Upgraded, if you can call it that. Swaddled in a coating of fake flesh. Big eyes. Wide mouths with gleaming metal teeth. It's like by trying to make them look more human, they only succeeded in making them look less.

Cael looks up. She can see the moment when clarity hits— like he's suddenly got focus, purpose, determination.

"Here it comes," Bhagram says. The other men vibrate in anticipation. Gwennie doesn't have to wait long to see—

Cael's head has this barely visible twitch, and . . .

A dark shape sails out of nowhere, from way behind them. Blurry, at first, spinning. Then Gwennie realizes: it's a cob of corn.

It hits one of the *evocati*.

Whonnnng.

The soldier spins toward it. Two of the mechanicals pivot, too, their hip joints whirring and clacking as they train sonic cannons on nothing.

That's when Cael yells: "Wanda, run!"

Not *Gwennie, run.*

Wanda. It's Wanda Mecklin. Jeezum Crow, she looks different.

And then Gwennie watches what unfolds next with a nauseating mixture of fear and excitement. Equal parts *Cael is alive* and *why in the Lord and Lady's good green earth is he with Wanda?*

As the soldiers spin and Cael calls to Wanda—

She turns, starts to break away.

The stalks of corn all around them begin to whip about—

The *evocati* draws a thrum-whip and cracks the lash back toward Wanda just as a stalk of corn rips out of the dirt, borne on a lurching perch of spider-leg roots, and catches the whip. The coil lashes around it instead—

A flash of a corn-leaf, and Cael's bonds are cleaved in twain.

His hands are free.

Which means so is his Blight-vine.

One of the mechanicals wheels on him with its sonic cannon—

The vine coils around it. Cael pivots, turns hard, the gun jerking suddenly to the side, re-aiming it at the last moment as a sonic blast punches the *evocati*'s golden armor like an invisible battering ram, denting it so hard and so deep the breastbone beneath must also be broken—and given the pained look on the man's face, seen clearly despite the grainy blur of the video, that's about right. Then Cael rips the mechanical's arm off and uses that arm like a bludgeon to smash it back to the dry, dead earth.

The other mechanical, though, is fast.

And its cannon is still loose.

And pointed at Cael.

Gwennie actually cries out, as if this is happening live, or as if her voice calling to warn him could travel back through time and change what's coming. Then, she thinks, maybe it does.

Because even as the cannon tracks him, Wanda is there— running fast, her mouth open and—oh, gods. Tendrils, dark tendrils from her mouth like a hundred rat-tails squirming. Except they're not tails. They're vines.

She's got the Blight, too. Wanda leaps on the mechanical's arm. Her head dives toward it and then wrenches back—

The arm snaps off in a shower of sparks as Wanda—looking now like some feral thing, some monster out of a storybook—jerks her head sideways, sending the arm flying into the shuddering corn. The men in the bar hoot and clap and gawp as she rips into the mechanical, her vines tearing it into sparking bits.

The last *evocati*, the one with the whip tangled in the corn, has freed a sonic rifle from his back—

Cael points at him. An accusing finger.

And following the line of that finger, his own Blight-vine flies.

The vine punches clean through the man's helmet and out the back of his head. Dripping red before sliding back through, retracting to Cael and once more winding back around his arm.

Again, a roiling mixture of emotions. Gwennie is happy that he's safe, but scared of who he is, of what he's become. And Wanda . . .

Cael, on the video, points toward the boat—toward the camera *on* the boat.

Wanda joins him in facing the lens.

Both of them raise their hands and all the stalks shudder and suddenly launch from the ground like rockets firing—their image on the screen is lost to all the motion and clamor, and then everything tips over and lists sideways.

Static remains on-screen before clicking over to darkness.

One of the men, a thick-browed thug with a nose like a lug nut, raps on the bar. "Play it again. Play it, play it."

Another man, hollow-cheeked and with an archipelago of dark melanomas rising up the side of his face, shakes his head and whistles. "I dunno who to root for there, boys. Blighters freak me out, but the Empyrean can suck Old Scratch's bung—"

"Ish called a *win-win shit-u-a-shun*," Horgo the drunk mutters. His breath is so bad she has to recoil, holding her own breath lest she lose that sweet apple all over the bar-top.

Bhagram spins the visidex around, goes to press play again, and the whole thing starts all over. She can only hear it now, the crunch of cornstalks underfoot, the sound of the cob hitting a helmet, *Wanda, run* . . .

Then a quick crackle of static. She can't see exactly what's happening—the angle doesn't allow it—but she can tell that the video has been replaced with a face on-screen. A visidex call.

She recognizes the shape of the head, and the voice confirms it.

It's Solow, the Mercado Maven.

Round, bulbous, like some corrupted fruit.

"Looking to round up a posse," he says, speaking like he's talking through a mouthful of wet rice. "One of those kids from the east came to me—Bayland or Boylan or whatever, the big one, the thickskull . . ."

Gwennie's blood goes cold even in the warm, dank air.

Solow continues: "Said he's out there growing fruits and

veggies that damn sure ain't on the list, wanted to make a deal, blah blah blah, who cares. I looked him up, though, and you know the girl he's with? They're all wanted. Check the visidex, look at the reward board. Piles of ace notes—"

They all slowly turn and look at her.

Dark, suspicious eyes narrowing to slits.

They've figured it out.

On the screen, Solow must be following their gaze. "What the—? Whaddya lookin' at? Oh. *Oh.* Jeezum god, are they there? The kids?"

Bhagram is the one to say: "We got this, boss."

Then he turns off the screen.

They all stare at each other like that for a while. Nobody moves. Only sound is the mouse-fart squeak of shifting floorboards underneath everyone as they tense up, ready for something, anything, to happen.

"You said you don't like the Empyrean," Gwennie says, trying to put as much steel and gunpowder in her voice as she can manage—but fear is a hard river running right through her. She remembers being in the tunnels in the Saranyu's Engine Layer, chased by that man and that boy. The things they wanted to do to her. The intent here in the eyes of these men seems to be greed more than it is lust, but she doesn't trust it to remain that way. Then, someone saved her. Now, she won't be so lucky.

"We don't," Bhagram says.

Melanoma grins, his mouth full of rickety teeth, like the cob man's teeth. "But we *do* like ace notes, little girl."

"Solow was right," she says. "We *are* growing fruits, vegetables. Proper ones. We can share them. There's money in there—and the garden keeps growing. The ace notes won't stop with one harvest."

"To hell with nancy-pansy fruits and vegetables," Lugnut grumbles. "Sounds like a lot of work, tending a garden. You, though . . ." And there it is. The flash of lust like light across a knife's blade. "You don't look like much work at all, do you, girl?"

Girl. The way he says it. He doesn't think anything of her except that she's a poppet doll to be flung around and used for his pleasure.

"You don't wanna do this," she says. A last warning.

"We do," Melanoma says.

"And we will," Lugnut adds.

Horgo scurries backward, looking frightened, like he doesn't want to be involved in any of this. So much so that he covers his eyes.

Bhagram lifts up something from underneath the bar: a sonic pistol. Dinged up and pitted like it had been in an explosion. Probably another gift from the fallen Saranyu: the crashed flotilla serving as an overflowing cornucopia of Empyrean *things*.

He lifts the pistol, casual, as if he has all the time in the world, and gently turns the dial—probably to stun, she thinks, unless the reward is for her dead or alive. The dial clicks and she thinks: *This is the only moment I have.*

She can't run. If she runs, she'll end up with a sonic round discharging in the middle of her back.

So that leaves her with only one option.

She executes that option before she even finishes thinking about it.

Melanoma gasps as Bhagram's head jerks from the knife—a

knife that was in her hand just a moment before and now sits buried in the gelatin of his eye, all the way back to the brain. Drool creeps from the barkeep's lips.

Then he drops.

"You killed our bartender," Lugnut growls.

He and Melanoma charge at her.

Melanoma pirouettes and tumbles. Lugnut's heels skid out from under him, and he topples backward like a stack of milk bottles hit with a rock. The thinner man has a knife sticking out of his chest. Lugnut has one in his throat.

The thinner man lays there, narrow belly heaving with what will surely be his last breaths. Lugnut gives one last bubbly wheeze before dying.

Gwennie bites back panic. Tries not to scream. Tries to regulate her own breathing even as her vision narrows. *Think of your mother. Of Scooter and Squirrel.* Solow will come here. Sooner than later. She has to move.

They all do.

BLOODLINES

LANE PACES. Everything feels buzzy and awful. He has to stop every ten feet or so, as vertigo threatens to drop him to the ground. Nausea tumbles. The lean bridge across his shoulders feels tight, like a clove hitch knot pulled too taut. His mother. *His mother.*

He almost killed her.

Maybe he did kill her.

He hasn't slept well these last couple of nights. Hell, he hasn't slept hardly at all.

The hallway in which he walks belongs not to a hospital but to what was once an Empyrean residence. At one time the floors were black glass, but they've since shattered, the fragments held together by—well, he doesn't really know. Some kind of plasto-sheen or floor glue (probably made from corn, because oh, hey, isn't everything?). The walls, alabaster, also ruined—not shattered like glass, but with lean cracks running end to end, giving them the look of fractured bone. Everything is dusty and in disrepair: a clamshell light hanging off the wall, tube wiring dangling, bits of ceiling pulled down. The city fell, and it did not land well—though, Lane supposes, it fared better than most things that drop from the sky. The fact that the Sleeping Dogs have been able to put Pegasus City together out of the Saranyu's wreckage is a testament, he thinks, to Empyrean engineering.

There. A moment of peace. Away from the thoughts of his mother.

But of course, once he realizes that, it's like shining a flashlight in a dark corner—and suddenly he sees the creature that waits there. A conflicted creature of guilt and anger. A spider with Lane's face.

Someone behind him. He turns—it's Killian.

The pale raider comes up, throws his arms around Lane, kisses his temple. Shushes him. Strokes his hair. "It's all right, Mister Moreau. It's all right. Everything's gonna be all right. Just fine, just fine."

Lane feels angry, but his tone can't muster it: "It's not going to be fine, Kill. Where've you been?" He suspects he knows the answer to that question. *Finding Pheen.* "That's my mother in the other room. I shot her. Do you get that?"

"Hellfire, I wish you'd shot *my* mother," Killian mutters into the space behind Lane's ear. "She was a whore. I don't mean that as an insult. I mean, quite literally, that she gave it up to whoever had an ace note to stick up her dress. My father could've been any number of motorvator repairmen or corn processing linemen from Blackgable to Freehold."

"I didn't know," Lane says, pulling away. "My mother was

no picnic, either. Went off to be a . . . a godsdang Babysitter, of all the things." *Traitor to the Heartland.* But there, then, that iron spike of guilt through the back of his mind, hitting like a headache. *She's still your mother, you animal.* "And now she's here. I thought . . . I don't know what I thought. She was dead, maybe. Or just so far from here that I didn't have to think about her."

Lane pats his side, finds the small cigarette case he has there—sterling silver, though tarnished, with an enamel Pegasus inlaid in the center. One of the many treasures given up by this ruined place. He pops the lid, finds a twisted cigarette—this isn't ditchweed, this is something they grow, or grew, here on the flotilla. It smells piquant. Fresh earth and dry cherry. He wraps his lips around it, doesn't light it. Just fiddles with it, waggling it about with his tongue, tasting the dry paper.

The door down the hall moves—all the angles are wrong since the buildings fell, and it sticks in the frame, has to be shouldered open.

The doc comes out. Nika Vellington. Broad-shouldered woman, looks like she could pull a motorvator through the corn all on her own. Skin darker than any Lane has seen—rumor is, she has blood of the Shattered Coast folk in her. A year ago, Lane hadn't even *heard* of the Shattered Coast, didn't even know that there existed a world beyond the corn.

He expects an absurd scenario—her emerging with hands slick with blood—but the only sign of her work is the line of sweat on her brow and her sleeves rolled up over her thick fore-arms and knotty elbows.

"She'll live," she says.

A sigh of relief escapes Lane's lips. And swiftly after, a match tip of anger pressed to the back of his mind sets the whole thing aflame, burning up any shame or guilt he had there. How dare that woman. His *mother*. Showing up here. Showing up *now*. "Thanks, Doc."

"That's your mother?" she asks. The ghost of an accent haunting her words: *Dat's your muthah?*

"Yeah. Yes. In name anyway." He fumbles for a lighter but can't find one and winces. "She awake?"

"The sonic did a number on her. The pills I gave her got teeth, and she'll be out cold rest of the day, maybe a week or more."

Killian perks up. "What, ahhh, what pills are those?"

But he swallows the question soon as Lane shoots him a look.

"But she'll live?" Lane asks.

"She'll live," the doc says.

Lane offers a hand. The doc shakes it. He says to her, "I know you weren't one of us before, but your services are . . ." He's looking for the word, but he's frazzled. He tries to sound *leaderly*, tries to conjure the tone and the words to sound properly *mayoral*. "Valuable. *In*valuable. And I just want to say, also—" Here, suddenly, whatever he was going to say has gone out of his head like a sheet blowing off a clothesline, caught on a wind, *poof, whoosh*—

Behind the doc, he sees his salvation:

Luna Dorado, striding up with purpose.

She pushes past the doc because—well, because that's Luna. "There's a sitch," she says to Lane. Ignoring everyone else in the room, as is her habit. "You need to deal with it."

Killian says: "We're a bit busy here—"

"Lane," Luna says. "Situation."

And then she pivots heel-to-toe and storms off. Like a hard wind blowing in one direction, unwilling or unable to be deterred.

They stand on the wall. It wasn't there when the Saranyu floated, but it's here now because Killian had the idea to build it: He said they were going to need protection beyond just the guns, and so he set all the ships and motorvators they could muster to dragging the rest of the flotilla wreckage back to Pegasus City so that the barrier could be cobbled from the remains. It's a patchwork wall of varying colors and building materials, giving it the look of a brock-turtle's mottled shell. That is in fact what some folks call it: the Shell.

Up here, a hundred feet above the Heartland, the wind whips. The corn looks like little blades of grass, gently swaying.

Lane thinks how far he's come from *Betty* the cat-maran.

He misses those days, in a way.

"What am I looking at?" he asks.

Luna points. Out over the wide-open green, a small ship hovers. A skiff of some kind. Empyrean, obviously, because Heartlanders don't have skyboats.

Then she hands him a visidex. A zoomed-in look at the skiff—again, definitely Empyrean, though beat to hell and back. Which is curious.

"The guns are trained on the ship," she says. Above the wall, at the corners, and then below, running laterally, are the guns of

Pegasus City—massive sonic cannons that once hung below the floating city or along its edges. Meant to deter an enemy attack from below, they repurposed them to repel attacks from above and from the side, thanks to Rigo's suggestion. It gives them one hell of an advantage, because they can shoot anything out of the sky that comes for them. The Empyrean don't have a ship that can get in range.

"It's an Empyrean scouting ship," she says.

"How do you know?" he asks.

"Because I'm not an idiot."

Well, okay, then.

Behind them, the ragged breathing of Killian, who's finally catching up as the meager platform that passes for an elevator disgorges him.

"Thanks for waiting, everybody," Killian rasps. "No, really, I'm fine, it's good, not dying over here or anything."

Luna shoots him a look, then rolls her eyes. Back to Lane: "Shoot it down. Then we'll check it out."

"You sure that's what's best?" Killian says, still doubled over, hands on knees. He straightens, holding his side with the flat of a hand. "I'm all for decisive action, really, truly, I am. But I find it a bit of a barbed burr to swallow that this ship out there is Empyrean. It's just hovering there like a fly. A harmless little puzzle."

Lane's about to speak, but Luna jumps in:

"Harmless. Harmless? Do you know who my father is?"

"Oh, here we go," Killian moans. "Of course we do, girlie. *Obviously.*"

And yet she tells them anyway, because that's how Luna is.

"My father is Carlton Dorado. Legacy member of the Captains' Council. And what he always said was *expect the unexpected*—"

"Oh-ho-ho, and how'd that work out for him?"

Lane winces at the sting. Because Luna's father is dead. Dead because one of the other captains on the council—Hvin Jarlskoenig—assassinated three of the other captains, betraying them for the Empyrean. (Reportedly, the Empyrean did not welcome Hvin with open arms so much as they threw him off one of the flotillas when he arrived expecting a hero's welcome.)

It's been a hard year on the Sleeping Dogs. They're ascendant now. Bigger than they'd ever been. But the chaos of the Heartland puts them all in precarious positions, and the ground continues to move beneath everyone.

Luna's jaw drops, then everything tightens up as if she's preparing to attack them both. "I let . . . whatever *this* is between you go on. Your little relationship? I don't judge. I don't care who sticks what in who. I care that things get done right. That we keep everyone safe and that we *collectively* stick it to the sky-bastards any chance we get. Now, Killian—"

"Think before you speak," the pale raider says.

"I appreciate your service to our people. I do. You were a helluva captain once upon a time, and Daddy admired you because you got things done. But now, you're a flower gone to seed. Drunk on the Empyrean's left-behinds: wine and Pheen from what I hear. And that means you're fuzzy around the edges. But I'm sharp. And Lane needs sharp to keep this city—"

The visidex beeps.

Lane looks down as the others both give him—or, at least, the screen—an irritated look. *Holy hell.*

"They're hailing us," Lane says, surprised. "They want to communicate."

"So talk to them," Killian says.

"It's a trap," Luna says.

Lane cocks an eyebrow. "How could it be a trap?"

"They send a virus over to corrupt all the visidexes and that jumps to what few computer systems we've managed to get running. Or they hone in on our frequency and fire a homespun rocket right up our dresses. Or they—"

Killian reaches for the screen. "Oh, for the sake of all the sweet Saintangels, answer the damn call."

Luna snatches the visidex from Lane's hands, then cancels the call. With a quick spin of her fingers she pulls up the gun cameras and command screen.

"Shoot them down."

She hands it back to Lane.

He turns to look.

The ship is still out there, hovering. He wants to think that means they're innocent, but Luna's filled him with these ideas. He can't be naive. He has a whole city to protect. One lapse of judgment brings this whole place down. Everything he's built here is balanced on the tip of his finger. One twitch and—collapse.

He pulls up gun controls on the visidex. The nearest cannon at the corner tower pivots, leveling a long barrel that looks not unlike the barrel of an Empyrean pistol, except built for the hands of a giant, not a man. The cannon thrums to life—

Just as the ship begins flashing its forelights.

Lane's finger hovers over the fire button.

"Oh, what now?" Luna asks, annoyed.

Killian just scowls and watches.

The lights flash intermittently. Not just a steady flashing, either, but in an erratic pattern: one flash, then a few seconds, then a long flash followed by a couple quick pulses and—

Lane freezes, watches the pattern go once, twice again.

Lord and Lady.

Lord and Lady!

He whoops and laughs and closes the gun camera screen.

"Let 'em land," he says to Luna. She starts to protest, and he just yells over her with a happy cackle: "I said, let 'em land!"

SUMMIT

RIGO LETS OUT a moan of relief. He wipes sweat from his brow and leans forward on the skiff's console with his elbows. "I thought we were dead."

"I began to worry that myself," Pop answers. He reaches over and musses Rigo's hair. "Using Bug Code was a good idea, Rigo."

He can't help it—Rigo feels a swell of pride. He was never able to please his own father, but maybe that doesn't matter. Maybe Pop's the only father he ever needed. The father he'd in fact had all along.

"*You* taught us Bug Code," he says. Way back in Boxelder, when Cael first started the Big Sky Scavengers with Gwennie, Lane, and Rigo, Pop said he wanted to teach them this code—a code that could be heard or seen, a code in dashes and dots. He called it Bug Code, and for a long time Rigo thought it actually had something to do with insects—something about wing patterns or their clicks and chirps. But later on Pop told them it had to do with a Vibroplex, a little device that generated the code for you, a device that everybody called a "bug." They learned the code to communicate with one another in situations where they couldn't speak, either at a distance or as a cipher when others— like Boyland, that big donkey—might be watching or listening.

So, Rigo hoped that the Lord and Lady hadn't seen fit to steal that memory from Lane's mind—and that Lane was out there watching them in the first place. Since nobody wanted to pick up their transmission, and since the guns all swiveled and pointed right at them, he had to think quick.

(Here he looks down at his missing leg and at the clumsy artifice that has replaced it, and he realizes that he'd much rather be able to *move* quickly than to *think* quickly. No girl will ever want a hobbling cripple like him. Not even a young hobo girl like Beryl—who doesn't even like boys anyway, as it turns out. He's never gonna find a girl. Never gonna have kids. Be old and alone and legless. Even more useless than his own father. Shoot.)

It isn't long before ships emerge from Pegasus City. A couple sloops with low-swept sails, the sigil of the Sleeping Dogs on each.

Again, Rigo tenses.

Pop must sense this, though, because he says: "It's all right. They're not attack boats. I think we just found ourselves an escort, Mister Cozido."

Meeting Pop in that theater back in Curtains changed everything.

First, well—first, Rigo thought he was dead. Thought maybe that those two bullies had beaten him to death in the alleyway with his own foot and that his fever dream before finally dying was to see Arthur McAvoy. Pop, like one of the guiding Saintangels to help him leave the dusty, corn-cracked earth and ascend to the sky to take his place in the manse of the Lady and the Lord.

But then he saw: Pop had changed. This was no idealized version, no heavenly illusion. The man had a scruffy half-beard. His face, even in the dim light of the old theater, showed lines deeper than Rigo remembered. Like he had aged more than just a year. Like he had aged *ten* years.

The man looked like a hobo—appropriate, as it would turn out.

Pop embraced Rigo and they hugged like that for a while. Arthur's voice cracked as he told Rigo how glad he was to see him, how seeing a friendly face from Boxelder meant the world. How he didn't expect it here at the far-flung fringe of the Heartland, but how it had helped him.

Neither of them spoke of Cael at that moment.

Instead, Pop showed Rigo what he'd been working on.

It was Martha's Bend all over again, except bigger. Below Curtains was a whole network of tunnels—many of which Pop hadn't dug out because they already existed. He said they once used these tunnels to smuggle people in and out of the Heartland, into the murky, swampy jungle beyond: a place Pop called Bleakmarsh. He said they seized on the original tunnels and built more, too. He didn't do it alone, of course.

He had help.

Jeezum Crow, Pop had a whole dang *army*.

Hobos and Blighters. Just like in Martha's Bend. But others, too—simple folk. Regular Heartlanders gone hobo. If Pop had dozens of folk with him in Martha's Bend, here he had hundreds. And the tunnels beneath the town went well beyond the borders of Curtains, stretching out a couple miles into the dirt beneath the Heartland. Pop said they even had a few tunnels that ran to other towns, too, and they planned on digging more.

It was a small society.

They were growing food.

They were building things: radios, water purifiers, corn-boats, motorvators repurposed to dig underground.

And they were stockpiling weapons.

A few sonic shooters. Couple thrum-whips. And a lot of bladed weapons: sharpened shovels, corn scythes, moon sickles, machetes, knives.

Pop didn't say much about that.

Instead, he took Rigo down a long, narrow dirt-wall passage.

He took him to a room at the end with a simple cot at the far wall.

On the bed lay Filomena McAvoy. Cael's mother. A body besieged by tumors. Worse than before, by the look of them— her face was lost to them entirely. The tumors across her flesh were like sandbags stacked upon her.

Sitting by the bed was a woman—

A woman who turned toward Rigo and Pop as they entered, a woman who Rigo saw with no small surprise was Merelda, Cael's sister.

She was never particularly nice to him—nor was she mean, really. Mostly she just ignored Rigo, treated him as if he were a minor irritation, like a slobbery dog or something. But here, he saw the tears brimming in her eyes, and next thing he knew she was up and hugging him. And the moment was like a cork popped out of a bottle, letting out old, stale air so they could breathe again.

Because suddenly they were all gathering around the bed and sitting down and talking about . . . everything. About how Pop came to the edges of the world, where the Empyrean's gaze was weakest. About how Merelda found her way here after hearing about a man named Arthur who was recruiting hobos—"scooping them up," she said. About how everything has changed, how the Empyrean have gone on the offensive after the Saranyu fell (and how that was more of an excuse to continue what they had already begun with the Initiative, to turn Heartlander men and women into mechanicals), how the Sleeping Dogs have staked out Pegasus City, how the Maize Witch is real and drawing the Blighted to her as if she were the flame and they were the moths.

Rigo told them how he came to leave Pegasus City—"Every day for weeks the Empyrean kept sending new ships, new soldiers, and we just kept shooting them down. We were living in ruins. Folks were trickling in, sick, injured. We started hearing those stories about more towns like Tuttle's Church: people turned to . . ." There he let his voice trail off. "I just had to go away." *I couldn't stomach it.*

And it was then that Merelda talked about Cael.

She told the story of them on the Saranyu. She and Gwennie and Scooter and a couple others Rigo didn't know. She said how Cael and Boyland (together!) showed up, and how Cael saved Gwennie's little brother. And then, as everything fell to hell, Cael fell with it.

There it was.

The truth of the thing.

Cael was dead.

Merelda's brother. Pop's boy. And Rigo's captain. Dead.

It crushed Rigo. Crushed him right into the dirt, like one of Lane's cigarettes smashed by the toe of his twisting boot. He tried not to cry, but dangit he was never really good at stoppering that bottle, and the tears came and so did the snot, and the weight hit him all at once. All the things he'd lost: his home, his leg, his family, his friends. His future, even.

Pop patted his back. Told him that grief was okay.

But that it would have to come later. And Rigo looked up, confused and, for a moment, angry. Because Pop had had time with the news about Cael. Pop was allowed to grieve, so why should that be robbed from Rigo?

Then Pop said, "We'll have time to mourn, but for now, we've work to do. Are you ready to work, Rigo?"

Gamely, numbly, Rigo nodded.

"Good. Because we need to pay a visit to our old friend Lane Moreau."

Lane sees Rigo hobble down out of the skiff and his face erupts in a big smile, and he claps his hands and begins a long stride to meet his old friend—

But when Pop comes down after, Lane stops, breathless for a moment. Then the whoop that comes out of him is loud enough and happy enough, you'd think he just found out the Empyrean took off into outer space with plans to never come back. He breaks into a swift run and collides into Pop so hard his own legs kick back and catch air, and Pop has to steady himself against the door, wincing. But he laughs, too, and hugs back.

"You're alive," Lane says, smile so big it looks like half his head's on a hinge. "Old Scratch and King Hell, Pop! You're alive!"

Pop laughs again, but this time it's the laugh of someone who's been through it all and come out the other side: a laugh with the paint worn off, a laugh with rust on it. "Guess you found me out, then."

And then it's on to Rigo, picking him up and shaking him like he's full of money or candy. Lane squeezes him so hard Rigo thinks he might pop.

All around, onlookers stare. A young girl stands nearby, pouting. Near to her is someone Rigo almost doesn't recognize: Killian Kelly. Once one of the captains, he now looks almost like a ghost. As if something vital has been sucked out of him. Sallow, thin, more a bedsheet twisted up than a man.

Rigo can sympathize.

Others stare from the decks of the two sloops that escorted them in. Above, on catwalks and balconies, other Heartlanders watch. They don't look suspicious, but they damn sure aren't welcoming, either. If Rigo had to describe them, he'd say they look weary. Maybe a little scared. A whole lot burned out.

And he can sympathize with that, too.

"C'mon, c'mon," Lane says, finally pulling away. He claps his hands. "Welcome to Pegasus City, gents. Who wants a tour?"

Nightfall. Rigo's tired and sore. He feels the skin around his prosthesis is chafing, raw as a corn husk. Pop must be feeling it, too.

His hobble had gotten worse as the afternoon went on, as Lane took them through the shattered streets and crooked buildings of Pegasus City. The whole thing has changed since Rigo left it, since he walked away from this place knowing that he couldn't be a part of whatever would happen here. Lane and the other raiders have made strides he couldn't have imagined. It looks like a proper city, almost, like one of their own towns given a high-grade fertilizer—everything grown up and out, towering over him.

Even ruined, he understands now the majesty of the Empyrean. What they have up there truly is the Seventh Heaven.

It's just that they think they deserve it.

And that the Heartlanders don't.

Lane showed them everything he could: the tortoiseshell wall, the massive sonic cannons (Rigo takes special pride that it was his idea to put those there), the housing district (repurposed apartments from the Empyrean), the machine shop, the green-houses (all the glass shattered, but plants growing), the docks and hangars where they stow their corn-ships and skyboats, and finally, what Lane says is the most important thing: the engines. He told them that the engines failed and fell separate, and most of the Engine Layer was just scrap. But, he said, the engines themselves—the humongous hover-panels in particular—were reparable. Now fixed, they wait only for the fuel necessary to power the generators. Fuel that will come from the corn.

Now they sit around a white crooked table in a tall white tower—inside what looks to be a big damn birdcage, iron-wrought with an emerald patina.

"Used to be one of their jail cells, I'm told," Lane says, getting out a decanter of a liquid so red it's almost black. With one hand he manages to claw-grab three glasses and he plunks them on the table, starts messily pouring. "This is wine. Like, actual wine made from actual grapes. They grew all kinds of stuff up here. Potatoes and grapes and funny fruits like rangpurs and bloodberries and papa-yuzus. Like I always figured they gave us their scraps as rations. Worse than scraps. Food pastes in tubes and mechanically separated meat goop. Just eyeballs and butt-holes mashed up. Poison, basically. But this stuff"—he swills the bottle and it goes *gloonk gloonk gloonk*—"this really is the top of the pops, the uppermost level of heaven itself."

Three glasses, one going to each of them. He lifts a glass and walks around, clinking it to each.

Lane finally sits.

He laughs. "I think you're supposed to, like, smell the wine or something. . . ." He pauses, shrugs, then takes a big long gulp.

"Pegasus City is one of the most impressive things I've ever seen," Pop says. "I'm proud of you for what you did here."

Rigo watches Lane stiffen. His old friend tenses up, like he's suddenly uncomfortable in his own clothes, in the chair, like maybe the wine tastes bad, too. The smile that arrives looks forced. "Thanks, Pop."

"I bet the Empyrean are hungry to get their hands back on the fallen flotilla. They made attacks?"

"A few in the beginning. The first wasn't an attack—it was a salvage mission." Another gulp of wine, finishing the glass. "They thought they'd be hauling the city back up into the sky, but they were shit outta luck."

Pop leans forward. "Were there Empyrean folk alive after that? After any of the attacks or even when it fell?"

"There were some." Lane smacks his lips now, looking guilty, like a child being interrogated by a teacher. Or a parent.

"What'd you do with those people?"

"Some of them are in prisons like these," Lane says, gesturing with the empty glass to the prison bars all around them. "Some of them didn't . . ." He clears his throat. "Some of them didn't quite make it."

Pop nods. "I see. Lane, it's time maybe to talk about why I'm here."

"Sure, sure, okay."

"Remember what I was doing in Martha's Bend?"

Lane leans forward, eyes narrowed. "I do. Hobos and Blighters. A fresh garden. That was something special."

"I'm doing it again."

Blink, blink. Like a silent bomb going off—all concussion, no sound. Rigo detects—well, he doesn't know what it is. It's tension, but possibility, too. Lane's got gears turning behind his eyes as he thinks this over. He pours himself another glass of wine and drinks it.

"How many?" Lane asks. "People, I mean."

"Two hundred and fifty-six."

"That's a big number."

"Big enough. What do you have here?"

"Not quite two thousand."

"My people would add to that. In a big way."

Lane nods. "We have the infrastructure. To support them, I mean. The Saranyu has resources out the wazoo."

"I could bring my people here."

"That would be . . ." Lane laughs. "That would be incredible."

"But there's a catch."

"Okay . . . ?"

"I need you to step down."

Lane smiles like it's a joke, but he fast figures out that nobody else is joining him. "I don't understand. Step down from . . ."

"Being mayor of this place. I respect what you've done here. But you're still a boy, Lane. The world can't rest on your shoulders for long, or it'll flatten you like a tin can under a motorvator tread."

Lane stands up. Not quite angry, by the look of it, but Rigo can see he's getting there. Right now, he stammers: "But—but you said you were proud of me. Of what I did here. This place is all me. I'm . . . I'm the guiding hand!"

"And it's time to step back. Let someone else take over for a while. You'll still have control, not like you're a cow pushed out to pasture."

"Let someone else take control."

"That's right."

"Like you."

"Like me." Pop sighs. "Lane, son, I know this is difficult—"

"I'm not your godsdamned son. You had one and he's dead. He was a selfish kid, *Arthur*. You didn't teach him to care about the Heartland, you taught him to care about himself. But you, on the other hand, you used to be somebody. You think I don't know that you used to be one of the Sleeping Dogs? That— that—that hell, you helped *found* the Dogs? And now you wanna waltz on in here and take the captain's wheel outta my hand as if you'd never left?"

"Lane," Rigo says. "C'mon, just . . . just calm down for a second."

But Lane's hand falls to his hip, to the sonic pistol dangling there.

"I oughta back out of this cage," Lane says, "and lock it behind me. Traitors. Treating me like I'm still just some dumb kid. I'm not! I'm old as you were when you started this damn thing!"

Pop says softly, "And that's the problem. I didn't do it right. I was . . . blind to a lot of things. Because I was young. I wasn't ready."

"Get out."

Again, Rigo tries. "Lane, c'mon—"

"I said get out. Get in your skiff and go back to your . . . gardens."

Pop grunts as he stands, leaning into his hip. "I'll go. But I need to ask you first: What do you plan to do with all this? The city. The raiders."

"We're not raiders anymore. We're liberators."

"Supposing that's true, what's next?"

Lane grins: a smile empty of humor and heavy with malice. "We're going to fly this thing. Have a flotilla of our own. Conquer the skies."

A moment goes by, and Pop seems to consider this. Then he nods a sad nod and gives Rigo a look.

Rigo knows what's coming.

Pop leaves. Lane trails after, roving and zigzagging behind them like he's already a bit drunk. The long trip back to the skiff is silent and about as uncomfortable as trying to sleep with sand in your ass-crack. By now the crowd that watched Pop and the two sloop boats come in has dispersed, but folks still mill about, many of them working on repairing the shattered city: a heavy woman spreads some sort of white goop across a long crack in pale brick while a man below her tinkers with a plasto-sheen machine.

Comes the time, then, to get on the skiff.

And Rigo's heart hurts. Because of what happened up there in that tower, sure. Because Lane and Pop are fighting, and that's like watching your own family fall apart in front of you. But his heart hurts, too, because of what comes next. Rigo prayed to all the gods and angels and devils that this wouldn't come to pass, but the mission is the mission.

"I'm not going with you," he tells Pop.

Lane seems taken aback. Pop turns, looking confused. A rehearsed look. "*What?* Rigo, you already left once. And I need you. We have work to do."

But between them, an unspoken transmission: *This* is *the work.*

Rigo says, "I think Lane's on the right side of history. Thanks for taking care of me. And for bringing me back here. But I'm staying."

The look on Pop's face isn't real, Rigo knows that. He's acting. A mask to serve a purpose. And what he says next isn't real, either, but it still cuts to the quick: "I thought we were family, Rodrigo. But I guess we're not."

A TIGHTENING NOOSE

"WHY?" SCOOTER ASKS. "Why do we gotta leave, Gwennie?"

"Because," she says, kicking open the boxes next to her bed and bundling up what few clothes she has here. "Because they know who we are. And they're going to come for us. Is Mom packing?"

"I . . . I dunno."

"Well go!" she says, clapping her hands. "Go check, now. Go on."

Scooter darts out the door, ducking past someone as they approach.

It's Balastair.

Gwennie sees him, his dust-lined face, dirt under his nails. A far cry from the prim, crisp man she met on the Saranyu. He scratches at the patch of facial hair along the bottom of his chin.

"Gwennie," he says. "Maybe this is all . . . blown out of

proportion. We're just starting to really make something of ourselves here."

"You and Cleo, you mean."

"What? No. All of us. All of us! Maybe you misinterpreted—"

She wheels on him. "No. Don't do that to me. Don't try to make me feel like some foolish schoolgirl who doesn't know the tip of her finger from the back of her ass. They were gonna kill me, Bal." She hesitates, feels a tremor run through her. "So I killed them first." She bites back tears then looks away, goes back to packing with her teeth gritted.

Balastair is silent for a moment. Like he's chewing on what to say. "H-how? How did this happen?"

A shadow darkens the door to the room.

Gwennie turns. "Because of *him*."

She flings a wad of his clothes right at Boyland, who catches them not with his hands but with his face. "What's going on? What happened?"

Gwennie tells him. About going into the bar. About how Solow was planning—probably still *is* planning—to send men here.

"This is your fault," she rails. "So desperate to be a big man like your father that you've gone and nearly got us all killed. Now we have to leave. What little we have we have to throw away, start over somewhere else."

Boyland pushes past Balastair.

"Gwennie, I'm sorry. I didn't know. But maybe they won't find us—"

"They'll find us," Balastair says. "Maybe not tonight, but soon enough. Only a few outlying homes here in the shadow of the mountains. It won't take them long. Especially if the Empyrean join the hunt."

Boyland catches her wrist. He looks deep in her eyes. "We can fight them. We can hold our own, hold 'em off—"

She wrenches her hand away. "Pack your own stuff. I'm done helping you. I'm done with you in every way. Won't be any wedding. This is over. You're a big, dumb, horrible boy."

"Please. Don't say those things." His jaw works like a millstone, and she knows that he's angry. But behind the anger is sadness, too, hanging there like a ghost hovering. "Let's sit down. Godsdamnit, Gwennie. We can figure out a plan."

"Oh, I have a plan."

Both of the men look at her.

"We're going to Pegasus City. To the Sleeping Dogs. And once we're there, I'm gonna go back out and find Cael McAvoy. Because guess what?" She pushes past Boyland. "He's alive."

SWIFT FOX

THE TALE REACHES Arthur's ears over a drink. He's in a small farmhouse just outside the town of Dooley, maybe five miles past Fort Calhoun—it's a town where everybody's scared. They're scared of the raiders. Scared, too, that the Empyrean will come for them like they did so many other towns: first Tuttle's Church, then others like Brickbriar, Dry Springs, Blanchard's Hill. Here, folks have remained dutiful, working hard for the Empyrean to show that they don't need to be taken over, no, sir, no thank you.

That's on the outside.

On the inside, the fear that's gathering is turning to something meaner. Like a hound slowly going feral because his owner has abandoned him.

He meets up with an old ex-raider there—big fella named Pressman. Arms like a couple of old-timey iron-shot cannons, like you'd find on pirate ships in old picture books. Pressman's been out of the Sleeping Dogs for a long time, long as Arthur's been. His wife, too—a woman earthy and round and dark like a clay pot. Pressman says, "Got too strange there. Didn't like it when they turned from rebels to raiders. Became selfish and mean." He chews on a root.

From the other room, his wife, Kallen, agrees: "I don't cater much to violent people. I wanted to change things, not burn it all down." Her words come alongside the sounds of dishes clanking as she scrapes food off them.

"I appreciate dinner," Arthur says. He holds up the glass. "And the fixy."

"Fixy's mostly just piss, but that dinner." Pressman whistles. "That's on you. You brought us the vegetables. Empyrean figure out what you're doing, they're gonna bring the hammer down, Arthur."

"They have bigger rats to catch," Arthur says.

"Hear they got a boy in charge of that city."

"I just met with him." Arthur hesitates, but then says: "I know him. He grew up with my son. He's a good kid, but . . . out of his depth." Leaving Rigo behind pains him far worse than the bone spurs at his hip ever could. And it was clear that Rigo didn't want to stay, either. But that was the arrangement they made: If things went south with Lane, as Arthur feared they would, Rigo had to stay behind. Arthur would be in touch with him soon.

"We were young once."

"We were, at that."

They clink jars and both polish off the fixy. Tastes like corn, cuts like razors. Appropriate, perhaps, given Hiram's Golden Prolific with its thirst for blood and its slashing corn-leaves.

"The rest of the seven," Pressman says. "They're all dead, aren't they?"

"I think so."

"Black Horse."

Arthur winces at the name. "Eben Henry."

Pressman spits into his glass, scowls. "Long may Old Scratch fill his every space with burning ash and biting ants."

"That's if he's dead. Heard stories he's still out there."

"He was. He was looking for you, I'm told."

Arthur straightens up. "For me."

"Mm-hmm. Can't tell me that's a surprise. He cut Charlie up in a washtub. Shot Neddy in the dang back." He puts the root back in his mouth, chews on it. "But now they're ghost stories, because Eben Henry is gone from this Heartland, moved on to whatever waits for him in King Hell."

Pressman must see Arthur's face, because he adds: "They found his body, Arthur. Some say the Maize Witch done it. Trussed him up out there at the edge of the dead corn, body swollen with roots pushing in and out of him. But some passersby said he had another wound, like someone stuck him with a knife." He shrugs. "Who knows, maybe it's all a legend. Maybe he's been dead for years. Maybe he's still out there. Can't be bothered by spooky stories."

"I suppose that's true."

Still. Eben Henry. Been a long time. Once they'd been so close. But Eben had other ideas about how things had to be.

It stays with Arthur, even now.

"I guess you came here for something," Pressman says.

"I did. You still have it?"

"Of course. Ned told me to hold on to it and so I did."

"You could keep it."

"Eh. Pshh. Wouldn't know what to do with it. My scrapping days are done. Me and Kallen, we ain't young. Worst we're gonna do to someone is hit 'em across the back of the head with a shovel, and then I'm outta tricks. You hold on, I'll go get it."

He disappears into the other room, comes out a couple minutes later. He returns with a rosewood case, big as Arthur's lap. He sets it down and hands over a little golden key.

"There you go, Swift Fox," Pressman says. "A gift from my cousin, Iron-Red Ned Pressman."

Inside is a gun.

Not a sonic shooter, but a long iron revolver. The back of the barrel pregnant with a cylinder thick as Arthur's wrists. It's not just a gun; it's a damned hand-cannon. Ned was a gentle heart for the most part, but he said that when he carried a gun, he expected it to get the job done and then some.

Below it is emblazoned a name, inked on a slip of parchment and pinned to the felt. *Heavenkiller.*

Arthur doesn't know that he'll need this. Certainly it's not the way he wants things to go: The Heartland plunging into violence will do nobody any good. People start lighting fires, the whole place will burn, and before long they'll be stacking up bodies of good people like cords of pulpwood.

Just the same, if he needs it, he wants to be ready.

"Thanks," he says, closing the box and snapping it shut.

"Ammunition is just underneath it. Lift out the tray, and there's just shy of a hundred rounds of .50–70 rounds. Ned's special bison-killers."

Not that any of them have ever seen a bison. By the time Arthur was born into this world, the bison had already been dead for forty years.

"You could come with me," Arthur says, standing up.

"What? Come on down to—shoot, where you at now?" But before Arthur can speak, Pressman shakes his head. "You know what, don't tell me. We ain't coming, and I don't wanna know in case the Empyrean think I do. We have a home here. We're tired."

"Speak for yourself," Kallen calls from the kitchen, then comes out, flinging a rag over her shoulder. She's a stocky woman, built like a broad maple tree. Pretty eyes, though. Gray as a storm cloud, but bright, too, like the sun's poking out behind the troubled skies. "You leaving, Arthur?"

"I suppose I am. Sadly. Thank you for dinner."

"It's not a thing. We're happy to have company these days." She sniffs. "World's coming apart at the seams."

Arthur shrugs. "Maybe that's a good thing."

"Hey, lemme ask you. You really got Blighters working for you?"

"I do. Good people."

"They're not all going crazy or anything?"

"Nope. Long as they're working the soil and tending to plants, that seems to keep the . . . noise at bay." He hesitates to mention that they don't even need seeds anymore. The Blightborn have learned to produce the seedlings themselves.

From their own flesh.

"You see what that one Blighter did earlier today?"

Arthur *hmms*. "We talking Esther? The witch?"

"No, nuh-uh, a boy. And a girl, too, actually. Here, I'll show you."

Pressman rolls his eyes. "Oh, by the old gods and the new, woman, don't bring that thing out again." But it's too late, because here she comes with a visidex she dug out of a small trunk in the corner of the room. Pressman looks at Arthur and he says, "I think the Empyrean spy on us with those things. They aren't just letting us have these toys—oh, sure, sure, they say they come from that fallen city of theirs, but I don't buy it, I think they're—"

Kallen grunts and just thrusts the visidex between them. "The show is queued up, just hit the funny little triangle button there."

And then Arthur sees.

A young man and a young woman.

Both Blighted.

Taking apart a quadron of Empyrean—two mechanicals, two *evocati augusti*—like it's nothing.

"Cael," Arthur says, the word spoken in a quiet hush, somehow both pained and happy at once.

"Cael's your son, right?" Pressman asks.

"What about him?" Kallen says.

Arthur squeezes his eyes shut. "On the visidex. That boy is my son. That boy is Cael, and that girl is his Obligated, Wanda Mecklin."

Back at the skiff out back of Pressman's house, Arthur stops, leans forward on his elbows, and presses his head against the cool metal of the ship. He breathes in and out, then finds a laugh crawling up out of him like a frog from its hibernation hole. A laugh that quickly morphs into a sob as the full weight of what he saw hits him.

Cael is alive.

Cael has the Blight.

Cael killed two Empyrean soldiers.

These last two pieces cannot diminish the first, but still they overwhelm. Guilt chews at Arthur like weevils stripping a corn-cob of its kernels. He never wanted Cael to have to grow up into this. Merelda, either. Both his children now plunged into a world like the one he grew up in—thrown into it too early, forced to grow up fast, made to do things that no adult should have to do much less any child. He thinks again of Lane running a city all on his own. Rigo having lost a foot. Wanda with the Blight, too. And what of Gwennie? Hell, even Boyland, or any of the other children in Boxelder. What happened to them? Were they turned into metal men, doing the bidding of the Empyrean?

Controllable workers. Docile to their handlers, violent to their foes.

Arthur draws a deep breath. He quiets his tears.

He has a shot still. Of helping his kids get to a normal life, or some semblance of it. It isn't over for them. It's over for him, maybe, mostly, but for them—life goes on. Many years ahead.

It's up to him to make sure those years are good ones.

The father's creed.

That means he has to get to Cael. *Now.* Cael is nearby. Or nearby enough. The visidex showed a stamp not too far from here. He'll fly over, canvass the area. Though that probably means the Empyrean will be doing the same, but he has to take that chance. Cael needs him.

Their family can be reunited.

He opens the skiff door, gets in, starts to sit down—

A blow to the head knocks him sideways into the next seat.

His ear rings. He senses someone hovering over him; Arthur takes the case with the gun, Heavenkiller, and whips it upward even as his vision distorts and drifts into double, triple—

But the person deftly ducks out of the way, then catches the box and yanks it away. A voice reaches him. Female.

"The Empyrean requests your presence."

He knows that voice. He swears he does.

Slowly, his vision drifts back together, like two leaves in a puddle drifting closer and closer—and it's then he sees Simone Agrasanto standing there, hunched over inside the skiff, scowling. One eye hidden behind an eye patch, the rest of her face wearing the deep lines of a perpetually pissed-off person.

"You," he says.

"Me," she answers.

And then she hits him again.

CROSSING THE PERIMETER

AS HE WALKS through the endless corn, Cael knows he should be scared. And sad. And ashamed. Two more men, dead by his hand—well, not his *hand* precisely, but at this point he believes that the Blight-vine coiled around his arm is still under his command.

And yet he feels invigorated. More alive than he's felt in a long time. It's not the taking of lives that did it—there he admits to a pang of guilt with a thread of horror twisted around it. But rather, it's the power.

The things he was able to do. Cutting through his own cuffs. Launching corncobs like they were dang bottle rockets.

What else can he do?

Wanda is just as cranked about it as he is. She skips around him, giggling, and at one point she stops him in the corn and grabs his collar in her hands and she kisses him so hard it feels like she's trying to eat him or be eaten herself—swallowed up whole so that the both of them can be together.

He pulls her into an embrace, and she whispers in his ear: "We can do anything, Cael. The Heartland is ours. Together."

Her tongue finds his ear and a shiver moves over him.

This isn't the Wanda I knew, he thinks.

A distant, frightened thought. Strange, but then his body reacts, and he feels the heat rise to his cheeks. And once more he can feel all the little lights inside her (Blight-lights, he's taken to calling them) twinkling like the parliament of stars that will soon be overhead as the sun sets and the moon rises. Her hand drifts to his stomach. His hand slides over the small of her back and she presses into him—

He feels it before he hears it.

The corn, disturbed. Aware in its own way—and that awareness shared with him. Thrust upon him.

Someone's coming.

That's when he hears the *snap*.

And the voice that follows.

"Thought I saw something out here."

Cael pulls Wanda to the ground. He urges her against the earth and flattens himself there, too. In the sunlight that shines at a slant, pooling there like rainwater, he can see Wanda's face—it's bright, electric, alive, her eyes dancing, her mouth twisted in a strange smile.

Out there, a shape. Thirty feet away. Barely seen through the stalks.

A voice crackles over a radio: "If you don't see anything, come back. Need help with the perimeter."

The other voice, not on the radio: "Mm-hmm, yeah, yeah."

And then the body retreats through the corn.

Once more, Cael and Wanda are left alone.

"We can take them," she says.

"You're awfully eager."

"We have power they don't understand."

"They don't need to understand it to get in a lucky shot. We're still just two cornpone yokels to them. And they're the Empyrean. Two of them out there now, but not sure how many others might be there."

"So let's go find out. And if they mess with us—"

He sucks air through his teeth: "Dang, you gotta relax for a minute. One of us can go. If we both go, that gives them a better chance of spotting us."

Wanda smiles, changes the conversation suddenly. "The corn doesn't touch us. Have you noticed that? It tries to bleed anyone else who goes through it, but us . . . it stays away."

"Yeah. Yeah, I noticed."

"We can use that. We can be quiet."

"*One* of us can use that. I'll go."

"Are you going because you think I'm not capable?" Her chin is lifted up, and the smirk on her face suggests a challenge. That, too, is unusual for her. The Wanda he once knew was a leaf in a stream, going whatever way the water wanted. But now she seems to be planting herself in the current like a rock. He can't help but admit: he kinda likes it.

"I'm going because one of us has to, and if someone's gonna get hurt I'd rather it be me than you."

She smiles sweetly. "My hero."

"Heh. Yeah. All right. You good here?"

"How will you find me again in all this corn?"

"I can feel you. I can find you."

Her smile shines like a mad beam of light.

I can feel you. I can find you.

Wanda's burning up. She's like a field on fire. Her brow feels cool, but inside she's got this bonfire crackling, fingers of flames reaching for the heavens and threatening to pull everything down upon her.

The Blight—no, she thinks, the *Gift*—is inside her. Like a hundred little roots, a thousand tiny tendrils pushing their way into every inch of her, just underneath the skin, beneath her tongue, at the ends of each finger. Like flower buds straining to bloom, like eyes waiting to open.

She feels different.

Part of her thinks: *I am different.* Like she's not even Wanda.

Another part says: *You're just getting smarter. More sure of yourself!* Cael seems to want her more now that she's confident. Owning who she is.

And here a voice of doubt creeps up from her deepest places:

Who are you, though, really?

What are you becoming?

Are you even human anymore?

She tries to let those questions go. She concentrates very hard to tamp them down, shove them back into the dark from whence they came.

Instead, she just breathes.

Feels the corn out there, swaying. Feels its thirst for water, for blood, feels its need to spread out and consume everything. Roots pressing into earth like greedy, grabby fingers, drinking everything up.

It's a magnificent creature, the corn. She adores it and hates it in equal measure. Wanda marvels at its power and its design. And fears and loathes what it's done to everyone and everything around her.

Mother Esther wants to kill it. That's all right by Wanda.

Fact is, Mother Esther gave her everything. She gave her this Gift. With two warm hands she held Wanda's face. Craned her head back. Forced her mouth open. Told her to close her eyes . . .

The vine choked her. She gagged and tried to bend forward to puke, but the woman held her fast, and soon it was like the vine was a part of her. She felt it inside her like a snake slithering around in her belly. Then heat rose. The fires began. She fell asleep for three days. She dreamed of Esther. Felt the woman inside her, crawling underneath her skin like shoots and runners threading through dirt.

Then Wanda awoke, transformed. It was scary at first. But soon it felt natural. Beyond natural. She felt gifted, special, different in a way she never had before. Used to be she was boring old Wanda. She can see now that she was needy. A scaredy-cat. Afraid of being alone and lost, desperate to let others stand for her, happy to hide in their shadows. That's not her. Not anymore.

Now, she has power.

A part of Esther, given to her.

Cael is coming.

Like he said: he can feel her, he can find her.

And she can do the same with him.

He shines like sun through a prism. A hundred beams, fractured. In her mind's eye he's almost blinding.

Her awareness picks him up when he's still way out there.

She loves him.

She knows that.

She no longer *needs* him. Not like she used to. The need is gone, and it's replaced with something so much more interesting: Want.

Her desire for him radiates like a house on fire.

He comes through the corn, then—it eases aside for him, as if the thatch of stalks is a door that opens in his presence. He comes alongside her. It's only now that she notices it's nighttime—the moon already at its peak. How long was she sitting there? How much time was lost?

Cael says, "All right, here's the bad news. The wreckage of the Saranyu is that way—" He points to the direction they were headed. "We were going around, but it turns out it wouldn't much matter. They're setting up a damn perimeter. Empyrean soldiers and a whole lot more of those . . . mechanicals." He hesitates on this, and Wanda suspects he's thinking the same thing she is: *There might be Heartlanders encased in those metal bodies.* "I don't know how far it goes, but I went up and down the line, and it keeps on far as I can see it. Seems like they're starting to close off access to the Saranyu. Surprised they didn't do it before now. Something must've triggered it."

"Us, maybe."

"Could be."

"So," she says, interlacing her fingers into his. "Is there good news?"

"There is, yeah."

"Well?"

"I think I have an idea on how to get past. But I'm gonna need your help because I'm not sure I can do this alone."

Her heart does a somersault inside her chest. Like all of her life has been building to this one moment. They're going to go out there and do something together, because that's the only way it can be done. *He needs me.* And suddenly she rethinks it: *Maybe I do need him. Maybe we need each other.*

"Name it," she says.

He tells her what they're gonna do.

Then he adds: "Like you said: we can do anything."

She smiles so hard, it's almost painful.

Jezmin Reese is a guardsman of the *evocati augusti*. He stands at the base of the ketch-boat's gangplank, his horsehead helmet tucked under his arm. He's a young man, just nineteen, already past his final Name Day. Been a guardsman for a year now, and in that year, things have gone topsy-turvy.

He joined the guard thinking that his job would be, well, to *guard* people. That's what the *evocati* did. They wore their helmets and stood vigil by anything that needed the protection. They guarded city squares. They walked the flotillas, looking for the rare few hopheads or Pheen addicts. They sometimes came down here, to the dust bowl, accompanying those who needed the attachment: proctors, praetors, assayers, whoever.

But all that changed when the Saranyu fell. Now the *evocati* are troops more than anything, soldiers who were never trained to be soldiers.

His friend Seena, she says that really, their job is to be escorts. Escorts for the mechanicals.

That's new, too.

The flotillas have always had their metal men. Elevators. Bartenders. Gutter-sweeps and nanny-cams and fruit-pickers. Anything to take the burden off the men and women of the flotillas. But this is different.

One of the mechanicals nearby stands stock-still. Inert, like there's nothing there, nobody home, no mind or computations at work. Staring out over the corn with all the stillness and concentration of a light-post.

Empty.

But Jezmin knows that isn't exactly right. It isn't empty. It isn't even just a mechanical anymore.

Because there's someone in there.

A human being. A Heartlander.

He represses a chill even though the night air is warm.

Everything's changed. The failures of the peregrine and Frumentarii have left them scattered and toothless. Rumors of something new keep rising like whispers on the wind: a new flotilla constructed out there in the mountains. And a new group of soldiers, too. Girls. Young girls. Trained as killers. *Insanity*, he thinks. Who would let young girls be soldiers like that?

The mechanical's head suddenly lifts with a clockwork tick and turns with a flywheel whir. The round mirror eyes pivot with little *vvzzt vvzzt* sounds. Its flat jaw opens and from within its metal throat a speaker buzzes.

"A pollen drift is incoming," the metal man says.

"I doubt that," Jezmin says. "We'd know. We'd have seen it on the scans." He feels strange, suddenly, for even speaking to this thing. It's not the *talking to it* that's the problem. It's communicating with it as if it's his equal. As if he's just having a conversation rather than telling it to polish his boots or hang up his thrum-whip for him. "The perimeter has been formed." Again he says, now as if he's arguing with the thing: "We'd *know*."

The perimeter: a wide circle of guardsmen and mechanicals formed around Pegasus City to prevent anything coming in or going out. Most importantly: to keep the Heartlanders from harvesting corn, gathering fuel.

Then, when the time's right, they'll close in, crush the city.

The perimeter stretches on for miles.

If a pollen drift—what the Heartlanders call a "piss-blizzard," though that's a term a bit too profane for him—was incoming, they'd know.

"It's local," the mechanical says, bulky metal chin lifted as if it's sniffing the air. "They would not have detected it on their sensors."

Jezmin is about to protest one last time and tell this clanking mechanical idiot that it's clearly broken and will have to get sent back to the flotilla for readjustment—

But then a few streamers of golden pollen cascade down.

As if out of nowhere.

The pollen whispers against the helmet in his hand.

Well. The mechanical isn't broken after all.

He's not allergic, not like some of the men. Sometimes, the pollen really gets to folks. Eyes go puffy, noses run like faucets. Still, it'll limit visibility. But where'd the storm come from? How could it be local?

Then he understands. Because all around him, the corn shudders like a frightened mouse. Tassels like fingers tickle the air, and from them he watches faint shimmering ribbons of gold cough up from the stalk-tops without a sound and catch on the faintest wind. Strands of pollen, as insubstantial as spirits, rising and lifting in concert. After only a few moments the sky glows golden, the gilded curtain swallowing the night.

What's frightening is how it takes almost no effort at all.

Wanda and him, holding hands there in the corn under the fat-bellied moon. Together, fingers meshed, vines braiding, they glow bright. Not so that anyone can see but so that each of them can feel it.

They reach out and they find the corn. A thousand spears of light thrust up out of the dry, dead ground. Hiram's Golden Prolific.

Together, they become one with the corn.

He can feel them getting lost to it. A chorus of whispers— corn-leaves hissing against corn-leaves, a faint hum of blood-hunger, a thirst to drink up what little is left in the ground. Just as the corn wants to taste their blood he feels like it wants to swallow them up, just *slurp* them up out of their bodies.

But he thinks:

We're in control here.

And then he hears Wanda's voice inside his head:

I know.

She heard his thought. And responded to it.

Terror and bliss hold hands inside his heart.

They command the corn as one.

They tell it to shake and shudder. To spread itself, to cast its genes out to the world. A display of botanical lust, tassels shaking, pollen growing, unmooring, flying free on the wind. First from just a few stalks, and then from a dozen more, and then from ten dozen.

The pollen drifts.

They just made a piss-blizzard.

He opens his eyes, and there it is. A curtain of gold washing out the moon and brightening the night. He hears Wanda inside his head: *We did it.* He feels her happiness. Her lust. Her love.

Cael pulls his hand away. She casts a look at him, wounded, and he tries not to show the relief he feels at her not being inside his head—and not being inside hers. He can't handle that right now. Instead, he gives her a smile and echoes the sentiment: "We did it." But then he adds: "We have to move."

She nods. "Right. Yeah. Of course."

He waves her on. Into the corn. Toward Pegasus City. Hidden under the guise of the storm they made.

BLOCKADE RUNNERS

LANE WALKS THE SHELL.

He paces like a shuck rat along the outside of a barn, desperate for a way in. He feels like a rat slinking along. Feels, too, like he's got rats in his belly, chewing up his insides to make a nest.

For a while there, everything felt right on. Like all the stars were lining up in the sky for him, easy-breezy—all he had to do was draw a finger between them and connect the dots. He built this place out of wreckage. Secured a fuel source and started the motorvators harvesting, got the facility back up and running. But now things are creeping in at the edges, the way a slurry river pulls apart the earth, eroding the dirt and carving a channel for its filth.

So many things feel wrong.

He killed those people.

Killian still isn't right.

Arthur McAvoy showed up, made him feel like a fool-child.

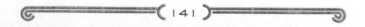

And he almost killed his mother. A woman he hasn't spoken to or seen in years. A woman who cozied up to the Empyrean and who now sits—awake, or so he's heard—under the care of their doctor, Nika Vellington.

Now, as a hawked-up loogey atop the shit sundae he's been served, the Empyrean is out there, circling the wagons. Trapping him in a fence made of men, ships, and, worst of all, mechanicals. Already they've been cut off from the harvesters and the facility of Fort Calhoun. The Saranyu doesn't have the capabilities to process corn into fuel because—oh, what a shock—the Empyrean didn't want that to poison their precious air. So they stuck all the facilities down on the ground. *Let the Heartlanders deal with it:* the skyborn motto, it seems.

Out there, he can see the shimmer-haze of the Empyrean ships. They're out of gun range. The sonic shots would dissipate and never reach the targets.

They know that, surely.

The one thing he has right now, the one person he can count on, is Rigo. He looks toward the lift door, where Rigo leans. Poor kid occasionally winces and shifts his weight, trying to get comfortable on his one leg.

"You know, Obligations have stopped," Lane says. He means it as small talk, but as soon as the words land he's pretty sure it's the opposite of that.

"What?" Rigo asks.

"Yep. Used to be a proctor would come down, like Agrasanto, and facilitate. But that's done. The Empyrean have shut all that down because they're clearing house. Town by town. List as long as my arm now—towns I've never even heard of. Some I have. Like ours. Boxelder is gone."

Rigo hesitates. In a quiet, mouse-fart voice he says, "I heard." He suddenly blurts out: "Now I'm never gonna get a woman."

"Oh, jeez, Rigo, don't say that."

"This is my year. Or should be. If we were back in Boxelder right now I'd be coming up on a brand-new Obligation Day and they'd hand out the names and I'd be paired with someone. Sometimes I wonder who that might've been and what that life might've been like with that person. Like, if I ended up with Haley Oakes, maybe I could've moved right in with her family out by the gulley. But I heard her father was a hard man, and I don't need any more of those. Or what if I ended up with Fessie McDonald? I always used to feel bad for her because of her one leg being so much shorter than the other, but Jeezum, who am I to talk now?" He laughs a little, but it isn't a happy sound. "Really, if I ended up with anybody, I hoped it woulda been Wyatt Sanderson's little sister, Savannah. She was always so nice to me. Picked me up out of the dirt one day after Boyland had beat the actual snot out of me. She stayed with me for a while and acted like she didn't realize I'd been crying. They had a cat. I don't much like cats, but I could've learned."

Lane picks a nit of tobacco from between his teeth. "Hey, now. Wouldn't you rather be with a girl who likes you for you than a girl who got your name handed to her on a slip of paper drawn by some soulless Empyrean proctor?"

"I dunno." Rigo shrugs. "I figure that'll never happen so Obligation was probably my best bet. I mean, dang, look at me."

He presents his hands like he's offering the saddest prize chicken you ever did see. Featherless, headless, covered in welts and boils. "Ta-da. Rodrigo Cozido. Got the body of a one-legged barstool—"

"And the heart of a godsdamn Saintangel, brother."

Rigo smirks. "I don't think the gods would damn a Saintangel."

"Well, whatever, I'm not all that interested in horse-ass theology." He pinches the cigarette and flings it over the wall: a pinwheel of embers in the night. "I don't care about much of that old crap. That stuff's meant to keep us down here, pressed into the dirt like a cigar under a boot. Like—the Obligations? I always wondered, what was the point? Why make us marry each other—and why choose for us? First I figured, you know, okay, it's just control. They're control freaks and they like puppeting us around. Then I thought, maybe they're trying to give us something to do. Keep us from getting bored and restless. Like the Lottery—which turns out is rigged anyway. It's an event, a . . . a thing to *care* about. A distraction, really. But then you know what I settled on? You know why I think Obligations exist?"

Rigo leans in, a big curious question mark across his face.

"Livestock," Lane says. "You get a couple cows or goats together, first thing you wanna do is breed them so you get more of the same. Then you have more animals to milk, eat, or breed. For a long while the Empyrean needed us to do their work down here. Manage all the machines. Keep the motorvators running and the processing facilities open. But all that's falling away. They're killing us. They're *replacing* us." Lane pulls another cigarette out, though he doesn't yet light it. "I don't know what to do," Lane says. "About . . . all this."

"Maybe you need to sleep on it. You look rough around the edges. You lost some weight, too, and you were pretty beanpole, before."

Lane knows he has lost some weight. He feels loose, light, airy. Like he might just slip away. And sleeping isn't high on the list, either. He's busy, too busy. When he has time to actually eat, he feels sick. When he has time to sleep, his thoughts run laps with long rope, tying him tight.

"I gotta prove that I can hack this," Lane says. "That I'm not just gonna fold up like a tent, like Pop thinks I will."

"You don't have to prove it, that's the thing. Let someone else have it. You got everyone this far. Maybe it's time to back off a little."

A part of him wants to do that. Gods, what a great sigh he'd breathe—to just be able to open his fingers and let it all fall through them. He can't, though. Too much at stake. He's put too much of himself in this.

This is what he's always wanted, he tells himself.

A chance to do something. To change things.

To spit in the eye of the Empyrean.

"I can't let go," he says. "I just can't." More pacing. Like something's chasing him. Like he's chasing something. "I want to reach up and tear those bastards right outta the sky. They've had us in a noose for too long. It's time for us to tie *them* in knots, you understand?"

"Yeah. Yeah, I do."

Lane turns. Plants his hands on the wall, looks out over the moonlit corn. A new fire burns in the deep of his belly, coals stoked by this very conversation with Rigo. He suddenly feels strong again. Anger renewed.

Then, out there at the edges, at the blockade the Empyrean is forming, he sees something. Lane calls Rigo to the wall and points.

"Look at that."

"A piss-blizzard?"

"Yeah. Small, though. Local. Like a . . . golden haze just hanging there."

"That's weird."

Suddenly, the golden cloud lights up, like flashes of lightning pulsing behind a thunderhead. The distant warble of sonic weapons discharging reaches them. Lane shrugs. "Well, that's even weirder."

Cael and Wanda sneak past the perimeter like it's nothing. The air suffused with yellow, a hanging miasma that hides their presence almost perfectly. One minute they're on one side of the Empyrean blockage—the next they're on the other, creeping through the corn. Silent, because the corn doesn't want to touch them or be touched by them in turn.

Each can feel the other's excitement. Like two kids that just snuck past a schoolteacher's window, or managed to smoke a cigarette and share a bottle of fixy as their parents slept. They dart into the corn, toward the distant Saranyu. Cael whispers to her that it shouldn't be long now, just another couple miles to walk and—

Behind them, a clamor. Shouts from a guardsman. A warning Klaxon.

And then sonic weapons going off left and right. The air filled not just with a fog of pollen but with the warbles and shrieks of sonic blasts.

Wanda, between blasts, says: "What the hell is going on?"

"I dunno." Cael grits his teeth. *Keep moving. Just keep moving.*

"It doesn't involve us, right?"

"I don't think so."

"It's good cover." She echoes what's in his head: "We should keep on moving, c'mon."

She starts to pull ahead, but he catches her hand.

"What if someone needs our help?" he asks.

"Are you crazy? *We* need our help."

"It's you who said it. We can do anything. The power we have. What good is it if we don't use it to help? They're damn sure not shooting at each other! Someone could be in danger."

"It's gonna put us in danger."

He shrugs. "I think we ought to get used to that."

Then he darts back through the stalks toward the perimeter.

Once more crammed into a skiff, the journey forward was silent as the vessel drifted over the corn-tops. Boyland piloted the ship. He kept throwing furtive glances to Gwennie in the back, but she wasn't having any of it, turning her gaze away at every opportunity. She sat with her mother, Scooter, and Squirrel. Balastair and Cleo were stone-faced in the middle seats, Cleo scowling, Balastair looking mostly tired.

And then suddenly: a few strings of drifting pollen.

"Piss-blizzard," Boyland called back. "Gonna lose viz."

And then they were in it. The gold-shimmer haze was a wall—they went from darkness to moon-shining pollen. For a moment, all was quiet but for the hiss of pollen against the skiff and the thrum of the engines—a vibration felt in her bones, in her heart.

Then: a sonic shriek.

The side of the skiff pitched upward like a table flipped.

Next thing she knows, her mother is screaming, holding on to her as the skiff goes sideways—the belts hold them in, and suddenly the fear hits her that the belts are *trapping* them, because if the skiff flips, they'll be pinned beneath, crushed like skeeters on a windshield—

But Boyland keeps the skiff going—not upright, but on its side.

He hollers out, "Protect your eyes!"

And then the skiff dips hard into the corn. The thrash-cracking of stalks like the sound of a motorvator. The skiff side bangs against the earth, and next up is the sound of wrenching metal—the golden air filled with the blue sparking light of hover-panels shattering. Then it's over. The skiff plonks down back onto its bottom.

For a moment, all is still.

Gwennie looks around. Her mother is shell-shocked, trauma-blasted, mouth working soundlessly. Scooter starts to scream.

Squirrel shushes him, a sound that rings not of sympathy but rather of irritation. Boyland starts to curse. Balastair turns around: "Is everyone okay?"

"Sonic blasts," Boyland says, prying himself out of the seat, swiping away a searching frond of corn. "Empyrean. Gotta be. Get out! Get out of the boat!"

They all scrabble to pull themselves out. Gwennie's feet land on the ground and she kicks away a broken stalk, starts helping everyone out of and away from the skiff.

She takes Cleo's hands. The woman's eyes search hers. "Empyrean," Cleo says. Not a hateful word. Wistful. Longing.

"C'mon," Gwennie says. "Let's go, let's go!"

"Let's go," Cleo says, her words almost dreamlike.

Then Cleo shoves past Gwennie and begins to scream.

"Help! Help me! I've been taken against my will! I'm Empyrean, like you, I'm a captive—"

A keening sonic shriek. Cleo spins like a top. Blood sprays into pollen.

Balastair screams.

Everything plunges into chaos as sonic blasts cut through the corn, shearing stalks, sending cobs spinning in the air. Gwennie shoulders hard into Boyland and yells: "We need to flip the skiff! On its side again!"

He looks confused for a moment, but then he gets it.

The skiff will protect them.

Together, they pivot the craft and lift hard—and for a moment, it's too damn heavy. But it gets a whole lot lighter when Balastair, looking like he's been run through a laundry wringer, presses his shoulder and helps them lift.

The skiff forms a small wall. Gwennie races out to fetch Scooter.

The corn ahead of her flattens. A shadow emerges.

She picks up Scooter, pulls him behind her.

A chain-rattle, a gear-tooth whir—the mechanical raises its sonic arm.

A knife flies free from her hand. It chips the metal man's mirror eye—the ocular lens splits, breaks in two. With a brief shake of its boxy skull, the mirror parts fall away.

Then the sonic cannon glows bright.

Gwennie hunkers down, spreads out her body wide as she can—just as the skiff forms a shelter for the others, she acts as a shelter for Scooter.

But the blast never comes.

Instead, all she hears is a wrenching, ripping sound.

She opens her eyes in time to see a lashing shape fling the mechanical's decapitated head into the piss-blizzard.

Cael.

Everything seems to unfold in slow motion, like delicate fingers gingerly unwrapping a gift only to find something horrible within. Wanda already felt unsettled, watching Cael run into what was suddenly a pitched battle, but then it's like an iron weight drops through her stomach and out the bottom of it, tearing her like tissue paper. Because there is Gwendolyn Shawcatch. Cael's first mate and first love.

And suddenly Wanda is rooted to the ground, feet planted hard as sonic blasts cut apart the cornfield around her. Her eyes fixed to Cael and Gwennie as they realize who the other is, as they hurry toward each other amid the chaos, moving nose-to-nose as her little brother hurries behind the skiff, as the two of them mouth each other's names and turn to fight together.

The guardsmen emerge, mechanicals alongside, and Cael and Gwennie step forward to fight them. *Gwennie.* The Blight-vine lashes, snatches a thrum-whip from a guardman's hand, puts it in Gwennie's. The whip cracks. The *evocati augusti* goes down.

A dead woman lies nearby. The corn bends to drink the pooling blood. Wanda can feel it. Can taste the coppery tang. She wants to puke.

A mechanical lurches out of the corn, cannon pointed toward Cael—her Obligated doesn't even see it, he's too busy. Wanda flicks her wrist up, and a snare of roots like a crushing hand pulls the cannon-arm down. The sonic blast goes off, digging a deep shovel-hole into the earth. It's enough of a warning—Cael spins, and the Blight-vine knocks the metal man aside like a hand batting a doll off a shelf.

It's then Wanda thinks:

I could kill her.

An absurd thought, one that horrifies her, but the horror of the idea doesn't make it go away. She can't dismiss it. It would be so easy.

Wanda could choke her with a vine.

Slam a stalk across the back of her head.

Use roots to break her bones.

Pull her apart like warm bread to feed the corn.

Jeezum Crow, who am I?

Wanda, who feels guilty when she swats a fly.

Wanda, who just thought about murdering an innocent girl.

Big hands grab her, shake her from her reverie. She hears a voice, loud, booming, familiar: Boyland. "King Hell. *Wanda?*"

She turns, snapped out of it.

Just as a thrum-whip coils around his neck.

His eyes bug.

Boyland screams as the lash begins to vibrate. His thick fingers claw at the whip but come away smoldering at the tips. His teeth chatter so loud they sound like a woodpecker hammering on a barn wall.

At the other end of the whip is an *evocati augusti*, sneering beneath his helmet.

She raises a finger and points it.

Something struggles underneath the flesh of her fingertip, like a grain of rice pushing its way out of her skin.

It's a seed.

A tiny little seed.

She flicks her finger.

The seed flies true and goes where she wants it. The guardsman's head shudders, and suddenly his one eye is shut, his face wrinkled and wincing beneath the horsehead helmet. Because he has something in his eye.

Something that's about to grow a great deal bigger.

It happens fast, faster than is natural—fast enough that as the seed pops and the root-tangle explodes out, it sounds like a rifle shot. His head jerks. Both eyes are gone, erased by thrusting roots, his mouth wrenched open by tendrils to make way for a stalk of corn jutting from his now-shattered jaw.

The whip uncoils from Boyland's neck. The flesh there is seared—some of it bleeding. He looks up at her with horror. He says something, but whatever it is gets swallowed by the sudden roar of hover-panels as a massive trawler—flags of the Sleeping Dogs rippling in the winds of the pollen drift—emerges, firing sonic cannons, taking out mechanicals and *evocati augusti* like some kind of pirate ship savior.

She wonders suddenly who the ship is saving.

Them from the Empyrean.

Or the Empyrean from them.

VALKYRIE

HERON YONG looks nervous, but Enyastasia cannot care about him. Because *she's* trying not to be nervous. Her middle is a jar of starving flies shaken up and then opened inside of her.

Together, the two of them stand atop the seventh circle of the Luzerne Garam Ilmatar—the tallest tower on any flotilla the Empyrean possess. The tower is an architectural marvel, with four sides that twist, giving it a liquid look. Even the windows warp and bend with the gentle spiral.

One floor below them is the Architect's Aerie—a meeting place for all the Grand Architects. While each Empyrean flotilla is allowed to do as it sees fit, for the most part, each is still connected to the whole—and certain decisions must be made together, not apart. Like how to increase cornfuel production. Or how to deal with unruly Heartlanders.

Or how to deal with *her.*

"They must know what you've done," Heron says, voice shaking.

"*Shhh*," she says. "Lower your voice."

"The wind is catching it. Nobody can hear us."

"Just the same." She pauses. Heron needs to be controlled, lest he tells them what happened. And that's not an option. "And it wasn't what *I've* done. It's what *we* have done. Together. You're in this."

He looks at her. Fear shines there in the mirrors of his dark eyes. She can see hers reflected back. He's afraid. So is she.

That fear cannot be allowed to guide them. Not now.

Heron opens his mouth. She can see the thoughts rising, about to reach his lips. He's about to say that they don't have to be in this together.

He's about to threaten her.

And so she does what she does best. She stares, emotionless, like one of the mechanicals: her face a cold, inert mask. The mask of a killing machine, a machine that has never known mercy and will never compute it.

"Of course," he says, bowing his head.

Good boy, Heron.

"We're very close now," she says. "They have no choice but to consider what I'm saying. The Frumentarii are broken. The peregrine is done. Eldon Planck, the Initiative's creator, is missing, somewhere down amid the Saranyu's wreckage. Berwin Luzerne . . . had an accident. The way is paved and the door is open, and all we have to do now is walk through it with steady feet."

"We're not ready for this. You're a child. I'm . . . not much more than that. I don't even know if I believe in what we're doing."

She reaches for his hand and takes it.

"You don't have to believe. You just have to trust. Have faith. Like in all the old gods, the gods of the sky, the ones we name the flotillas after. But have faith in *me*."

Enyastasia squeezes his hand. Not in a loving, comforting gesture. But in a way that grinds the knuckles like iron bearings. Heron's knees buckle.

She continues: "Don't make the mistake of losing your faith in me. Because the gods don't like it when you stop trusting them."

Her grip relinquishes his hand. He yanks it away and shakes it, sucking in breath and whimpering. "You're scary."

"I know."

And with that, she hears the elevator doors crank open, hears the Elevator Man announce the uppermost floor to whoever has come to get her and deliver her to the chambers below.

"It's time," she says.

She and the young architect head to the elevator.

A massive, sprawling room. Black table. Red carpets. Drapes the color of pressed wine. An ugly space. Enyastasia is sure it has some name, a name that harkens to some period of design that the Empyrean glitterati all know about—but Enyastasia just thinks it looks old. This was the first flotilla, after all, and it hasn't seen much updating while Luzerne was at the head of this table.

Ten Grand Architects sit around the table. Seven men. Three women. Most of them old—though, really, Enyastasia wouldn't use the word *old* so much as she'd call them all "decrepit skin-kites aloft on the winds of their own gaseous emissions."

Two chairs are empty.

The head of the table: Berwin Luzerne.

The other side: the chair reserved for her grandfather Stirling Ormond.

Heron hovers behind her, nervous energy bleeding off him like heat vapors off a hot hover-panel.

The architects share a series of uncomfortable looks. Miranda Woodwick, who looks quite a bit like a constipated stork, flits a gaze toward the round, toadlike Ernesto Gravenost—who had seemed to be melting into his chair but now perks up at her nervous stare. He shrugs. She jiggles her head as if to say, *Someone, please speak.*

Someone does. Fentinue Crisler clears his throat, steeples his fingers, and leans forward with his elbows on the table. Everything about him looks tight, as if he's a corpse left in the sun, its flesh drawn tighter and tighter as all the moisture dried up.

"Thank you for coming today," he says, his voice with a crisp edge to it. As if someone is giving him a slight pinch whenever he reaches the end of a sentence. "You, too, Mister Yong—"

"Can we dispense with all the polite folderol and get to the matter at hand?" Enyastasia asks. "Is Project Raven allowed to continue or not?"

Again more looks at the table.

Fentinue speaks, almost as if he's irritated nobody else will. "The untimely death of Berwin Luzerne"—she hears the slightest sigh of relief from Heron, behind her; relief, most likely, that they're not on the hook for murder—"has left us reeling and grasping for a way forward in this dark time. But we are prepared to continue with his recommendation despite his demise, that Project Raven be canceled. We have a way forward—"

"You're weak," she says. A collective gasp from the table. The regal old Jorum Grantham looks like he's about to foul his seersucker pants. "I came here days after the Saranyu fell. Days after my grandfather died because of an attack by a cell of terrorists you were incapable of identifying and incapacitating. And I said to you that I had a plan. One part of that was the creation of a warflotilla, and I recommended this bright young architect to build the Herfjotur. The other part of it was the commission of a new band of soldiers. That was Project Raven, and I am to be its head."

They're still staring at her, shocked by her impudence.

Ernesto Gravenost finally speaks, and when he does it's all wet flapping and rheumy lung-grumble, as if every word first has to pass through a filter of pudding. "We already have a two-pronged approach. We have the Initiative, and we have Herfjotur, which, yes, yes, we have you to thank for that idea and for sending Architect Yong in our direction. We are most gracious. We are prepared to offer you a notable tract of real estate in the Palace Hill District of the Oshadagea—a vineyard, a stable, a small sky-yacht—"

"I don't *want* a vineyard, or a boat, or a bunch of godsdamn ponies. I want what I have been building to for the last year. I am Dirae to my Harpies, and we are prepared to go to war." She sneers. "Have you seen the visi-feeds? Have you seen what the animals are up to down there in the dust and the pollen?

Yes, the metal men of the Initiative set up a blockade around the Saranyu's wreckage. But look what happened! The terrorists attacked it. Broke the line. Destroyed a dozen mechanicals. Destroyed a ketch-boat. Killed a dozen more of our guardsmen. Does that *feel* effective to you?"

Ernesto blusters: "We will soon have utter supremacy of land and sky with our Initiative in place and the Herfjotur flying in less than a month—"

"Even if you had those a year ago, would it have stopped the Saranyu from crashing to the Heartland? You can't stomp ants and think you've killed the colony. You need to kill the queen. They have our flotilla and have claimed it as a city. They have the love of the Heartlanders. And now they have *Blighted monsters* fighting for them—monsters who can take apart your precious metal men with barely more than a thought. But sure, of course, let's keep pretending that every problem is a nail and we have the hammer." She leers, wild-eyed, feeling a fire going wild inside her. "Sometimes, you need a knife."

"And you're that knife?" Fentinue asks.

"Not me. I'm just the handle. My girls, the Harpies, are the blade."

"But you *are* just girls," Ernesto says—contained within that sentiment she hears incredulity, but also anger. She can practically hear his thoughts: *How dare these girls think that they can be soldiers for the Empyrean?*

She's about to let fly with some choice profanities, but it turns out, she doesn't have to. One of the women present, Miranda Woodwick, lifts her cranelike head and narrows her eyes: "What's wrong with being female?"

The other two female architects present—Isme D'kard and Ginger Wellington—both nod their heads in agreement.

"Well, it's not—it's not just that!" Ernesto blubbers. "They're *girls*. Children. It's not fitting for them to become . . . a . . . a *weapon*."

"I designed the Kingfisher model of ketch-boat when I was fifteen years old," Miranda says, chin lifted. "What did you do at fifteen, Ernesto? Eat, drink, be merry on the deck of your father's yacht?"

Ernesto blubbers. "Not all children are eager. I came to my role and my talents in time—"

"I have come to mine now," Enyastasia says, voice raised. "So let me use my talents for the good of the Empyrean. This is not the time to be soft-handed. I am the handle of the knife. Wield the blade, godsdamnit." With that last word she pounds the table with the flat of her hand.

They all quietly look to one another, shifting uncomfortably in their seats. Ernesto biting a thumbnail. Jorum squirming like something's trying to burrow into him from below. Fentinue looking left, right, left, right. "I think it's time to vote, then, on Project Raven."

And they vote.

Below, clouds snake along the streets of the Ilmatar flotilla. Some drift up and over the buildings, like a consumptive force. Enyastasia wonders what it would be like to jump. To fall. To *whiff* through those clouds and die a half-moment later. She's considering it, her hands on the edge, her feet itching to pick her up and carry her over. *Kill yourself. Die. Show them what they lost in you. Let the guilt destroy them.*

But that's not what would happen. They'd all moo and cluck and bow their heads and shrug. They'd say she was troubled. They'd say her grandfather was addlepated. They'd say her father was a monster.

And then they'd go on feeling plenty justified for voting her down, for killing Project Raven before it ever took flight.

Enyastasia quakes.

Heron is down there, being congratulated. Handshakes pistoning his arm so hard it's probably about to fall off at the elbow.

All she's done. For nothing. Just to prop him up.

A presence behind her. A part of her thinks: *Doesn't matter who it is. Just spin around, grab them, throw them off the edge.* Because whoever approaches isn't her ally. She has no allies but her Harpies. The scarred-up girls who are daughters to those who died on the Saranyu. Survivors. Like her.

Instead, she waits.

The voice that speaks surprises her.

"I'm sorry about that in there," Miranda Woodwick says.

"You voted for me."

"So did a few others. But the numbers just weren't there."

"No." That word spoken with a clenched jaw.

Miranda steps up next to her. Cranes her long neck out, looks down, following Enyastasia's own gaze. "You're different than all the others."

"Different. Yes." She hesitates. "Broken. I'm broken."

"Broken does not mean ruined. Are you familiar with the art of *golden joining*?" Enyastasia shakes her head, and Miranda continues: "When a ceramic pot, or vase, or cup is broken, one may mend it with a resin mixed with powdered gold. The broken pot then regains its utility and gains an even greater beauty."

"I like that."

"Me, too." Miranda looks her up and down. "I'd always heard rumors about you. Stirling was tight-lipped, never wanted to say much. Your father—he was the one, wasn't he? The one who broke you, I mean."

Enyastasia offers a stiff nod. She's not used to talking about this. Nobody ever asks, probably because they don't want to know. Nobody up here in the sky wants to be forced to think about troubling things. They'd rather flit away like swifts on curved wing, ducking and dodging.

She says, "My mother died in childbirth. Leaving me with a father who didn't want me, a father who was the son of Stirling Ormond, a Grand Architect who had no time for him, and so my father had no time for me. Problem is, he had already burned so many bridges on the flotillas thanks to his behavior that nobody wanted him around. He took his yacht—the *Argus*—and in a fit of drunkenness took me with him. I was three at the time. He wanted to live his life: women, sometimes boys, gin, poppy-smoke. So me, he just locked away. A yacht isn't big. My bedroom was a box."

"Did he . . ." The words trail off.

"No, he didn't. But if I dared to speak up or cry out he beat me until I was quiet. I stayed in that box for so long my legs began to atrophy." *And that's why I learned to be strong.* She doesn't say that, for some reason. Given the votes, it feels suddenly unearned. "Eventually my father killed himself. Drunk, he fell off the yacht. Or so I'm told."

"You didn't kill him, then."

"I wish I had."

The wind howls, filling the silence between the two.

"Men always want to put us in boxes," Miranda says finally. "They want to keep us there, out of sight, out of mind. Make our limbs weak so we can't fight back. They would very much prefer us to be props—a rack, perhaps, to hold up their hats, a shelf to display their trophies. I am pleased to hear that you are not so easily contained."

Enyastasia raises an eyebrow. "Oh?"

"What if I told you that Project Raven can still continue?"

She turns her whole body to face Miranda. "Then I'd say I'm listening."

"Good." Miranda leans forward, lowers her voice. "The ones in there who voted against you are men. They are empty-headed old cowards who will die sooner than later. I'm old, too, but wise enough to know that I'm not the future. I see that change is upon us. You're the change I want to see. They're putting you in a box. It's time to get out of the box, Miss Ormond."

Enyastasia is about to say something, but then the older woman takes her hand and peels the fingers back—Miranda presses a small piece of paper into her palm.

"What—?"

"A list of locations. Where those men in there lay their heads at night. Take away their voices, take away their votes, and the raven will fly again."

PART TWO

PEGASUS CITY

BIG SKY BROKEN

HE'S ALIVE.

Lane's mouth is dry as hardtack. His hands are sweat-slick.

Cael is alive.

Lane wants to be happy. And he is—but that happiness is a small flame in a roaring wind. A wind of great worry. A wind with teeth. Last time they saw each other, Cael killed Billy Cross, Killian's first mate. Then Cael disappeared out the back of the trawler, breaking through the window in Killian's chambers— and then he was gone.

Rumors had persisted. That Cael was alive out there. That he was on the Saranyu when it fell. Lane tried not to give too much to those rumors—as if he didn't already feel guilty enough about the things he'd done to remove the Empyrean yoke from the Heartland's neck. He tried to tell himself that back then, on the trawler, things would've been different if he just could've talked it out. If he'd been there to help mediate between Cael and Killian. Gods, that feels like forever ago.

He walks through the center of the city. Folks are up and out today. They're happy. He can feel the energy. Over there, a couple kids have set up a line of enemy soldiers made out of buckets and boxes—one bucket has been painted like a horse's head, another like the dead, leering face of one of the mechanical men. The kids take stakes and sticks and use them like they're pretend sonic weapons and swords, and attack—shrieking and war-whooping, knocking buckets up in the air and whacking them again on the way down.

Couple tents away, a few raider women sit outside a fixy still—plastic jugs and medical tubing and glass bottles. The smell coming off that contraption could burn the hairs right out of your nose. Any fly that gets within fifteen feet of that thing is gonna drop dead of drunk. The women laugh and sharpen machetes, and as Lane passes they give him a respectful nod and two-finger half-salute, half-wave.

As he walks, that's the reaction he gets. Nods. Waves. Smiles. Chins up. Chests out. Like they're proud of themselves for following him, which is even better than them being proud of him alone.

And yet he feels like an imposter. Like somewhere in the backs of their heads they might still have little drawers of judgment reserved just for him, and at any moment they might open those drawers and let the bad thoughts out. *You don't belong here. You're too young. Too dumb. You're no captain, no mayor, no nothing. Stowaway. Pretender. Naive little faggot.*

Though he wonders:

Is that judgment coming from other people, or from himself? *Shit.*

He chews on a birch stick, nods, and waves, and tries to muster a smile. Ahead, in what passes for the city center—Boxelder Circle—he sees the lunch wagon set up. Sign hand-painted above it: SULLY'S KITCHEN. Someone painted a likeness of Sully the Cook on it—a bit cartoonish-looking, the cheeks too round and red, the eyes big like a puppy's eyes. Of course, the truck is Sully's only in name, only in memory. Sully's dead now. Made into a red mess by the mechanicals of Tuttle's Church.

All around the wagon, raiders and Heartlanders gather. Lots of laughing and big voices booming from men and women alike. The rhythm of stories going around—the words lost as the voices compete, but Lane knows the rhythm of a tale told. He spies a few bottles of Micky Finn's gin going around in a circuit, and a few bottles of Jack Kenny whiskey.

In the center of it, there he is.

Cael McAvoy. Captain of the Big Sky Scavengers.

Once, one of Lane's best friends.

Still is, right? that voice asks.

Way it asks, it doesn't sound so sure.

Suddenly, a presence presses up against him, preceded only by a moment's worth of septic breath. Killian. He reaches for Lane's arm and holds it tight—the man's skin is almost prickly-cold, yet somehow damp.

"Your friend has returned from the dead," Killian says in Lane's ear.

"It's a good day," Lane says.

"Is it? He's a Blighter and a killer. Don't forget Billy."

"Billy was your first mate, not mine."

"Yes, but *I'm* yours. First mate, best friend, and everything else," Killian sneers. "Cael McAvoy is a bad seed from whence grows a devilish tree. He's got the stink of Old Scratch about him. Chaosbringer. Hellhound. Shit-stirrer."

"Control yourself, you're drunk," Lane hisses.

"More than drunk. High as a skiff, I am." Killian grins.

Lane pushes past him into the crowd. Killian remains behind, though his words chase Lane like a hungry ghost.

Folks see Lane coming through, and they stop and say his name then step aside—cutting a path for him that leads right to Cael.

Everyone goes quiet.

Cael isn't alone. My gods. *My gods.* It's Gwennie. And Wanda! He feels a fishhook tug at the corner of his mouth, a grin he can't help emerging into the light—a grin that quickly stalls when he sees the faraway look in Gwennie's eyes; the shining green leaf-scale running up Wanda's neck like a swirl of mold on a fence-board; the pulsing, twitching vine braided around Cael's arm. Just behind them: Rigo, with the same bombed-out look as Gwennie, with his one leg long gone. And so Lane's initial surge of *the gang is all here* quickly dies back and he's left with a hollow feeling. Boxelder feels suddenly very far away both in distance and in time. A thousand miles and a hundred lifetimes between them. But Lane keeps the grin, tries to hold it there, pinned to his face like a sign nailed to a wall—

He hesitates, hangs back a little.

Cael does no such thing.

Cael barks a laugh, the kind of laugh that isn't forced, that sounds like it kicked its way out of him like a foot through a rotten door. He springs up and collides with Lane and wraps his arms around him. Lane can't help it—he goes with it, feels a kind of buried love and brotherhood surge through him. The two hug for a while, squeezing each other so hard it feels like one of them is going to pop. And yet, Lane feels it—the Blight. It's there, too, like a third person trying to get in on the reunited lovefest. He can feel it throbbing along the margins of Cael's lower back like a dull heartbeat.

Then there really *is* a third person in on the embrace—Rigo, slow to move but surely eager to join, is grunting happily as he joins the hug. And then Gwennie's there, too—hanging slightly back like she's unsure of herself, like she doesn't know if she belongs anymore. But Rigo hooks her and suddenly they're not so much a bunch of old friends but one entity, one mind, one crew: the Big Sky Scavengers.

"That's it," Lane says. "We need to have a proper reunion. All of us Boxelder types. Big Sky crew." He laughs, pulls away. "C'mon, you three."

Cael hesitates, then says, "Wanda, too."

Lane gives him a look, like, *Really?* Wanda's standing off to the side, looking—well, he can't quite tell what. A little sheepish, but there's something else there, too—anger and jealousy, maybe, the two feelings warring for dominance. Or maybe calculating together, he can't say. She's changed. It's not just the Blight. She looks taller not because she's actually gained height but because she's *standing* taller.

"She was crew with us for a little while," Cael says. "And she's crew now." He waves her on. Lane notes that her face brightens, though her eyes do not.

Seems they all have stories to tell.

The red wine goes 'round and 'round. An hour in, their lips are purple. They're all telling stories. It's silly, but they're not talking about the last year. They're talking about back in Boxelder. Rigo tells the story of that time they convinced Wyatt Sanderson to take a shit in Pally Varrin's hat. Gwennie and Cael talk about when they saved her little brother from that rat-trap processing plant out near the dead town of Bremerton—they both tell the story in tandem, each giving one piece after the other like a team. When they're done, Lane opens a new bottle of the red stuff and pours everybody a new glass while recalling for them the day that they managed to convince Boyland and his crew of the "priceless scavenge" that was really a busted-up motorvator full of bees—that was back before all the beehives went dead thanks to who-knows-what, chemicals maybe, or some unseen defense mechanism developed by Hiram's Golden Prolific.

"Boyland beat the snot outta me," Rigo says, laughing.

Cael nods. "Yeah, he lit me up like a bug zapper. Gods, man, he beat King Hell out of all of us time and again. But that day . . ." He whistles. "That day it was worth it. I woulda taken ten beatings like that just to watch him slinking back to town covered in hundreds of those bee-sting welts."

"He's here, you know." It's Wanda who speaks up. She doesn't look to be having as much fun as everyone else.

Lane straightens. "Boyland Barnes Jr. is in Pegasus City?"

Gwennie nods. Cael does, too. Rigo's the only other one who must not have known. His jaw hangs loose like its hinges are busted.

"Godsdamn," Lane says. He knows it's the wine talking, but he licks his lips and says: "I say we all get up from this table, go find his ass, and beat him till he's blue. We whip his hide like he's a dirty blanket hanging on the line."

"I'm in," Gwennie says. Her voice slides a little, like a foot planting down on greasy mud—bit of a drunken slur creeping in. "He slunk off with my mother and brother and the others. I owe him a beating, I think."

Wanda speaks up: "I saved his life out there, and I'd rather it not be for nothing. If you don't mind." It's then Lane notices: She hasn't touched her wine. When he poured her a second glass, he just filled her old one to the brim—wine on top of wine.

"He's a turd clogging up the pipes," Rigo says. "Man I wanna break bad on him something fierce."

"Wanda's right," Cael says. "We should leave him alone."

"He almost got us killed," Gwennie says. "He almost got *you* killed up there on the Saranyu. I almost had you. And then he—" Her voice breaks. Anger, sorrow, Lane can't tell.

Cael sighs. "Maybe. He also saved my ass. You boys remember that hobo? Eben Henry?"

"How could I forget him?" Rigo says, mouth a mean, flat line.

"He, ahh, he tried to kill me." Cael seems rattled, revisiting this. "Put a knife through my hand and pinned me to the ground. Told me that he hated me, hated my family. Said he was one of the original raiders—one of the Sawtooth Seven with my father. Maybe with my mother, too, I'm not really sure—everything from that night kinda runs together like spilled paint. He said he was gonna take from Pop what Pop had taken from him: a son. Boyland saved me. Plain and simple. Beat him down with an oar and then I . . ." He puffs out his cheeks but doesn't say any more.

"Pop is alive," Rigo says.

Cael lifts his head. "What?"

"He's alive. I just—*we* just saw him. Couple-few nights ago. Your sister, too. Merelda's with him."

It's hard to tell if something has just been taken from Cael or given to him or some measure of both. He looks to be reeling, like a great big twister lifted him up, whirled him around, and tossed him back down to the ground.

His eyes gleam, wet.

"That's good to hear," Cael says. Like he's trying to keep it close to the vest and not wear his emotions on his face. "That's real good."

But then Gwennie erupts. She bursts out crying. Great, gulping, sudden sobs. Her hands ball into fists and she presses her forehead down on them. It's so abrupt nobody seems to know what to do with it. Rigo is first to her, putting his hand on her back.

"My father is dead," she blurts out through a spit-slick mouth. She wipes at her eyes with the back of her forearm. "Lord and Lady, they . . . they killed him, and they did it to get to me. They took him and marched him to the end of the gangplank and dropped him off. I saw him fall." She turns a piercing stare toward Cael, her sobs damming for a moment: "Just like I saw

you fall. You fell, Cael. I don't know how I'm sitting here looking at you."

Cael struggles for words, but it's Wanda who speaks.

"The Blight," she says. "It saved him. I know you're all scared,
looking at us the way you are. I can tell it freaks you out. But it
saved his life same as, in a way, it saved mine."

"I brought down the Saranyu," Lane says.

That revelation—that *confession*—comes up out of him without his blessing. Like a snake teased out of its hole. Drowned out
of its nest by a few glasses of red wine.

Predictably, everyone stares.

"It wasn't my idea," Lane says. "Cael, you know that. After
you . . ." *Killed Billy Cross and escaped the trawler.* "The plan was
still the plan, and we came upon that town, Tuttle's Church, and
the Empyrean had already . . . taken over. The people weren't
people. They were machines. They attacked, and several of us
died, but me and Killian, well. We, ahh, we made it down below
the street and found the control mechanism and—" He winces
like this hurts to tell. "I was the one who put the code in. Trans-
mitted it to a raider on the Saranyu. So I guess he was the one
who really did the deed, but it came from me. So I'm on the hook
for it. I know that it . . . killed a lot of people and didn't do any of
you any favors, and I'm sorry. That wasn't what was supposed to
happen." A surge of resolve rises in him: "But I'm glad I did it."

It's like everyone has had their throats cut. Silence and a few
small sounds like the bubbling whisper of an opened neck.

Cael's the one to finally say something. He nods, like he's
found his own resolve (though here Lane wonders if his friend
ever really lost it—Cael isn't known for being wifty about

whatever path he's walking on, even if that path is about to drop him off a cliff). With a sniff and a shrug, Cael says: "Well, so here we are, then. All together again. Guess it's time to tell you what I want."

Lane sits forward. "What *you* want?"

"Mm-hmm. Much as I like seeing everybody again, me and Wanda have something we need to do. And I need your help, Lane."

"Name it."

"Somewhere on this flotilla—now, this city—there's a laboratory. Belonged to an Empyrean woman named Esther Harrington. She thinks that her lab still contains a . . . well, I dunno what it is, but it's a weapon. A weapon to use against the Empyrean."

"Harrington," Gwennie says. "Like Balastair Harrington?"

"His mother, I believe."

"Why would an Empyrean woman create a weapon to hurt her own people?" Lane asks. "That doesn't add up." He swills and sloshes the bottle of wine, takes a pull straight from it. His head buzzes, numb. "And where'd you meet this Empyrean lady anyway? Down here in the dirt? Something smells like road-killed rat, Cael McAvoy."

Cael and Wanda share a look.

Then he says: "It's the Maize Witch."

Gwennie, grief-addled and obviously tired, suddenly laughs. "The Maize Witch? That's a joke, right? Wait, wait, I can do it, too: me and Jeezum Crow were hanging out at Busser's Tavern with the Mother of Milk Teeth and the Saintangel Miriam, and then the Lord and the Lady stopped by—"

"She ain't a dang fairy tale," Wanda snaps. That seems almost as much of a shocker to the room as Lane claiming he brought down the Saranyu. Wanda? Angry and snapping? Looking mean as a stepped-on snake? "She ain't a witch, though. Her name is Esther, like Cael said. She's the first to be gifted by the Blight. We need to listen to her because she's the way forward."

"*Pegasus City* is the way forward," Lane says. "But okay, fine, whatever. Let's say there is some kind of secret weapon here. What's it do?"

"Well—" Cael starts to say.

But Wanda gives a sharp shake of her head and what sounds like a warning: "Cael—"

Cael, though, has always been a bull with blinders on and keeps charging forward. "It'll kill the corn."

"Kill the corn."

Rigo offers a low, *holy shit* whistle.

"Yup. Don't know how, but she swears it'll kill every last stalk of Hiram's Golden Prolific. Then the Empyrean won't have fuel for their ships. It'll be like cutting their knees out from under them. They need the corn, so we take the corn away. Lickety-split."

King Hell and Old Scratch, Lane thinks. The wine now has him pickled good and proper, and he almost seizes on what Cael's saying like a dog smelling chicken blood, because my-oh-my what a glorious thing. To rob them of their fuel. To destroy what's been a plague upon the Heartland: the godsdamn corn. Hiram's bloodthirsty invader. *Kill it all. Burn it. Laugh as all the flotillas fall out of the sky like birds popped with slung shot.*

But then he hears Luna's voice in his head. And Killian's

voice. For once they seem to agree inside the echo chamber of his own skull, and they remind him: The Sleeping Dogs need the fuel. If they're going to fly this flotilla again, if they're gonna take Pegasus City to the skies, they need the corn. They need it for all their air-ships. All the motorvators. Every last bit of it.

Better to steal it from them than to destroy it.

And so it is with some surprise that he hears himself say to Cael: "I can't let that happen."

Cael goggles. He looks like he just got punched. "Sorry, what?"

"We need that corn," Lane says. "For now, at least. The fuel runs things for us, too, don't forget. Hell, even now we got this extruder machine? Makes plastic out of the stuff. Soon as we break that dang blockade, we'll get back to Fort Calhoun and get the motorvators running again."

"You're an ass," Cael says. "We used to talk about this as kids—*oh yeah, hurr hurr, we're gonna spit in the Empyrean's eye and kill all this fool corn.* Swatting at the stuff as it sliced at a leg or a bicep, took a taste of blood from us. Back then it was just some dumb fantasy, but suddenly it's maybe really for real and you're pissing all over it? What in King Hell, Lane?"

"I grew up," Lane says, sticking his chin out. "Became an adult with real responsibilities instead of running around like a sheep-headed idiot. Maybe you oughta do the same, McAvoy." He pops air from his lips—lips he can't feel, lips taken by the wine. "Everybody, get out. Go on. This little reunion's over."

"Lane—" Rigo starts, but Lane waves him off, too.

"You've changed," Cael hisses.

Lane nods. "You bet your ass I have."

AN IDEA OF SALVATION

"I KNOW WHAT YOU DID," Pop says. He winces when he speaks, as if the dancing light of the fire hurts his eyes.

Agrasanto looks up, a glop of gruel ration on the tip of her thumb, then pops that thumb into her mouth like a lollipop to suck it off. The taste is bland, like eating wet clay. Hunger is hunger, though. "Do you, now."

"Boxelder. You helped those folks."

"Did I."

He leans forward—she can see that he's changed since last they met. There's a wildness to him now, like he's just a hair more animal than man. Or maybe that's how he always was, and all this has brought it back out. *Don't worry, Arthur, I've changed, too.* He says, "Some of the Boxelder folks ended up with me and my people. They told me what you did for them. Those who left survived. Those who stayed, they were turned into—"

"I know what happened to them."

"You obviously don't approve. Or didn't then."

"Still don't." A shudder runs through her at what the Empyrean has been doing to people. She's seen it, at a distance. Wrangling up Heartlanders. Marching them onto these . . . processing ships, ships that look like black beasts dragging fat bellies across the tops of the corn. They do the processing right there in those boats—they don't even bring the Heartlanders onto the flotillas anymore. Security risk. The screams that come out of those ships . . . the fire can't make her warm, can't burn that memory out. Instead, she reaches down, picks up the wooden gun case, runs her thumbs across the snaps. "The Initiative is a brutal solution. Inhuman."

Pop chuckles, a dry, raspy sound, like footsteps on dead leaves. "Last we met you were brutalizing me pretty good, Proctor. Getting your kicks in. Calling me a terrorist. Threatening me and my family."

"Then you may also remember that I said your people were not dogs. They were children. You were to be a lesson for those children."

"What happened to you, then? What changed? I bet I know. You got a little Heartland dirt under your fingernails, on your tongue. In your blood. You started to see maybe we weren't all bad."

"Don't presume to know me." *I'm not a book you can read.*

"Why'd you help, then?"

She hesitates. "I don't know, Arthur. I did what I felt was right."

"Does it still feel right?"

"It does, but *feeling* right doesn't always *make* it right. Doing the right thing is a good way to get wrong." She sniffs, tells him: "They came, that night. My people. They found me there in your little rotten cob of a town, and they took me up and interrogated me—politely, painlessly. For a little while my lie had traction. But eventually they gathered up some of the others from your town and put them to the question, and they owed me little, if anything, and so someone sold me out. The Empyrean hurt me. Jailed me. Were going to hang me, actually. That's what they do to traitors. They hang us from the bottom of the flotilla until the birds pick us apart." Her mouth forms a stern line—a knife-slash of anger. "But I escaped."

"And now you're an exile."

She snaps open the lid on the gun case. "I am between worlds, Arthur. A one-eyed queen in the land of the blind. Caught between the clouds in the sky and clods of Heartland dirt. That means I have to make a choice. I have to pick a side. Truth is, I'm just not that strong. I want to go home. I want to talk to my husband again. I want to look down on you all with the cocksure contempt I was born with."

Pop shrugs. "They say you can't go home again."

"They better be wrong because I'm going to try."

Agrasanto removes the fat-barreled revolver. Her hands bow under its weight. "Heavy. Really very inelegant. A man's weapon. Men always think they need something more than they really do. They want the ax instead of the scalpel. The big gun instead of the *effective* one. Still." She thumbs open the chamber after some fumbling, begins slotting bullets into the cylinder. *Click. Click. Click.* When it's full-up, she eases it shut with the heel of her hand. "I admit it's impressive. 'Heavenkiller.' Some name."

"A promise, maybe."

She points the gun at him, then thumbs the hammer back.

He stiffens. But he sticks his chin out anyway—she's not sure if it's faux bravado or a courage that even she doesn't possess. King Hell, maybe it's something deeper, something worse. Maybe Arthur McAvoy just wants to die. No—she doesn't buy that. He knows his son and daughter are alive. He must want to remain so, too.

"If I was meant to be a lesson for children then," he asks, "what am I now?"

The gun barrel hovers, its black eye staring beyond the firelight.

"A ticket back to heaven."

"How's that?"

She decides to tell him. She doesn't owe him, but the night is long and dark, and this conversation is a stone to break up the river.

"You're a terrorist, Arthur. A wanted man. Now more than ever. I can buy my way back in with you on a pewter platter."

"Alive? Or as a corpse?"

Her finger curls around the trigger like a worm around an apple stem.

"The gun has a lot of power," she says. "I can feel it. I get it now."

She removes her finger from the trigger, eases the gun back into the box, still loaded. She closes it, then says:

"You get to live, Arthur. Things are changing up in the skies, and I don't yet know who will be the one to take you off my hands and give me my pardon. But as soon as I figure that out,

I'm taking you straight to them, and they can do what they want with you. Ask you questions. Cut you open. Throw you off the back end of the new war-flotilla I keep hearing about. I don't care. I don't care about anything anymore except putting all this behind me."

"What you want is a dream," Arthur says. "You can't put the snakes back in the can, Proctor."

She shrugs. "I'm going to try."

FOUR CONVERSATIONS
AND A FISTFIGHT

SLEEP IS A GHOST Cael chases but cannot catch. The room they give him here in Pegasus City isn't much more than a closet—the towers of the Saranyu crumbled and collapsed when they fell, and what remains standing are stunted, broken fingers, crooked and strange. The rooms shoulder against one another like old wooden fences that would fall to pieces if they didn't have the others to lean on.

His thoughts run laps around him. And his Blight-vine is itchy, too. It burns at his chest, from where it originates. It tightens and loosens around his arm, sometimes sliding along the underside of his arm and reaching up and grabbing his hand. Leaves tickle the insides of his knuckles. Sometimes it feels intimate. Other times it feels insistent, urgent, like it wants him to get up and go *do* something.

Lord and Lady knows he's thought about it.

He could go out. Midnight. Throw around the Blight-vine

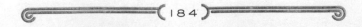

like it was nothing. Tear his way through this so-called Pegasus City like it's nothing more substantial than a moldy old bedsheet. But for what? He doesn't know where he has to go. Or if Esther's secret weapon is even here in the city, or if it fell elsewhere. Too many things he doesn't know.

What he does know is that everything has changed.

Or, worse:

Every*one* has changed.

That bothers him. Cael was never like Lane. He never wanted to go out and completely change the world—just wanted to change it for him and those he cared about. Set them up, get a little garden going that the Empyrean couldn't see. He never wanted to be part of something bigger.

Just something a little bit better.

He doesn't like change. It leaves him feeling weird, like the world went its way and didn't think to bring him along with it.

His mind keeps revisiting Lane. Lane was always the firebrand, but always one who followed his captain. Now he's a captain all his own, and Cael respects that. But he's having a helluva hard time dealing with it.

His mind goes there, but his heart—well, his heart hurts. Keeps thinking about Gwennie. And Wanda. And back to Gwennie. He thought he'd never see Gwennie again. And Wanda . . . she's his Obligated. Which still means something, right? Or maybe it never meant anything at all. But she has changed. She changed *for him*. That scares him. It scares him because he likes it, he likes that someone would do that, but deep down he also knows how wrong that is. That someone would put herself in danger, would allow the Blight into her body, just for him?

Is that what love is?

Or is that something altogether stranger?

Is it just obsession?

Jeezum Crow, does Wanda love him? Is she *in* love with him? Does he love Gwennie and does she love him? Gods, to see her again was something, wasn't it? Spying her there in the corn, even as the world was going to hell all around them, even as a godsdamn mechanical was about to draw down on her . . . he shudders. Irrepressible.

Because he knows that mechanical wasn't all mechanical.

He knows that when he ripped the head off, the vine tasted something. The vine tasted blood. Human blood. What the Maize Witch said was true: The Empyrean is taking people and making them into machines. Soldiers. Workers. Puppets. It wrings Cael's stomach like a rag.

And with that he goes back to thinking about the Blight again, and how the others see it, and how the others have changed, and Gwennie and Wanda and Pegasus City and the Empyrean and, and, and—

Circles and circles. Thoughts tying knots around other thoughts.

Sleep kept at bay by the chewing rats of bad ideas.

Morning comes with a knock at the door. It isn't a friendly knock.

Whomp whomp whomp.

Whole building seems to shake with it. Dust streams down. Cael, shirtless, rises not from sleep but from some cobbled-together half-sleep where his waking thoughts mingle with dreamlike ideas. He rubs his eyes and goes to the door.

The whole frame is crooked and the door sticks. But he manages.

Standing there, two people.

The man he recognizes. Killian Kelly. A withered specter of what he once was, like a healthy stick whittled down to splinters. He's pale and pasty. Got a cock-eyed lean to his body—favoring not just a leg but one whole side of him, like half of himself is somehow rebelling.

The woman—a girl, really—Cael doesn't know. She's pouty. Lips in a pointed sneer. Long blond hair bound back in a pony-tail, with a hard slash of bangs across her forehead as if someone trimmed them with a bowie knife.

Both of them have sonic pistols. Killian's is a fancy one, too—a lean, elegant Rossmoyne, by the look of it. Hers is more utilitarian. Dinged up, scratched. But that maybe means it has seen more action.

Cael grunts. "Good morning. You the welcome wagon? Whatcha got for me? Couple nice pastries, maybe, cup of hot dandelion tea?"

"Look at that," the girl says, staring down at Cael's arm. The vine there is not one vine, not really, but three: each emerging from a barklike patch in the center of his chest. Sometimes he touches that spot—it feels like a bit of tree bark on spongy ground. Floats the way a kneecap does when you push on it. The vine pulses, as if liquid sluggishly runs through it. "That's a helluva thing you got there."

"Yes," Killian says, never taking his eyes away from Cael's own. "Something of a marvel. Last time I saw it, it was a good bit smaller, and yet, the damage it did. You remember that, Mister McAvoy? You remember my first mate, Billy Cross?"

"I remember how you shot him," Cael says. He knows he's poking the beast on this one, but it's like tonguing a broken tooth: he just can't help it.

"That's a rather deliberate misinterpretation of events," the raider captain says, showing his teeth.

"You tried to shoot me. I turned the gun away and yet you still fired the weapon. And your first mate took that bullet. I was defending myself."

Killian points a finger, leans in. "You're a *monster*—"

The girl plants a hand on his chest, eases him back.

"My overeager friend here . . ." She stops, looks up, then laughs a little. "Funny to be calling him my friend, because up until yesterday we didn't agree on much. And then you showed up. Common enemies are a wonderful thing in times of trouble. Gets everybody on the same page. Turns out, Killian and I agree on one thing, at least: we don't care for you."

Cael frowns. "I'm sorry, and you are?"

"Luna Dorado. Right-hand man to Mayor Moreau."

"You don't look like a man."

"I got balls bigger than yours, I bet."

"You might, at that. Listen, I didn't sleep for squat last night, so if you don't mind cutting through the clouds and getting to the point—"

"You're welcome to stay," Luna says. "Lane has made that clear."

"*But*," Killian adds, "you're not to disrupt what we're trying to accomplish here. This is a good place, a *necessary* place. But things still hang in a delicate balance, and the last thing we need is some Blighted punk messing it all up. Do you understand what I'm saying, Mister McAvoy?"

"You don't sound like a raider anymore. You sound Empyrean."

That does it. Lightning dances in Killian's eyes. "Shut up. Shut your crass mouth. You go about your business and you leave Lane's alone. If not . . ." He lets his words go, one hand resting on the Rossmoyne shooter at his hip.

Cael thinks, but does not say: *I could break both of your necks before you even cleared the holster.* He's not sure that it's true. He feels confident. Overconfident, maybe. And he's not looking to stir the soup, so—

All he does is nod, then ask: "We done here?"

Before they answer, he slams the door.

He waits for them to leave. Then he goes to find Gwennie.

The hallways are like the hands of some big giant that reached down and gave them a twist. Shattered marble floors rising here, sinking there. Walls cracked and split. Light fixtures hanging—though they have power. Some spark and pop, little firefly embers hitting the shattered tile and dancing before dying.

He thinks they put her on the other side, around the square.

The building groans and shifts as he walks.

He wonders if it's safe, if Lane has done enough to keep this place stable. Maybe he hasn't. Maybe he doesn't care. Would

Lane put Cael in an unstable building just because he was pissed? That seems callous, even for Moreau.

It's Gwennie he's looking for, but it's Rigo he finds.

Rigo, outside Gwennie's door, with a small bundle of flowers. Cael doesn't know what they are, but the blooms are big, round as his fist. Pink petals like the crinkly material of some girls' Obligation Day dresses.

"Rigo," Cael says. He can't help but smile—no matter what changes, Rigo still seems like Rigo. A rock in the stream.

"Hey, Cap. I was coming to see you next."

"I can head back to my room—"

"No, no, this works. Sorry you're in such digs. They're setting up new apartments, and this place needs serious renovation, but it's far down the list." He must see the look on Cael's face because he says: "It's not dangerous. They put in supports, and Empyrean construction is pretty powerful stuff—heck, half these structures survived the fall."

Cael sniffs. "I saw some of it fall, you know? I was up there. Some buildings were buoyed by these big balloons so they fell slower. Others weren't so lucky . . . dropping out of the air. Like holding a vase in your hand and then just opening all the fingers." He mimes the motion. "People were in those buildings. These apartments all belonged to people who are now dead."

"Yeah. I heard they had . . . a lot of bodies." Rigo shifts uncomfortably. "I hate the Empyrean as much as the next guy, but I dunno." He visibly swallows. "I'm sorry about last night."

"What, Lane? Yeah, it's all right. He's gotta do what he's gotta do. And he was a little drunk, I think. I just hope—well, I just hope he knows what he's doing. I know I couldn't handle the horse he's riding."

"Pop worries about that, too."

"Yeah?"

"Uh-huh. That's why he came here. To see if he could partner with Lane and join forces. Pop's got a whole new grow operation. A hobo army a lot bigger than last time. Lane and him got into it pretty good and . . . I stayed behind. Pop asked me to. He wanted me to keep an eye on Lane and maybe see if I could . . . change his mind about things. But I dunno."

"Well. Shit."

"Yeah." Rigo looks down at his feet, the one that's real and the one that isn't. "Are we gonna be okay, Cael?"

"You and me?"

"Nah, I know you and me are square. I mean everyone else."

"Not for a while, I don't figure. But maybe one day."

Rigo suddenly perks up. "Oh, jeez, I got you something, too." He reaches behind him and pulls from the hem of his pants a small, flat screen. A visidex. Chipped on the one end, and the back is pocked with tiny craters—some of them still home to tiny bits of stone. He hands it to Cael. "This is from the Saranyu. Everyone up there seemed to have one and so there are quite a few floating around. This might have a map of the old flotilla on it. Maybe it'll help you find what you're looking for here."

"Thanks, Rigo. I don't know what to say."

"Just keep me in the loop. Don't brush me aside. I'm here to help."

"It means the world," Cael says, and means it.

"The Maize Witch. Is she really real?"

"Yeah. She's something. I don't trust her, exactly. But I'm alive because of her, and I guess I owe her a chance, at least."

Cael's heart jumps as the door they're standing in front of opens.

Gwennie stares out at them, hair mussed up, one eye wide, the other eye wincing. She smacks her lips. "Lord and Lady, you boys are chatty."

"Sorry," Rigo says. He thrusts the flowers at her. "Here."

She raises her eyebrow and takes the flowers. "Aw. Thanks, Rigo."

"They're called King of the Flowers. I dunno why, but they're pretty."

Gwennie leans forward, kisses him on the temple. As she pulls away, her eyes meet Cael's. She smiles at him. The smile is sad.

"Oooh, hey!" Rigo says suddenly. "You guys want food? I can scare up something, probably. Dang, I should've thought of that."

"I'm starving," Gwennie says.

Cael says, "I could eat."

And like that, Rigo gives them a pair of thumbs-up and he's off like a shot. It's painful watching him hobble. Cael may never get used to that.

"Surprised to see you at my door," she says. "You never were much of a morning person."

"Things change, I guess."

"You don't like change."

"I like it about as much as I like blisters on the bottom of my feet."

She laughs. "You haven't changed much, then."

He doesn't say anything, but gives himself away by looking down at the vine coiled tight around his arm. Her own gaze follows his.

"You wanna come in?" she says.

Her room is about the same as his, but cockeyed in a different way. The floor bulges up and the ceiling bows. The cracks on the walls look like birds.

She sits on what passes for a fainting couch. He leans up against the wall.

"I thought you were dead," she says finally.

"I maybe was. Or close enough to it."

"But here you are."

"In the flesh."

He wants to tell her how sorry he is about her father, but he's afraid to say it. He doesn't want to take them down that path, but he wants her to know he's here for her. So he keeps it bottled up. Makes him feel like a fool and a coward. *Godsdamn you, Cael McAvoy.*

"I missed you," she says.

"I missed you. Seeing you up on that flotilla . . ." He laughs to cover up his embarrassment. "I thought I'd never see you again, after your family left. They whisked you away up into the sky and everything went to King Hell down in Boxelder."

"It went to King Hell up there, too. The Sleeping Dogs. The Pegasus Project." She sighs. "They put me on display, like I was some kinda . . . freak show. *See the Heartlander girl with dirt under her nails.* Bastards."

He chews at a fingernail. "Lemme ask you. There any good people up there? Or is it just a skyful of monsters?"

"Hmm." She thinks about it. "There are. Good people, I mean. I met a few of them. Balastair is one of them. Some of them aren't good but aren't awful, either. Just . . . confused. Ignorant, I guess you'd say. They've been fed a line of cow-shit about us Heartlanders, too. We think they're monsters and they think we're savages. . . . I had one woman ask me if we killed each other for food. Saw another dress like some kinda corn princess, as if that's how we all dress. That was some party. That's where I found your sister."

"Mer was at that party? Jeezum. What'd they do to her?"

Gwennie rolls her eyes. "Nothing, 'cause they didn't know she was one of us. She had a whole scam going. Hooked up with this nasty length of rope called the peregrine. Guess she was kinda his . . . mistress."

Cael flinches. "Really?"

"She lost her way up there, I think. But I guess she found it again. We came back down to the Heartland and . . . the bunch of us set up outside a small town. But after a month she decided she didn't want to stay. I don't blame her. Our little farmstead was tense. She didn't have a place there."

"Merelda was always like the pollen. Went where the wind took her."

"Can I ask you something?"

"Sure."

"Wanda."

His mouth goes dry. "That doesn't seem like a question."

"I guess it isn't. I know how she found you."

"You do?"

"Yup. Boyland told me about the posse Agrasanto threw together."

"Oh, right." *Boyland Barnes Jr., you sonofabitch.*

"I just wanna ask . . . you and her a thing?"

He wants to lie. That's the thing to do. Tell her, *Nope, no way,* and then fall into Gwennie's arms and go tell Wanda, *Sorry, that other thing you thought was a thing wasn't a thing at all. That's life in the Heartland, Wanda.*

But he doesn't. Which means maybe he's changed a bit, too.

"I think so. I don't know if it's a thing as deep as an Obligation or if it's a thing that'll last, but . . . she stayed by my side for a year. I almost died and she left home and left her whole life behind. And she became like me to be closer to me, you know? That worries me a little, but it doesn't change what she did for me. So, for now, I guess we're something."

Gwennie smiles and nods, but he can see that she looks like she just got slapped. "You love her?"

"I don't know. Honestly."

"You love me?"

He's about to tell her *yes, yes, I do,* but she quickly stands up, shaking her head. "No, don't answer that. This isn't important. Lot of things going on, and the last thing we need to be worrying about is pawing at each other like we're kittens looking for milk. This can wait."

Can it? Life feels awfully short all of a sudden.

But instead he just nods and says, "Yeah, yeah, of course."

Of course I love you.

"I'll help you get what you need from this place." She offers her hand, like she wants to shake over a deal. "I still get to be first mate on your crew, right?"

He takes her hand. Holds it there for a while. She doesn't flinch at the Blight-vine that shifts and squirms.

"Damn right," he says.

The held hands linger a little longer, and then finally she pulls away. "Jeez, you hungry? I'm hungry. Where's Rigo?"

Cael swallows, finds it hard to push words up out of his throat, but somehow he manages.

"I'll go find him," he says.

He winds his way through the shattered halls of the old apartment building. Cael knows he's finding his way toward the exit because he can hear the industrious sounds of Pegasus City rising in volume. Hammers hammering. Machines grinding and grumbling. A woman yelling something muffled, but Cael can tell it's some kind of command, a call to action, to work.

Rounding a corner, he sees the doorway out—it's like something from a warped dream, a portal with no right angles. He heads toward it, his own hunger now pecking at him like an insistent bird.

Suddenly, a hand falls on his shoulder. A heavy, meaty paw.

Even as he's whirling around, he knows to whom it belongs.

The fist connects with his face. His skull snaps back on its mooring, and for a moment all he sees is a rain of starlight—and then vertigo hits him as he's falling from the Saranyu all over again. When his vision clears a half second later, there's Boyland Barnes Jr. standing there, fist cocked again.

"You mother-loving freak," Boyland slurs, then throws another punch.

Cael catches the incoming fist. The vine coils fast around Boyland's wrist and twists upward. The big teen cries out like a wounded rabbit, and the tension goes out of his one knee as he winces and whimpers.

"I'll let you have that one hit," Cael says, tasting blood. "Just that one. Because we got a lot of complicated history, and I figure I'm probably owed a punch. But the second one ain't allowed. I could break this arm. The Blight *wants* me to. I can feel it. It'd be giddy as anything to snap your limb like a mouse's neck in a snap-trap. But I'm not gonna let that happen, long as you don't see fit to pitch another one. We square?"

Boyland growls.

Cael increases the pressure. Boyland yelps—his whole body goes slack, and suddenly the Blight-vine is the only thing keeping him standing.

"I said—*are we square?*"

"Yeah, *yeah*, Jeezum Crow on a salty cracker, just *let go*."

The vine unspools.

Boyland staggers backward, manages to catch himself before falling.

"The hell's this about?" Cael asks. "I was just minding my own business, staying out of yours."

"You just came from Gwennie's room."

"So?"

"You're back with her. I can smell it on you. She's . . . my wife. Or was gonna be. You sonofabastard." Way he says it, his voice is sludgy, muddy. That's when Cael realizes.

"You're drunk, you buckethead."

"What? I'm not d— I'm not drunk, *you're* drunk, McAvoy." Cael gives him a look and Boyland shrugs. "Oh, whatever, Mister Holier Than Thou. Always so dang cocky, like the world owes you a favor, like you got it all figgered out. Asshole. So what if I managed to swipe a bottle of Micky Finn's?"

Boyland slumps against the wall.

"Go on back to your room, Boyland. Sleep it off."

"You love her, dontcha?"

"Her who?" Though he damn well knows who.

"I love her. I do. Not just an Obligation thing, either— because, you know, I really think she's like, a, a . . . shoot, I dunno, like a flower or something, a pretty, pretty flower." He *urps* into a closed fist. "I can't even put my words straight to how I feel about her, but how I feel about her is that I love her."

"Lemme ask you something."

The buckethead gives him the side-eye. "Go on."

"You let me die up there. On the Saranyu."

"And yet, here you are, Miracle Man." Cael can feel the anger there.

"But you didn't know that. You had to figure on me taking the dirt nap after a fall like that. Gwennie almost had me. But you came along, pulled her away, which meant I fell." He licks his bottom lip, tastes blood from where Boyland popped him. "You did it for her, I get that. But I wanna know: you do it because you were afraid she was gonna fall, or did you do it because if I survived, then you were afraid she was gonna fall *for me*—?"

Boyland grinds his teeth. "Honest answer?"

"Honest as the day is long."

"Both. It was both. Not like I had a lot of time to think about it up there, but I had enough time to see the ways of it. I knew if we kept trying to save you she might go over the edge with you. And I knew if we *did* save you, well, I knew I probably was out of that picture. As I am now."

Cael grunts. He wants to be mad. But it's like hunting rats and only kicking up dust—he's just not feeling it. "Forget it. Go get some sleep."

"We square?"

"I reckon we're pretty godsdamn far from square, and seems to me that however all this shakes out, someone's gonna be unhappy, whether it's you or me or both of us at the same time. We ain't square, and we may never be square, but it is what it is and we'll go on pretending it isn't."

With that, Cael turns around and heads to the door.

By now, his head's spinning. His heart, too, and both of them seem to be whirling about in opposite directions. He can't seem to find his balance here—Lane going against him, Rigo working for Pop, Gwennie wanting to be with him just as he's with Wanda, Boyland being all slobbery sad and talking to him like they're buddies or something.

He heads out of the building, his lip still smarting, his mouth still tasting the tang of his own blood. The city is awake and working—sparks rain down as someone welds beams together up above his head. Couple young kids nearby—one of them with a face blackened by some kind of tumor mask—doing mortar-work to assemble a wall, the tool scraping loudly as it presses the sloppy goop against the crooked bricks.

Someone calls his name, someone off to the side.

He keeps going. Whoever it is, he doesn't wanna talk.

But the voice is louder and more persistent, coming at him.

Well, crap.

He stops, turns, throws up his hands, and says, irritated, "What?"

It's Balastair. He almost doesn't recognize the man at first—he's not gone full-on Heartlander yet, but his hair's shaggier, pulled back in a ragged warrior's tail, and his face is scruffy with growth. Still, though, the rest of him—even guised in the clothing of a Heartlander—is crisp and well put together. He lifts a finger and calls after Cael:

"Mister McAvoy—a moment?"

"Sure, fine, yeah." Cael rolls two fingers together: a gesture of impatience. "And seriously, just call me Cael, okay?"

"Cael. Yes. Of course."

Up close now, Cael can see the man looks like he's been rubbing poison ivy in his eyes. Puffy. Bloodshot. Red nose, too.

"You don't look so hot," Cael says.

Seemingly taken off balance, Balastair looks embarrassed as he dabs at his eyes. "I . . . lost somebody. I'm grieving. In the sky we are usually afforded a long period of mourning. Days-long funeral processions. Weeks away from work, when one is allowed to grieve in isolation or with a chosen few."

"Down here, we aren't usually afforded the time for that. I've seen men die in the field, taken down by a motorvator, and still the work goes on." Suddenly he feels stupid and insensitive. "I'm sorry for your loss. I heard it was your ex-wife?" He remembers meeting her up there on the Saranyu. She didn't seem particularly friendly.

"Killed by our own. She ran to them thinking they would help her and . . ." He shakes his head. "Cleo and I were a mismatch, perhaps from the start. I had a lot of anger for her, but still, she was once my wife and . . ." His voice cracks. "I didn't come to talk about this, so I should adopt a Heartlander's toughness. I came to talk. And offer my help."

"I'm sorry?"

"I . . . knew your father. A little bit anyway."

Cael blinks. "How's that? You're not that much older than I am."

"He . . . knew my mother. I don't know all the details, not exactly. I know that your father as a young man was on one of the flotillas—though I don't know how or why that was. It was there he met my mother, and later on they reconnected here, in the Heartland. When she left the flotilla, she reached out to him and . . . again, a lot of this is hearsay, but she seemed to think he had lost some of his, ahh, rebellious edge. He wanted to settle down, and she wanted to do the opposite. But she contacted me—back when we were still talking. Had me help him a little."

"The seeds," Cael says.

"Yes. You knew about them?"

"Found out, yeah." Cael laughs. "Honestly, that's what started all this. The dang seeds. The secret garden." He shakes his head. All of this came from that. All the good. And all the bad.

"Little seeds grow big forests," Balastair says. "Something my mother used to say."

"Pop used to say things like that all the time."

Balastair offers an awkward raising of the brows. "Well. So. I ahh—" He clears his throat. "I understand that my mother wants you to get something for her. Something secret."

"She does. I don't know what it is, exactly—it's a secret to me, too."

"Certainly sounds like my mother. She's not keen on giving more information than she feels is absolutely necessary—a philosophy I myself do not share. All told, if whatever she wants is here, I'd like to help you find it. I used to live on the Saranyu. I know its places and spaces, even . . . destroyed and reassembled like this. I'd like to help, if you'll allow me. I've long kept myself out of my mother's . . . dealings, but at this point it seems time to pick a side."

Cael thinks: *I don't even know if I've picked a side yet.*

He keeps that to himself and instead offers a hand. "Works for me."

Balastair takes it and shakes it.

"We should begin in earnest."

Cael nods. "Won't be easy, though. Seems Lane and his people don't want us poking around."

Balastair nods. "Then we'll need to find a way to poke around, unseen."

NIGHT OF THE
GOLDEN JOINING

ERNESTO GRAVENOST EATS. It is one of his
greatest pleasures. The sensations of eating are paramount to
him: tonight, the cracking of bones, the sucking of marrow.
The warm insides of a pheasant's egg. The slurp of noodles and
pickled cabbage. Hot salty broth on his tongue. The cherry
and pipesmoke aromas in this decanter of wine. All the flavors
mingle and play inside his mouth, leading to the fullness of his
round, bulging belly.

It goes beyond sensation, though: Part of it is knowing that
he has what others do not. Even here in the Seventh Heaven he
is granted pleasures that few are allowed. He has first pick of
the vintners' wines. The brewmasters' beers, too. He can choose
his own lambs to be slaughtered, or goats, or geese, and once a
week he receives a box of fruits and vegetables that are unparal-
leled, even on the other flotillas. For he has chosen this flying
city—the Gravenost Ernesto Oshadagea—as one that provides

the finest food for the rest of the Empyrean. (That, one of the many advantages of being a Grand Architect.)

It all starts here.

And he gets first taste.

Below them, in the corn-taken Heartland, are people who will never taste the things he has tasted, who will endure great hardships for no reward. Even the smallest thing—a cup of coffee, a soft pillow, comfortable shoes—are pleasures he is allowed and they are not.

Cruel, he supposes. But thrilling, too.

Having something that others do not is always a secret delight.

As a younger man, he felt the Heartlanders should be treated better. The flocks and herds of beasts tended to here upon the Oshadagea are well-kept creatures. They are fed the best food so they become the best food. And so he felt that the Heartlanders should be treated well so that they would work well in return. But the Heartlanders rebuked that notion. The more you give them, the more they demand—they're greedy, that way, like hogs. It's why Ernesto enjoys eating pork most of all. It feels deserved.

And so they began to take away things from the Heartlanders, removing choice and opportunity first. Bit by bit, cutting them down, boxing them in. Now, the Empyrean is removing their humanity.

That sits poorly with him sometimes. If only because what joy will he get of taking pleasures that mechanical men cannot have? He's never been excited by the notion of having something the elevator could not possess, or a mechanical window-washer.

A man cannot find pleasure in one-upping a blender, or an oven, or a harpsichord.

Thoughts like these are in fact robbing him of the pleasure he should be feeling at this meal. The visidex in front of him is screen after screen of unpleasant news: Yes, the Empyrean have taken more towns, rounding up the inhabitants and . . . scooping out whatever it is that makes them *freethinkers* and shoving them into their new metal bodies. But the Heartlanders are fighting back. Pockets of resistance here and there, and then one big bright tumor in the center of it—a tumor like a beating heart, the wreckage of the fallen Saranyu. They should've taken it back when they had the chance a year ago, but those terrorists had already taken it, had already manned the weapons, and now . . . the chance is gone.

A little voice inside him says: *Maybe you should've listened to that girl.*

The girl.

Hnnnh. No.

That Ormond girl, too young, too foolish. Too *strange* by a sky-mile. All those scars on her face. Why do that? Sure, the boys and girls of the flotillas are wont to . . . express themselves as individuals. Odd tattoos—some made to glow like the winking tails of lightning bugs. Hair wild like a bird's tail, or shorn to the scalp. Teeth dyed. Tongues cut into serpent forks. Fingernails painted, extended, teased over time into corkscrew shapes or staircases or sine waves. Last year one of the fashions was drawing faces over your existing face—how disconcerting. And a few years back, "suicide chic" was in play: nooses worn about the neck, makeup made to mirror the striations of life expired, fake scars on the wrists and throat, devices made to leak blood. Shocking and mad, maybe, but it was all fake. Boys and girls taunting the mortality they would one day face.

The Ormond girl found that line and danced right over it.

Not surprising, given her father. And given how little her grandfather did to rein them in.

No, it was best they rebuked her. In time she'll see that.

He pokes at the gooey pheasant egg with a fork. It leaves treacly golden trails across the white plate. Gone cold by now. Ugh.

Time yet to reclaim some pleasure.

The young woman who cooked this—what's her name? Sistina? Sastina? Hmm. It's a pretty name, whatever it is. He calls her "Dumpling," though, an ironic name given how small and thin she is—like a graceful little bird. The nickname has its value: just last week she asked him, *Do you think I've put on weight?* and he hmmed and cleared his throat and didn't say yes, not with his mouth, but he *did* say it with his eyes even though it wasn't at all true.

It makes her more pliant in the bedroom. A woman weakened of her value and resolve will go far to try to reclaim it.

Soon he will be done with her. But he has things he wishes to try first.

He pushes the chair back and wipes crumbs out of the thatch of chest hair poking out of his unbuttoned, high-collar shirt. He begins to unbuckle his belt, and as he fidgets with it, he totters toward the bedroom and nudges the door open with a knee—

The bedside lamp clicks on.

His breath is snatched away by the hand of surprise.

Dumpling sits by the bed, a pillowcase over her head, hands bound behind her, the spiderweb negligee hanging on her as she leans forward, trembling. She's afraid. And now, so is he.

Because next to her, sitting cross-legged on the bed, is the Ormond girl. She looks different. Her face. The scar-lines etched there have been inked, tattooed so that they seem to glow with golden light.

"You," he says, his voice quiet and crackling.

"Me," she says.

Sitting in front of her is a sonic pistol.

"What do you intend to do with that?" he asks.

"Shoot you," she answers.

He quakes. Looks around. Sees the curtains blowing. The window has been removed—not broken, just removed. Cut out.

She must see him staring that way because she says: "You're thinking a young girl like me couldn't have possibly come in through the window. We're so high up. No way you would've anticipated me scaling a building like that. But I did. That's my strength and your weakness. You underestimate me because I'm a girl and because I'm young. It's your doubt in me that gave me the open door through which I walked."

"You're a monster. A broken little monster."

"I was broken, but I am fixed. All my girls are joined with shining gold." She echoes Miranda's words: "We have our utility and we have been made all the more beautiful."

She reaches for the pistol but doesn't take it. Just lays her hand across it.

A threat, or a promise?

"You disgust me," he says.

"And you disgust me. That summarizes our entire relationship. I know why I disgust you. I am a young girl with power over you. Let me tell you why *you* disgust *me*. You are old and self-indulgent, a man who uses his power to crush bugs and eat rich meals, who gets fatter and fatter while ignoring all the problems. You're weak, ultimately, flabby and grotesque. The only way a beautiful girl like Sestina here would ever deign to let you press yourself against her is because you force her through the power granted to you."

He begins to protest, stammering, gurgling: "Now, just you wait, nobody granted me my power, I designed this flotilla and—"

"You designed it the way my grandfather designed his. You copied those who came before you. And now you are lord over a ship that has reduced value in this time of terrorism. There are enemies clawing at our undersides, and all you want to do is grow fatter on grapes and sausages. I will change that by removing your vote."

He leers. "You will kill me, and then all the others will turtle inward. They'll *hide*, you see? They'll see that I've been executed and they'll shrink away into boltholes or protectorates and their votes will remain safe."

"That's true," she says, running her finger along the length of the sonic shooter. It's an elegant gun—he's not really much of a fetishist when it comes to weapons, but this one looks brass, smooth, as much a needle as a pistol. "Unless, *unless*, I executed you all at the same time. Unless I had been training a regiment of smart, deadly young girls who I could unleash on one night to dispatch every vote that countered Project Raven. Wouldn't that be something? Like a sword blade cutting a line of candles in half in one blow." She uses the shooter to mimic the motion of the blade. "Whoosh."

His blood turns to cold syrup.

"You wouldn't dare. Spare me. I'll help you. You have my—"

He does not get to say "vote."

The sonic shooter screams and cuts through his middle.

His meal paints the wall behind him.

MOTHER AND SON

LANE PACES LIKE a nervous barn cat, his hands clasped in front of him—one fist nested inside the other, the fingers trying to pry open the other fist in an anxious gesture. Here, the door. Behind it, his mother.

Nika leans forward: "You can go in now. She's awake. And aware."

"Just hold on," he says. "I need to think."

"He needs to think," Killian says. For once the man's eyes are bright and clear as a glass of water. The ex-captain steps in front of Lane and stops him from pacing by planting both hands on the sides of his arms and holding him there—not a cruel, forceful gesture, but a gentle urging to stop. "You don't have to do this now. It can wait. *She* can wait—" And then, under his breath: "She damn sure waited long enough as it is."

"No, I need this," Lane says, then corrects himself: "I need to *do* this."

He's queasy.

Everything feels like it's slipping through his fingers.

Pop rebuking him.

Cael coming here and demanding things Lane cannot give him.

Luna's been cold.

Killian—at least *he's* been good. Been staying out of the Pheen, away from the poppy, even off the whiskey and gin these last few weeks. His face no longer the hue of cigarette ash, his eyes no longer cloudy.

The ex-captain puts his forehead against Lane's. "Go, then. Time to get this over, perhaps. Better to rip the stitching out than to extend this misery."

"You'll wait here?"

"I'll wait here." Killian leans in, kisses Lane's temple.

Lane has a moment where it feels like—well, when he was a kid, he jumped off Burt and Bessie Greene's barn roof. Beneath him was a heap of corn-leaf hay, just a pile of dried dead Hiram's, and just before he jumped off that roof, he felt the same thing that he's feeling now. Fear cutting through him like a cold knife. His stomach trying to crawl up between his ears.

He didn't break anything, but the dried corn-leaf cut him something fierce. His walk back home with the rest of the crew saw him covered in a slick brown sheen of his own blood.

Thing was, that day, he jumped off the roof for a reason.

He told Cael and Rigo that it was because he wanted to see if he could do it. Ballsy, bold, doing it on a dare that nobody actually dared.

But the reality is, he wanted to jump.

He wanted to hurt himself.

Not because he wanted to die.

Not because he invited the pain.

But because he hoped, secretly, that if he hurt himself just badly enough, his mother would come and find him. She would leave the Babysitter life and come to him. And tend to him. And make it all better.

That never happened, of course. It was Pop who tended to his cuts.

"I'm ready," he says, and he opens the door.

She looks small as a bird, sitting there on the cot.

His mother, Mitzi Moreau.

Time hasn't been kind to her. It's held her fast, carved lines into her face, pushed her eyes back into their sockets, painted shadows where there were none before. She's not skeletal, not exactly, but she looks withered, winnowed, pared down to a smaller, more concentrated version of who she once was.

Mitzi sees her son enter, and she stands. The sound that comes out of her is halfway between a laugh and a sob. Her face softens; the lines warp and melt. She hurries over to him with small, squirrel steps, calling his name through that ongoing laugh-sob, but he throws up his hands and takes a step back to match her steps forward—

"Wait," he says, firm, cautioning.

"Laney," she says, her hands physically pleading. "It's me. It's your mama, sweetheart."

"You don't get to say that," he says, each word cold and half dead. "You want to call me anything, you call me Mayor Moreau. You want to call yourself something, maybe you should try *traitor to the Heartland.*"

Her face is like a sky of falling stars. Everything sinks and sags. She takes a few ginger steps backward and sits down on the cot, looking numb.

"Oh" is all she says.

He didn't want the conversation to go this way—at least, not so swiftly—but it feels like he's already stepping off the edge of that barn roof again, so he lets himself fall into it.

"You betrayed the Heartland." *You betrayed me.* "You turned against your own people and worked for the skybastards of the Seventh Heaven against them. You can't do that and not be held accountable."

"Lane, we all worked for the Empyrean. Every one of us."

"I didn't. And I don't."

"I did it because I needed the ace notes. *We* needed the ace notes. Once your father died—"

"Don't you mention him. This isn't about him!" He scowls. "And it damn sure wasn't about the ace notes. How many ace notes found their way back to me, to the farmhouse, huh? *Huh?*"

"I should've sent more—"

"You should've sent *some*. Any! Anything at all! You went and took a cushy Babysitter job halfway across the godsdamn Heartland and the only thing it did is put ace notes in *your* pocket. It didn't benefit me! It didn't do anything for me except leave me alone in a rotting, ruined house on the edge of nowhere—if I didn't have friends I would've *died*. Died because my father was too stupid to live and my mother was too greedy to stay!"

"I wasn't greedy!" she protests, again standing up. "I wasn't. You have to believe me, Laney, I . . . I left because I didn't know how to raise you."

A gulf of silence between them, like two townsfolk standing in the wreckage of their home after a tornado has come and gone.

"What . . . what the hell does that mean?"

She says, "Some women, Lane, they have a calling to be mothers. They understand their children. I never had that. Your father understood you. He was half a boy himself. But you were always a strange creature to me, some little needy thing who wanted me for reasons I just didn't get. I left 'cause I figured I was going to screw you up."

"No," Lane says, stabbing an accusing finger in the air, punctuating each word. "You left because you figured I was gonna screw *you* up."

She looks down at her feet. "Maybe you're right."

"You're a traitor to the Heartland."

"I was a traitor to you, you mean."

"Whatever. Anybody else, I'd sentence you to death. But I figure you worked for *them* for so long, maybe you can work for *us* now that we've got you back. I'm putting you to work building this city for us."

"That seems fair."

"You don't get to tell me what's fair and what's not."

She takes a step toward him, but the look on his face must stop her.

"Just remember," she says, "at the end of the day, we're family."

"I have a family," he says. "And you're not it."

DIGGING IN THE DIRT

MOTHER'S EYES are flat matte, lifeless, and without spark, each a dirty spyglass looking nowhere, seeing nothing. She still gets up, moves around, speaks to Gwennie, but her words are dull and mumbled. Her shoulders hunch forward. She looks like she's trying to push herself inward—farther and farther, perhaps, until she is able to simply disappear.

"Everything's okay?" Gwennie asks. "With Scooter and Squirrel?"

"They're fine. We're fine." The woman fritters about the half-collapsed apartment, scooping up little piles of dust as if that'll fix it.

"Well, where are they?"

"They're out . . . playing." The way she says this last word tells Gwennie she doesn't really *know* where they are.

Gwennie goes to the window—a window with the glass pane broken out of it—and looks down. The sound of the two children playing reaches her ears: it's almost musical. Down below in a small lot lined with pulverized rubble, the two children come running. Scooter with a doll made of corn husk, Squirrel with . . . what looks to be a spear made out of a broomstick, some tape, and a shard of gleaming glass as its tip.

Squirrel is not very good at playing.

"Squirrel has a spear, Mom."

"Oh. Okay." Barely a reaction.

It's like something has been bombed out of her. The ground blasted.

"It's your job to keep them safe—" Gwennie starts to say.

Mother snaps. "I couldn't keep Richard safe. Neither could you. Neither could any of us. We're not safe, Gwendolyn. None of us are *safe*."

And then she composes herself as if that never happened— her body again shifts inward and she continues pushing dust into her open palm.

Gwennie almost wants to cry, though a part of her thinks: *At least she got mad. At least she's still in there, somewhere.*

Sigh.

She points to the basket over by the side. It's full of food: she sees the green mop-tops of carrots, the bulge of tomatoes, a long, lean twist of bread. "Well. You have food. I'm going."

"Fine."

"Fine."

She moves to give her mother a hug, but it's entirely one-sided. The best she gets is that the woman leans into it a little. Another small sigh escapes her.

And with that, Gwennie's back out the door.

Outside, she listens to the sounds of distant working as she faces the back end of the building. It opens up to the giant wall that surrounds the city, a mottled tortoiseshell wall that sometimes feels like protection, but just as often feels like a prison.

Somewhere around the side she hears the two kids laughing—which is good, because it means Squirrel hasn't stabbed anybody today—and she goes to follow after it. But around the corner, she doesn't find the kids.

She finds Wanda Mecklin.

Wanda. Standing there, arms folded over, nervously chewing her lower lip. "There you are," she says.

"Here I am," Gwennie answers.

And then neither one of them says anything.

Gwennie watches Wanda. The signs of Blight upon her are small—but she can't help but look at them. The girl's tongue hides behind her teeth, but even with evening coming Gwennie can see the sheen of the green leaf that tips it. Her fingernails are like little rolled-up leaves. The smell coming off her is floral—strongly so, almost aggressive.

"I need to find the kids—" Gwennie starts to say.

"Cael left."

"Left? What?"

"He snuck out."

"I don't know what that means."

Wanda sighs as if she's dealing with a stupid child. "He left with that other one, the Empyrean man, and they snuck off."

"Empyrean? You mean Balastair."

Wanda shrugs, looking irritated. "We weren't introduced."

"That means they're going to look for the . . . well, whatever it is that the Maize Witch sent Cael here to get."

A defensive sneer. "Sent Cael *and* me to get."

"Right. Of course. Sorry."

"It also means he went off without the both of us."

That echoes Gwennie's thoughts perfectly.

It stings her. He could've at least *told* her! Dangit.

Wanda starts to say, "Cael and I—"

Gwennie snaps: "I don't care, Wanda. Don't. Care. You and Cael have a thing, and I'm not going to mess with it." *Godsdamn do I want to mess with it.* "I don't wanna talk about Cael. Girls can get together without talking about boys, you know. We're more than trophy cases to hold them up."

Hard to read how Wanda takes that. Her face goes through some calisthenics—a scrutinizing frown to an eye-rolling *whatever* to, finally, a softer countenance that might just indicate acquiescence.

"Okay," Wanda says.

"Okay."

"So, whaddya want to talk about?"

"I dunno, Wanda." She's exasperated, but realizes that she's the one who made the offer, so . . . "You miss Boxelder?"

"Not really."

"I miss it. Sorta. I miss some of the people."

"I miss my family." Wanda suddenly hugs her arms to her chest and rubs her hands over her elbows. "I don't know if they'd like who I am now."

"My mother doesn't like me, I don't think."

"Imagine what she'd think if you were Blighted."

"I thought you liked being . . . that."

Wanda pauses, seems to think on it. "I do. I feel strong. It's a gift, not a curse, but I also know that most folks don't think of it that way. Even here, where it seems like everybody's an outcast now, they still look at me like I got two heads on my neck or a lizard tail whipping around."

"Sorry."

"I asked for it. I wanted this. I still do want it. It's their problem, not mine. I went through my life thinking that everyone else was better than I was and that I was always trailing behind, trying to be like them. But now I know that I'm just me and they're gonna have to deal with that."

Gwennie thinks but doesn't say: *And yet you became something else in the process.* Or maybe this is who Wanda was all along. Maybe the Blight is bringing something out of her that was always there, just buried.

Maybe it's doing that for Cael, too.

She shudders.

PALACE HILL

EVERY FLOTILLA HAS a Palace Hill, Balastair said.

And he was right. Even this one—even after its fall.

Cael and the Empyrean man creep through the streets of Pegasus City as the moon crests high in the sky, signaling midnight.

Balastair described Palace Hill as a thing of beauty—but everything he described is in wreckage. There are the cobble-stone streets: piled up in heaps and mounds, the stones cracked. Cael sees elegant marble and rare wood, much of it blasted to rocks and splinters. Scattered glass, bent chrome pocked with rust, trellises leaning on trellises.

And yet, many of the homes remain. Half collapsed, some partly imploded, a few entirely sound in terms of structure and shape—but if you squint hard in the light of the night sky you can see the shape of what the homes once were, manses of some expanse, born of craft and skill and looking like nothing Cael

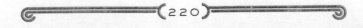

has ever seen before. The Heartland doesn't have homes like these, shattered or no.

This area: cordoned off. Daily the Sleeping Dogs work through the space, rebuilding. But no one sleeps here. Not yet. It hasn't been declared safe—not a lot of value in populating an area if it's just going to kill those who stay here. Pegasus City needs its people alive, not mashed to a red mess under a crushing wave of broken stone.

"I don't get it," Cael says in a low voice. "I fell with this city. Most of this stuff shouldn't be here. How the hell does a floating city fall from that height and stay together? Hell, some of the buildings back toward the city center are still tall towers—I'm not my father, I'm not smart like he is, but that don't seem to make a lick of sense."

Balastair sighs as if he doesn't feel like talking about it, as if remembering it all is a chore. "It's a combination of factors. Part of it is the engineering. Many structures are designed to absorb all kinds of shock—a flotilla isn't so much a single city as it is a series of buildings and areas chained together and allowed to float, and they constantly push and pull on one another. Once in a very rare while, a chain snaps—no small feat, given the size of these chains—and the buildings smash into one another. And yet they remain whole. Foamcore walls behind the stone. Nano-width web-mesh infusing the building material. Everything tested for tension and tremor. The other part of it is, half the city didn't completely *fall*. Parts were protected by massive inflatable buoys—balloons, really. Not strong enough to keep buildings afloat, but enough to make their descent gradual rather than . . . *apocalyptic*." He sighs suddenly. "This was my home once."

"The flotilla."

"This area of the flotilla. I grew up here. With my mother."

"What was that like, having her as your mama?"

Balastair groans as they push on through the ruins of Palace Hill. "It was something I don't really want to discuss." And yet here he goes, discussing it: "She was a strange woman, consumed by her work. I never knew my father—she didn't deem it *vital* information, didn't think him necessary at all. I believe her phrasing was 'vestigial.' Like a tail or one's far-standing teeth." Cael is nimble enough to make it through the wreckage, but Balastair keeps almost losing his footing on scree and broken stone. "Oof. Walking this hill made me tired enough then. Now, it's downright torture."

"You think that house is still here?"

"I cannot say. If it is, we'll find it."

"And if it ain't?"

Balastair shrugs. "Then we do not find what my mother hopes you'll find. And whatever plan B is, she will enact it."

"You think she's got a plan B, huh?"

"I think she has plans A through Z, and then one through a hundred, and several more lined up after that." He picks up a cracked, chipped balustrade—part of two horses, each winged, one Pegasus with its nose against the tail of the other. He groans again and tosses it to the cobble, where it snaps in half like a clod of dried mud. "The way she told it, the Blight—strictly speaking, Brunfels Molecular Mutation Syndrome—was an accident, an unexpected hazard of the work she was doing. She blamed the Empyrean, said they were pushing too hard too fast, ignoring risks for the sake of progress. But one night, while wreathed in poppy-smoke, an assistant of hers—a woman named Ursula Aldrovandi—said that it was intentional. A design by my mother and tested on herself first above others, probably because she wanted to be as powerful as the Grand Architects, but no one would allow her that. Or maybe just because she had seen something in the skies of the Seventh Heaven that she didn't like. I don't know. Whatever it was, she didn't share it with me. One day she was my mother, the next she was taken into custody, and the next after that she had escaped, thanks to the help of a small cabal of Blighted agents."

"Can I trust her?"

"Esther?" Balastair moans, pinches the flesh above his hawk's-beak nose. "I honestly don't know, Cael. I myself cannot decide if she's a noble martyr, a brave academic, or a villainous monster. Or some strange helical twist of all three." He pulls his hand away from his face, and Cael sees his gaze narrow. "I suppose we're about to find out, though, because . . ."

He points toward a half-collapsed house of beige brick, a house enrobed in a mesh of dead, withered vines. Desiccated flowers dangle from trellises snapped like broken bones.

"That's it?" Cael asks.

"That's it," Balastair answers. "Shall we?"

The ghost of home haunts him. This place was his, long ago—his and his mother's, though since lived in by someone else. (He recalls, just now, passing by the window the day he visited the Lupercal and seeing a small boy standing there behind the glass, looking out.) Still—the specter of this place, of their lives here, is an almost tangible presence. There: the mantel on which sat a silver brazier in which she burned incense. In the corner of the room he no longer sees, the birdcage that once sat there, but the memory of it is so powerful he feels like if he were to reach out he'd be able to touch it—maybe even hear the chirps and burbles of Erasmus not long after hatching.

Oh, Erasmus.

He suspects this Heartlander—Cael, who seems a bit . . . well, not *simple*, but *straightforward*—wouldn't find much sympathy in the bird's death. So Balastair bites back his grief the way one swallows bile.

Images of his mother dance like wraiths behind his eyes.

Esther, passing through, always passing through, rarely stopping to eat dinner, never cooking a meal, sometimes tending to the lilacs that lined the windows or the wishful-bashfuls hanging off the trellis. Her corn-silk hair, her pale eyes with too much knowledge dancing in them, a mouth ever twisted up in a small smile or down in a scrutinizing scowl. Early on, in her lab coat, always in her lab coat. But as time went on, her dress changed—gone was the coat, in came a diaphanous dress. Her hair ceased to be pulled up around her head and ears and flowed over her shoulders: golden, like sunlight striking waterfalls. She changed, then. Became obsessed with plants. With lineage and legacy.

With mutation.

He shudders, remembering the first sign of her Blight—they were out back, in the small garden terrace. He with the young Erasmus (no longer a hatchling but not far past it), training the bird not to speak, not yet, but to modify its sounds for a different purpose—a chirp for food, a shrill trill for warning, a fluty warble for play. She was moving white bricks, making a new planter and—

He still remembers the tiny snap.

Her fingernail broke off. Clattered on the bone-bleach pavers beneath them.

He looked over in horror as she held her finger aloft—the index finger on her right hand. The nail was gone altogether.

In its place, a small puckered pink hole.

A pea-shoot tendril rose from that hole.

It uncoiled, twirled in the air, testing it the way an inchworm does before taking an uncertain step. Balastair yelled out, a moment of weakness he still recalls. And he recalls that she did *not* cry out.

All she said was a small, curious "*Oh.*"

"What're we looking for?" Cael asks, interrupting Balastair's reverie of memory. "This place looks like a picked-over corpse. Can't even get upstairs."

Sure enough, the stairway up is so collapsed it's unusable.

"We'll still have to check up there," Balastair says. "Which means finding our way to climb out and up."

"I'm game for that."

Cael stretches out his right arm, and the vine coiled there relaxes, like a snake lazily removing itself from a tree branch. Balastair realizes he watched his mother take to her own mutation that way—any fear that Cael may have once had over what had happened to his body was fading away. Now, it's becoming a tool. And soon, Balastair suspects, it will become part of him rather than something outside him. A transition that should come with fear, but won't.

McAvoy steps out the front door once more. From inside, Balastair watches as the young man does a few stretches, cranes his neck a few times, then reaches his hand to the sky.

The Blight-vine follows the line created by the arm. It extends upward, and Balastair can't see what happens to it—but he can see the look of surprise and glee on Cael's face.

"Well, King Hell and Old Scratch, look at that!" Cael calls, then grits his teeth and disappears as the vine pulls him upward.

This is the boy Gwennie was pining over?

He supposes he gets it. Cael is—how to put it? A creature of action. Impulse and impetus. He *does* things. Balastair was always more internal, living an intellectual life, one of imagination and infinite possibility. Making a choice changes the nature of possibility, doesn't it? Before acting, a thousand options remain open.

Act, and your options winnow to one.

That's what Cleo always hated about him. She said he was too afraid to do anything, too afraid to take a step for fear of how the ground would move when he did.

Cleo, gone from him now.

Her death leaves a hole in his life. He knows that abstractly he's good to be shut of her—she was a vain creature. Not a monster, but eminently selfish. Like too many of his fellow Empyrean citizens. A traitor to him in so many ways and yet he hoped to rekindle something with her. Though here a small voice reminds: *You wanted to rekindle that only to make Gwendolyn Shawcatch jealous, isn't that right?* And it is right, though he'd never admit it out loud.

A vision again of Cleo spinning around, killed by what she hoped would be her own saviors. Spun body. Blood.

He shudders, tries not to cry out. A hand over his mouth to prevent it.

A quick shake of his head to clear out the spiders that have nested there, and then he's out the door, looking up. Cael waves down, extends his hand, and the vine reaches for him. Balastair has to repress the feeling of discomfort watching this braided, veiny vine slide through the air silently toward him. Cael calls down: "Take it, I'll pull you up."

Balastair begins to reach upward—

Something moves behind Cael.

A shape taller than he is.

McAvoy hears it. The vine starts to retract. Balastair calls out a warning—but it's too late.

The mechanical man steps out from the shadows of the room above and knocks Cael backward with a hard metal hand. Then a sonic shriek cuts the air, and suddenly he's tumbling out of the second-floor window, catching the lip with the Blight-vine—a save that doesn't last long as Cael spits blood and falls two stories, cracking hard against his shoulder, head snapping against shattered cobblestone. Balastair yells, runs toward him—

But a shadow emerges from the side.

He catches the glint of a pistol. It clips him in the side of the head—his heel skids out from under him, and before he even realizes it, the ground is rushing up to meet his tailbone. A sudden flashback hits him—coming out of the Lupercal, the falcon tearing into Erasmus, turning the little bird into a red pulp. The peregrine descending, shooting him, leaving him wrecked.

Even as the shock travels up his spine and he rolls over onto his side, a sharp, angry thought cuts through everything: *But I showed him, didn't I?* Percy the peregrine, dead by mechanical Pegasus.

And yet, some fear haunts him, some fear that the person walking toward him now out of shadow, out of night, *is* Percy—the peregrine returned from death, vicious and vengeful—

But it's not.

It's just a girl.

A wild-eyed, sharp-faced girl with a sonic pistol. He doesn't recognize her at first—though then he remembers seeing her when they first landed here, rescued from the blockade and brought to the wreckage of the Saranyu.

Luna is her name, isn't it?

"You've got to—I don't—" he stammers, trying to find words. A trickle of blood crawls down his temple, clinging to his jawline.

"I don't have to do anything," she says.

And then she shoots him.

The front of Balastair's shirt is gummy with vomit. A few feet away, pressed up against the wall, sits Cael—cradling his shoulder, his nose rimed with dry mucus, eyes red. McAvoy looks unhinged: teeth bared in a feral gesture, flinty eyes darting from Luna to the two metal men that attend her.

Balastair recognizes the mechanicals. One is a Bartender-Bot. The other, a Constructor: meant for building things, fixing things, and demolishing them in turn. Both repurposed. Each with sonic shooters fitted to the arms.

The young girl twirls her pistol and chews on a stick.

"You naughty little princes," she says.

Cael spits. His lips and tongue smack drily. "I hope you're Obligated to Old Scratch, you little brat."

"Ooooh," she says, then whistles. "Little brat. Big words for a Blighter." Balastair watches Cael tense up. The vine seems to tense with him. Luna points the pistol at him. "Oh no, no, no. Keep that abomination tucked tight, or I'll find cause to pull this trigger again."

"This was once my house," Balastair says. His words are mushy, muddy—the results of having been hit by a sonic blast. One that was thankfully set to be nonlethal. "I have a right to be here."

"You have no right except what I say is right. This house is property of the Sleeping Dogs, Harrington. And, see, that's how I *beat you idiots here*. I do my research. I learned pretty fast how to use those visidexes. Didn't take long to search your name, find the places here you once called home. Killian is at the other location in case you showed up there."

Other location? Then he realizes: his home. The one before everything went to ruin. He hadn't even thought of it still existing, that's how distant that life seems to be now.

"Just let us find what we're looking for, and we'll be on our way," Cael says. "You can kick my ass back out into the corn if you want."

"Oh, we'll throw you to the corn all right," she says. "You'll be food for it, you Blighted—"

A sound, outside, and she looks over her shoulder—

Killian Kelly comes in through the front.

His face wearing a sneer-smirk.

"Like rats in a trap," he says. "Shame neither of you are particularly keen on following the rules that have been set out before you."

He clucks his tongue.

Balastair rolls his eyes. "Might I point out the irony that you're raiders and rebels whose *very existence* relies upon not following rules?"

Again the pistol rises, and Luna's finger eases toward the trigger.

Balastair's hands fly up, and he's ashamed at the cowardice in his voice when he says: "Sorry, sorry, sorry."

"Lane will be very displeased with his old friend," Killian says.

"Who says he has to know?"

It's Luna who asks that. Balastair puzzles at it—but Killian is already ahead of him, frowning. "You sure about that?"

"It would be easiest. No fuss."

"I don't understand," Balastair says.

"They're gonna kill us," Cael growls.

Oh. *Oh.*

"I don't like it," Killian says, "but it would be easier. Lane doesn't need to know about this. He has enough to worry about. This treachery would wound him far more gravely than my own physical injuries did me."

"It's decided, then," Luna says.

She raises the pistol.

Balastair winces. Another act of cowardice—he is sure that Cael is meeting this fate with eyes open, face forward, chin thrust up in defiance, and again he's reminded why Gwennie likes him.

He hears the click of the dial on the side of the weapon.

And then:

A sonic shriek.

It's Killian who cries out.

Balastair's eyes jolt open.

The girl, Luna, drops to the floor on her knees, hands planted against the cracked marble. She makes a *hurrk* sound. Vomit splashes the floor.

Balastair doesn't even realize what's happening until the young mayor of Pegasus City steps through the door, long-barreled sonic rifle in hand.

"Lane," Killian says. "How—?"

"Get out," Lane says to him, his face a mask of rage.

"They were—" Luna tries to say, but she gags again and presses her face into the crook of her elbow to hold it back.

Killian steps in front of Lane. "They defied you. You see that, right? This callow cur, supposed to be your friend—"

"*Get. Out.*"

The older raider reaches for Lane, but Lane tugs his head away, then says: "And take her with you."

GIFTS FROM OUR MOTHERS

THEY FIND NOTHING in the house. The three of them now—Balastair, Cael, Lane—climb and clamber through the remains of his onetime home, and they find nothing. It has been pored over, picked through. And still, Balastair looks. And thinks. And listens.

He listens to the two others talking outside. The acrid, heady tang of one of Lane's cigarettes—an Empyrean brand, if Balastair's nose has it right—rising up through the broken windows and off-kilter frames.

Their voices drift up to his ears.

Cael: "I thought . . . I thought we were done, man. I thought maybe you didn't trust me anymore."

Lane: "I trust you, Captain. I do. But I also have this place and . . . I was afraid to do wrong by the people here in order to do right by you. The greater good and all that." The sound of an

exhale. Another plume of blue smoke against the black window. "Like I know anything about the greater good."

Cael: "Me neither, man, me neither. I don't know what's right or wrong or upside down or sideways anymore. I feel like I don't know rat-crap from my right foot. I'm just . . . going day by day. One step at a time, which means I'm going somewhere." He laughs. "I just don't know where."

Lane: "I hear that, boss, I hear that."

Balastair kicks aside a broken light fixture: a brass seashell, dented and pocked and pitted. He follows the wires, finds where the fixture once hung, peers into the black. It's just more crumbled mess—a guillotine of stone. If this was the hiding place—and it isn't, because it's too simple, too easy—then it's long sealed off. They'd need to demolish this place first and sort through the fragments piece by miserable piece before they'd find what it was his mother thought they should have. A worthless, futile endeavor.

Maybe that's a good thing.

Because really: What kind of weapon did his mother hide here so long ago? Wouldn't someone have found it by now?

No. She would've hidden it well.

Hmm.

Outside: the *fing* of a lighter opening. The crackle-hiss of flame touching a cigarette. Lane: "My mother's here. In the city."

Cael: "Whoa-dang. Your mama's here?"

Lane: "Mm-hmm. She got rounded up with a couple others and brought here and . . . well. She and I had a conversation, and that's when I realized: She's not my family, not really. You guys are. You were always there for me when she wasn't. Pop, too. But this past year put blinders up and—well, shit, it took her to rip them back off again, get me seeing straight."

Cael: "I'm still floored she's here."

Lane: "Yeah." A pause. "Yeah. Anyway. I just wanted you to know I'm putting my ace notes on the table. I'm all in, brother. I just had to remember who my real family was."

Remember family.

A feathery tickle in the back of Balastair's brain.

Cael and Lane keep talking, but his mind wanders like a sick rat through the pipes and walls of memory. Back to that time when his mother first saw her own Blight. There in the back garden. On the stone terrace. That small word.

Oh.

That moment is a splinter in the skin of his memory.

And surely it was one in hers, too.

Can't go down the steps, so instead he heads back to the window—the one Cael fell out of only an hour before—and climbs out over the edge. And here, another memory, because didn't he do exactly this one time? *One* time he thought he'd be a rebellious little tit and flee home as a young boy, only twelve, running out into the night. That, the first time he discovered the Lupercal . . .

His muscle memory of that adventure has long gone from him, and his foot slips and he almost falls—

But still, he manages. He dangles. Drops.

"Shoulder still hurts—" Cael is saying, but his words cut short as Balastair lands in an awkward crouch. "Hey, uhh, Bal. You okay?"

But Balastair barely hears the question. He moves past them, alongside the house where the stone accordions and a hole sits in the side like a mouth puking up a frozen tide of bricks. There, then. The terrace. Bent iron fence, trellis cracked and snapped like little bones.

The terrace. Built right off the foundation of the house.

The homes here in Palace Hill did not fall individually—it was the whole hill that fell, buoyed by the inflatables that surely opened the moment the engines failed and chains broke. Some of this is still intact.

Balastair drops to his knees, starts prying up bricks. It's slow going, but not hard—the bricks aren't held together and sit crooked against one another, leaving little gaps for his fingers. But then he reaches in and feels a sharp lance of pain through his finger, to his wrist—

He retracts a hand already bleeding. The nail bent back, half torn, beads of blood dotting the edge like the round heads of red pins. He winces, sucks it into his mouth.

Next thing he knows, someone's easing him aside. Cael.

Cael has part of the iron fence.

So does Lane.

They begin to dig. And pry. And crack bricks in half. Where they pull things apart, Balastair reaches in and removes the bricks. And yet, nothing. They're finding nothing at all but more brick, or corn shoots already crawling up through the dead city. (Hiram's Golden Prolific is damn near indestructible, and suddenly Balastair thinks, *It knows, it knows we're hoping to kill it, and so it's trying to beat us to whatever weapon my mother wants us to have*, but that's absurd, the corn doesn't think, it just *does*.)

And then suddenly—

Thunk.

Cael's bar hits something.

Something that sounds like metal.

He pulls it away, and Balastair leans into the hole, begins to cart out broken bricks—his blood spattering in the bone-white dust—and he reaches in, finds the margins of something. A box. A crate. Big enough that he asks them to get back in there with the iron posts, to clear it away and lift it out.

This feels like a holy moment. The two young men levering the box out of its crater. Bricks crumbling and tumbling away.

Lane squints over his pinched cigarette.

"This it?" Cael asks.

Balastair says: "I think so."

It's a metal crate with rounded edges.

Three feet square, roughly.

Balastair leans in, wipes dust off of it. He finds a latch that's been taped shut with yellow tape. That means—

No. *No, no, no.*

He feels around him, palms a small flat chip of brick and brings it up to cut through the tape—it slices with a whisper. He pops the top of the box.

Lane and Cael peer down into the box.

"It's empty," Cael says.

"Wait," Lane says. "Something's in there."

Balastair reaches in, finds a small slip of paper. Even before he reads it he can feel the embossed Pegasus at the bottom, the Empyrean seal.

"Property of the Empyrean," he says without even having to read it.

"I don't get it," Cael says.

"It means they have it. Whatever it is my mother wanted you to find, they possess it. They have the weapon, Cael."

Cael growls, cries out, pitches the iron bar like a spear.

And that ends their hunt.

REPATRIATION

"YOU DON'T HAVE TO DO THIS," Pop says.

"I'm afraid I do," Agrasanto answers.

The skiff hums as it rises toward the flotilla. At first there's just empty sky, and then the blue is blotted, the sideways sun casting into shadow as the Grantham Jorum Tempestas fills the window. First the glowing hover-panels, the grimy underlayer, then the skiff eases forward and ascends through the drifting islands and tilting structures of the flotilla—each chained together or held fast with telescoping bridges, strung up with wires and cables. Something about it feels like being reborn, resurrected, drawn up through tangled root and rich grave-earth before emerging out into the light—to glass and chrome, to silver and steel, to statues of Saintangels and Pegasus wings. Flat ribbons of morning sunlight shining bright, trapped in mist and slowly burning it away, pooling in windows like paintings inked in glowing magma.

The chains bind Pop's wrists and loop through an eyebolt under the skiff's dash. Agrasanto's hands are bloodless on the wheel, and stick.

"Will your husband be here?" he asks her.

"I hope so. Rutan's the one who set this up for me. He is a man of leisure but still has political connections through his family."

Pop nods. "So you will be able to buy your way back in."

"It seems. Rutan knows the Granthams. So that is who will receive you: the Grand Architect of this flotilla and the praetor, Mydra Alamene."

"You've already negotiated the deal, then."

She nods stiffly. "I take you in, all charges against me go away."

"I thought you were different," he says. "Thought maybe you'd changed, saw the error of your people. I know the Seventh Heaven isn't populated with monsters—many of you don't like what's being done to us, haven't liked it or understood it for a long time. I'm a little disappointed, to be honest."

"The guilt of a parent," she growls. "Don't bother. I already have it. My mother was good with all that. Guilt. Shame. Regret. But it is what it is. I've made my decision. Maybe I can change things from up here. Maybe I can work to alter the landscape from within."

"And if you can't?"

"Then I go on living my life. I have coffee in the morning while Rutan drinks his tea. I read the visidex over fresh fruit. My husband tends to the house, the garden, the dogs. And sometimes I look down at the Heartland, and I feel a pang of sadness, for the

Empyrean shadow cast upon you is long and dark." She shrugs. "Then I go about my day and think about happier things."

"Will it really be that easy?"

"It will," she says, though the way she says it, he's not so sure.

Ahead, an octagonal platform. Each point of the platform marked by a flashing orb in a brazier shaped like an inverted eagle's claw.

The proctor presses forward and eases the skiff rails to the platform.

The skiff hisses as it depressurizes.

"I'm sorry," she says.

"Are you?"

"I am. I'm sorry I convinced you I was someone I was not. I'm just as selfish as everyone else. It's not that I don't care. It's that I want what I want, and that outweighs any sense of blame."

He frowns. "At least you know yourself. Others would justify it. They'd dance circles around it until they forgot what they'd ever done wrong."

"The question is, have you justified all that you've done wrong?" On her face: a smile flashing like the beacons around them.

Pop doesn't answer.

She gets up, grabs the case with the Heavenkiller revolver, then begins to unlock his chains.

He thinks: *I can take her.*

But it's an illusion. He can't. And won't. He's not an old man, not yet, but the balance of his life has tipped the other way—he's getting slower, not faster. She's still quick, still tight and tough as a cinched belt. And even if he succeeds, then what? People will be here waiting for her. He hasn't been on a flotilla in—gods, how many years now? Twenty, at least. Where would he go except to the edge of the city and down to his death?

The last hope of him wrapping the chain around her neck and killing her leaves him—like seed-wisps stolen from a dandelion's crown. *Whoosh.*

Proctor Agrasanto binds his hands behind him.

And she leads him out of the skiff and onto the platform.

The winds kick up when they land, howling. The sensation hits him—one he remembers from a long time ago but whose memory is more academic than tactile—where the entire ground beneath his feet seems to be shifting, sliding side to side subtly, reminding him that his feet aren't planted on hard earth, but defying some natural order, standing way up in the clouds, in the sky, closer to the sun and the stars than any of his friends and family in the Heartland below.

It's a feeling both wonderful and terrible—buoyant, in a way, but it also makes him queasy to think about it. Anxiety prickles the back of his neck.

"Come on," she says, marching him in front of her.

Ahead, a set of steps down off the platform. And then a sky-bridge leading to an elevator with a set of accordion doors and an auto-mate next to it on a pillar.

The elevator dings.

The accordion doors slide open with a rattle.

A young girl steps out. At first Pop thinks her face is just in shadow—because it is—but as soon as she steps farther out onto the skybridge and a band of morning light reaches the side of her face, he sees that she's scarred. A labyrinth of puffy tissue. Each raised ridge painted gleaming gold.

She's alone.

Agrasanto hrrms, pulls him forward and down to meet the girl.

"Girl," Agrasanto says, "you don't belong here."

"Don't I?"

Something about the way the girl says it. She knows something. She's playing a game—acting cheeky and cruel at the same time.

Pop feels the proctor tense up next to him.

"I'm meeting people," the proctor clarifies. "Important people. And if you're here when they arrive, I imagine they won't be happy—"

"You're meeting Mydra Alamene?" she says. "And Jorum Grantham?"

Further tension—like a spring tightening. Agrasanto nods. "I am."

The girl sucks air between her teeth. "Except you're not. I'm afraid I'm here instead. My name is Enyastasia Ormond, Dirae of the Harpies."

"I don't know what that is."

"You've been gone awhile, Proctor Agrasanto."

Pop suddenly has the sense that things have shifted here in the skies—like one of those slide puzzles in reverse, the squares moved by a diligent thumb until the image is no longer discernible.

"How—?"

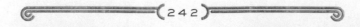

"I told you. I'm Dirae of the Harpies. I have military command."

"You have—what? The Praetorial Council—"

"Is less than the Grand Architect Council, and it's them I went to. They denied me, of course, which is why men like Jorum Grantham had to die."

Agrasanto seethes. "That's mutiny. You can't usurp power like that in some bloody coup! You're just a girl—"

The girl moves fast.

So does the proctor.

The skybridge is five feet wide, maybe—Pop has nowhere to go unless he wants to slip off the edge and down into the wind-scoured bowels of the flotilla's underlayer—and so instead he shields his face as two sonic blasts scream past each other like a pair of shrieking raptor-birds.

The proctor and the girl stand there a little while longer.

Each with her gun up and out.

Agrasanto's weapon wavers, sun sliding along the shiny barrel.

It's then Pop sees the blood. Spreading from her midsection, like a towel soaking up the oil from a busted motorvator.

Agrasanto looks at him, tries to say something—

But then her heel slips out from under her, and she falls off the edge of the bridge. Silently, as if she were never there to begin with.

Pop wheels on the young girl—the young *cruel* girl, a girl standing there, grinning ear to ear like that fox that just figured out the lock on the henhouse door. He bares his teeth, but she just laughs.

She turns down the dial on the pistol as he charges her.

The sonic scream hits him in the chest.

His thoughts warp. His guts churn. The sonic blast unsettles every molecule inside him—his marrow like worms burrowing, his veins like corn roots pulling apart all the dirt that composes him—

His own heel skids, slips, and then it's over the edge for him. But—

His descent, quickly halted.

A hand catches the chain binding his hands behind him.

As the winds die back for a moment, they're replaced with her disgruntled sigh. "No, no, no, Arthur McAvoy. You don't get to leave us just yet. You have a head full of information that I'd very much like to have."

He cries out, and she lifts him back up onto the bridge, dry-heaving.

PART THREE

THE SEVEN

FLIGHT

HIS HANDS SHAKE. Cupped inside them, the little gray bird dances about, shrugging its wings. Balastair peels back both thumbs so that the tiny thing can look up at him with its beady eyes, the feathers atop its silly head mussed as if it just woke up, its beak offering an incredulous, disbelieving look.

Up here, at the wall, he feels almost like he's in the sky again. The corn, far below, wind pressing shapes into it. In the distance, the blockade, now bolstered and reinforced by many men, many ships. And a line of mechanicals—here they're impossible to make out, except when one of their exposed metal parts gleams in the sun. But he's seen them through the scope: their rubbery flesh, the way they move in herky-jerky steps, their dead eyes and flexing mouths. It gets worse when you consider that actual men and women are encased in those things.

He shakes his head. Can't care about that right now.

This is not his fight.

What *is* his, however, sits cradled in his hands.

"How are you feeling, Cicero?"

The bird chirps a fluted song.

He found the young bird a week ago down near the Boxelder Circle—the little thing was unable to fly, hopping about and burbling and squeaking. Some Heartlander—a builder, someone who works on the very wall on which Balastair stands now— was about to stomp on it, but Balastair waved his arms (making very birdlike gestures all his own) and caught the man's attention before the boot came down. Since then, he's been feeding the little bird, getting it back to strength.

The bird quite likes him, and he quite likes the bird.

The bird's been able to flit about the room—from chairback to chairback, from one side of a railing to another. Now, it's time for a test.

He opens his hands. The bird hops out onto the edge of the wall.

Hop, hop, hop.

Singing a little song. *Warble-woo-chirpy-twee.* It makes a sound like a visidex ding. Then a cat meowing. Then a motor-vator hum before going back to its little singsongy trill.

"Go on," he says, giving the bird a little nudge. "It's time."

One more song. Sounds like a question mark.

He pokes the bird in the butt.

The bird tumbles off the edge, wings pinwheeling.

And then the bird is gone.

Gone.

He expects the bird to flutter back up—a dark blur, a gray puffball shape against the blue expanse.

He waits.

Waits.

Nothing.

Oh, by the gods.

No.

Horror fills him.

The fledgling didn't fly. Cicero wasn't ready.

No, no, no!

He imagines the little bird down there in the corn—body broken, if not dead. Food now for the corn. Balastair buries his face in his hands and weeps.

There we go.

The long case sits on his bed, dark wood like swirled chocolate, golden clasps like monkey hands. Lane slides his hands along it.

This is gonna make a helluva surprise.

A little bit of good news in a bad time never hurt anybody.

He hoists the case up, turns around—

And about jumps out of his skin.

Killian stands there. A withered, winnowed shape. A specter, really—a skin-kite with deep-set eyes and dry gums. Half-lidded eyes stare out.

"Didn't think you'd come back this time," Lane says stiffly.

"I always come back to you, love."

"Love." Lane scowls like he's eaten a spoonful of dirt. "That's a good one, Kill. Precious." He takes a sniff of the air. "You smell lovely."

"You want to make out?" Killian says, leering. He lurches forward a few steps, a lusty look crossing his face.

"You smell like cat piss and rank sweat. Be still my fluttering heart, O Killian Kelly," Lane sneers. "I'd rather stick my tongue in an anthill."

Killian faux pouts. "We used to be something, you know."

"Used to be, yes."

Now, a real pout. "I could use your compassion. A little empathy wouldn't fucking kill you, would it, Moreau?"

"I tried compassion. Same thing as feeding you more rope for hanging. Didn't work, and so I'm done with that. Now it's tough love."

"Tough love?" A small smirk. "So you *do* still love me."

"Get bent, cornstalk."

Killian laughs. It isn't his bright, bold laugh—it's a greasy, muddy sound, the laugh of the drunk and defeated.

Lane asks, "So, what was on the menu this time? More Pheen, I'm guessing." Fact that the corners of Killian's lips tug up into a playful smile tells Lane he hit the mark. It's been three months of this. Gotten worse of late, too. The onetime captain has been disappearing for days on end now, coming back worse and worse every time. He's diminishing. And Lane feels powerless to stop it—and is increasingly unsure whether he even wants to keep trying. "Where do you find the stuff anyway?"

Killian just grunts and grins like the cat who ate the canary.

"Have you seen Luna?" Lane asks.

"That little shank-blade? She's hiding in some bolthole somewhere. Or maybe the rumors are true—maybe she really did leave."

"We didn't find any missing ships."

Killian shrugs. "Whatever. I don't really care. Never liked her much—always found her a bit *childish*. I was surprised you picked her as your right-hand girl. Still don't understand that one."

"I already explained this to you."

"Yes, yes, wah wah wah, similar childhood, parentless orphans, a shared hatred for authority." He fakes a yawn. "You know why *I* think you did it? I think you did it because you didn't want to work with me. Or you're still ashamed of who we are to each other. Didn't you yell at me about that, once? Hmm. Easier to hide me away than make me a proper adviser."

"You don't know what you're talking about." And yet, his words ring in Lane's head like a votary tolling his bell—a loud gonging echo that won't quit. Is he right?

"What's in the case?" Killian asks, leaning up and over.

"Nothing." Pause. "Something for Cael."

"Your new boyfriend?"

"He's got his own relationship problems without me piling on."

Killian grins, tongue in the pocket of his cheek. "And yet, you *would* pile on, wouldn't you? You love him."

"I love him because he's my friend."

"Sure it's not more than that?"

"Sure you're not just jealous?"

"I admit it. I admit all manner of things—I admit I'm jealous, I admit I'm an addict, I admit I am half or *less* of the man I once was. What is it you'll admit, Mister Mayor? Hmm?"

Lane asserts once more: "Move."

"Gladly."

As Lane passes by, he looks at the man Killian has become—he's almost a transparency, as substantial as fog.

"I don't want you in here anymore," Lane says. "We're done."

With that, he leaves, case held up between him and Killian—a wall constructed, temporary but effective.

"Still nothing?" Cael asks the visidex screen.

His sister, Merelda, shakes her head. "No sign of him, Cael. I'm sorry."

After leaving Pegasus City more than three months ago—just before Cael and the others arrived—Pop hasn't been heard from. Not back at Curtains. Not anywhere. Best the hobos could figure, they tracked Arthur to the house of a pair of old raider cohorts—Pressman Horner and his wife, Kallen—and after that, vanished. No skiff in the corn. No body. And Empyrean spies have been hard to come by, but there are rumors of some dramatic changes up there in the Seventh Heaven. Some political shift that Cael doesn't understand.

"Shit," he says.

"They're gonna scrub the line soon." Takes a good bit to hack a new signal pathway to other visidexes—took them a while to even figure out how to do it, though Balastair was a big help in showing them how the dang things worked in the first place. Whenever they carve out a new connection, the Empyrean comes along and "scrubs" the line—wipes it of data so all that comes across is a garbled transmission. Warped visuals, distorted audio. Like trying to watch something on a broken Marconi.

"Yeah, I know." He hesitates. "How's Mama?"

"Same as she ever was. Not much changes for her, I guess."

"Give her a kiss for me." He massages his temples. Tries not to think about his poor mother. "And you? You good there?"

"We get more folks every day. Things are changing."

"Yeah, no, I mean, how are *you*?"

He sees a twitch at the corner of her lips. "I'm good." He knows this isn't her life. Not the one she pictured anyway. Once she imagined a life of opulence—and she almost had it on the Saranyu, according to Gwennie. But now here she is, hanging out literally underground with a small army of Blighters and hobos? Hell, she's pretty much *in charge* until Pop gets back.

If Pop gets back. *If.*

He tries not to show the anxiety on his face just as he wagers she's trying not to show hers. He says, "I'll see you soon, sis." *I hope.*

"We're still trying to figure out a way to break the blockade—you're too far to reach underground but ffzzzzjrrr—"

The image warps and distorts, as if pulled in a hundred different directions. Merelda's face pixilates, and the words go wonky.

Cael curses and ends the connection.

A hand slides over his biceps, up to his shoulder, and down to his chest. His breath catches, startled. The vine around his arm tenses, then relaxes.

He knows her scent. The soap.

"I didn't hear you come in," he says.

Gwennie bends down and they share a quick kiss.

Then he looks behind her, sees no one. She laughs. "Don't worry, no one saw me."

"You sure?" he asks.

"I'm sure," she says.

They kiss again. Warm, soft, slow. She moans against him. He pulls her down toward him as her tongue slides into his mouth.

The dream comes again, as intense as it always is. Wanda wandering a blasted, cracked land. Fissures forming in dead earth. Black vines snaking from the gaps—vines of white thorn and red sap, twisting, curling, twining. Men and women speared on those thorns. Thorns jutting out through their hands, their feet, their eyes, their mouths. Lifted as the tendrils rise.

As Wanda walks this dead space, her feet crunch—on stones, on corn, on little bones.

Whispers chase her.

You're failing.

You've done nothing.

Everyone hates you.

Who are you?

You're different.

You're not like them.

The Heartland is sick.

Time is escaping.

The whispers grow louder and more insistent, repeating the same things over and over again—accusations of mutation and monstrousness, of total inhumanity—until soon she's running and the voice is screaming. Vines thrash at her face, thorns tearing at her cheeks, her eyes, her lips. That's when she starts to change.

Her fingers fall off—it's bloodless, this act, they're just like handles that come off a drawer, and in their place are unfurling leaves. Her teeth fall out and seeds remain. Her throat is full of milky sap. The skin on her feet suddenly splits like the seam of a small shirt pulled over the trunk of a fat man—and what's left is a squirming pile of roots that suddenly fix her to the ground. The roots burrow like chewing worms, and she can run no farther—instead, she falls forward, hands hitting the ground. The finger-leaves bury in the dirt, too, and a thick vine pushes up past her throat and out of her mouth and plunges into the cracked ground, and she gags as the vine pulses and fluid courses within it—

All that is Wanda is slowly lost.

The ground cracks, opens, a yawning chasm strung together by roots pulled taut like stretched stitches in a ripping wound—and the dirt crumbles beneath her heels and then she's falling, falling, forever falling until—

She hears Mother Esther laughing in the darkness of her mind.

We are one, child.

The baby twists inside of her.

The child as long as a night crawler, squirming inside her belly.

She sits up, bathed in sweat, clutches at the space beneath her stomach as a wave of pain radiates out from that spot. Wanda winces, bites down on her cheek, rolls onto her side, and curls into a ball. . . .

The pain fades, cast to the wind.

For a while, all she hears is her breath.

Chest rising. Inhale, exhale. Inhale, exhale.

Around her, the Engine Layer is quiet, dead, doomed. A blackened, charred place—when the Saranyu fell, it must've broken apart and caught fire. She wasn't there, but she can imagine the way the flames pushed through these tight channels—through the wire mesh, through the ductwork, through all the pipes and around all the hard corners.

She found corpses. They hadn't cleaned them out yet. Burned up like briquettes. Hard and flaky like a shuck rat left too long on a campfire.

For three months, Wanda has slept here. She gave up the room they had her in—she wanted to get away from everyone. The dreams started, dreams like the one from which she just awakened. But everyone looked at her strange. The folks of Boxelder always treated her a bit like a special case—gawky, awkward girl, too eager by a Heartland mile, a flower that was both too delicate and not pretty enough.

It's different now. They still treat her like a special case. Except now it's the opposite. She's not the delicate one. *They* are. They are afraid of what she'll do to them. What the *Blight* will do to them.

They don't seem to have this problem with Cael.

It's because he's a boy, she tells herself. Men with power are routine. Women with power are not. People are frightened by change. Which means they are frightened by women with power.

But it's something else, too. Cael hasn't changed. He's still the same—a patch of Blight on his chest, a vine leading from it to his arm. His Blight is singular, unchanging, itself a kind of status quo.

Wanda, however, has changed.

Is changing, even still.

She feels it in her belly. A twitch. Like a root poking through stubborn dirt.

And there's something else, too. The power swells within her and, like in the dream, she can hear—no, she can *feel*—Mother Esther laughing. Not a mocking laugh. But one of pleasure, of kinship, of celebration.

She picks up a shard of mirrored glass she found poking through the ruins of Empyrean homes. Then she looks at herself—this, an act she performs every day, sometimes every few hours.

"I barely recognize you," she says to herself. Leaf-gloss tongue flicking. Face now comprising many hard angles: cheekbones, brow line, lips, nose, chin. The veins in her eyes are no longer veins but, rather, tiny pea-shoots. Her eyes have gone from brown to green. Underneath her strawberry-colored hair is a fine layer of dark purple tendrils forming a kind of mesh— she almost wonders if her hair will soon grow *real* strawberries, and as the thought reaches her, a real strawberry plumps up just above her ear, hanging there, tugging on the skin like a heavy weight—then it drops off, rolls down her shoulder and into her hand. A hand she didn't command to catch it.

Reflex.

She thinks to eat the berry, but then her stomach roils. It came from her, didn't it? Wouldn't that be like eating your own hair or fingernails?

The strawberry thuds and splats against the wall as she throws it.

Even without meaning to, another berry grows in the space between her neck and her jaw, and she feels them hanging heavy there—she can grow fruits and vegetables like this. Sometimes she controls it. Sometimes she can't.

Something she's seen only one other person do—

Mother Esther.

Strange, that.

Wanda bows her head, says a small prayer of thanks to Mother, asks for her help in this dark time. She wipes away tears.

Again the baby inside her moves.

It's Cael's. She knows this because he is the only person with whom she's ever been intimate, though a little voice inside her nags her with a series of troubling questions: *What if you created the baby out of nothing? What if the Maize Witch did it? What if there's no baby at all and truly you're just going mad, you dumb, daft girl?*

No. *No.* Those simply aren't options.

The child is Cael's.

He doesn't know. Yet. But she's going to tell him today. She's going to tell him that the baby is healthy and will be happy with them and that the baby *is* human, but yes, the baby is Blighted. She knows this because she can feel this. The first true Blightborn? Wanda doesn't know. But she likes to believe it.

She will tell Cael this, and she will also tell him that she knows he's back with Gwennie. Despite everything. She will tell him that it's okay, that she forgives him because in his heart, Gwendolyn Shawcatch came first.

But she will not be his last.

That is reserved for Wanda.

Because Wanda is his Obligated.

And Wanda is the mother of his child.

A gasp, and then the ragged sheets are kicked off, and Gwennie looks over, sees Cael launching himself up, pawing at the air. She grabs his hands, his wrists, holds him still. She presses her forehead against his cheek, shushing him. Then she kisses him there. Kisses his jawline. Wipes hair slick with sweat from his brow—he leans into it, eyes closed, and his breathing calms.

"Dream again?" she asks.

"Mm," he says, "yeah."

"Same as usual?"

"I think. Trying to remember it is like trying to catch a moth. But I feel it. Something talking to me. Dunno if it's the Blight or Hiram's Golden or if it's *her*—" The Maize Witch. A name that still scares Gwennie, if only because the old stories had some truth to them. "But, shoot, it feels like it's mad at me. Mad because I'm not . . . *doing* something. And I dunno what." He turns toward her. He looks scared. "I think maybe this is what drove Earl Poltroon mad."

"Is Wanda having the dreams, too?"

He looks sheepish and afraid.

She sighs. "You haven't talked to her at all, have you." A statement, not a question.

"Not in a bit, no. Been a few weeks, I think. She . . . she's off on her own."

"She knows, doesn't she? About you and me."

"I have no idea."

"Lord and Lady, Cael."

"I should find her. I've been a jackass."

"What else is new?" she says with a small smile. He doesn't return it. "Hey, I've been an ass, too, McAvoy. She and I talked a while back, and I was all like, *We don't need to care about boys and who needs Cael anyway*, and now that . . . this is happening again, all that rings hollow. Like I was just setting her up to forget you so I could swoop in."

"You *did* swoop in," he says—and there's that smile.

He's not wrong. A month ago they were out on the wall, looking out across the corn at night, the moon shining in slivers of shining leaves, and they had found a bottle of something called Old Bumbo Rum, and Cael uncorked it with his teeth, and the two of them took turns drinking and talking about the past, and that lit a fire inside her, a fire so warm and so pretty all she wanted to do was spread it as far as she could, and so she walked up to him, took the bottle out of his hand, and kissed him hard as she was able.

And then before too long, clothes peeled away, and the two of them leaned against the edge of the wall, the infinite Heartland and endless sky around them, and they did what they hadn't done in what felt like an eternity. It felt right. And familiar. And new, too, in its own way. When his Blight-vine coiled around her arm and pulled her close, she felt scared, but being scared felt good, too, and now it doesn't bother her at all. It's just part of who he is.

"She's probably hurting, poor girl."

"Yeah," he says. "Dangit. It's just—you know, all that talk of being Obligated. Like that matters anymore? I just . . ." He grunts in frustration—a sound with which she's definitely familiar. Cael is not always the best at expressing himself. "Aw, man. It was a lot of pressure. She changed for me. And then those times we . . . you know, we *did* it, it was like something else entirely. I could feel her light up like all the stars in the sky. It was like it wasn't even just her and me, it was like the Blight was there with us, binding us together."

Gwennie listens to him, tries not to acknowledge the knife-twist of jealousy that sticks in her when he talks. He and Wanda shared something she and he never could. Does she light up like all the stars in the sky for him? Or is being with her like reading a book in the dark?

"You gotta talk to her," she says.

"I will. After the Council of Seven."

"You promise?"

"I promise."

"Funny," she says, fingers playing across his chest.

"What's that?"

"Last time we were together was before Harvest Home, back in Boxelder."

"It was at that."

She ponders. "Us doing a proper Harvest Home here in Pegasus City is a good idea. It feels a little like the way things used to be. You think we can ever get back there?"

She knows the answer. He doesn't even need to say anything. All Cael does say is: "Better get dressed, unless we feel like showing off our . . ." He *ahems*. "Assets."

She laughs. It's nice, the laugh. For now, in this moment, she's happy.

But happiness is a curious thing, she thinks.

Hard to catch, harder to keep, she thinks. What did Cael say about remembering his dreams?

Like trying to catch a moth.

Tonight Wanda is going to the Council of Seven. Less official name: the Boxelder Seven—a misnomer, maybe, since one of the group is an Empyrean man, but the rest all come from the same place. Cael, Wanda, Lane, Rigo, Gwennie, and Boyland. Boyland sometimes doesn't bother showing up. And neither does Wanda. Which makes it more of an unofficial Council of Five, but nobody wanted to call it that—something about the group that founded the Sleeping Dogs being the Sawtooth Seven. Lane said, "I like the parity," and so it was decided.

She doesn't feel much a part of the group, though she wonders if that's more her doing than anybody else's. Is her exclusion real? Imagined?

In their heads, or in hers?

Probably doesn't matter. Nothing to be done now. She tried to tell Cael that: Once they didn't find what they were looking for, they had to go. But the hooks were in him again. His friends. His old life. He forgets how different he is. How different *they* are. Wanda's wondering if she should leave, too. And yet, she remains. For him.

Cael. Sigh.

She's about to exit the Engine Layer—through a hole where

a massive chain fell, cutting this hallway ring clean in half—when she hears a voice just outside.

A girl's voice.

She doesn't recognize it at first—it's been some months since she heard it. But then it clicks: Luna Dorado. Once Lane's adviser—since then, she's been missing. Rumors said she left, fled Pegasus City for . . . who knows where?

Wanda presses flat against the wall. She listens, but catches only the end of the conversation:

"You have everything you need. The deal is the deal. Don't screw me on this. You have *no idea* the risk I'm taking."

And then a chime—the sound of a visidex call ending.

Wanda thinks: *I could just kill her.*

That has been a thought creeping into her mind with some regularity these days—and that chills her to the bone. Any problem she sees or imagines, she thinks: *I could choke it, break it, tear it apart, let it feed the earth.*

Or, sometimes, more simply:

Blood makes the grass grow.

By the time she peers out the rift, stepping over a rusted chain that's twice the thickness of her thigh, she sees no one. Luna is gone. Maybe, Wanda thinks, she's going mad, and Luna was never there in the first place.

Madness is almost more comforting, isn't it?

Balastair feels gutted. He's a doll whose stitching has popped, whose stuffing has been pulled out by a cruel child—a cruel child named *life*, and suddenly that common refrain of this place,

That's life in the Heartland, echoes in his mind, and for a moment he feels infected by it. Like this place has gotten into him, into his blood and bones and every one of his cells. This emptiness, this hopelessness, is altogether worse than the Blight, he realizes.

Because at least with the Blight, you can use it.

This . . . this *feeling*, it has no value. Just a slick-walled hole, grim and lightless. No way out. Just a place to stand and wait for the dirt to be piled atop your head. Even though he's walking through this so-called Pegasus City, he feels like he's standing still in his own grave.

This used to be his home, this place.

And it is, once more. But not in a way he recognizes.

Dirt beneath his feet.

Shattered remains of buildings.

The memory of his mother following him. The ghosts of all who died when this place fell. Cleo, too. Manifesting as a whisper.

Who is he? What's his point? He's helping these people with their infrastructure. Helping them with the visidexes and with the greenhouses so they understand how to actually *grow* food instead of just consume it. (At first he blamed them for being so stupid, which he realized was rather judgmental given how the Empyrean have helped to ensure that this knowledge was kept as far from the Heartlanders as the moon, sun, and stars.) Even still, he feels like a hanger-on. An Empyrean freak. Was this what Gwennie felt like on the flotilla?

People wave as he passes—friendly enough. They smile, too. Though it's not the same treatment that other Heartlanders get. They get hugs and handshakes and good-natured insults and angry arguments that end in a night of drinking and laughing and, sometimes, crying. He gets the polite nods, the *toodle-oo* of the fingers, the short, crisp language.

He waves back. Smiles back. Keeps walking, hoping they don't see how upset he is. Upset over . . .

Over a little bird.

Over little Cicero. Tiny catbird fledgling.

He curses himself. It was too soon. The bird should've biologically been able to fly—but it had no mother, it had only him, a man who thought he could do for this bird what he did for a little grackle named Erasmus. Of *course* the bird wasn't ready to fly. He pushed it off the ledge and—

No! No. Thinking about it is about to push *him* off a ledge.

There. Dead ahead. A prison tower that Mayor Lane Moreau has taken as his office. It's where they meet for their so-called council, an advisory group to which he knows he doesn't belong. They, the Heartlanders from a small town. He, an Empyrean man a world apart.

He sighs.

Begins to walk toward the door.

Then—a surprising thing.

A little sound in the air. A *warble-woo*.

He turns, shields his eyes from the sun with the flat of his hand. And then something *lands* on that hand. Little feet. A flutter of something soft.

Balastair brings the hand down.

The bird, Cicero, shrugs its wings and shakes them. Then it chirps a strange, discordant song.

The bird never died.

Cicero is alive!

Balastair laughs and nuzzles the little bird. It jumps up onto his head and he strides toward the elevator, feeling suddenly alive, buoyant, and bewildered.

THE BOXELDER SEVEN

THE MEETING STARTS. Five of them sit around the table underneath the ornate human-sized birdcage. Lane stands at the head of the table, leaning forward, hands flat. Rigo sits to his right with a visidex—the boy has changed since taking on the right-hand-man role to Lane. He's leaner, sharper, seems more confident. His new leg doesn't hurt, either; Balastair found a proper replacement in the crumbling wing of the old hospital. This leg is strong, metal, with bold scrollwork and real leather straps. It's as much a thing of beauty as it is a thing of function, and it appears to have given Rigo renewed purpose.

Balastair also seems to have brightened up. He's looked so sad, so lost, for so long that Cael half expected to find the man hanging from a rope somewhere one day. But now? Cael watches him across the table—a little bird hops from the back of one hand to the back of another, then to a finger, then to his wrist, occasionally interrupting the proceedings with a little song. When it does, Balastair chuckles and shushes the creature.

The real surprise is that Boyland showed up. Drunk as a skunk in a funk, his lower lip hanging open like the mouth of a broken mailbox. Occasionally he seems to focus, then he snorts loud through his nose, smacks his lips, and goes back to staring off at nothing.

Though sometimes he straight up stares at Gwennie.

A sad, hard glare.

Cael doesn't much like that look.

Underneath the table, Gwennie bumps her knee into his. At first he thinks it's a mistake, but it's not—she presses up on him harder, moving her leg against his, knee sliding up and down, then in circles. Just that small touch sends heat to his brow and sweat to his palms.

"Tonight is Harvest Home," Lane says. "Rigo had the right idea, I think—I know it's not the right time of the year, but people are already perking up about it. We've got boxes of whiskey, gin, 'shine. Got a chicha beer stand set up and a few games going, plus a band calling themselves—"

"Itself," Rigo corrects. "Not themselves."

Lane rolls his eyes. "Calling *itself* the Pegasus City Irregulars—they're actually a bit all right. Got a banjo, washboard, keytar, accordion. Shit, what else? Rigo, what am I missing?"

Rigo goes on: "I think it's pretty well covered. Dancing. Drinking. A lottery—a real lottery, like, folks don't win a trip to the sky where they get treated like freaks and animals."

Gwennie laughs, but Cael feels her tense up at the mention of it.

"Don't forget drinking," Boyland mutters.

Everyone shares a look.

But Cael notices that Balastair and Gwennie are sharing their own look. A long gaze, too. He thinks, okay, maybe they're each reliving a memory from when they were both on the flotilla. Gwennie doesn't like to talk much about what happened up there, but Bal probably already knows. They shared something there.

Suddenly Cael is wondering: *Just how much did they share?*

Jealousy sinks its teeth in—a rat-bite looking for blood.

But he doesn't have long to think about his own jealousy, because the elevator dings, and the door opens.

Wanda steps into the room.

Underneath the table, Gwennie's leg suddenly pulls away from his own.

Everyone turns. The looks of shock are obvious—eyes wide, jaws slack. She hasn't come to a meeting since the beginning. Some haven't even *seen* her since then. Wanda's changed. She seems . . . taller. Thinner in her limbs, her neck, even her fingers. Cael can't put his finger on it, but she even *moves* differently, like she's a praying mantis considering its next meal. The Blight has taken her. The undersides of her forearms are ridged and textured like tree bark. Red flowers thrust up from behind her ears—not stuck there, but *grown* there, out of her hair or from the back of her neck. The whites of her eyes are shot through with green, her fingers tipped with thorns.

She stands there for a moment, regarding all the eyes upon her.

"Sorry," she says.

Wanda closes her eyes.

And her flesh changes.

Thorns shrink into fingers. Her eyes clear. The flowers bloom in reverse, shrinking, imploding, disappearing. The bark on her arms shudders, ripples, then becomes a stretch of pale pink flesh—raw, as if it had been abraded.

Jeezum Crow, Cael thinks. *She can reverse it at will?*

She looks more like Wanda used to.

But every inch of movement remains calculated and considered with an eerily confident certainty. She comes around the side of the table and stands behind Cael. She puts her hand on the empty chair next to him.

"Can I sit here?" she asks.

Cael looks up. He smiles sheepishly, moves to pull out the chair.

She sits, turns her head toward him, and smiles. "Hi, Cael." She leans forward and gives him a kiss on the cheek. Just that small connection sends up a fireworks display of lights behind his eyes—and again he is reminded of her presence, thrumming with life that is both hers and the Blight's. It's stronger now. No longer is she just a field of fireflies or a spread of stars across the sky—now she's bright as a hundred moons.

He swallows hard. "Hi, Wanda."

Wanda looks past him.

"Hey, Gwennie." She utters a gawky, awkward laugh—the one Cael knows from back in Boxelder, the one that sounds like

Wanda. But Cael fears it's an act—like she's *trying* to convince them that's who she is. "Aw, jeez. Sorry, everybody, didn't mean to interrupt."

"Godsdamn, Wanda," Boyland says, breathy with awe. "You know how to"—he *urps* into his hand—"command a room."

"Nice to see you, too, Boyland."

Silence breeds. Everyone shares uncomfortable looks.

Lane says, "Uhhhh. Whh-where were we, Rigo?"

"Well." Rigo clears his throat. "We were talking about Harvest Home tonight and all the—"

"I saw Luna Dorado," Wanda says, interrupting.

Lane, suddenly flummoxed, asks, "What did you say?"

"I saw her. Not an hour ago. North end of the city, by the Engine Layer. Well, to be more accurate, I *heard* her, I guess. Talking to someone on a visidex. Not sure what it was about—I came in a little late to the conversation." Then she gives another of her gawky laughs, like she's really playing it up. "Sorry?"

Rigo hands Lane a visidex, and Lane puts out a call to his security team to go search the Engine Layer for Luna.

"We had to assume she remained in the city," Balastair says. The bird bounces up his arm to an elbow he's extended. "It was never much of a possibility that she could get past the blockade." A blockade that everyone knows has only grown in the last few months.

Cael speaks, finds his voice a bit croaky—he's nervous sitting between Gwennie and Wanda, as if all of a sudden the two of them might start pulling him apart like they're dismantling a malfunctioning motorvator. "That blockade is like a noose around our necks. They've pushed in again. Upped their numbers *again*. Gonna be a point they make a move, and when they do, I'm not sure the cannons will be able to stop them all."

"Cael's right," Gwennie says. "The blockade is killing us. We can't get new people in. Can't send new people out. We can't access Fort Calhoun."

Rigo stands. "We're working on bolstering defenses. Training people with weapons. Setting up an emergency network through the visidexes. If they push in, if they attack, I've run the numbers—I think we can push them back."

Wanda seems to watch it all with rapt fascination. Again she gives off the vibe that she's a visitor from the outside, from above them. Or worse, a raptor studying a rat as it scurries to and fro.

"We need an edge," Gwennie says. "We need a plan."

"If only we had my mother's weapon," Balastair says.

Cael shrugs. "Whatever that even was."

"Doesn't matter," Lane says. "We don't know what it was, or more importantly, *where* the damn thing has gone—"

Boyland says something, something quiet. Everyone keeps talking past him, because they all probably assume he just mumbled something grumpy and drunk—some mush-mouthed insult, some half-witted half-ass commentary. But Cael thinks it was something else. He shushes the room and says:

"What'd you say, Boyland?"

"Oh, lookit that. Captain Cael wants to hear what I have to say."

"Crow on a cracker, Boyland, just spit it out."

"Yes, Cap'n, yessir. Shit. This is the first time y'all have paid attention to me in months. Forget I was here, didja? Don't mind me babysitting your kids long as I stay out of your hair, but soon as I speak up and have something you want, then suddenly you all remember I'm alive—"

Rigo's brow furrows so deep you could plant seeds in it. "Boyland, if you have something to say, just say it."

"The Luzerne Garam Ilmatar," Boyland says. "Happy?"

"What the hell's that?" Cael asks. "Another flotilla?"

"Yes," Balastair says. "First in the fleet."

"'S'where the . . . *weapon* is, the one you're looking for. The one the kooky Blight-bitch sent you digging for like a well-heeled doggy."

Cael feels his Blight-vine twitch at that. He wills it to calm. "The weapon is there, on that flotilla? How do you know?"

"Because I gotta lotta free time. Didn't take me long to find enough booze to keep me brined till the world falls apart, so I had to occupy myself in . . . *other* ways. Turns out, didja know there's a whole series of administrative offices? Files and folders full of paper. Paper! You believe that? Shit that's not on the visidexes but is handwritten on godsdamn paper." He guffaws, suddenly. "Empyrean savages!" He wipes his nose with the back of his hand. "Anyway. I got to reading and found a whole cache of notes about the Blight-bitch—*Esther Harrington* and her darling boy, *Balastair*. Whole folders on the witch. One of them was about the contents of her home after a search by someone called the 'peregrine.' They took everything they had out of that place and sent it to the Ilmatar flotilla. Including one 'package' marked as 'cylinders—purpose unknown.' A package that the notes said was dug up out of the terrace after it was found via something called a 'bio-scan.'"

He burps again.

Once again, the room is stunned to shocked looks and stammering silence.

"I never thought of that," Rigo says. "They kept paper records."

"Not so smart now," Boyland mutters. "Huh, Rodrigo? Shoot. I should be mayor of this place."

"Your father made a helluva mayor," Lane says, scowling. "A drunken baboon falling asleep at the Harvest Home podium—"

"Hey!" Boyland says, standing up so fast he knocks his chair out. "Godsdamnit! I figured this shit out with the . . . with the Ilmatar and none of you did, so maybe you wanna gimme a little rope, huh, Mayor McFaggot—"

What happens next surprises everyone. A visidex flies across the room, beans him in the head. Boyland yelps, bats it away, and by the time he's turning back around it's *Rigo* who's all over him like moths on lamp-glass. He hobbles fast, hits Boyland like a cannonball in the chest, knocking him back over his own fallen chair. Boyland yelps and tumbles. Rigo gives a twist to his hip and, faster than anybody figures, has his fake leg in his hand, raised above his head like a club—

A whipcord of vine lashes around the leg and holds it steady.

The vine, emergent from the middle of Wanda's palm.

"Let him go," she commands, a surprising amount of steel in her voice. "He's drunk. He helped us. End of story, way I figure it." Then with a cold smirk she adds: "Besides, you wouldn't wanna get blood on that pretty leg."

Rigo, looking suddenly embarrassed, pulls away.

The vine uncoils from the leg, disappears back into Wanda's outstretched hand as if it never existed in the first place.

Cael thinks: *Okay, she's scary.*

Boyland stands, dusting himself off. He rubs the side of his arm and then laughs. "Damn, Rodrigo. You got more stones in that pouch than I remember." Rigo scowls, then retreats. Boyland holds up his hands: "Sorry about that, folks. That was just the liquor talking. Lane, you do what you like, ain't no business of mine or anybody's. Rigo, thanks for straightening me out, Wanda, thanks for . . . whatever it is you just did. I'm gonna sit now and go back to not doing shit. Okay? Okay."

He sniffs, straightens his chair, then sits back in it. Arms behind his head, he leans back, closes his eyes.

Thirty seconds later, he's snoring.

"Uhhh," Cael says.

"All of that was rather unexpected," Balastair says.

The bird chirp-warbles and pecks at his hair.

Lane presses the heels of his hands into his temples. "All right. Let's get the wheels back on this cart. We know the flotilla. We just gotta get there."

"The Ilmatar isn't far," Balastair says. "It tends to hover in what is roughly the center of the Heartland. The problem is the blockade. They have ground and sky supremacy. Efforts to get past them . . ."

Cael says: "We use the trawler."

"Huh." Lane perks up. "*Huh.*"

Cael goes on: "That thing's built like a fist, man, so let's use it like one. Haul it back and—" He punches a fist into his open palm. The Blight-vine shudders with the hit. "*Boom.* Knock a hole right through it."

"The problem," Gwennie says, "is that soon as we do that,

we'll bring the whole blockade after us. They'll break the line and trail us like flies after a dung-wagon. We may get through them initially, but that can't last. They'll take pieces out of us until we keel over."

They all pause. Cael feels the hope sucked out of the room once more. Like sails without wind, hanging limp and lifeless.

That is, until Rigo claps his hands.

"That's exactly right," he says, suddenly excited. "The trawler *will* draw them all out. They'll break the line and leave a big-ass, no-fooling hole—and when the trawler kicks that door open—"

Cael snaps his fingers. "We sneak through after."

"That's genius," Lane whoops. "Big Sky Scavengers, at it again!"

Boyland's voice drunkenly booms: "You all better hope it's worth it. Could be a hot bucket of goat shit"—he coughs and burps—"dummies."

Once more, an awkward, uncomfortable silence. Cael—and he figures this is true for everyone—wrestles with that question. He's pissed at Boyland for even bringing it up, but the lunk-headed thug is right. They take this shot, that's it. If it's the wrong one, it's wrong in a big, big way.

"We have to try something," Wanda says.

They all nod.

It's Lane who speaks up: "We'll go over it again tomorrow. Chop this thing up into little bitty pieces, make sure we have it right. For now: may Old Scratch piss on all this, it's time to get ready for Harvest Home!"

26

GIFTED

CAEL'S ON THE WAY OUT of the room when Lane hooks him by the elbow.

"Hey, Captain," Lane says. "Hang back a sec."

Both Gwennie and Wanda turn and give him looks.

Then they walk out together.

Lane whistles. "That was something."

"Yeah, I think maybe I dicked up real good."

Lane winces. "I can't help you with that—my own romantic track record is hardly exemplary. But I might be able to brighten your day just the same."

"How's that?"

Lane reaches under the table, pulls out a long wooden case. Freshly oiled. Golden clasps like paws closing it. Cael sizes up the mystery box, and Lane eggs him on. "Go ahead. Open it. It's a gift. Sorta."

Well, shoot, Cael likes gifts.

He steps over to the table, pops the case—

Lickety-quick, his breath is gone, stolen away by the sight of his father's lever-action rifle sitting there. Last he saw the weapon, it had been broken in half on the floor of Killian Kelly's chambers just before Cael leaped out the window and into the corn. He assumed the gun was gone, destroyed. Here, though, it's been mended. Gilded brass plates holding the two pieces together. Each of those plates carved with images of a fox running fast, ears back, legs outstretched in either direction. *Swift Fox*, Cael thinks. Pop.

He runs his hands over the oiled wood, the polished barrel.

"You still have it," he says.

Lane nods. "Yeah. Took it back from Killian. I hoped one day I could get it in your hands again. When you came to Pegasus City and we sorted through our bullpuckey, it seemed high time to give it to you, but I didn't want to hand you a broken-ass rifle. There's an old raider here, gunsmith name of Mutu, and I paid him to do it."

"It's a beauty." Cael picks it up. It feels good against his shoulder. It feels proper. *Righteous*, even. Slowly, the Blight-vine slides along the back of his arm, then his hand, until it winds its way around the stock of the gun. Feels firm, snug, stable. He jacks the action, opens the chamber with his hand, the vine holding the weapon in place.

"Almost forgot," Lane says, and pulls out a small cardboard box of bullets. "You left those behind. Only a handful left."

Cael uncoils the vine and sets the rifle in its case.

"Thanks, Lane."

"My pleasure."

"I'm sorry about everything that's happened. Feels like Boxelder was a lifetime ago."

"A lifetime? Three lifetimes. Four! *A hundred.* I don't feel like the same person I was three months ago, much less three years. I'd wager a stack of ace notes that Busser or Doc or Bessie Greene wouldn't even recognize us."

"No fooling." *I bet they really wouldn't recognize Wanda.* That thought strikes him as cruel and petty, somehow. He needs to be there for her. He's the only one here who understands what she's going through, and he's been avoiding her like she's a distempered dog. "We gonna be okay?"

"Who? You and me? All of us?"

"I dunno. Any of us, I guess."

Lane laughs, though it's not precisely a happy sound. "Cap, I sure as shit don't know. I suspect it's gonna get a lot worse before it gets better. All of it just depends on if we can get through the bad parts in order to see the good ones. That's the rub, as they say."

"That's life in the Heartland."

"If we do our job right," Lane says, "in a hundred years they won't be saying that anymore. One day maybe folks won't be able to recognize the Heartland, either."

"I'd like that very much."

"Me, too, Cap. Me, too."

Cael steps out of the elevator—and into a scene he doesn't yet understand.

Wanda stands, arms crossed. Looking worried.

Gwennie sits nearby on a heaped mound of steel chain. She looks like she's on the verge of tears. Not uncontrolled sobbing, not the kind of weeping where you grab fistfuls of hair and yank them out of your head—this is a dam breaking, a wall whose cracks are plainly seen but can still hold back the water. She meets his eyes once—then looks away.

"I do not know what's happening right now," Cael says.

Everything feels loose and slippery—a rope sliding through his hands.

Gwennie stands and walks over to him, head bowed.

"Congratulations," she says to him, then gives him a smile that has all the strength and certainty of a wilted leaf—lips crinkled, pressed hard together again, like she's trying to hold something back.

Then she pivots, heel-to-toe, and hurries away.

Leaving him alone with Wanda.

In the distance, he sees everyone setting up for Harvest Home. Stakes, tents, ropes. A few Heartlanders roll a big wheel painted into colorful pie slices—a game of some kind, a game of chance. He watches Gwennie duck between those tents, and then she's gone.

"What did you say to her?" Cael asks, suddenly angry. He knows the anger isn't fair, but who said anything was fair?

"I'm pregnant," Wanda says.

A fist to his middle.

Hard to get air—

"Wh-what?"

"I'm pregnant, and it's yours."

It feels like he's on that wheel now, spinning around and

around, watching the world whip past. Faster and faster, all the bolts and screws coming loose, like he's about to break down and fly apart at any moment.

"How?"

A sharp bark of a laugh. "I think you know how."

Wanda hugs herself tight, rocks back and forth on her heels. Her brow is knitted, her lips pursed. She looks worried. Cael thinks, no, it's more than that. She looks *human*. Right now, she looks more like Wanda than she has in a long time—and any anger he had vanishes in the wind of that revelation.

"I gotta sit," he says.

He goes and sits on the giant mound of metal—taking Gwennie's seat. The metal is still warm. He sets the case with the rifle by his feet, almost as if it's a wall between him and the news.

"You don't have to be involved," she says. She stares at him. He can't tell if she's sad or mad or what. Probably both. "But you needed to know."

"I'm just a kid. A kid can't have a kid. I'm only seventeen." He pauses, thinks. "Damn, I'm probably eighteen, aren't I? I missed my birthday in that . . . Blight-pod or whatever it was. King Hell. *King Hell.* I missed your birthday, too, didn't I? Aw, man. Happy birthday. I'm sorry I missed it. Gods, I'm *not* too young. Pop wasn't much older than this when they had me. Folks get Obligated, they're expected to . . ." *Gulp.* "Be expecting. Is that the word? Expecting? King Hell!"

Wanda rubs her arms. "You're rambling."

"Hell yes, I'm rambling! This is—" He makes a noise that isn't a word but more of an animal sound. "This isn't how I thought today would go."

"I'll leave you to think about it," she says. And then she takes a few steps backward—a slow retreat. She wants him to stop her. And he wants to stop her.

"Wait," he says, standing up. "We're having a baby?"

A hesitant nod.

"Okay. Okay. *Okay*. Is it . . . uhh, healthy?"

"You tell me." She comes over to him, takes his hand, presses it against her middle—a middle that hasn't yet grown, really, a middle whose expanse is still a flat stretch of skinny girl. Wanda moves his hand underneath the hem of her shirt and against her skin—flesh that is oddly cool—and then . . .

He's aware of her once more, all the bonfires of life that compose her, all the pulses of energy—bursts of verdant vitality like bright blooms on dark vines. But then he senses something else in there.

A small flame nested. Like a lit match burning in a ring of fire.

It doesn't belong to her. Not really.

It belongs to itself.

Another life.

He gasps, almost pulls his hand away, but she grabs his wrist and holds it firm. He feels further for the little creature without even meaning to. Cael can detect the baby's margins. Gods, it's not *even* a baby yet. It's not much bigger than his thumb. But it has a heart beating. Dark little eyes searching. Little fingers searching. Fingers that have fingerprints.

Fingers that bloom into little flowers. Petals fluttering in the fluid.

Cael says quietly: "Is it human?"

"Partly," she says. "And it's not an *it*."

It's a she, he realizes.

"A little girl." He says this with some awe and a great deal of fear. Boys, he gets. Girls—oh, gods, they're a mystery to him. Cael suddenly thinks: *I'm going to be a father. And a terrible one, at that.*

"A *pure* little girl. That's what she is. Pure. You and I, we had to be changed into what we are. But she didn't. She's perfect. Half you, half me. But also: She has the Gift from the beginning. It's part of her." Wanda smiles. "The power she'll have. The glories she'll be able to give the Heartland . . ."

Cael leans forward, presses his forehead against Wanda's. "They'll judge her. The Heartland. The world. They won't understand."

"Then she needs us. Together."

He swallows. "Together. Okay."

She kisses him on the cheek.

He smells strawberries. And honeysuckle. And rotten blossoms long fallen off their tree.

The metal plate grinds as he shifts it aside.

A yawning black tunnel awaits.

"This goes out to the corn," Lane says. "Few know about it."

His mother blinks, rubbing her wrists. "Honey, I don't understand."

"You need to go. Go back to your Empyrean friends."

"I . . . they're not my friends. . . ."

"They're more your friends—gods, more your *family*—than

I am. You're not welcome here. But I also hate to see you on work detail like you're some kind of prisoner." *Which you are*, he thinks. "So. Go. Be with them. Join their ranks. Their time's almost up. Maybe you can pass a message along for me? Just tell them *ticktock, ticktock*. Mm?"

"You don't have to do this," she says. She sniffs, wipes her nose with the back of her hand—he's not sure if she's really about to cry or if it's all just part of her act. "We could work this out, you and I, we could . . ."

"Do you wanna go back to the Empyrean or not?"

She hesitates.

And doesn't say anything.

And that silence says *everything*.

Lane steps aside. He crosses his arms. "I'm going to bolt this thing shut once you're through. After you're gone? You won't be a part of my life ever again. Not that you were to begin with, so you won't miss it."

"I'm sorry," she says, her voice small as a fly, and just as welcome.

"Go."

And just like a fly she flits away, gone through the hole.

He feels something tumbling around inside of him, and he knows suddenly what it is: It's his voice. A plea to her. He wants to yell, wants to call to her as she hurries through the tunnel: *No, don't go, you're right, we can figure this out. I love you.* But he swallows that. Digs a hole, buries it deep.

He blinks away tears that he tells himself are from dust or pollen or rust flakes in the air. Then he closes the metal plate.

CURRENTS AND CURRENCIES

ARTHUR'S MOUTH IS A DRY, cankerous crater. His tongue, sandpaper. Eyes, too—they feel dry as grapes gone to raisin. He hangs in the cylindrical chamber, a room sound-proofed against his screams with spongy, textured foam. Arms spread out. Legs tucked back. Scalp burning from where the probes have been left for so long. They should be infected by now, but once a day someone comes and applies a spray of Annie cream to fight any disease taking hold.

He doesn't know how long it's been.

Weeks. Months.

Years.

He gasps. Wheezes. He has no sense of anything. Is he still on a flotilla? Hard to say. He's been hooked up to this machine, in this blank room, for so long sometimes he wonders—maybe he's back in the Heartland. Maybe he's up in the air. Or on a yacht. Or somewhere far-flung from the borders of the Heartland—maybe

on an island somewhere in the wind-churned Sea of Angels. He's never been there, never seen the Shattered Coast. So much of the world kept away from him. And from his family. He never even told Cael and Merelda about the world because he was afraid.

Afraid they'd want to see it.

He tried to protect them, and now he worries that he did the opposite.

He always relished information and knowledge. It was his desire to know everything and to share what he knew—he told his own father that way back when, and that formed the fundamental rift between the two. Arthur's father wanted the boy to keep his head down, fly straight. Arthur thought the Empyrean were trying to control them too much. He didn't like that they were restricting information, withholding knowledge. Arthur railed against that, struggled against its bonds. That was part of what the Sawtooth Seven was about. Coming together as part of a shared goal—a shared goal that itself grew out of an incident, an incident where an Empyrean proctor died by their hands: an accident of sorts. They meant to hurt him but not to kill him. . . . And suddenly, just conjuring that memory brings it fully to bear against him, and once more Arthur feels himself standing there in a ring of corn, the ground blasted beneath him, Proctor Posilack clutching at his ruined throat—and he thinks, *Oh, by the gods, it's happening again, everything turns and tightens and I'm back here*, and there's Eben Henry, Black Horse, a feral grin on his face—and there's his lover, Bellflower, and Iron-Red Neddy gone pale, and Corpse Lily staring down at the writhing, bleeding man, stone-faced . . .

Light shines in.

The door to the chamber opens.

Merelda walks in.

Chin lifted. Shoulders back. He feels the proud father—but he feels scared, too, because that means she's no longer with him anymore. She's here, part of the Empyrean, here to punish him, here to *hurt* him. Unless she's here for other reasons . . .

"Are you here to save me?" he says, his voice a whisper full of fiberglass and small sharp stones. "Is Cael all right?"

The girl sniffs. "I am here to release you from the machine."

That voice. Not Merelda at all.

The cruel girl. Face with the golden scars.

"You," he croaks.

"Yes. Me." She begins to feel along the top of his scalp. She begins to unmoor the probes one by one. Each feels like she's ripping a clump of hair out of his skull. "Your time here has been well served. What you know—the breadth and depth of your entire life—has been plucked from your mind like a cat pawing the guts from a frog's belly. It has been cataloged and sorted through. Your life as a series of books. Or software on a visidex." She stops, chuckles. "It's really pretty cool, honestly."

"You're a monster."

"I am. I won't disagree. Sometimes the world needs horrible people. Though really, it's all a matter of perspective, isn't it? I mean, consider that to the weeds in the garden, the gardener is a monster, viciously yanking them from the dirt. What horror! Such cruelty! An apocalypse of weeds!" She begins unhooking his arms from the cables that encircle them. "And yet, it's a job that needs to be done, right? That's me. I'm the gardener. Your people, the Heartlander terrorists: you're the weeds."

He falls forward. She doesn't bother catching him. Arthur crumples like a handkerchief thrown down upon the ground.

"It's really amazing," she says, "how little you people appreciate us. We feed you. We clothe you. We give you purpose. The corn down there in the dirt is an amazing thing. A beautiful crop that saved your lives. It kills mosquitos that spread bonebreak flu. It kills the blister flies that come from Bleakmarsh. It stabilized the climate. It can be made into fuel, plastic, food additives, anything and everything."

"It's a disease. You're a disease."

She makes a disgusted sound. "Ugh. You know, some of us up here in the sky have gotten soft about you. It was a fad for a time to dress like you, to pretend to be like the salt-of-the-earth Heartlanders. There began this . . . idea that you were these noble workers, toiling in the dust for us. But we've disproven that, haven't we? You don't work hard. You're not the shepherds— you're the sheep. You barely tend to the motorvators. You work the processing lines, and a third of you get injured or die from it because you're clumsy. Meanwhile you keep reaching up to the heavens, waiting for a handout from us." She sniffs. "My own father was like that. He was Empyrean, *obviously*, but what a waste of space. Not a contributor. Content to live off the dole."

Arthur chuckles, laying his cheek against his own forearm. "So that's what this is about. You have daddy issues. You're ruining the world because you're mad at your father." His laugh almost becomes a sob. He struggles to keep that bottled up. He doesn't want to show this horrid girl any weakness.

"Whatever helps you sleep at night, Arthur. And you don't have many nights left. You've been scheduled for execution. Seven days. I thought it might be more fitting to have you become part of the Initiative—after all, you're already halfway there, aren't you?—but I'd rather make a show of it."

"Kill me. I don't care."

She *hmms*. "I might believe that, actually. You're pretty beaten down. But I bet you'll care when I tell you about your son, Cael."

Cael. *Cael*. He turns his face toward her. One eye staring at her so hard he hopes the hate he's projecting is a transmission that can kill her—an invisible laser that will cut her apart, dissect her into her pieces.

"What about my son?" he hisses.

"He dies. Tonight. We have all we need from you. My girls are trained. We have the map, the technology for our descent; we even have someone on the inside—and in fact, it was you who showed me the way. Showed me a weak link in the chain: someone who had cause to battle with Lane Moreau, that erstwhile 'mayor.' I was able to contact this someone thanks to the information contained inside *your* amazing mind. And it is amazing. You are far smarter than most of your Heartlander companions. You should've been born Empyrean."

"My son . . ."

"Is the walking dead. Thanks to you."

Arthur weeps as the scarred girl snaps her fingers. Other shadows descend upon him. Hands reach for him and drag him into the light as he calls his son's name.

Miranda waits for her outside, like a heron watching for fish by a stream.

Enyastasia tries not to register her surprise. "Miranda."

"I just came to wish you good luck tonight. I still think it's premature."

"They're having a celebration. The chaos of their festivity is our opportunity. The door is open. I'd like to walk through it."

Miranda's mouth tightens into a firm line. "It's a risk. A very big risk. Especially with you going along—let your Harpies go. You can remain behind. If you're injured, or worse . . ."

"My girls are the knives, and I am the one wielding them."

"And who is wielding you?"

Enyastasia twitches. She tries not to, but there it is. What is Miranda playing at? Is Miranda suggesting that *she* controls Enyastasia? Or that she wants to? Or that nobody does—and that's the problem? *Shake it off.* "You have to trust me. I won't fail at this. Someone has to go into that nest of vipers and cut off their heads." She hesitates. "Do you trust me?"

Miranda purses her lips.

Enyastasia thinks: *I don't want to have to kill you, too.*

But the architect nods. "I trust you. Go. Bring us back their heads."

Later, Enyastasia lays out seven ace notes, each one flipping forward with an audible *thwip*—"The currency of the filthy Heartlanders," she says. "But now, these seven cards are *our* currency."

Suddenly, the yacht takes a hard bump. The air: choppy today. Winds moving in. Somewhere, she figures, a twister is etching a line across the corn and the yacht is catching a taste of it way up here.

The yacht can handle it. It was her father's once.

She pulled it out of storage for just this purpose.

That pleases her. To take something that was his and to subvert it to her own purposes. This was where he kept her. Where she was forced into a box and made to stay. And listen. And weep. And foul herself.

He is dead now, and she is alive. Her father was a stain on the legacy of the Ormond name, a legacy she reclaims tonight.

Across the table, seven pairs of eyes watch her.

Seven girls, standing stock straight. Hands clasped behind their backs. Faces painted, scarred, branded. Guns at their hips, knives strapped to legs.

My Harpies. Each without a name. Oh, they had names once. But those names are erased. Willfully forgotten. Identities eradicated—these girls become one. Each just *Harpy.* They sleep together. Eat together. Live together. They are one entity, not seven separate.

In the old stories, it was the Harpies' job to take revenge on those who killed their sisters, their families, and snatch up the evildoers and deliver them to the nest of the Dirae. All of them, sky-spirits and cloud-creatures, half-bird, half-human. Diviners of the law. Executors of justice.

And so it is today.

On each ace note, a name and a sketch.

"These are the ones calling themselves the Boxelder Seven," the Dirae says. "They are villains. Evildoers of the highest order.

They are parasites inside the body of the fallen Saranyu, repurposing its corpse and defiling it for their own purposes. What do we do with evildoers?"

In unison, the girls say:

"We claim them with our claws, we throw them to the wind, we break their bodies and water the corn with their blood."

"Again."

"We claim them with our claws, we throw them to the wind, we break their bodies and water the corn with their blood!"

"Again!"

Claws! Wind! Bodies! Blood!

All these girls: they will be the justice she wants.

(A small voice inside her says: *To be the justice you* need.)

Justice for a world where her legacy—the flotilla, the Ormond Stirling Saranyu—was swatted out of the air and robbed by brigands and idiots.

"These seven are the heads of the hydra. These heads must be taken for the beast to die. When they die, the city they have built from the bones of our home will die with them." To think, the old fools wanted to just send the Herfjotur there, start blasting away. As if that would matter. To kill a colony of bees, you must find and extinguish its queen. To win that simplest, stupidest of games, Checks, you had to kill the queen. You don't kill kings and queens with hammers. You cut them from the tapestry with fine razor blades. Enter the Dirae and her Harpies. "Are we ready?"

In simultaneity: *"We are ready, Dirae."*

She gives a sharp nod.

The girls each step back. They raise their arms into the straps hanging above them—each tugs on a circular chest plate, a narrow metal ring molded to their bodies with shimmering blue glass in its center.

Cut from hover-panel tech.

They tighten the straps. This happens mechanically, the Harpies timed almost perfectly to one another. Enyastasia thinks with stifled surprise: *They really* are *one entity. They move as one, think as one. I did it. I win.*

Each reaches down, pulls red-lensed goggles from their hips.

They put them on, too.

Enyastasia mirrors their movements: She steps back, grabs the straps, puts on the hover-plate. She denies herself the goggles. She wants to see everything. Wants to feel the sting of the cold air and hard wind in her eyes.

She nods again, then says:

"Let us descend."

They shout together: *"Let us descend!"*

The Dirae reaches up, finds a handle there—

She pulls it.

Several gunshot bangs in quick succession—

And then the floor is gone. Falling out from underneath them.

They fall down through the night. Stars streaking. Wind whipping their hair, chapping their exposed skin.

Together they fall toward Pegasus City, far below them in the Heartland.

REAPING WITH THE SWEEP
OF THE SCYTHE

IN GWENNIE'S HEAD, it's a twisted mash-up. Like two motorvators that crashed together and became one. *Or like a Heartlander suffering the Blight*, she thinks. On the one hand, this is Harvest Home. It looks like Harvest Home: the stands selling food, the booths running games, the people carrying bowls of chicha beer. It feels like it, too: the twang of a banjo, the smell of roasted corn, the dizzy, drunken feel even before she's gotten properly dizzy and drunk.

But then—the Empyrean feeling bleeds in, like water soaking a towel. She sees the signs and sigils and remnants of the Seventh Heaven: a statue of a Pegasus with its hooves up and out as if it's about to crush some poor Heartlander, a woman laughing and gnawing on a carrot that's big as a baby's arm (carrots, after all, were not on the list of acceptable foods back in Boxelder), the shine of visidexes, the clink of liquor bottles once too good and too rare for all but the most influential Heartlanders.

It's Harvest Home, but gilded with an Empyrean edge. A Heartlander tradition in chrome and silver, given wings, made to fly.

She wanders into the crowd, feeling suddenly alone. Some of these people she knows a little bit—over there, one-armed Wesley Wong stands behind the plywood booth running a wheel of chance, and behind the big line at Sully's Kitchen wagon is the hefty-chested Benigna Batts. But all told, these people are strangers to her—familiar for their *Heartlanderness*, perhaps, but no more her townsfolk than the people who lived on the Saranyu.

It's then that she misses Boxelder with an ache. Like something's been removed from her—some unknown vital organ between her stomach and her heart. Her grief over its loss is suddenly so *real* it feels like it's about to knock her legs out from under her. And then, when she thinks about Boxelder and that loss, the door is open to thinking about Cael, and what Wanda told her . . .

Rigo suddenly jostles up alongside Gwennie.

"Oops," he says, fake bumping into her. He holds up a bowl of chicha beer. "Got you this!" The foamy, sour beer almost sloshes over the lip.

She waves it off. "I think I'm good. Thanks, though, Rigo."

"Oh, come on! We have some celebrating to do—Boyland rubbed together his two brain cells and came up with the location of the Maize Witch's *secret weapon, ooooob*. And maybe we have a plan to break the blockade. And I notice that you and Cael have been getting a little chummy again—"

"Cael doesn't own me. We're not a thing." She hears her own voice and realizes she's protesting a little too loudly.

"I didn't say—wait, what?" Rigo's face is a house of cards, collapsing. "Oh no. Oh, jeez. What happened?"

"Nothing happened," she says, stern-faced. Then takes the bowl of beer and tosses it back. Foamy, spit-slick, sour. Just like home. The rush that goes to her head is more from the lack of oxygen when guzzling it, but just the same—it's a nice precursor of the drunk she now decides has to come. "Nothing."

"I don't understand—"

She says the words without even really meaning to let them out—it's like closing the barn door halfway and then finding a horse slamming them open once more before bolting.

"I felt differently this time," she says. "In Boxelder, we got together because . . . because we were two dumb kids, and it was a lot of fun, but we always—or at least *I* always—knew it would end. Obligation Day and all that. And then everything went sideways, and I ended up on the Saranyu and . . . I saw him that one last time. He'd still been carrying a candle for me and almost died doing it." Her volume rises to compensate for the crowd. "Lord and Lady, I thought he *did* die! And that killed me. *Killed me.* I realized, I think I love this dumbass. Gods, can you believe I almost married Boyland? Jeez-dang. Then: here. Pegasus City. I was the one who started it with Cael. It was me, okay? Not him. I was playing like it was no big thing, but it *was* a big thing because suddenly the rules had all gone out the dang window. I looked forward. I could see a life where he and I were together, a real team! Maybe we had kids, maybe we ran some scavenger crew somewhere picking through the Empyrean bones, maybe we'd leave the Heartland and see a world that two years ago we didn't even know *existed*. But all that's done and gone now. Window's shut. Door's closed."

Rigo blinks, and his face wilts. "I only heard, like, half of that, but I got the gist. I'm sorry. Maybe it'll still work out between you two. . . ."

"Yeah." A big, empty laugh. "No."

She wants to yell: *Wanda's pregnant. Pregnant with what, I dunno. Maybe she isn't even pregnant at all. Maybe it's all a ruse. A lie to keep me out of the equation.* The girl was nice enough when she told her. She almost seemed human again. Until the end of it, when she said to Gwennie: "I'm sorry this happened. But if you try to ruin things, like you tend to do, then I will kill you where you stand." Before saying once more: "I'm sorry, again."

Rigo reaches up and hugs her. Gwennie almost spills her beer. She leans forward, catches the rim of the bowl and sucks down any of the near-spillover.

As they're embracing awkwardly, a third body pivots and hip-checks them—at first she thinks it must be someone else from the Boxelder Seven, maybe Lane, or even Boyland (certainly not Cael, not now), but it's someone she's seen and doesn't know—a haggard ragman, an old hobo whose mouth is a ruined cupful of broken dice. He gestures at them with a jar of something that smells strong enough to strip the fur off a shuck rat and yells:

"I saw stars falling! The stars falling right upon us—"

Rigo shoves him back. "Bortigan, this isn't the time, you old drunk."

"Blue lights, streaks of blue lights—bright as the blue blazes!"

The weather-beaten hobo mutters as he wanders into the

crowd, swilling his jar of paint stripper, white-lightning whiskey. He tumbles away like a wad of blowing trash.

"I gotta go find Scooter and Squirrel. I think Mom should be here by now. . . ." Her words fall apart in her mouth, and she really just wants to say: *I'm gonna go find a blanket to hide under and cry and drink this awful beer until the sun rises or sleep finds me or the world ends or whatever.*

That, however, isn't an option. Her mother really is here somewhere with the two kids.

Without saying anything else, she pulls away from Rigo and heads into the throng, putting on the bravest face she can muster.

"Why the long face, goat?" Lane asks.

Cael lifts an eyebrow. "It's why the long face, *horse.*"

"Yeah, well, we ain't got any horses, do we?" He smiles—a big, boozy grin. A few Heartlanders pass behind him and shout—*Mayor!*—before clapping him on the back hard enough that he spills a bit of whiskey from his glass. "Haha! Good men, good men." He pops his lips. "Hey, besides, goats have long faces."

"You're drunk."

"I am *in my cups*, as they say." He gives a woozy wink. "Oh, what? Come on, this is Harvest Home, Cap'n! This is like all the grand old times getting secretly drunk around the adults, except this time, *it's not so secret!*"

Cael finds a small smile at that: "It wasn't much of a secret then, either."

"Ha, probably not, probably not. Still, it's nice to be the ones in charge for once, isn't it?" Lane narrows his gaze, looks Cael up and down. "You look like a man with troubles on his shoulders. An ox with a too-heavy yoke."

At first, Cael isn't even sure if he wants to tell Lane. The lanky beanpole has enough to worry about: running a city, trying to undermine an Empyrean blockade, navigating the emotional bramble-patch that is Killian Kelly.

But Lane's his friend. And he needs someone to talk to. Badly. "Wanda's pregnant."

It takes a second to pierce the miasma of inebriation, but the news finally gets there. When it does, Lane's jaw hangs loose like a door knocked off its hinges. "Holy shitfire and damnation. You're gonna be a father. You're gonna be a father!" He guffaws and slaps Cael on the arm, then wraps himself around Cael like creeper ivy up a crooked tree. "I don't know whether to be happy for you or scared for the world. Look out, Heartland, another McAvoy on the way!" He whistles and loops his arm around Cael's neck, then pushes his glass of whiskey to Cael's lips.

Cael sighs and goes with it, lets the whiskey leave a trail of burning caramel down the back of his throat.

"I'm gonna be a shit dad," he says to Lane.

"Nonsense. Cease those shenanigans, Captain. Quit it right damn now."

Cael shakes his head. "No, seriously. What the hell, man, I'm no good for anybody. I'm a dope, a dumbass, as much of a donkey as Boyland Barnes Jr. is. I don't know squat about squat, and I make good decisions, ohh, about half the time—and that half is because I got lucky, not because I got wise."

Lane leans in, says loudly in Cael's ear with the intimate proximity drunks so often favor: "The fact you recognized this fact? Shows you're gonna be just fine. You're the captain, Cap. Your crew's just growing by one is all. We'll figure this out together. We'll all be the kid's family."

"You mean that?"

"Of course I mean it. Way I see it, that means I'm gonna be an uncle. I can't wait to meet the little—er, boy?"

"Girl."

"Haha, oh, by the sulfurous balls of Old Scratch, you are in *trouble*. I can't wait to meet her, seriously. Cael. Cael. You listening?"

Cael sighs. "I'm listening."

"You got this." He leans forward, kisses Cael on the temple. "Now, I notice that both you and I are without a drink, and I have a bottle of eighteen-year Moon Isle malted whiskey squirreled away in a nearby bolthole. I don't know what it is or what it tastes like, but I want to crack the cork and try it with you. Can I go get it?"

Cael grins. "You got my blessing, Mayor."

Another kiss to the temple, and Lane is off, pirouetting through the crowd, clapping shoulders and cackling like a happy madman. Cael's glad they mended fences. Lane's a true friend. That boy is *bona fide*.

Lane's fingers search under the shelf of rubble—they touch something cold, something that spins a bit away from his probing digits.

"Ahh, dangit, get . . . over . . . here." His fingers spin the glass.

I hid this thing too well.

It's away from the crowds. The pile of rubble is one that still hasn't been cleaned up, though it's been drawn on with paint and chalk by some of the few children who are here in Pegasus City. In the distance someone yells: "Hey, Mayor, you lose something? The keys to the Mayormobile or something?"

Folks are laughing and he knows they're laughing with him, not at him, but growing up where he did, any laughter still has the chance of making him feel oddly small and unwittingly persecuted—but he can give as good as he gets, and so while looking under the rubble, he lifts his free hand and gives the catcallers a well-extended, up-thrust middle finger.

He won't let it ruin his good time. They don't mean anything by it. Lane's just drunk—booze can turn one's mood the way wind turns a mill. Tonight, though, he has a great deal to be happy about. The city has come together for Harvest Home. A city he helped build with an event he helped put together. Heartlander solidarity on display—all with the help of the Boxelder Seven. Old friends. Even Boyland, that brick-headed dunk-tank. And now Cael and Wanda having a baby—

There! *There.* His fingers finally get atop the bottle and manage to pull it in the right direction. The bottle rolls out into his hand.

The label is weathered, worn, yellowed. A blue ink moon like an old raider tattoo next to a sketch of an island chain. *Moon Isle.* The number *18* handwritten at the bottom of the label. The cork sealed into the bottle with wax the color of blue spruce. The whiskey sloshes, and for a moment Lane thinks: *Maybe I'll visit*

Moon Isle someday. Wherever it is. There must be people there, right? Certainly the fish aren't bottling whiskey!

When all this is done, when he's a bit older, a journey is in order.

Bottle in hand, Lane stands.

And there stands someone right behind him.

He turns, frowns. "I don't know you. Thought I knew everybody."

The girl looks up—the electric lights strung up all around illuminate a face that looks almost like broken pottery. Her scar tissue—the "cracks"—painted with a shimmering gold, or bronze.

The knife-blade flashes.

Cael kicks a bit of broken brick. Not far away, the crowds seem whipped up even more than they were before—lots of laughing, lots of drinking. This was a good idea, Harvest Home. When Rigo came up with the idea, Lane thought it would be a mockery—as much a facsimile as a scarecrow, fake and obviously unreal, but damnit if it wasn't a thing people really *needed*. He looks around. Folks venting steam. Letting it all hang out.

It's nice to see.

More laughing around him. Somewhere: yelling, hollering.

A scream, too . . .

His vine tightens around his arm, cutting the circulation. He tells himself: *Just a few revelers getting out of hand.* Though even that could be a problem. Heartlanders aren't exempt from monstrousness. A few drunks going after some poor girl, maybe. An odd thought: *One day you'll be protecting your daughter from drunks like that.* Daughter. Lord and Lady!

He takes a step forward when, from off to the side, he sees Lane coming up. Cael flags him over. "Hey, Mayor—you got a plan in mind in case folks get *too* riled up at this thing . . . ?"

But Lane suddenly staggers into him, almost knocking him over.

Oh, gods.

His middle is wet. Gleaming red. Parts of his guts bulging out, cradled in his one arm like a just-born baby. In his other hand, he's holding a broken bottle upside down—bloodless knuckles wrapped around the bottle's neck, the base of it jagged and bloody.

"Gave as good as I got," Lane says. His words are gummy, throaty, and when he licks his lip, it leaves a trail of blood so dark it's almost black.

"Godsdamn, Lane, what the hell—" Cael catches Lane before he falls, props him up, gets his arm around his friend. "Who did this to you?"

"I don't know who she was," Lane says, voice cracking, eyes wet. "Got rats in the walls, Cap'n. They're in. They're here. This is them." He lifts his trembling eyes skyward. "Am I dead? Am I gonna die? Shit. *Shit.*"

"Gonna get you some help right now, none of that dying talk," Cael says. But then Lane points a finger and says:

"Her."

A girl. Younger than Cael, maybe, but not by much. She's

coming up from the side, her skull bloody, the glass shards stuck in her scalp catching the colored lights. The knife in her hand—bloody.

She's got her teeth bared. Her stare is as dead as a crow's eyes. The girl marches forth with her body tilted forward, as if some grim gravity—some unbreakable tether—drags her toward them.

Cael thinks: *She did this to my friend.*

He wishes he had the rifle. But for now—

He reaches toward her. The Blight knows what to do. It lashes out, quick as a whip, and coils tight around her neck—then it stiffens, halting her momentum and fixing her to the spot.

Her eyes bulge. She makes a sound like a rabbit, screaming.

Then the knife flashes.

It cuts clean through the vine. Pain like Cael has never known recoils through the remaining vine, to his shoulder, to his mind—as the vine thrashes about, spraying dark sap, he feels the strength go out of his legs, and he drops to his knees. Lane collapses with him, crying out.

The girl tosses the Blight-vine aside.

She leaps for Cael, the knife hissing through air.

One minute, Gwennie is leading Scooter through the crowd to go find Balastair—because, as Scooter puts it, "he wants to see the little bird, teach it some tricks," but the next thing she knows, she's on the ground, flat on her back, and her little brother is screaming.

A scarred girl, her hair shorn to the scalp, sits atop her chest, perched like an owl on a roof-peak.

She has a long knife. The blade twirls in her hand, and suddenly it's hilt up, blade down, and the girl plunges the weapon toward Gwennie—

Gwennie jerks her head aside. The knife sticks in the ground. The girl growls, "Your bodies will break! Your blood will water the corn!" then wrenches the knife upward—

But Gwennie spits in her eye, then rolls her whole body to the side. The girl yelps, scrambles off like a spider before she topples.

The girl is up fast—too fast, improbably fast, like all her muscles have been trained to be less a girl and more *some kind of nightmare,* and the knife drops to the ground and a pistol is in her hand—

By now people are screaming all around—

The shooter goes off, screaming a sonic wave—

But before it does, the hand jerks to the side, and the blast craters the dirt inches from Gwennie's head.

A small knife-blade sticks out of the girl's hand. The gun drops.

A shape moves fast from the side. Squirrel screams, leaps bodily atop the girl like some kind of shrieking demon, and begins to stab at the scarred girl with a knife—

The attacker makes no sound. She twists her body and flings Squirrel off her. The smaller girl hits the ground hard and rolls, the knife clattering away as she remains still. Gwennie yells for Scooter to run—"Go find Mom!"

Then she scrambles to stand. She manages, just barely—

Turns to run—

The girl yanks the other knife from the back of her own hand. A jet of blood follows in its wake, but her face barely registers any pain at all.

The scarred girl turns the blade around, then comes for Gwennie with it.

Gwennie picks up a hunk of dry earth and wings it toward the girl—she bats it away like it's nothing, because it is nothing, and suddenly Gwennie is thinking, *Don't let her kill you, you can do better than this—stay alive!*

The girl emits a banshee wail, then runs forward with the knife twirling, dancing, cutting air with a whisper-hiss—

But before she reaches Gwennie, she's whipped up into the air. Legs kicking, arms thrashing—

A thorn-studded vine coiled around her head and neck.

Gwennie remembers a time when Cael's father caught a rock dove out by their chimney. Fat-bellied birds. He said a small apology to the bird before covering the bird's head with his hand and giving the bird a little shake—same way votaries of the Lord and Lady's manse might shake holy water onto those they are attempting to bless—the bird's neck broke with an audible *snap*.

This is like that, but worse.

The vine gives the girl a hard shake like she's just a toy, just a doll. The neck breaks like the sound of a tent pole snapping. The head goes sideways, and the vine tosses the body down like it's naught but a broken tool.

Wanda steps forward, eyes gone all green.

The vine comes from her open, outstretched mouth.

It retracts into her maw. Her throat bulges as it becomes part of her.

"Oops," Wanda says.

"Thank you," Gwennie says, gasping, trying to find air. "For saving me. I know you didn't have to."

For a moment, Wanda just stares. Then, shaken from it, she says: "Check on the girl. Then we need to find the others."

It hurts less than it should, all these cuts, all this blood, because Boyland Junior's so deep in his cups that even his teeth are numb. He squeals and staggers backward, his big arms thrown up in front of him like a wall—beyond his arms, the knife slashes again and again, cutting through his flesh and muscles, maybe down to the bone. Blood comes off his arms in red curtains.

He's not even sure what the hell is happening. One minute he was standing there looking into the crowd of people, letting his mind wander and his vision drift so that every person had a ghosted doppelgänger—one, then two, then three. *Four of everybody*, he thought. *My own version of King Hell.*

Somewhere, people started screaming. He registered that, but couldn't quite pull any meaning out of the mire, nor any concern.

Then four versions of one girl stalked up to him.

Took a second to pull his gaze back together, and by the time he did—uttering something that sounded like, *Wuzza, who you?*—she started moving her arm in a figure-eight motion like she was trying to hit him all fancy-like, except he realized all too late that her hand wasn't empty and, in fact, held a very sharp knife. A knife that, even now, is slicing his arms up like they're lamb sausage.

His heel suddenly catches on something—a crumbled bit of rubble, a tent peg, a stubborn shuck rat—he has no idea what and never finds out. All he knows is first he's vertical and then he's horizontal.

The girl, this knife-wielding psycho, stands over him. She's not smiling. No sign of her being happy about this at all. Her face is just a scarred-up mask of grotesque indifference. His father, the Boxelder mayor, used to look *happy* when he laid into him with a belt or a book. (*Only thing a book is good for*, the elder Barnes said, *is beating the donkey I call a son.*)

Gods, just thinking about that, thinking about his father—thinking about how right now his arms are slick with blood and maybe he'll never use them again, thinking about how Gwennie is lost and gone and how all his life has broken apart like turds out of a goat's ass—

He starts bawling.

His head flops back and he sobs so hard it's like the grief is being pulled up all the way from his toes to his heart and then to his eyes, a journey that hurts. A strange thought goes through him:

Grief is poison.

Then for a half second, the tears clear and the hitching sobs stop, because the girl is just . . . standing there. Struck dumb by his display.

A look crosses her face.

He knows that look. His own mother's worn it in the past.

He mumbles, words so slurred he's not even sure they're words:

"Don't you feel bad for me."

And then something slams into the side of her head and knocks her over like a scarecrow. Takes a little bit for Boyland's brain to catch up to what he's seeing, but he licks his lips and wipes a ropy strand of snot away from his face with a blood-slick arm, then asks: "Cozido?"

Rigo stands there, holding his leg like a bludgeon. Same way he held it earlier that day when he almost brought it down on Boyland's head.

He hobbles a bit, then stoops and refits the prosthetic to his stump.

He offers a hand. "We have to go," Rigo says. "We're under attack."

The girl with the golden scars screams as she leaps for Cael— her shriek is a wildcat's cry, a sound that contains multitudes. Cael's there on his knees, and a thought flashes crystalline in his mind—*I have to stay alive.* His daughter needs him. She's just this little thing without any protection of her own. A tiny un-person who needs him and who needs Wanda, too.

Wanda.

He's going to have to kill this girl.

The Blight-vine's flopping uselessly by his side.

The rifle's back in his room.

But he's got the old standby.

He reaches back, feels the slingshot tuckcd in his back pocket and draws it, scrambling with his other hand to find a piece of stone or shattered brick, and he scoots backward as the girl rushes him—

His hand finds a stone, but then fumbles it—

The stone drops away—

At her feet, fast movement.

Lane.

The mayor of Pegasus City slashes out with the broken bottle—

The girl howls as the glass cuts across the back of her ankle—

She drops. Lands hard on her shoulder. The knife flicks away.

Part of Cael thinks: *Grab her, throttle her, ask her who she is.*

But there's no time. Because Lane is bleeding out. His guts are shining under the electric lights. If he's going to save his friend, he has to move fast. Cael gets under Lane, lifts him up carefully as he can, and begins to move.

The Harpy was once named Bellique Killane. She was a child of great privilege—her mother, an engineer on the Saranyu who ran a team of programmers (a team that also contained her father) responsible for crafting the network by which visidexes communicate with one another. Twenty years ago, that was not a possibility between flotillas. Today, it is.

Because of her mother.

Because of her father.

Both of whom lived on the Saranyu.

Both of whom are now dead.

Bellique was not on the Saranyu at the time—some who were on the flotilla escaped with their lives, hurrying to yachts or skiffs as it fell. She was with her sister, Chantal, on the Oshadagea, learning how to be a vintner. That was her dream, and her parents supported it. Because that is the glory of the Empyrean. See what you want to be. Be what you want to be. All of life infinite in its potential. Until the attack on the Saranyu changed that.

It robbed her of her family.

It robbed her of her name.

No. That's not correct. She *gave up* her name.

There are some days she cannot even remember it, but she remembers it now as she creeps into the room to kill an Empyrean man. A traitor to the Seventh Heaven, as much a traitor as the Saintangel Cipher was to the Lord and Lady (Cipher thought he could fly higher than they could, build a house so far into the sky that it was a manse not in the clouds but in the stars, but he learned that wings made of wax melted under the heat of the sun).

Here, this man: Balastair Harrington.

Sitting by a window in his chamber, separate from the rest of the celebration. Already she knows her sisters are down there, doing what they must under the directive of the Dirae. This is their calling. The Harpies have died along with the Saranyu. They are now waking ghosts. Angels of vengeance. More monster than man.

He sits in shadow. Lights off. Just a silhouette.

Bellique—no. *No!* She has to stop thinking of herself as somebody. As a *person* with a *name*. The Harpy—that's it, yes, just the Harpy—creeps forward, drawing the knife, a knife whetted with an electron-sharpener, a knife so sharp it'll cut through bone if allowed the chance.

Her feet are silent on the floor. Silent even in the rubble.

They are silent because she has been trained to be silent.

Trained for over a year now. To stalk. To creep. To kill.

Deep breath.

She slices out with the knife.

The blade meets little resistance.

The man's head comes off at the shoulders and rolls to the ground.

Everything seems to go slow. It's chaos now. They've stepped over bodies. Hurried past them. Squirrel is with her. Scooter, too. She's holding both of their hands, pulling them through the crowds, Wanda following close behind. More screams, somewhere. Sonic trills. She can't find her mother. Doesn't want to lose her. A little voice says, *You've already lost her, you pushed her away after what happened up there, you've left her alone*—but she can't go down that path, not now, not with everything going on—

The power goes out. The electric lights go dark one by one in quick succession. More gasps. More screams. Raiders yelling, *We're under attack!*

Then the lights come back on, flashing, strobing. Electric buzz-snaps—crackling, popping, hissing above their heads like locusts in a burn barrel. For a moment, the crowd parts—

And there stands Rigo and Boyland.

Boyland looks like the walking dead. Gray-faced. His arms dark with blood. Face, too. All of him, soaked and sodden. Red lines, darker and deeper, mark his forearms, his biceps. Cuts. It runs off his fingertips like runoff from rain-gutters. He's looking in her direction in horror, and so is Rigo, and then both of them are calling out—

But they're not looking at her. They're looking past her.

Gwennie turns, sees Wanda standing there.

Clutching an opened throat, her eyes bulging. Fingers grasping at the wound, coming away wet with red.

One of the girls stands there, teeth bared, knife out.

The girl raises the weapon again—

Gwennie's wrist flicks before she even realizes it.

A small throwing knife embeds in the scarred girl's temple.

The attacker lists sideways and hits the ground, dead.

Wanda. Throat slit. The child inside her—Gwennie hurries over, crying out, everything going slower and slower. She rushes to Wanda, catches her by the arms, holds her up. The girl's eyes are unfocused, going empty, her tongue lolling out over her lips. There's this moment, and Gwennie recognizes it because it's *right there on Wanda's face*, when Wanda realizes what's happening, and this look of utter sadness crosses her face—everything crinkled up like she wants to cry but can't, and she makes a sound in the back of her throat, a terrible animal sound.

Gwennie hears herself saying, "Wanda, Wanda, Wanda, no—no! You can't, you have to, oh gods, no, please—"

Wanda's eyes snap to focus.

They look at Gwennie.

Clarity. Awareness. Fear and sorrow wiped away.

It doesn't even register at first—Gwennie thinks it's just more blood, or some strange effect of having one's throat opened, but what she sees there in the hissing, blood-bubble gap isn't human. Little tiny tendrils—small vines like searching threads, like inchworms venturing off a leaf's edge. They rise from the bottom of the wound and reach down from the top of it, too.

They meet in the middle. Little stems and shoots curling around one another, tying in knots—

Pulling taut.

She's fixing herself.

Or maybe: the Blight is fixing her.

The wound suddenly closes up. A scar, ragged and green as moss, marks the space where her throat had just been opened.

Wanda blinks.

Then clutches at her middle.

"The baby," Gwennie says.

"She's fine," Wanda says. "I'm fine."

She pushes past Gwennie, moving toward the others—but all Gwennie can think is: *None of this is fine, and none of us are ever going to be fine again.*

The Harpy turns away from the Empyrean man's corpse.

The air is suddenly filled with this sound—she recognizes it as the rustle of bird wings followed swiftly by panicked squeaking—just before something hits her in the face and begins to peck and claw at it.

She swats at it, but the little bird is far faster than she expects. It flies up, around, left, then right, then back to her face again, pecking, scratching.

Another whistle from beyond the bird.

And then the little creature is gone.

When the Harpy regains her vision once more, she sees him standing there. The Empyrean man. Balastair Harrington.

The thing she thought was his severed head—really just a hollow container—rolls at her feet.

"Who are you?" he asks her.

"Vengeance," she says, but the word suddenly rings hollow.

"What have you done?"

"Blood feeds the corn."

She sees the sonic shooter in his hand.

He fires.

Kill her, Balastair thinks. She's just a girl, though, her face cut up like a patchwork quilt. Hard to be too angry—she's kneeling there, gagging and spitting and crying. The sonic blast did its number on her, but he set it to stun, and even now he looks at the weapon and thinks maybe he should turn up the dial, set it to kill, and put her out of her misery.

"You came to kill me," he says. Then he leans down. "But I won't kill you. I can't. Don't make me regret this decision."

Then he extends his finger into the air.

"Come, Cicero."

The bird lands on his finger.

It's time to find the others.

Cael thinks: *There's a doctor here somewhere. Nika something.* She treated Lane's mother. And he tells Lane that, too—he says,

"I'm gonna find that doc you were talking about. She's gotta be here, man. Gotta be here somewhere. Then we're gonna get all of you stitched up and put back together—I just—" His words, drowned out by someone yelling. Ahead, a group of raiders fire sonic weapons into the air at another girl somersaulting above them, a pistol in her hand, too—by the time she lands atop the peak of a nearby tent, the raiders who fired at her are all dead or dying on the ground.

Not that way, then.

Cael pulls Lane sharply right, behind the now-overturned Sully's Kitchen food wagon. His friend's feet drag limply, and as Cael pulls Lane down he says, "The doc. Where do you think she is?" But Lane doesn't answer.

Lane's head rocks back, mouth open, eyes wide.

No. *No, no, no.*

Cael's heart catches in his throat like a frog in a cat's mouth, and he pats Lane's cheek and feels under his friend's throat—there's nothing there, no pulse, no feeling at all but the cold and clammy skin. Lane's chest isn't rising or falling. What was once there is now gone. Some presence, fled. Cael knows that but can't admit it, can't believe it. He grits his teeth and cries out, screams Lane's name, holds his friend close. He rocks him back and forth. He begs for him not to be dead. *Come back to me, brother. Don't be gone. Don't leave me alone. We were just figuring all this shit out.*

He doesn't know how long he sits there like that, blubbering and keening and holding Lane's body close. Cael doesn't care. Can't care. He barely recognizes Balastair's voice at his ear—"We have to go. Come on, Cael. We will mourn him later, but please, we have to go *now.*"

29

CHOOSERS OF THE SLAIN

I HAVE FAILED.

Enyastasia, Dirae of the Harpies, limps into the crooked alleyway between two crumbling buildings. A trail of blood marks the ground behind her—the tendon on her left foot is sliced to ribbons. Her head, too, is cut up, bits of glass still stuck under the skin of her brow, her scalp.

That foolshead mayor did this to her.

With one bottle.

She stinks of blood and white whiskey.

Tonight was supposed to be her crowning glory. A proof-of-concept moment that showed the necessity of Project Raven. It took a great many sacrifices to get here—it was supposed to have been worth it!

Already she's formulating excuses. *I didn't have enough time. We didn't have enough support. The old men who run the flotillas . . .*

No.

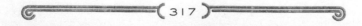

Don't do that.

She needs to own her failures. If this were a success, she'd certainly claim it—she'd wear it like a shield and mantle, parade it about for all to see. Failure must be that way, too. Failure must be an instructional manual written in scar tissue. That's what her face was always meant to represent—the ugliness of Empyrean failures put forward for all to witness. A revelation of weakness.

Enyastasia slides down behind a fallen stone pillar.

She looks at her sonic pistol. Thinks what it would be like to place the barrel in her mouth—what would she hear as the sonic blast tore off the top of her skull? Would she hear the shrill cacophony of crows screaming? Would she hear a secret song—a lullaby sung to her by the Lord and Lady as she entered their sacred sky-manse? Would she hear nothing at all?

Again: no.

No!

Suicide is for the weak. It's meant to be a demonstration, a cry for help. Or worse, an escape into something bleaker and blacker: the sucking gravity of helplessness and lost hope.

She will not make excuses.

And she will not end herself.

What she does instead is hope. Hope that her Harpies accomplished more than she herself managed. That the blood on their hands is predominantly from others and not from themselves. And she hopes they will not judge her too harshly for what must happen next.

She takes a small communicator from a strap around the inside of her thigh—she presses the red button. Into it she whispers:

"Miranda?"

The woman answers: "You're alive."

"It's time."

"You're still down there. Extract yourself first."

"I said it's time! *Let the bombardment begin.*"

Up in the sky, above the Heartland, a black shape hovers.

Soon, wind turbines—silent and black matte—spin to life.

The black shape begins to drift forward, sliding across the night like a starving vulture, desperate for death.

DOOM FALLS

THE TREACHERY doesn't sit well with Luna. It's a heavy beast upon her shoulders, hunched there, pecking at the back of her neck with a grave persistence. But Lane Moreau was weak. Her father always said, *Don't truck with pussies*, and she started to seriously question whether the erstwhile mayor of Pegasus City was always a pussy or was just becoming one.

(Of course, her father was a serial abuser, and her mother was dead from a cancer that ate half her face so early in Luna's life that she barely remembers the woman.)

Either way, Lane didn't have the stones to keep doing this thing. He was compromised. Tainted by the presence of his mother and the appearance of his so-called friends—folks who, way she saw it, only wanted to keep him down.

Even Killian saw it that way.

Not that she much cares for him, either. He was just one more anchor wound around Lane Moreau's ankle.

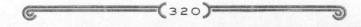

She feels guilty.

Would that there was a better way to handle this.

But there damn sure wasn't.

The other girl—the Empyrean one with the scarred face, those scars glittering with gold—contacted her on her visidex. Said her name was Enyastasia Ormond, and she told Luna that a very important opportunity had presented itself. The girl said, *Things are shifting up here. A changing of the guard. But that means I need a changing of the guard down there, too. Maybe with new blood in control, we can end this struggle. We can stop it before others die.*

Luna asked what that meant—

It meant information. Anything she could tell Enyastasia about Lane, about Pegasus City, about his friends. The girl grew more and more frustrated until Luna mentioned the Harvest Home celebration.

That, the scarred girl said, was all she needed.

She said to prepare, because after Harvest Home, Luna would become mayor of Pegasus City. And then together they would end this struggle between the sky and the land below.

And now she stands on the wall of Pegasus City. Beneath her, the screams have died back. So, too, have the sounds of sonic weapons discharging.

This is my city now. She'll go down soon, clean up the mess, proclaim herself the interim mayor. Luna will do a good enough job of it that they'll look past her age or the fact she's just some girl, and they'll let her keep the position because they'll see that she'll do what has to be done to keep them strong. And no one will ever know she sided with the enemy once—just this once— to achieve that end. Because soon the two sides will talk. Soon they'll find common ground. The deaths will cease. The block-ade will break apart.

She'll be a hero.

Her and her new friend up there in the sky.

The deal now sealed.

Or so she believes.

The imaginary badge she's placed upon her chest does not last long in her mind. Because she looks up one last time at the moon—her namesake, really—and no longer finds it there. Nor does she find the stars that normally surround it—the glittering panoply gone dark.

Dark, because something drifts across the sky.

Dropping lower and lower.

A ship, she realizes.

Or is it? No ship is *that* big.

It occurs to her then—she's been betrayed. This isn't part of the plan.

She pivots to bolt and head back to the elevator—

The first sonic cannon fires into the wall. It tears through the cobbled-together barrier like a child's fist through a pile of blocks. Her legs bicycle, carrying her face-first into the elevator accordion, slicing open her brow. She grabs a hold of it as everything grumbles beneath her.

She thinks: *Is anyone manning our own defenses?*

Then the wall crumbles beneath her, and all goes dark for Luna Dorado.

31

THE WAKE

RIGO REMEMBERS THUNDER, lightning, and rain.

They're a distant memory. Artifacts from when he was a little kid, because of course it doesn't rain anymore. He hasn't seen the forked flash of lightning or heard the ground-grumbling boom of thunder since he was just a boy.

But he remembers being scared by the flash, bang, and clamor. Terrified, actually. It made him feel tiny and more vulnerable than he already was. The sky tumbling and drumming, the heavens opening up and pouring buckets of water—it felt like he had no control at all. Like he was exposed to the elements: a shivering little bird in a gale wind. His mother's soothing didn't help, because he wanted to scream at her: *It's you, too! You're just as small and tiny as I am! You can't make it stop!* And of course his father's only response was to scowl and grouch at him, call him names or, if he was really in the bottle, laugh at him until he cried.

It was Pop who eventually made him feel better by explaining what was actually going on: electricity built up, discharged from ground to heaven, the sonic wave of air like hands clapping in reverse. Still scary in its way—great bolts of lighting ripping the sky in half!—but no longer a terrifying mystery.

A few years later it wouldn't matter anyway. Because then the Empyrean announced that all that pesky rain wouldn't fall anymore. No more thunder, no more lightning. Hiram's Golden Prolific would drink its fill from the tables of water a hundred feet below it—hungry, searching roots cracking the earth like hands breaking bones, like tongues sucking out marrow. (Though how long the water there would last? Nobody knows.)

Now, he feels it all over again as the city shudders and booms, bombarded by sonic blasts from above—nobody knew what was coming for them, and when they finally saw the moon and stars blotted out, it was too late. Already most of the north wall is crumbled. The city's defenses—their own sonic cannons—have been taken out prematurely. All but one anyway, whose valiant attempts to take out the specter above their heads has been worthless, because it's too far away for their own cannons to make any difference. Which means the cannons the Empyrean are using must be something new.

Another boom and crackle.

He wants to stop what he's doing, curl up, and cry.

But he can't. Because right now, he's the *only* one keeping it together.

It took all night for everyone in the group to finally find one another, thanks mostly to Balastair, who used everyone's visidexes to coordinate. Now, they all sit huddled in the charred remains of the Engine Layer. Wanda said it was pretty well protected, and she wasn't wrong. Hard steel encases them. A building already half collapsed sits on top of them. The sonic blasts can't get here.

Yet.

Rigo takes stock: Cael, Wanda, Boyland, Balastair, Gwennie— and her mother, and the two kids, Squirrel and Scooter. Then a half dozen other Heartlanders picked up amid the chaos and the crumble.

And Lane.

There—Lane's body under a raggedy quilt. Too tall to fit, so from the one end emerge his boots. And from the other, a wisp of his dark hair.

Rigo quakes. *My friend is gone, my friend is gone, my friend is gone. . . .*

He has to bite into the meaty pad of his thumb and palm to keep from crying. *Not now,* he tells himself. *Later.*

What *is* happening now is that Rigo has a map of the city sprawled out in front of him. It's a work in progress, because Pegasus City was itself a work in progress. All hand-drawn, with lots of scribbles and question marks added by himself and others: initially part of an effort to get organized.

Now part of an effort to get the hell out of here.

"These cuts are deep," Gwennie says. She cinches the last bit of cloth around Boyland's other arm and tucks it underneath the wrapping. He's not soaking them with blood anymore, so that's good, though pink lines already crisscross the wrappings, one line to match each wound.

For a while, Boyland just wept, rocking back and forth like a baby.

Now, he's quiet, his face the color of concrete dust. "Am I gonna die?"

She offers a small smile. "Not today, I don't think."

"Glad you found your mama," he says. He looks across the way, where Gwennie's mother lies sleeping, Squirrel and Scooter lying on each side of her, using bundles of rags and dirty blankets as bedding.

"Me, too." *Maybe you can start treating her right*, Gwennie thinks.

"Cael okay? He and Moreau were close."

"I don't think any of us are okay."

"I love you," he says.

"Boyland, I don't know—"

"No, nah, wait, hear me out. We might not survive till morning, and if that's the case I'd rather just say what I wanna say before it's too late. I know I screwed things up for us. I'm not a big thinker. I don't see ten miles down the road like some of these other guys. I'm clumsy and selfish and, ahhh, at this point—" He clears his throat, swallows hard. "It's pretty clear I got a drinking problem. I don't know that I'm ever gonna be a *good man*. But I know that for you I'd give it my all. Maybe I'd never be good. But maybe I could be better."

Her face warms. A bloom rises to her cheeks. "I know, Boyland. But right now I don't think we should be thinking about—"

"I said hold on. Hear me out. I want to be with you. But I don't want you to be with me."

"What?"

"I don't want you to be with me or with anybody. Not now. You're smarter and stronger than most of these boys who fawn over you. That's why they—uh, *we*—do that. You ain't like a lot of the other girls. You pop like a firecracker. You're strong like an iron bar. You've always done your own thing, and being with me—being with anybody—will take that away from you. Nobody should take anything away from you. Least of all me."

She leans in, kisses him on the forehead.

"Thanks, Boyland, that's . . ."

His eyes go unfocused. And stare off at a middle distance.

"Oh, gods," she says, a sob struggling in her chest to be free. "No, no, no, you buckethead, you can't "

He jostles back to awareness with a snort. "Huh? What?"

"Jeezum Crow," she hisses, and swats him on the knee. "I thought you were dead, godsdamnit."

"Oh. No. Just resting."

She almost laughs, then slides up next to him. "Asshole."

He shrugs as if to say, *It is what it is.*

Cael, with a gentle hand, lifts Wanda's chin. "You gonna tell me what this is about?" He runs a finger across what looks to be a scar—it's pink along the margins. Skin, except in the middle, where it's like a braid of tiny roots and shoots.

"One of those . . . *girls* slit my throat."

"Ho-holy heck." He feels suddenly dizzy. "Wanda, whaddya mean?"

She lifts her eyebrows like, *Hey, no big thing*, even though this sounds like it's the biggest damn thing Cael ever heard. "She cut my throat and almost popped my head like a bottle-top. It's okay."

"It is *not* okay. Are you all right? Is the baby—?"

Again she grabs his hand, presses it against her belly. His awareness of the child flares inside his mind. Her little hands searching, big eyes staring. An umbilical cord like ivy—a tether gently turning and twisting.

"You can always touch me to see her," Wanda says.

"I didn't want to presume. Your body isn't my property."

"Your property? Naw. But I'm a part of you and you're a part of me now." She lifts her chin. "Literally. You have permission. She's yours. You wanna check on her, just reach over and check on her. Stop acting like she ain't yours—because she is. Before, us being Obligated was maybe a little bit of a fantasy, at least for me. But our little girl changes that. This is for real now."

He nods. "I know."

"I don't know if you really love me. And if you do, I suspect you'll never love me the same way you love her." *Her.* Gwennie. "But we're in this together no matter how it shakes out. You hurt me, I might be able to get over that. You hurt our little girl, and I'll bury you so deep even the corn won't be able to find you. We square?"

"We're square. Also, you're scary."

Her face softens. She looks suddenly sad. "I know. I don't mean to be."

"I know."

"I'm changing."

"I know that, too." *It isn't just the baby.* Hell, she's seemed more human since she told him about their daughter. "You can do things I can't."

"I'm sorry about Lane."

Just a mention of his name sends something wriggling up from inside his chest, and suddenly his bottom lip is shaking, and he has to bite it all back. Eyes shut tight, fingernails digging into the flesh of his palms. "Thanks."

He pulls her hand up and kisses it.

She rests her head on his shoulder.

Boom. The Engine Layer shakes. Dust and ash drift down. Balastair moves along the line of survivors, offering them water and what little food Wanda already had squirreled away here—a few apples, some pro-bars, a bag of spelt crackers. He can't help but turn and look at the corpse underneath the quilt. Balastair did not know Lane Moreau very well, but death is death and Lane seemed like a good fellow, and he can't help but feel dragged down by all of it.

Forward, he tells himself. *There's work to be done, Bal.*

He stoops down by Cael and Wanda. "They're blocking the visidex signal, but I was able to get an encrypted message to your sister."

Cael nods. "She okay?"

"Sadly, it was not a two-way transmission. Just a single communiqué. Otherwise, I fear the Empyrean would've intercepted."

Cael nods.

Balastair offers them an apple. "Only two left."

"I can grow more," Wanda says.

"Oh." *Oh.*

He suddenly feels strange. Like how he did sometimes when he was speaking to his mother. His mother would wear a warm smile but seemed otherwise alien. He used to joke that he thought she might be a spider in human skin, but that's not really what it was. She had been losing her humanity for some time and was less a spider and more the human embodiment of a Venus flytrap—a carnivorous plant with a human mind. Or a human with the mind of a carnivorous plant? Did it even matter?

"Thanks, Bal," Cael says.

All Balastair can do is nod as he moves on, zigzagging among the survivors. Until he gets to Gwennie and Boyland.

He tries not to show what he feels for her. There's no point in it. Not now. Perhaps not ever. But even in trying to conceal it he can feel the awkwardness, the stiffness, and when he speaks he stammers:

"I, ahh. I've got apple—I've got *another* apple, one more, umm."

He holds up the apple and shakes it.

Gwennie takes it. "Thanks, Bal."

"Of course."

She takes his hand. "I'm glad you're okay."

"Yes." He offers a stiff nod. "I'm glad the, ahh, the both of you are okay, too." He pulls his hand away gently—though maybe not gently enough, given the way she flinches a little. Then it's on to Rigo.

The poor lad is hunched over, a temporary light hanging above his head. A trembling finger scans a hastily scrawled blueprint of the city.

He doesn't look up as Balastair approaches, but he speaks:

"You get in touch with the Ilmatar?"

"No—but I did talk to some of my people on the Mader-Atcha. They were able to protect the transmission from their end." He hesitates. "I think."

"You think?"

"Well, none of this is very *certain* is it? It's like playing Checks in the dark." He hears the irritation rusting the edge of every word, and he tries to scrape some of it off and soften his tone. "This is all quite up in the air, but I think the transmission went undiscovered. My people can meet us on the Ilmatar in a day. If we make it. Can we make it?"

Rigo puffs out his cheeks in an uncertain sigh. He's about to say something when his eyes flit to the other end of the room. Before Balastair can even turn, he hears a mournful wail rise up.

It's Killian Kelly. He takes hesitant steps toward the body of Lane Moreau.

The distant booming rocks the room.

Killian pulls his hair back and loops it with a ragged strip of cloth. His face is dusted with ash, the ash streaked with tears.

The raider is like a man with a noose around his neck suddenly kicking the chair out from beneath him. Killian drops to his knees hard, hard enough so that the whole room shudders when he falls. He buries his face in his hands and keens like a river banshee.

Grief, Balastair notes, is a curious thing. It can be uncomfortable to witness when it's grief you don't share—it's awkward and strange, and it's easy enough to pretend that the grief is inappropriate, or odd, or ill-fitting. That's how the Empyrean tend to treat it—it's something you do in private, behind closed doors. But it's not like that here. Here, the grief is shared. Parceled out among them. These people have seen enough of it to know. They all understand.

And he watches these Heartlanders gather themselves together. They go to Killian—a man who's been chewed up by an old injury, who ran himself through a gauntlet of addiction (and may still be running that gauntlet even now)—and they gather around him and around Lane. They murmur words that Balastair cannot hear, but he hears the tone: sad, consoling, with a few hard spikes of anger punched through it all like bent nails. Cael hovers back with eyes of steel. Wanda doesn't watch the raider captain or the corpse, but instead watches Cael.

"You should go over there," Balastair says to Rigo.

Rigo looks up. "Not now."

"Your friends—"

"Need to get out of here alive."

A bit of steel in the boy's voice. Balastair warms to that. He has trouble finding his own spine sometimes, and it's nice to see others go through that struggle and come out tougher. "Fair enough."

"Tell me," Rigo says. "Why don't we have your people just go to the Ilmatar and find the weapon?"

"Because I can't trust them. I can't trust anybody who's not here in *this* room *right* now. I've no idea what weapon my mother has waiting. I can't put it in the hands of someone else. It's ours or it's nobody's."

"So, we not only need to get out of here, we need to get to the Ilmatar."

He sighs. "That is woefully accurate."

"Then the plan is still the plan. Just . . . harder." Rigo frowns so that the skin of his brow furrows like a freshly plowed field. "We still need to get to the trawler. No idea how safe the raider fleet is in the hangars. No idea who will even . . . captain the damn thing. But we send that out, draw their attention, pray to all the gods in the sky and the corn and the dirt that, oh, hey, the giant Doom Flotilla above our heads can't get a shot in, and soon as we have an opening we . . . sneak away. Except I don't like that part. *Sneak away.* Too vague. Still missing something." Rigo *hrrms.*

Balastair's about to say something, but whatever it is ends up lost to the Grade A freak-out across the room. Suddenly, Killian is storming madly about, bellowing: "I'm going to go out and find her, and I'm going to kill the little Empyrean slag for robbing me of him. And then—*and then!*—I'll man that one last cannon, and I swear on the grave of every Sleeping Dog that I'll shoot that flotilla down my own damn self—"

It's Rigo who cuts him short. "Wait!" he says, standing up.

Killian narrows his gaze. "What do *you* want?"

"You want to pay them back?"

"I very clearly do, boy."

"Then help us get out of here." That's when Rigo tells Killian—and the rest of them—the plan.

Upon hearing it, Killian smiles grimly. Through teeth clenched so tight it looks like they might ground down to powder, he growls:

"Then let's give my man one *helluva* fucking funeral."

A GARLAND OF LAURELS

ENYASTASIA WITNESSES the city that bears her name get pounded to rubble. Above, the Herfjotur brings screaming hell down upon the city—great night-shrieks that split the sky and hit the Saranyu like invisible boulders dropped by a callow, callous god.

She watches the destruction unfold while nestled into a half-collapsed nook above what was once the Halcyon Balcony. The Dirae knows that at any moment, one of the Herfjotur's cannons could point this way and end her existence—a blast of that size would vibrate her to scattered molecules. She would be reduced to a red mist.

It's not suicide, she tells herself. *Not if they do the job for me.*

Part of her is sad that the city will suffer this fate. Another part of her is glad. This, a child's reaction: *If I can't have my toys, neither can they!*

Between bombardments, she hears people: the citizens of

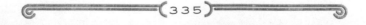

Pegasus City—some screaming, others crying. At one point she hears a man laughing: a mad, unhinged sound, as if this boisterous cackle is all he has left in the world.

Her ankle aches. And still bleeds.

Her head feels like she was born through a womb of glass.

At some point, she sleeps.

Her dreams are a dead place.

Then: a sharp intake of breath. Light shining on her closed eyes.

Morning.

She awakens. Drops down out of the nook onto the remnant of the balcony. Enyastasia looks up—the Herfjotur can now be plainly seen, flying lower than any other flotilla would. Shaped as a series of smaller octagons surrounding a larger one—each chained together, each a semi-independent battle station all its own. Should it be attacked or fail to hold together, its pieces can break apart and remain buoyant—mini flotillas, each with its own measure of firepower. A genius design. Her old friend Heron Yong did well.

She salutes him with no small measure of irony and disgust.

Nobody up above is going to want to deal with her anymore. She can already envision what happens next:

The sonic shelling is stopping, and the blockade will close in. The noose tightening around the neck. Until this nest of Heartlanders digs out of its hole and is killed in the unforgiving daylight. And then?

They'll come for her. They'll carry her back into the sky. And they will retire her. With a garland of laurels about her head, of course, because this was still all her idea (and because she executed those who might say otherwise). She remains an Ormond and will receive preferential treatment. They'll give her whatever she wants, and over time, people like Miranda Woodwick will distance themselves from her, and as the Heartland rebels are crushed and turned to metal men and as the flotillas continue to fly, she will feel more and more like she's in prison. And she will forever be haunted by her failure.

But it is then that she is afforded a new opportunity.

Across the field of rubble, one particular pile of crumbled stone and glittering glass shudders, a warbling screech buried behind it. Then it happens again, and again, until the pile blasts forth—bricks bouncing, glass clattering down in a shimmering sun-captured rain.

From the hole, the Sleeping Dogs fleet emerges from its hangar.

Two vessels, then four, then another four beyond that, until finally the big beast lurches free from its prison (losing the very top of its mast in the process given its reduced clearance): the massive trawler.

The ships power up, unfurl their red sails, and catch wind.

Heading toward one of the many breaches in the wall.

She grunts.

I can still complete my mission, she thinks.

She can still kill those she came to kill.

And with that in mind, she drags her numb, ruined foot behind her. The hunt will commence. It may kill her, this crusade.

It's a thought she finds eerily comforting.

ONE HELLUVA
FUCKING FUNERAL

KILLIAN SPINS THE WHEEL, then straightens it back out again. The trawler drifts through the ruins of Pegasus City, out over the collapsed wall with the other ships pushing ahead. And then, like that, they're out above the endless corn once more, pushing on toward the red sun bulging up over the horizon like a blood blister about to pop—

And toward the encroaching Empyrean fleet.

"Well, well, well!" He claps his hands. "They've gathered a rather robust welcoming party for us," he says to Lane. Lane, swaddled behind him in the crimson red of a Sleeping Dogs flag.

Lane, who gave his life for this life.

Lane, Killian's love.

Lane, who Killian failed. Again and again. "I always thought I was above reproach," Killian said. "It was me or the door, and even when I wasn't captain anymore I was still captain, and I knew I could get away with anything—"

The raptor-shriek warble fills the air—

Choom!

A sonic blast hits just behind the trawler, sending up a column of dirt, dust, and broken corn. The trawler rocks, but keeps on keeping on.

Killian war-whoops—a sound far angrier than triumphant. He pounds the wheel with the flat of his hand. "Stupid sky-bastards. Those cannons are slower than a salted slug—won't be able to hit us, I'm afraid, my love."

Another screaming wail in the air. Another blast hits—this one far ahead. Killian tells himself they won't calibrate a shot until it's too late. He wonders if that's a lie to make himself feel better, or an accurate assessment.

He wonders if it even matters.

The Empyrean fleet closes in. The noose is tightening as the blockade shrinks inward. Which means its ships are coming from every direction that he can see, except behind him—and even then, they're coming from the other side, too, ready to swoop in and take the city. Including whoever is left alive inside the walls of the fallen flotilla.

Chrome glinting in the morning sun. Ships above the corn. Some flying high, too—skiffs, yachts, ships not meant to do combat like those of the raiders—but beneath them, he knows that the mechanicals march forward, too. Metal monstrosities. Tinbodies with people shoved inside.

His side aches when he thinks about them.

"Ah, piss on it," he growls. "Lane, I love you. And I failed you. But I'll do my best to right things. And I suspect I'll join you soon."

He lifts his boot, stomps hard on the floor underneath him. That's the signal.

Whomp whomp whomp.

Above their heads, three stomps.

Cicero the catbird trills a nervous song.

Balastair shushes the bird.

"That's our signal," Cael says, rifle slung over his shoulder. The vine around his arm trembles, burning like someone's pressing a lit match to it as new tendrils push slowly up from the cut end. He can't rely on his vine to save him, not out here.

He and Wanda share a look, then reach down and lift the hatch on the floor. A breeze kicks in through the opened space. Corn-tops pass beneath them, firework tassels waving—as if they smell blood. And maybe they do.

Gwennie looks to her mother. "I've got them." She holds up both arms—she's got a grip on Scooter's and Squirrel's hands. Then she looks to each of them: "We ready to do this?"

Scooter nods, afraid.

Squirrel's eyes are shiny and alive.

Boyland, grim-faced, pale as a grub's belly, steps up to Cael, then offers a hand. "I got your back if you got mine."

"That's a deal." He shakes Boyland's hand.

"Time is wasting," Wanda says. "We gotta move."

"She's right," Rigo says, hobbling toward the opening. "Now or never."

And then, one by one, they drop out into the hungry corn.

It is in this moment that Wanda is reminded that she is a changed girl.

Once, and not very long ago, she was the flinchiest little thing. High-strung as a housefly—quick to wince, tense up; desperate to be liked; fearful of the world around her. Uncertain of her place in all of it.

What happens now, what unfolds around her and above her . . . it *should* unsettle her. The sounds of sonic cannons going off. The roar of the trawler's engines kicking up. The thrum of dozens of hover-panels vibrating the ground so hard her teeth rattle. The clanking and stomping of mechanicals.

But it doesn't.

All the people that she knew from Boxelder, they lie flat against the ground like scared children. Rigo presses his head into the dirt, hands clamped over his ears. Scooter tries not to cry, and Gwennie rolls onto her side, tucking the boy into her chest so that any sounds he does make are muffled (lest the mechanicals sense them and come to find them). Her mother, meanwhile, just weeps, the heels of her hands against her eyes as if that'll make it all go away.

Boyland looks lost. Like he's overwhelmed—a motorvator whose circuits have fried and now just sits in one space, engine revving but never going anywhere.

Balastair focuses on the bird, the tiny creature cupped in one hand, his face a mask of heartbreak as he pets the bird's head, cooing and whispering even though the sounds of the battle just beyond them drown it out.

Even Cael, poor Cael. Rifle held to the dirt, his forehead pressed against the wood of the stock, his back rising and falling with measured breaths.

The only one with Wanda's unswerving fortitude is the little girl, Squirrel. Squirrel is as her name suggests—she holds still and steady, but everything about her is coiled like a spring. Like she's about to leap into the fray at any moment. The girl is plainly mad. Broken at a fundamental level. The fact that Wanda relates most of all to this girl now says something about her, too.

I am not Wanda anymore.

The sounds going on all around her are a fascinating mystery. She finds herself listening, not just with her own ears, but through the vibrations reaching each stalk of corn. Here an unfinished joke crosses her mind, something about how corn has ears; she laughs a little, and Cael looks at her with a concerned stare as if to ask, *How could you find any of this funny?* and she wants to ask him in turn: *Don't you find it funny?* But of course he doesn't.

She closes her eyes and becomes one with the corn.

Some of it trampled under metal feet.

Some of it darkened by the shadow of the trawler, or the other raider ships, or the Empyrean ketch-boats.

Some of it searching, whirling, knowing there's blood in the air somewhere and desperate for a taste. (Wanda feels desperate for a taste, then, too—an ache on the back of her tongue where she wants blood to slide down the back of her throat.)

The raider ships aren't moving forward, she realizes, suddenly.

And they need to move forward if this is going to work. The line of Empyrean ships needs to be broken.

Her eyes jolt open.

Wanda reaches out and grabs Cael's hand.

He mouths the word: *What?*

She doesn't need to answer out loud. She knows that now. Instead, she lets the thought move through her—like a baby rabbit down a snake's mouth, like blood through an artery: *We need to help them.*

His eyes go wide. His mouth opens just slightly.

Message received.

The thought comes back to her like a boomerang:

Okay. Let's help them.

His eyes roll back in his head.

So do hers.

Killian roars. He spins the sonic cannon toward the ketch-boat coming up on the starboard side and lets fly with a screeching blast that knocks it off-kilter, punching a hole clean through its side. Then he rolls out of the seat, ducking a hail of blasts from within the corn somewhere—he has to get to the next cannon while this one recharges. He's a one-man war machine—he and the old blast-pocked trawler—and he cackles, half dizzy, body no longer hungry for the Pheen he's been sticking down his throat, but ravenous for retribution and violence.

But a little part of him knows this battle is lost.

The trawler is jammed up. The line of Empyrean just ahead is unyielding. He can't press on—can't push forward. And the others in the raider fleet are already dropping like flies. Even now he peers over the trawler's railing and watches a trio of mechanicals leap forward like metal rabbits and land atop the bow of a skiff—the skiff's nose dips into the corn, and the one poor raider captaining that boat (a young woman, Sally Forthright) screams as they drag her into the corn. The boat drops with her.

Killian bolts for the next cannon—

And a mechanical clambers up onto the deck right in front of him.

The raider captain skids to a halt.

"Out of my way, you soulless tinbody," he snarls.

The thing stomps a hard foot forward, aims its cannon-arm, and fires. Killian leaps out of the way of the blast—it shrieks past him, and something in his side stitches tight. Haunting pain from the ghost of his old injury (ironically, from the *last* time he tangled with one of these horrible things, he realizes). He hits hard on his shoulder, his head *gonging* against the deck of the trawler. He scrambles to stand as the thing pivots at its hip and points its arm once more, the cannon's tip wheeling on him—

There's a moment—a precious, strange, distant moment—when he feels Lane's fingers in his hair like a comb. Hands untying the cloth binding his hair in the warrior's knot. Tossing it aside. Breath on the back of his neck. Hand flat against his chest. Lane's whisper in his ear: *Come home, now.* Killian feels loved in this last moment. It washes over him like the warmth of the day's sun.

And then the mechanical's head jerks sharply right as a cornstalk spear pierces it. *Ka-chang!* Sparks fly. The sonic cannon never fires.

The metal man tumbles off the side of the boat.

"Crowsblood," Killian says. In awe of what just happened, but also with grief over what *didn't* happen: He failed to die and did not meet his love anew. Odd, that—to be disappointed in the lack of one's death.

But he has little time to consider it.

He hears the sound before he sees what's making it.

A ripping. Snapping. Breaking like bones.

Out there, in the corn.

Pollen begins to stream up and into the air, a haze of gold dust. Everything gone bright, so bright that he can barely see the shape that rises up out over the corn—a twisting, living thing. Like a lightning bolt that never flashes back to nonexistence—like a tree (*Remember those?* he thinks) that's shot up out of nothing and is thrashing its way through the stalks.

Then he realizes: It's not crashing through the stalks.

It *is* the stalks.

The corn is whipping about and joining a twister—a narrow tornado—made of more corn. Stalks upon stalks, corkscrewing together into a whirling, hungry thing—he watches it slam into a ketch-boat, splitting it in half before the sudden piss-blizzard swallows it all up.

He doesn't know how they're doing it, but they're doing it.

They're opening the door for him.

Which in turn opens the door for *them.*

Killian yelps, then hurries back to the wheel. He drops to

one knee, kisses the forehead of Lane Moreau through the drapery of the red flag, then swings himself back up to the wheel of the trawler. Hell with pain. Piss on what's lost. *It's time to get something back.*

The great beast, the Sleeping Dogs' trawler, pushes on through the hole—a hole in the blockade smashed open by the whirling twister given life by Cael and Wanda. *Wanda, mostly,* Cael thinks.

They hear Killian hooting, shouting, cursing.

And then the trawler charges forward. Three other Sleeping Dogs ships make it through, too, slipping through the opening.

It works. The Empyrean line breaks. The ships follow after while the rest move on to Pegasus City to pillage and plunder its bones.

"It's time," Cael whispers.

One by one, they get up and push on through the stalks.

PRESSMAN

"LAST I SAW YOUR FATHER," the old raider Pressman says, "he had just seen a rather peculiar video of you and your girl over there tearing the Empyrean a new hole. Seems he thought you were dead."

Cael nods. "I was awful close to it, sir."

"You don't need to call me sir, Cael. Pressman'll do."

The two of them sit together on the ruined, ransacked front porch of Pressman's house. The windows are broken. The front door, too. Inside, it's an even worse mess. "Sorry about your house."

"Empyrean want what they want. Least we were able to hide in the cellar when they came through. Most homes don't have cellars, and ours is hidden well enough." He sighs. "Thanks to your people for helping us put it back together again." Inside, the others help Pressman's wife, Kallen, straighten up. "How'd you find me out here?"

"Tracked Pop's movements through my sister. She knew he was coming here, so."

"I'll be sure to contact your sister. Let her know where you are and tell her as much as I can about what's happening." The old raider runs his hand over his scalp, sucks air through his teeth. "These are curious times. You really gonna go up on one of them flotillas?"

"We're damn sure gonna try. Ride should be here soon." Balastair secured them a skiff to the Ilmatar. Friend of his— some bartender named Kin Sage, survivor of the Saranyu; he got off the flotilla before it fell.

"I'd say that's it there." Pressman lifts his chin as a gesture. In the distance, a glinting shape.

"I suppose it is. Thanks for taking care of Gwennie's mother and the two kids. This ain't your obligation. We'll make sure you're square somehow."

"Boy, these days we all gotta be obligated to one another. If we can't do that, then we deserve to be turned into metal. Least then we'd work together."

He laughs, but Cael can't quite share in it.

"Thanks."

"You scared, Cael?"

"I am. But any fear I got going on is nothing compared to my desire to just see all this done and over with."

"I hear that, boy, I hear that."

Pressman and Cael hug. The man's rust-barrel arms hold him tight, and when he lets Cael go he claps the teen on the shoulders with big hands.

Cael sighs, nods.

Then he calls to the others: "Incoming. Time to catch that ride, y'all."

The Maize Witch watches. The corn truly has ears—and eyes, and all the senses and then some. With them she can feel Cael and Wanda and the others leave the small house in the middle of the swaying, shuddering Golden Prolific. Everything is in motion now. Which means she needs to get moving, too. And here her mind wanders not to the present or even to the past, but to a vision of an eventual future: Hiram's Golden Prolific, razed to the hard dirt. Little teeth and tiny legs. A squirming carpet of gleaming blue jewels. Her precious Blightborn finally having their day, finally claiming a place at the table. Thanks in part to her son and the genius—and rebellion—he manifested at such an early age. She quietly thanks Balastair, her dear child, and then she tells the others it's time to go. Mole asks if he can come, too, and she says: "Of course you can, my boy. What harm could it do?"

PART FOUR

THE HARROWING

THE ILMATAR

"COME," KIN TELLS THEM, waving his hands impatiently. "Come!"

The six of them bolt across the street, under the violet eventide sky.

Cael thinks: *We don't have doors like that down below.*

Then he thinks: *We don't have* anything *like this down below.*

Even poking through the wreckage of the Saranyu—or flying through it oh-so-briefly before the whole thing collapsed in the first damn place—he never really got the scope of it. The way the flotillas are layered upon one another. How they're not one whole city but rather several buildings and neighborhoods chained together and made buoyant.

Everything is lush. And *crafted*—none of it seems wild, nothing haphazard. All of it designed: the placement of every brick, of every flowering tree, of each softly glowing bulb. Statues at every intersection—many of some wispy, naked woman, her

hair blowing as if in a wind, her belly round like she's about to pop. "That's Ilmatar," Balastair said when they passed the first, obviously noting Cael's goggled eyes. "The mistress of the air, a virgin impregnated by the wind that blew up from the cold Atlas Ocean."

"You people are crazy as an outhouse cat," Cael said to him.

Balastair just shrugged and offered a sad smile before moving on.

They pass down narrow alleys. They cross over and underneath long bridges that look like mirrored scales, like each bridge is a snake dissected and stretched, its skin and bones forming a beautiful—if absurd—way to bridge the sky. While crossing, Cael feels his breath get trapped in his lungs—Gwennie tells him not to look down, but anything you tell him not to do, well, it's a good bet he's gonna do it. And sure enough, he does: He looks down long enough to see all the way through the Engine Layer to the green corn far, far below—corn lit by the setting sun, green leaves on fire—and for a moment, he almost can't move because he feels like he's falling all over again. Falling through clouds toward the endless waves of Hiram's Golden Prolific. All parts of him screaming in panic.

But then Gwennie touches his arm and says: "It scared the hell out of me, too, being up here. But we gotta keep moving."

That earns her a side-eyed stare from Wanda, but Cael gives a gentle shake of his head as if to say, *Don't worry about it.*

They keep moving.

And now, here they are.

Kin says: "This is it. The House of the Sky."

Ahead: a doorway framed with decorative flames cut from

hammered, etched copper—the door itself is round, and the flames around it make it feel as if they're entering into the eye of the sun itself.

They hurry through the door into a firelit room—the room shaped like the round bell of a clay oven. Pillows lining the edges of the room. Wooden birds—some small, some large, all of them almost skeletal in their construction—hanging from red threads above them. Gently swaying with the motions of the flotilla beneath them. Cael feels another bout of vertigo.

Balastair steps forward and greets a small woman, her skin the color of long-steeped tea. Her arms are inked with what look like words. Like passages from a book. Her purple dress—if it can be called that, Cael's never seen anything like it—is bound up with a sash the color of fire.

"I know you," Balastair says.

"Our meeting last time was informal," she says. "I'm Amrita."

He bows his head to her, and she kisses his forehead. Then he returns the kiss, too—Cael and the others watch this ritual unfold.

"The hell is this place?" Boyland asks.

"My friend's rudeness aside," Cael says, "I'm wondering the same."

Kin Sage—a small man with almond eyes and dark hair bound up in a fountaining topknot—says: "This is the House of the Sky. A temple devoted to the worship of the old gods."

The woman clucks her tongue. "Not precisely. Some of the old gods are gods of the hearth, the ground, the sea. We remain focused on those of the sky, the sun, the moon, the stars. Saranyu. Ilmatar. Oshadagea. Mader-Atcha. A pantheon of goddesses to which we are the priests and priestesses." She smiles. "Though your visit today is hardly spiritual, I recognize."

Rigo steps forward, gawping. "I'd like to hear more."

"Rigo," Cael mutters, "she's pretty, but now ain't a good time."

The boy nods, utters a nervous *hehehe*, and steps back.

"Something I need to know first," Balastair says. "Are you working for my mother? That question goes to you, too, Kin."

Cicero the catbird chimes in with what sounds like an accusing chirp.

Kin and the woman, Amrita, share a look.

"I'm not," Kin says. "Never did."

Amrita smiles, clasps her hands together as if in prayer. "I do her work sometimes. As I did when I visited you in the birdcage that night." She bows. "Your mother and I have different devotions, but our aims sometimes overlap."

Kin says to Balastair: "Why do you ask?"

"Because this is about her. She wants us to get something. But I don't know what it is, and she wasn't particularly eager to give up the ghost on it, either. We're grasping at straws, so we'll take whatever we can get. Things have gone completely off-kilter in the Heartland."

"It's chaos," Wanda says suddenly.

Everyone nods.

"Things have gone strange up here, too," Amrita says. "We are no longer allowed to be who we have always been. Many of the Grand Architects are dead. The flotillas are no longer guaranteed the autonomy they once were. We have been told that because we share the same sky, and because we share the same resource—the fuel to keep us aloft—then we must share the same ideals, habits, securities, rituals. Our freedom is being locked down."

"Piss on your freedom," Boyland erupts. "You all don't know a hard shit-squat what it means to have your *freedom* locked down."

Cael shoots him a look, but it's Gwennie who steps in. She puts a hand on his chest and says firmly, but kindly: "Not. Now."

Boyland growls, but he shuts up.

"No, the young man is right," Amrita says. "We don't know. This is only a taste of what the Heartlanders have been experiencing for a very long time, and you'll find that we are increasingly sympathetic to this. The winds of change are blowing here, two opposing gales—and it remains to be seen which is strongest. But even as the Dirae locks us down and demands further control, the people of the flotillas struggle against it, just as they have struggled against the Initiative and the Education Reassessment and the Lottery and the Obligations and all the other rituals that have been forced upon you."

Wanda's hand finds Cael's and squeezes. A gesture of love? A reminder that the two of them are Obligated?

"Who is this Dirae?" Balastair asks.

"The granddaughter of Stirling Ormond," Kin says.

Balastair looks taken aback. "Her? How is that possible?" He sees the bewildered looks of the others and says: "She was something of a scandal. Not . . . her, specifically, but what was done to her. Her father was an abuser. Kept the girl locked up in a box. They took her away. They said rehabilitation, but I always assumed she was locked up in some . . . floating asylum somewhere."

"She was," Amrita says. "At least, as I understand it. But there she made friends with other girls. She rehabilitated herself. Physically, at least. Emotionally, perhaps not so well. Later, she founded a small guild of girls—a cult, some would say—made up in part of children orphaned by those who died on the Saranyu. Orphans of the fallen city. She cut up her face and cut up theirs and . . ."

The woman keeps talking, but Cael feels the world dip and shift beneath him. Once more, that sense of vertigo, but this isn't physical—this is the vertigo of memory, the rushing sensation of standing at the apex of revelation, staring down into a dark pit of truth.

"I think one of those girls killed Lane," Cael says.

Balastair gasps and nods. "We were attacked by girls with scarred faces. . . ."

"The Harpies," Kin says.

Amrita leans forward. "Was she there? Enyastasia Ormond?"

Everyone looks at one another and shrugs.

Amrita clarifies: "You'd know her. Her face is scarred, too. Scars she's painted with . . . ahhh. Gold dust, I think."

Another wave of vertigo. Cael nods, mouth suddenly dry. "That was her. She's the one who came for Lane, then me." He lets out the breath he didn't realize he'd been holding. "Lane got her good, though. Broke a bottle over her head. Cut up her leg or foot. That's how we got away. Lane saved my life."

Kin and Amrita come together. "Maybe she's dead," Kin says.

"Even if she's not, she's hobbled. Literally and figuratively," Amrita says.

"The Herfjotur still exists—"

"But it can't attack *us*. Now's the time, Kin."

Balastair waggles his fingers. "Uh, hello? Time for what?"

"For revolution, of course." The way Amrita says it, it sounds to Cael like, *Uh, duh?* Kin nods and plants both hands on Balastair's arms, then says:

"The winds are shifting. We need to retake the skies—"

"Who cares?" Wanda blurts out. She squeezes her fists, and her arms ripple—the flesh suddenly studded with thorns. Her eyes are swallowed by a shimmering wave of green, and then a foul perfume rises up around her—an acrid, corpse-flower stink. "*Your* revolution. That's *cute*."

Cael sees her—thinks her look is beautiful, though the odor is foul. He doesn't know whether to bow before her or recoil in fear. He recalls a similar reaction when he saw the Maize Witch do her thing, too. Still. He wets his lips, nods for now. "She's right. Your problems ain't a damn thing to us. We've been fighting *our* revolution for a long time. Lane understood that. Took me a while to come around to it, but I did, and here we all are. You want to revolt inside your pretty houses and your robotic elevators, then you do that. But before you do, get us where we need to go."

Amrita takes a long breath, is about to say something when—

Wham wham wham.

A fist on the door.

A muffled command: "Open up. By order of the peregrine, Lirong Yau. Open up!" *Wham wham wham.*

"The Frumentarii," Kin says.

Balastair makes a frightened sound in the back of his throat.

"We can sneak you out the back," Amrita says, waving them on.

But then Wanda marches over to the door.

Cael hisses to her: "Wanda, wait—"

She flings open the door.

A squat man and a tall woman stand there, both clad in dark leathers—the man with a sparking baton, the woman looking down at a visidex.

The woman, lean and lithe with high-shelf cheekbones and purple eyes, is muttering: "No cameras in this area, but the Goddessheads have harbored refugees in the past—"

She looks up and gasps when the man's neck snaps.

From each of Wanda's fingers grows a cirrus of dark green—five strangling appendages, like tentacles searching the air. They slide silently away from the man's head and neck. The woman's about to cry out—but she never manages the sound. The finger-tendrils grab the visidex she's holding and smash the screen hard against her face. Blood squirts. The woman falls back.

Wanda never moved anything but her right hand.

Cael gently steps in, eases her back. Her eyes are a turbulent storm of colors—the green of leaves, the red of rose-bloom, the black of rot, the amber of sap—all swirling there. Hypnotic, almost. He wants to be lost in them. But when Cael holds her face between his hands and kisses her cheek, the eyes clear. Human once more.

"Now they'll know we're here," Amrita says.

Wanda wheels on her. "I don't care. Let them know. I will tear this place apart at the seams and fling each piece to the dirt if you don't give us what we came to get. Unless you don't have it?" She extends her right hand—the vines squirm and twist in the air like snakes.

"Wanda—" Cael cautions.

"No," Gwennie says, to Cael's surprise. "Let her. I'm tired of waiting, too. And don't mourn those corpses." She gestures toward the bodies as Kin and Balastair drag them through the door. "I don't know who this peregrine is, but the last one was a monster." To Amrita: "Give us what we want. Or we'll let her go all . . . angry tree-girl on you."

Amrita nods stiffly, then reaches into the folds of her sari. She produces a clear glass key—long as her palm and toothy. "This is the key to the Palladium Tower. I had to spend a great deal of . . . capital to get this. I hope what you're looking for is worth it."

"I suppose we'll find out," Balastair says, reaching over and taking the key. "Thank you, Amrita."

"There's one more thing," she says.

"Amrita . . ." Kin warns.

Amrita then turns to Cael: "Your father is Arthur McAvoy?"

That name sends a sharp shock to his heart. "Wh-what? Yeah, why?"

"Your father is here. On the Ilmatar."

36

THE PALLADIUM

"I DON'T THINK they should've gone off on their own," Cael says.

Above them: a massive bleach-white tower that looks like a bone spur, jagged and curved—a crooked talon. Two statues frame a pair of golden doors—two winged women, each with one wing pointed to the ground and a second wing pointed over the door, meeting in the middle.

Boyland laughs: a bitter, dry sound. "You're just upset because your two girls are off by themselves saying who knows what about you."

It was Wanda's idea to go off and find his father. She had good reasons: he would be well guarded, and if anyone was prepared to deal with that kind of threat, it was her. It was a thought that both disturbed him and filled him with pride in equal measure: this girl, once gawky and awkward and uncertain about every breath she took, is now a confident killing machine.

He told her no way, no how, that wasn't gonna work for him. Gwennie stepped in and said she'd go, too. That she'd keep Wanda safe. Wanda bristled at that, of course, said, "I'll be the one keeping *you* safe," but she consented just the same. Cael gave Gwennie his rifle. Said to give that to Pop—and, if she needed it, to use it. After getting directions from Amrita—the birdcage cells were nearby, just one bridge over—the two girls went off.

Rigo chose to stay behind with the other two Empyrean, Kin and Amrita. Not just because of his leg (which slows him down considerably when they need no such delay), but also because he can keep an eye on them. Make sure nothing hinky is going on.

Balastair steps up to the doors. He starts looking around. "There's no . . . there's no lock here!" Frustrated, he begins to slide his hands over the metal.

Boyland continues: "They'll be all like, *Oh, I think Cael loves me,* and then the other would be all like, *Cael doesn't love you like he loves me.* And meanwhile you sit back, arms crossed, picking and choosing which one you wanna make kissy-kissy with when they get back."

"It's not like that," Cael protests. Then, to Balastair: "Look, here—there's a mechanism in the middle."

"Uh-huh. Sure it ain't," Boyland says. "You're like a spider in the middle of a web, McAvoy. Are you good for anything?"

Cael wheels on him: "Wanda's pregnant, you ass!"

As he blurts that out, Balastair's hand touches the center of the doors, and a seamless panel hisses suddenly, sliding away to reveal a keyhole.

"Can we talk about this later?" Balastair says.

Cael wets his lips—lips dry from the air up here—and says, "Sure, yeah, whatever."

As the doors groan open and they step inside, Boyland shakes his head and says, "Well, heck-a-dang. Cael McAvoy, a father. We're gonna save the Heartland just to doom it again when your spawn gets here."

The auto-mate inside the elevator extends up from its pillar, waking the way a wooden fortune teller inside a carnival game might suddenly stir—lights flicker behind its eyes, and as its arms move, the wispy cobwebs strung between its elbows and its bell-shaped torso stretch and then break and then drift.

Folks haven't been inside this tower for a good while, Balastair thinks.

The Palladium Tower: a place where the Empyrean puts its odds and ends. Things that don't belong out among the populace, yet must remain kept and cataloged: old experiments, forgotten books, artifacts from the other parts of the world. When someone dies, if nobody is around to receive their estate, it goes *here*. Sealed away, like a tomb.

(Appropriate, given that just past the Palladium Tower is the Obol's Coin Tower—a needlelike structure that houses all the cremated ashes of the dead Empyrean citizens, each urn pressed with a coin minted to the family.)

Here, the auto-mate's speaker-mouth grinds and sparks and then comes to life with tinny, scratchy words: "Hello . . . Bala*stair* Ha-*ring*-ton!"

"Jeezum Crow!" Boyland barks, startled. "Kill that thing with fire."

"Calm down, it's just a dang robot," Cael says, though he feels the anxiety, too. Up here, they might not have human brains, but down in the dust, those metal bodies are melded with Heartlander flesh and blood.

Balastair says: "I'm looking for the property of Esther Harrington."

"*Esss*-tur Ha-*ring*-ton. Thirt*teenth* floor."

The elevator suddenly clangs and shudders. Gears squeal as it begins to ascend. Balastair watches the two young men with him—Boyland's still pale as an unmoored soul, and Balastair can see the striations of red peeking past the bandages. Infection may be setting in. Hopefully the antibacterial unguent that Amrita applied will save those arms. (At the very least, it smells pleasant, redolent with unusual spices: black tea, karak, khashamur pods, rose petal.) Cael just looks anxious, shifting from foot to foot.

At least, he thinks, *Rigo didn't come*. Nice lad, smarter than he gives himself credit for. But he's slower than they need right now.

"You all right?" Balastair asks Cael.

"Peachy," he says.

Cicero the catbird whistles a rough mimic of the tone of that word—*Whee-chee! Whee-chee!*

"A lot to take in."

"You think?"

"Are you ready for whatever awaits?"

Cael makes an incredulous sound. "Ready? I got a baby on the way that may or may not be human, with a mother who is cagier than a snake-bit hobo. Then I'm on a flotilla where I just found out they have my own father imprisoned for who knows why or for how damn long, and meanwhile I'm about to ignore all that and try to find some secret weapon for the Maize Witch— another mother whose humanity is wonky as hell—and for all I know we're waltzing into a trap that might end up being a recipe for her Heartland-renowned shoo-fly pie. That about cover it?"

The elevator bangs to a stop, jostling them all.

"I suppose it does," Balastair answers. "Let's see what surprise my mother has in store for us, shall we?"

The door opens to darkness.

And then a series of sharp *clicks* before bright fluorescent bulbs turn on one by one across the length of the room, illuminating an oblong space many times the size of Cael's own Boxelder home.

Ahead: plastic crates stacked high. Shapes that might be furniture (or, Cael thinks with a shudder, that might be metal men waiting to reach out and crush them with steel claws) hide under heavy tarps. Aisles radiate out from the center elevator, like the rays of a hand-drawn sun.

"Where do we start?" Cael asks.

"Where *don't* we start?" Boyland asks.

Balastair arches his eyebrows. "Mister Barnes Jr. is right. Start anywhere. We'll split up—cover more ground that way. And I choose"—he leans his head forward like a certain gravity is pulling him—"this direction."

The Empyrean man ducks down an aisle. Cicero hops off his shoulder and flies after him.

"Well," Cael says, "I'll go this way."

He heads down an aisle. He quickly notices that each box, covering, or bundle has a tag associated with it. Plastic tag on a little beaded metal chain. He lifts one up and peers down at it, and as he reads it, he calls out: "Hey, these tags tell you what's under the bundle. And where it came from. Look at the tags!"

He stands, and there's Boyland, all up in his orbit.

"We're splitting up," Cael says.

"I'm following you."

"That ain't the plan."

"It is the plan, farm boy. I don't wanna lift up some plastic blankie and catch a face full of some stomping mechanical, or end up breathing in a whiff of some weird experiment. I'm staying with you."

"Which means you ain't doing squat."

"By the Lord and Lady, Cael, I don't feel so hot, okay?" Cael gives Boyland a good long look and sees that his old rival is the color of a sun-bleached gravestone. Covered in a shining sheen of sweat, too. His tongue is pinkish gray and smacks as he speaks. "I think I got a fever."

"You look like something that came out of a goat's ass."

"Thanks, McAvoy."

Cael rolls his eyes. "All right, Barnes, sorry. Just hang with me. I figure that goop the priestess spread on your arms will take hold soon enough. Meanwhile, just . . ." *Hover there, like a skeeter.* "C'mon."

He heads down one aisle, then another, peeking under tarps—he sees bookshelves and lamps and, sure enough, an old auto-mate with ragged mop-head hands and giant suction cups on its knees and elbows. Boyland mumbles: "What in King Hell is that?" And Cael answers: "I think this thing washes windows. Look—climbs up using the cups. Arms got a couple extra joints in 'em, and those mop-hands look like they spin—"

He touches one, and the thing suddenly lurches to life—thrashing about, mop-hands whirring fast, too fast, smoke coming off them.

"Quik-kleen window! Gleam-shine spray!" Its jaw unhinges, and a mist spritzes from a hole inside its mouth, catching Cael right in the face. Cael flails, tastes chemicals, eyes burning—he trips over something, tumbling backward. *"Window-bot do a squeaky-sparkly job! You have a squeaky-sparkly day, Mister—"*

Cael blinks away the chemicals and opens his eyes just in time to see Boyland behead the thing with an old book. Dust flies from the book. More of the noxious chemical geysers from the thing's black-tube neck-stump.

Ffffpppsssss—then it sputters and goes dry.

"I hate these things," Boyland says.

"I'm not an admirer, either," Cael says, wiping his eyes again and spitting the chemical taste onto the floor. It's then he sees a glimpse of something just over his shoulder. A tag, dangling.

He picks it up.

He reads: *Harrington, Esther.*

Beneath it, the words: *Reclaimed goods from Palace Hill home; Ormond Stirling Saranyu.*

"Whoa-dang, here we go," Cael says, and he cracks the lid of a box. He calls to Balastair: "Hey, Bal—I got your mother's stuff here!"

He hears Cael calling. Faintly. And he calls back, "I . . . I've found some of her stuff, too." He feels a tightness in his throat and chest as he stares down at a gilded frame. Inside the frame: a picture of himself, his mother, and his grandfather Hiram.

In the photo, he's just a little kid. Ten, maybe twelve years old. Which means this isn't long before Hiram passed, before Mother began her . . . change.

He's holding a macro-oculus in the picture—they don't make them anymore, now it's just a lens that fits over the eye (uncomfortably, he adds), but as a child, this was his favorite thing. He decorated it with paint and stickers. Used it again and again to stare at the microscopic world and marvel at it. It was his first step on the road toward manipulating that tiny, unseen world—twisting helical forms and ushering forth replication and mutation.

Those days are gone, he thinks. *Aren't they?* The closest he got to doing any kind of science down in the Heartland was growing those vegetables at their little house. When Cleo was still alive. When everything had only just started to fall to pieces—he lies to himself, suddenly, pretends that he was happy then, but he wasn't. He knows it. He wanted things he couldn't have: a life back on the flotilla, a laboratory to do work, and Gwennie.

He takes the photo, then smashes the glass on the corner of

an old desk. With a circular movement he removes the rest of the glass using that corner, and once it's all gone, he reaches in, plucks the photo from inside the frame.

His mother looks young and happy.

Hiram looks magnanimous. A glow about him. Forked beard, proud smile, big and eager eyes. Balastair looked up to that man. Spent a lot of time with him, too—Hiram had retired, and Mother was always so busy.

Inside one of the desk drawers, Balastair hears something rolling.

He pops the drawer.

His oculus has rolled to the front.

Haha! He grabs at it. It feels so small in his long-fingered hands. But there, at the end, the dome shape with the crystal lens. He feels around, finds the switch, pops it—

A tiny blue laser emits from the front end.

He points it at a little tumbleweed of dust rolling across the desk, then presses his eye against the viewer—

The microscopic world made massive, blooming bright against his eye. Spherical, spiny shapes mingle with rods that look like shattered crystals. A dust mite, monstrous when seen so big, clambers across the tangle as if drunk.

He removes the oculus. Wonderful. Wonderful!

What other treasures await? His youth, contained in these boxes and drawers, suddenly laid bare and—

"I found it!" Cael calls from across the room.

"What?"

"Get over here! I think I found it!"

Balastair longs to remain with the nostalgia of his life on the

Saranyu, but for now, duty calls. He hurries down the radial aisle, reaches the center, then follows Cael's voice and finds him and Boyland standing over a crate wreathed in drifting steam—no.

Not steam. Dry ice sublimating to a gas.

Cael says, "Found this crate. Was wrapped up in all this red and black tape." Sure enough, next to the crate is a wad of the binding. Balastair sees DO NOT OPEN and lots of exclamation points contained inside triangles.

Icons of warning. That's promising.

And the crate's a good size—three feet by three feet.

What could be in there?

Cael waves him over. Down in the box: forty-nine cylinders, each glass capped with gleaming metal.

With ginger fingers, Balastair slides one out of its socket and places it atop the crate's lid. Inside the glass is—

"I don't know what that is," he says. And he doesn't. It's packed tight with something—some kind of material. Tiny little white orbs. Like tapioca blobs, though significantly smaller. In fact, they look like . . . "Eggs."

"From the world's tiniest chicken," Boyland mumbles.

Balastair shakes his head. "No, no, *insect* eggs."

It dawns on him.

No, it couldn't be.

Could it?

He takes the oculus, shines the laser against the side of the glass, and—

Yes. The cylinder is packed with tiny white eggs. He does some quick calculations in his head—the volume of the cylinder, the size of each egg. That means—a half million eggs in each cylinder. Nearly fifty cylinders. And if these are what he thinks they are . . .

"Don't open these," he says suddenly.

But even as he finishes those words, he hears the *click-hiss*.

He pulls away from the oculus, eyes wide.

Boyland stands over a cylinder, the metal cap in his hand. The open cylinder in front of him.

"Why not?" Boyland asks.

The cylinder starts to hiss and vibrate.

"Oh, gods," Balastair says. "What have you done?"

POPCORN

ARTHUR DOES WHAT he can to exercise his body. He stands and plants his hands against the wall and lifts his heels up again and again—his legs are wobbly, and they feel like they're on fire. He sobs doing it. But he needs to do it. If he has any chance of escaping the gallows, he can't be limp—can't flee on atrophied legs or with rubbery arms. While he works his body, he also works his mind: He thinks of his wife, his son, his daughter. He does math problems in his mind. Old problems from when he was just a student—hard ones, too, ones that took him months to solve. Symbols on a chalkboard. Sketches on paper.

He does this day after day.

Night after night.

His body aches. His mind feels like mud.

Everything in him just wants to give up—like an old dog who can't dog anymore. *I'm tired*, he thinks. *They have me. I'll never see the Heartland again, except as a corpse thrown off the edge of this flotilla.*

And that's if he's lucky.

Then comes the night when the wind howls through the bars of the birdcage prison they've placed him in, and two men come.

Frumentarii. Peregrine's Guard. He's already met the peregrine of this flotilla—Lirong Yau. An old woman. Bitter and wrinkled as an apricot pit. Dark eyes like chips of flint beyond pinched skin. She seemed tired during their meeting. Like all of this bored her.

Now, her men have come for him. Two men, each muscled beneath his leather. One looks young, naive, untested. The other is old, grizzled, a lantern jaw speckled with ill-shaven salt-and-pepper hair.

The old one mutters, "Your presence is requested, terrorist."

"By whom?" Arthur croaks.

It's the young one who answers: "The Dirae."

Then he opens the cage.

Arthur launches himself.

The older one deftly steps aside and brings a hard knee against Arthur's hip—right into the bone spurs that have haunted him since he was a young man. The pain is like sticking a screwdriver into the soft meat of a rotting tooth, except across his whole body. Everything lights up with excruciating agony, and Arthur falls down and crumples.

They haul him to his feet.

• • •

They step out of the elevator, and things happen fast.

Something lashes around the young guard's neck. He claws at it in the darkness, gurgling, eyes bulging. From around the corner steps someone with a gun held against her shoulder—

It couldn't be—

But it is. Gwendolyn Shawcatch.

She points the rifle, a proper rifle, a rifle Arthur recognizes as his own. The older Frumentarii reaches for the pistol at his hip, letting go of Arthur in the process, but having to do all that makes him slow.

And Gwennie is fast.

She jabs him hard in the solar plexus with the rifle barrel. As he *oofs* and doubles over, the rifle butt comes crashing down against the back of his head.

He drops, face-first.

And the young one slumps forward, too, in a lazy somersault against the other one's hind end.

The whip-cord vine around his neck withdraws as Wanda steps forward.

"I told you not to kill him!" Gwennie hisses.

Wanda shrugs. "He isn't dead, relax. He's just taking a snooze." She turns to Arthur. "Hi, Mister McAvoy."

He tries to find words, but none arrive.

Gwennie thrusts his rifle into his hands. "This is yours, I believe?"

He nods.

She smirks. "We gotta move, Swift Fox. Your son awaits."

COLONIZE

THE CANISTER FOAMS OVER.

All the eggs bubble up and out.

And they begin to hatch.

Cael doesn't know what the hell is happening. He steps back and curses at Boyland: "The hell are you doing?"

The buckethead scowls, looking suddenly nervous. "I don't know! I figure we don't have time to dally so let's, you know, pop the seal on one of these bad boys, see what's inside. . . ."

"What part of *secret weapon* do you not understand?" Cael looks at Balastair. "Do we need to cover our mouths? Run for the hills? What?"

But Balastair is frozen in place, eyes unblinking. All he says is:

"Ants."

"What?"

The eggs begin spilling over. And splitting as they tumble. Little white maggoty things burst out, doubling the volume of the eggs, making the whole pile grow and grow—and then the white maggoty things twist and throb, growing little rubbery leg-stalks and flicking antennas—

"They're ants," Balastair says again. "Oh, Mother."

"Kill 'em!" Boyland shouts, and takes a fist and brings it down on the growing pile of ants. They pop underneath his assault—sounds like a string of little firecrackers going off—and then Balastair is screaming for him to stop and is pulling him back, then Boyland is screaming—

The underside of his hand is blistering, growing red—

"Ow, ow, shit dang *gods it burns*." Boyland, shaking the larval corpses from the bottom of his hand, wiping them on his dungarees—where he leaves a smeary bug-gut trail, the fabric begins to smoke.

Cael grabs the hem of his own shirt, uses it to clean off Boyland's hand. His own shirt starts to smolder and fray. The scent in the air smells acrid, acidic, like the contacts of an old motorvator battery.

He affords another glance at the ants, still foaming over and spilling out of the cylinder in a white tide—

The little legged larvae start to change now, too.

They shimmer, iridescent like the blue of peacock feathers.

Ants. They're growing into ants. Hatching, pupating, swelling. Now what spills out of the top of the cylinder are proper ants, not just eggs, not just maggots—little insects, each the size of a pin's head.

They begin spilling out over the table. Thousands of them. More, even. Balastair and the others backpedal toward the elevator.

"Those little sum-bitches!" Boyland shouts.

"Bal," Cael asks, "what is happening?"

"Those are my ants," he says, looking horrified, shell-shocked. "They were my first. Mother said to begin with something small, something with a simple code, a creature that can breed quickly so that the results of my meddling would be plainly seen. She wanted me to work on little vinegar flies, but I said, oh no, I'll show her, I'll *impress* her—and I cheated. The first thing I changed inside my little ant specimens was how fast they bred. From egg to larvae to pupae in a matter of *moments*, not days or months."

"The hell's he talking about?" Boyland asks Cael, still shaking his hand like he just burned it in a campfire.

But Balastair continues: "Mother wasn't impressed, or didn't act that way, and so I kept pushing limits with these little ants. I kept making *changes*."

Across the room, the ants are spreading out, a shimmering blue pool shifting and rippling. They move fast. They're already at the far wall, crawling toward a metal vent like a stream of water defying gravity.

"I . . . used them to attack my mother's lab. I was angry. Impudent. I upped their formic acid content, concentrated it to create a defense mechanism against anything that would attack them—assassin bugs, other ants, even a crushing hand. Then I made it so that they hungered for the corn—that was what my mother was working on, and so I thought it would amuse me and upset her if their greatest desire was to tear apart the corn by stalk, by leaf, by root, and use it as material in their nests. And finally, I made it so they were attracted to anything electrical. They chew apart microchips. Eat wires. They form their own conduits, creating short circuits all their own."

Suddenly, the lights of the room begin to go out, one bulb at a time. Each buzzes, then flashes, then goes dark.

"All in an effort to hurt my mother." Balastair makes a desperate, sad sound: somewhere between a laugh and a sob. "I give you my first creation: the Blue-Jeweled Reaper Ant."

He turns and slams the elevator button once, twice, three times.

Bam bam bam.

"That's her weapon?" Cael asks. "Ants?!"

Balastair babbles: "She destroyed them. Or said she did. Gods, she kept them. And bred more of them. Colony after colony."

That's her weapon, Cael realizes.

"Do they hurt people?" he asks. Balastair doesn't answer him as they hear the elevator rumbling and clanging behind the doors. *"Do they hurt people?"*

"No. No, not unless you crush them. . . ."

Cael bolts back down the aisle, meeting the coming darkness.

He hopes the canister Boyland opened is now empty of its insectile payload—before the lights went out, he saw the ants streaming up toward not one vent, but several. In the dark, he feels around, finds the crate.

The witch wants her weapon.

And Cael's going to give it to her.

He hoists the crate—it's lighter than he expected—and heads back toward the elevator, half expecting his shoes to begin to smoke and melt.

In the center of the room, a golden square as the elevator opens.

The other two hurry in, and Cael slides in just as the doors close. Cicero the bird chirps at him, as if angry.

The Elevator Man rumbles to life. "Ah! Mister Ha-*ring*-ton. Your destination today, s-s-s-sir?"

"Down. Down!"

The doors shudder closed.

And the elevator begins to crawl downward.

"We may want to get off this flotilla," Balastair says.

"Why?" Cael asks.

"The ants. They'll get in everything. They don't—they're crazy! They don't colonize properly, they won't go to a single location and make a single nest—they spread out, and breed wantonly, and—" He pales. "That's what she wants. That's why they're her weapon."

The lights in the elevator dim.

"Aw, hell," Boyland says. "No, no, no, c'mon, c'mon."

The Elevator Man says: "I appear to be, be, be, be—appear to be, be, be having tech-*nick*-al diffi-diffi-diffi-*culllll*—"

Cael spies the little blue shimmer peeking through one of the holes in the auto-mate's speaker-mouth.

One tiny Reaper ant.

But there's never just one ant, is there?

A second ant head emerges. Then five more. Then *all* the speaker-holes have ants pushing out of them, and soon a whole stream of them disgorge from the auto-mate's mouth as if it's vomiting them, and it makes a sound like pollen hissing against a screen door—

"Don't move!" Balastair says. *"Do not move."*

The lights go out in the elevator.

Boyland screams.

THE HALF-LIFE OF
ANOMALOUS MATERIALS

"I ASSURE YOU," Lirong Yau says, scowling, "things are under control."

"They most certainly are not," Enyastasia says, stepping up to a bank of monitors splayed out in a beveled curve. Each screen is touch-capable, a visidex all its own, and she reaches out and begins to touch screens, bringing up maps, alerts, guard reports. The two *evocati augusti* guardsmen turn their horsehead helmets toward each other, giving a quizzical look and shrugging. "You have terrorists on board this flotilla. Might I remind you of the last time that happened? I'm sure if I could conjure the corpse of Percy Lemaire-Laurent, Peregrine of the Saranyu, he would tell you *all about it*."

"You are mistaken. And let me be the first to say I am disgusted by your assumptions—this is a breach of authority, *Dirae*." Enyastasia hears the way the woman says that word. In her head she translates it as: *You stupid little girl.* "I can speak for all the peregrines and all the praetors when I say we are growing tired of your micromanaging. You have not yet earned your—"

One of the screens flicker.

Miranda Woodwick's face appears. Her mouth is a severe line, her silver hair sternly, freshly trimmed almost down to the scalp. "There you are, Miss Ormond."

"Not now, Miranda."

"Don't *not now* me. You have to pull back. Our own people are rebelling. This is *too much* for them. You must see that. We have pushed too hard, and now they're pushing back—but we can stop this. We need to make some concessions; we cut out the tumors with a hard, sharp knife, but now it's time for a softer hand."

Enyastasia sneers. "I *am* your hard, sharp knife. I don't do 'soft hands.' You wanted all this? Now it's done. You don't just put me back in a box, Miranda."

"Enyastasia, please, listen—"

"No more listening."

She thrusts a finger at the screen and kills the call.

When Miranda's face is gone, she sees it—

The last report from two Frumentarii. "Look, Peregrine. Here. Two of yours went off investigating what they thought might be refugees from the Heartland. That was hours ago. Care to speculate on when they checked in to report last? When they called to let you know that *oh, false alarm, nothing going on here*—?"

"H-have they?"

Lirong Yau's bewilderment would be precious if it weren't so dire.

"No. They have not." She touches the screen of one visidex, calls up a hierarchical tree; she highlights two names on it, Bevins and Gormley. The two men she sent to procure Arthur from his cell—Arthur, who would be an excellent hostage to draw the Heartlanders out of hiding. She knows they're here. When the blockade closed in and the Empyrean fleet appeared at the shattered wall of Pegasus City, it didn't take long to hitch a ride and, on the way, look for docking anomalies—one appeared even as she was scanning for it. On the Ilmatar, of all places. She assumed they were coming to rescue Arthur McAvoy, and now that the two Frumentarii sent to fetch him have failed to answer, well, that *is* an answer all on its own, isn't it?

Rage claws its way up her throat. She growls.

"Get everyone," she snaps to the peregrine. "Every *evocati augusti*. Every Frumentarii. Then send a message to the other flotillas. Tell them they need to send reinforcements. This flotilla is under attack from the inside. We will go door-to-door. We will tear people out of their beds until they yield the terrorists to us. We've got rats in our walls, Yau. Go! Find them!"

The peregrine hesitates. She's not used to being bossed around by anybody but her own praetor.

But then she offers a clipped nod and leaves.

"And where will I go?" Enyastasia asks. She ignores the pain in her bandage-swaddled ankle, ignores the headache that feels like it's trying to rip apart her skull at her scar-seams. Again she pulls up a list of alerts.

What's that?

A contamination alert.

A little red pulse in the Archival District.

Right over the Palladium Tower. And spreading.

It reads: ANOMALOUS BIOLOGICAL CONTAMINATION.

"That is where I need to be," she snaps to the two horse-headed guardsmen on each side of her. "The two of you, come with me. I have something to get, and then some Heartlanders to kill."

BOTTOM FLOOR

"**NO ONE'S HERE,**" Gwennie says, pressing flat against the door of the Palladium Tower. She puts her hand on the door—nothing happens. Door doesn't open. No lock emerges. Nothing. "They should be here by now."

Arthur looks up. "Is my son in there?"

Wanda nods, because she can feel him. "He is." Somewhere in the middle of the tower, she senses Cael—a tangle of cells and neurons, each a shining diamond, a flickering firefly. His lights call to hers, and hers to his.

She can feel what he feels. Transmitting to her, bright and clean and sharp. Panic. She senses panic. Which raises her own panic level. But there's something else there, too—hope.

"He has what we came for, I think," she says. "But something's wrong."

Arthur stands, his face wearing the rictus of great pain, and then he feels around the winged statues. "Perhaps we can use one of these to lever—"

The door wrenches open.

It wrenches open because Wanda wants it open.

Another moment that strikes her as curious. *What I want, I can have. Just by taking it.* She marvels for a second, then continues to use a writhing web of tendrils like fingers to pry the door open the rest of the way.

Then she leans forward into the gap, bites down, and winces as she reaches up into the space—she closes her eyes. The vines snake up the walls, and what they feel, she feels. The smooth texture. The delicate rivets.

The bottom of the elevator.

She coils around the base of it and yanks.

Pain blooms in her shoulder, but she ignores it as the elevator drops down out of the tower. As if she dislodged food from a choking man's throat.

Cael, Balastair, and Boyland hurry out of the darkened, dead elevator. Boyland is whimpering—his one hand is covered in blisters, and a few stray blisters mark his neck, his cheek, his forehead. And his clothes are pocked with holes—as if someone took a burning cigarette and cooked away the fabric.

Balastair and Boyland swat at themselves, swiping their hands furiously against their bodies, panicked. Cael sets a crate down—gently—and does the same. "Godsdamnit. Godsdamnit!"

"Son, what happened?" Pop asks.

Cael stops mid-motion. He straightens up. "Ants," he says.

"Ants?" Pop asks. "That's a helluva thing. Why would ants—?"

But Cael doesn't give him time to finish the question. He launches himself at his father, and Arthur wobbles as he accepts the hug.

"I missed you, Cael," Pop says.

"Gods, I missed you, too, Pop." Cael pulls away, gives his father a good looking-over. "They kicked King Hell out of you, didn't they?"

Pop smiles, but Wanda sees that the smile betrays agony. "Don't worry about me. I'm just glad the lot of you is alive."

"Lane is dead," Wanda says.

Pop looks to Cael. Cael nods.

"We're gonna be dead, too, if we don't move," Gwennie says.

"Back to the temple," Balastair says. "Gwennie is right— we've little time to waste." As he steps forward, the Empyrean man puts a hand on Pop's shoulder. "It is good to see you again after all these years, Arthur."

"You've grown up quite a bit—"

Near them, one of the light-posts sparks and goes out.

Pop makes a quizzical sound. "Curious."

Another goes out, ten feet away. *Bzzt.* A flash, then darkness.

"Not curious," Balastair says. "Not curious at all!"

"It's the ants," Cael says again.

That, Wanda thinks, *is* curious.

41

TOOLBREAKERS

THE CORN BREAKS LIKE SNAPPED BONES.

The Maize Witch walks through the path she carves before her. Behind her, an army of her own Blightborn. To her side, Mole tottering along—a board in his hand, a board with a nail stuck through it, his weapon of choice. Ahead, in the distance, the sound of battle. Sonic shrieks. A *whumpf.*

She reaches out with her mind.

Cael and Wanda are above. As is her son. Twinkling lights in the sky—part of the shadow cast by the Ilmatar flotilla. They have her weapon.

It has begun.

Cael feels something tickling at his mind—not like the ants that had, only minutes before, been crawling all over his flesh (before

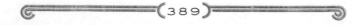

eventually moving on, as the humans held little interest for the swarming colony)—but rather, like tree roots pressing at an earthen cellar wall, trying to break through.

He knows what it is. Or, rather, *who*. Every time he blinks, there she is: the Maize Witch. Esther Harrington. *Mother Esther*. She's far below them, in the Heartland—straight down, right now. It's like she *knows*. She knows they've found the weapon. She knows they're close. She's ready to meet them.

As they hurry back toward the House of the Sky, Wanda presses her hand to his forearm. "That crate you're carrying. It's what Mother wants?"

He nods. "It is. But I don't know, Wanda."

"Don't know what?"

"If we can give this to her."

Wanda frowns. "But she's waiting for us."

Balastair, overhearing, steps in and says: "My mother is quite fond of irony. Ants, the hardest workers nature has offered us. Tireless creatures, thinking only of the whole, never of themselves as individual beings. And what is it that we fine citizens of the Seventh Heaven despise most? *Work*. Boring, ugly, endless work. Ironic that she hopes to undo us with such hard little workers. It's a message. Mother is fond of . . . messages."

"You guys *are* talking about ants, right?" Gwennie says.

Boyland shudders. "Gods, can we *stop* talking about ants?"

Cael starts to explain the ants—though Balastair takes over, tells the others what he told them up in the Palladium Tower.

Pop stops suddenly, holding his hip. "I need a moment." He unslings the rifle, begins to use it as a cane. Delicate, flinching steps forward. "There. Not what a rifle is meant for normally, but perhaps this is its *kindest* utility."

"You all right, Pop?" Cael asks, handing the crate to Balastair. He gets under his father's shoulder, helps him walk forward. The memory of doing the same to Lane—as Lane was dying—suddenly haunts him.

"Fine, fine, all fine." Truth is, Cael can hear the pain. Worse than it's been before. Watching his father like this—skinny as a starving cat, gray-faced, broken down like a hammered-on motorvator—is killing him. "The ants. How many colonies are in that crate?"

"One . . . *opened* already," Balastair says with no apparent pleasure, but also no apparent desire to throw Boyland under the wheels. "Which means we've got another forty-eight to go. Approximately twenty to thirty million ants. That's, of course, before they *breed*. And I assure you, the Reaper ant breeds with great alacrity."

Pop's face suddenly crestfallen. "They're a weapon."

"*Her* weapon," Cael says.

"Our mother's," Wanda says, pressing a hand to Balastair's arm—a move that makes Balastair flinch. Cicero tweets and hops away from her.

"They'll kill the Heartland."

"The corn," Cael says. "They'll kill the corn."

"No, no, no." Pop shakes his head. "Not just that. They destroy . . . electrical equipment. Electronics. And they're not easily dispatched?"

Balastair shakes his head. "Like Hiram's, they're . . . tolerant of most attacks that would try to destroy them. I don't know what would do it." He pauses. "Extreme heat. Or cold, maybe. But of course the Heartland has a moderate climate. No rain. Middling heat. It never gets cold, but rarely gets hot, either."

"Which means the ants will survive. They'll wipe out the Empyrean *and* the Heartland," Pop says. "No visidexes. No motorvators. No corn to run the engines, but no engines, either."

"Sounds like bad news," Gwennie says.

"Sounds like *heaven*," Wanda snaps. "Return us to the start. Like a chalkboard—just wipe all these foul scrawlings clean."

Balastair looks suddenly horrified. "You sound like her. My mother."

"Well, *good!*" Wanda says, sounding petulant.

Cael stops under the boughs of a massive tree growing up out of a ring of stones on the corner of this Empyrean street. He turns, stands in front of Wanda: "We're not her children. Okay? We can't just . . . accept what she says blindly. We gotta . . . think about this a little bit."

"*You?* Think?" Wanda barks. "That is not one of your strengths, Cael McAvoy."

"Hey!" he protests.

"You *do*. You *act*. But you wanna think this through? Okay! Let's think this through, Cael. We're slaves to the corn. And we're nothing but Empyrean pets. You know how they control us? Through all their . . . damn technology. Worse, now they're turning people *into* technology, sticking Heartlanders in metal bodies. We can end that. We can take their tools and break them over our knees. Technology doesn't have a soul. But we do. The plants of the ground do. So do the birds of the sky, and fell-deer, and even dumb shuck rats and moths. Even the ants do. So let something work for *us* for a change. Let's tear it all down."

He swallows.

Gods, she's right.

He presses his back up against the tree (and there, he can feel it—that "soul" she's talking about, like channels of light pulsing up through the ground, into the branches, to the leaves, back down through the roots again).

"The corn is evil," he says. "And maybe so is the technology that they use to make it. To enslave us. Lord and Lady, I never thought of it like that."

He suddenly sees it. If you take away the corn, their ships can't fly. But it's more than that, too—you have to take away everything they have, don't you? Their mechanical men. Their ships. Their screens. He thinks of how Esther lives: a simple house, a bounty of food always on the table, a community of people living together. Nobody enslaved.

And then it strikes him: nobody will hate him because of the Blight.

They won't even fear him.

Because the Blight—

It'll save the world.

What was a curse will be a blessing.

A bounty of food on *every* table.

He says it aloud: "They won't hate us."

"That's right," Wanda says. She walks over, cups his chin in her hands. When she does, he senses all the lights within her—hers and their daughter's. The little girl, swimming around like a tadpole. Turning like a seedling batted about by rain. Wanda kisses him. She tastes of honeysuckle nectar.

"They *will* hate you," Pop says, his voice dry and dark, a thundercloud blotting out a sunny day. "Think about it, Cael. Hiram's Golden Prolific isn't evil. A visidex isn't evil. Neither is a gun, a flotilla, a mechanical man. They're just objects. Tools. What matters is who *holds* the tools. Who has access and who doesn't? The tools aren't evil. Power is. Power over others. That's what the Empyrean want. And they use the corn and their wondrous marvels of technology to get it."

Cael steps forward. "So we break their tools. Then they can't control us."

"But then *we* can't have it, either. Don't you see?" Pop says.

"Maybe we don't need it!" Cael suddenly yells. He knows his voice is loud, too loud out here on the flotilla, and he knows that time is sliding through his fingers, caught on the wind like campfire ash, but his mind is going faster than an auto-train barreling down the tracks, and he needs this. "With the Blight, we will always have food, and once the corn is dead we can again tend the soil—"

"Cael," Gwennie says. "Pop's right. What happens when all of it goes away? Only those with the Blight will have power. The witch—"

Wanda snaps: "Don't you call her that. She's our mother!"

"She's *my* mother," Balastair says. "Not yours."

"She hasn't been your mother in a long time," Cael says. "Don't speak to my Obligated like that. She'll tear you a couple new holes—"

"Everybody shut the King Hell up!" Boyland yells. "Look!"
He points. Eyes follow.

The lights are going out. A growing wave of darkness creeping toward them. Darkness is cascading up buildings, too—where once a few windows had lights, they go dark. Up, up, up, the darkness climbs.

"The ants will bring this flotilla down," Balastair says. "Not quickly, but most assuredly. Boyland, for once, is right. We must move, and we must do it quickly. Agreed?"

"To the temple," Gwennie says.

They move out from under the tree. Cael lags back a moment, getting Pop situated once more on his shoulder.

Pop turns to Cael and in a low voice says: "This might fall to you, son. Don't make any hasty decisions. The fate of our world and the balance of power that controls it is far more fragile than it has ever been. Promise me you'll do what's right."

"I promise, Pop."

If only he knew what *doing right* meant.

THE BRIDGE TO NOWHERE

A CRASH OF GLASS. Ahead: panicked voices. Shouting. Someone snapping orders. They round a corner, and ahead they see horseheaded guardsmen dragging people out of doors, windows. Throwing them to the ground. *Their own people*, Cael thinks. *What is happening?*

Balastair says: "They're looking for us. There. Look. The temple—"

Frumentarii gather in a mob around the door. Blue smoke drifts from the doorway, already dissipating. A small woman, old and pinched like a clothespin, stands watching with her hands clasped behind her back.

"Where are they?" she snaps, her voice shrill and loud.

Guardsmen drag a priestess—an older, rounder woman, not Amrita—out the door and throw her to the ground.

"May the . . . sky bless you, Peregrine," the old woman says, coughing.

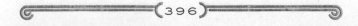

The other woman—the peregrine?—backhands the priestess.

"You were hiding terrorists!"

"I don't know who you mean—"

A sharp sonic trill—the blast empties the old woman of her guts. She cries, clutching her middle, before dying.

Balastair gasps.

"We have to go back," he says. "There's an alternate way—"

"But Rigo," Cael says. "We need Rigo."

"He's not there, I don't think. They'd have him on the ground already. At the first sign of danger, Kin was supposed to take him to the ketch—that's where you must go. I'll show you the way—"

"You're not coming with us?" Gwennie asks.

Cicero chirps, and it sounds like the same incredulous question—*tweet twoot twee woo?*

"This flotilla is in danger. If I can get to the control tower, I might be able to override the settings and deal with the Reaper ant contamination. Cold may kill them—I don't know, truly, but I have to try."

"Why?" Wanda hisses. "Let them fall."

"Because!" he retorts. "Because there are *people* here. And because more death isn't going to fix things."

"He's right," Gwennie says. "I'll go with you."

"Gwennie, no," Cael says.

"Let her," Boyland says. "She gets shit done, in case you haven't noticed."

From the direction of the temple, a cry of alarm. "Over there!" One of the Frumentarii points in their direction.

"Move!" Pop says.

• • •

Rigo hunkers down by the skiff. In the distance, he hears shouting, glass breaking. Under the spotlight of a streetlight, an *evocati* guardsman staggers into sight, bleeding at the head and neck. A young couple—he in a crisp white shirt, hair slicked back but for a mussed curl at the front; she in an iridescent dress with a gleaming silver umbrella—advances upon him. She clubs the guardsman with the umbrella. He kicks the *evocati* in the side.

"You don't have any right!" the woman screams.

"Tell your mistress she can no longer have the Ilmatar!"

The guardsman scrambles to stand, then hurries off—they pelt him with stones and coins before chasing after.

"I don't understand," Rigo says, breathless. "What's happening?"

"We're fighting back," Kin says. "The call is out. We hacked the visidexes. Everyone knows now. Tonight's the night we retake the Ilmatar."

Rigo scowls. "It had to be *tonight*?"

"Of course." Kin's smile is like a glinting razor. "The chaos you and your friends are causing makes a prime opportunity to reclaim what we lost."

"This could be putting my friends in danger."

"They'll be fine."

"And if they're not?"

Kin snaps: "Then they died for the greater good. Now stay quiet, will you? I'm still here with the boat. I'm not running off and joining the revolution. If they come, we'll get them off the flotilla safely."

• • •

They pass by chaos.

That's all it is, chaos.

Balastair understands. Kin and the others set this in motion. Frumentarii marching into homes. Sonic rounds shrieking from within. A horseheaded guardsman thrown out of a window. A gleaming pewter ashtray held in the hands of an old man as he bashes it down on the guard's helmet, crumpling the horse's head—the man cries out, gurgling.

They try to turn one way and instead meet a gout of gas-flame from a broken pipe. One Frumentarii thrashes, burning. A nearby *evocati* lashes his thrum-whip, catching a woman on the arm, flinging her into the gap between floating neighborhoods— her scream goes quieter as she falls.

"Can't get out that way!" Boyland calls.

Balastair eyes his options. They're dwindling—and they need to get to the skiff. They need to get *off this flotilla*. "This way!"

The gun is heavy in her hand.

Heavenkiller, Enyastasia thinks. Not today. This gun, pregnant with power, will not destroy heaven but, rather, save it.

If it kills anybody, it will be the devils. The devils who hope to pull the Saintangels down out of the sky. Bullets, blessed purely by her will to do right and exterminate evil where it roots like a gluttonous pig.

She likes that. She likes subversion. Taking someone else's weapon and turning it against them. It's practically poetic.

I should read more poetry, she thinks unexpectedly.

She and the two *evocati* march forward, toward where the peregrine awaits. It's then that she feels the tingle at the nape of her neck—

There.

Dead ahead, a hundred yards off.

Her enemies. The Boxelder Seven.

Well, six now.

She laughs.

Then raises the gun, cocks the hammer, aims, and waits.

As soon as they cross the arched bridge between islands—

She pulls the trigger.

Choom.

A cannon-fire boom like thunder rolling over dead earth. A fist-sized hunk of stone kicks up out of the bridge's railing just a second before Cael puts his hand there—the stone chips fly, sting his hand, arm, cheek, and he reflexively shuts his eyes and yanks his head back.

"Turn back!" Pop shouts—

But even as they turn, they see that retreating in the other direction is no longer an option—guardsmen of both the peregrine and horsehead varieties are closing in, first bolting at top speed, now slowing as they see they've got their quarry pinned on a bridge.

"We're doomed," Balastair says. "Trapped like mice."

Wanda stiffens. "No. Never."

Her eyes gleam green.

Whip-cord tendrils extend once more from her fingers—

But Cael knows that once she's loose, once she's given

over to the Blight, this will be a bloodbath. And there may be another way.

He puts a hand on her shoulder and says: "Wait. I have an idea."

Enyastasia growls. She heard the tales of Peregrine Percy Lemaire-Laurent's first attempts with one of the Heartlander irons—the recoil of the gun made him miss again and again before he finally met his demise. And she swore that the same fate wouldn't be hers. She was better, smarter, faster—but the gun is heavy, and it bucks like a malfunctioning auto-mate.

But she will not miss a second time, of this she is certain.

Once again, her small thumb drags the hammer back—

Cl-click.

Her finger snakes toward the trigger—

"Stop!" one of them shouts from the bridge.

The McAvoy boy. The Blight-freak. He's got something in his hand—a canister of some kind. He's holding his arm—and with it, that strange glass cylinder—out over the railing. "I'll drop it if you shoot!"

She's tempted to shoot anyway.

And yet—the terrorists have surprised them all before.

She eases her finger away from the trigger.

"I want to talk," he shouts.

She yells back: "So talk."

"This is a bomb," he says. A lie, but Cael doesn't really have time to explain the whole scary *antpocalypse* thing. "I drop it from here, it goes right to the Engine Layer. Then *boom*. Another flotilla lost. That what y'all want?"

Behind them, the guardsmen all share panicked looks. They take a measurable step back—as if that would save them.

"I'm prepared to accept your surrender," the scarred girl responds.

"No surrender," Cael calls. "Just let us leave."

Balastair shakes his head. "You don't want this, Dirae. You've already lost control of this flotilla. They're rebelling against you! Don't you get it? It's time to think about saving these people. There's a contaminant—a contagion loose in the flotilla. It'll bring this ship down, but I can stop it."

"What kind of contagion?" she calls out to him.

" . . . biological."

"Step forward."

Balastair looks back. "Trust me." Then he whispers: "Do *not* drop that."

The cylinder is suddenly heavy, and cold, and Cael's hand sweats.

Just drop it, he thinks.

For now, he tightens his grip.

She's just a girl.

That's what Balastair thinks. He can see that now. She's damaged—her mutilation made beautiful by the gold dust that paints her scars—but suddenly vulnerable. Her eyes are dancing about. With every scream in the distance, every pop of glass, every sonic trill, she flinches.

She's a girl, and she's human.

Balastair, having set down the crate on the bridge, steps forward. His hands are up as he approaches gingerly. In the distance he hears someone yelling for help. A guardsman? A citizen of the Ilmatar? He has no idea.

"We need to save this flotilla," he says as he closes in. "Or it'll crash. There are . . . insects. *Ants.* They will be a plague and they will—"

She interrupts him: "Why?"

"Why . . . what? Save people?"

"Why would you join with them? The Heartlanders. I don't understand it. It disgusts me. It literally makes me ill. The taste on the back of my tongue is like the blood after you bite the inside of your cheek." Her face twists up like a closing fist. Her humanity, a cloud passing in front of the moon—there and then gone again. He stammers:

"I-it doesn't matter, taking sides like this *doesn't matter*, when lives are on the line—"

Her arm flashes.

A gleam of moonlight on metal.

The gun smashes into the side of his head.

He drops sideways, to one knee—can't think, can't see—

Somewhere, someone is screaming—*No, don't shoot!*

Drop it!

Blood running into his eyes.

Drop the canister!

The barrel of the gun presses to his temple.

Cicero flies.

• • •

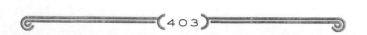

Balastair—!

Everything happens at once.

Gwennie moves fast—hands up, two knives. One flies, then a second—

Pop, too, is drawing the rifle from under his arm, hand flying to the lever-action, drawing it back, *ch-chak*—

Cael thinks, *All it would take would be for me to open my hand.*

The cylinder would drop. He could dump them all over—all the colonies, crashing down against the engines. Some spinning to the Heartland below. The plague of ants could begin. The corn would end.

The *Empyrean* would end.

Wanda hisses: "Drop it, drop it, *godsdamnit drop it*—"

But his hand tightens and he pulls the cylinder over the edge.

I can't. I can't do what Lane did.

I can't kill all these people.

The first knife sticks in the meat of her biceps.

Enyastasia shouts, her arm drops, the finger twitches—

The gun goes off.

A red bloom opens up on Balastair Harrington's chest.

The Dirae shrieks, sees the glint of the second knife—

She swings the gun upward, bats the flying blade away with the Heavenkiller revolver—the blade *tings* and spins away.

Gwennie watches that second knife knocked out of the air like a butterfly, and she curses herself for throwing too late, or too soon, or not fast enough, or—it doesn't matter, because the monstrous girl is still there, and Balastair is still dead or dying, and this she cannot abide.

She launches herself across the bridge—running at full speed, pulling the one last blade she has left tucked in the hem of her pants—

Ahead, the two *evocati* on each side of the scarred girl plant themselves and draw long, sparking thrum-whips. Their arms rear back and the whips crackle as they snap forward—

The girl between them sneers, bleeding, and points the revolver.

Right at Gwennie.

Cael extends his arm—

His Blight-vine, still stunted by the scarred girl's knife, feels hot, hot like scalding water in his veins, hot like a star going supernova—

The vine grows. Immeasurably fast, tendrils sprouting, braiding, weaving together into a larger vine, bulging and pulsing—

He lashes it, curls it back just over Gwennie's head.

Both the thrum-whips catch his vine instead of her.

Gwennie ducks under them, just as the whips begin to vibrate, chewing through his vine once more.

Cael screams.

Balastair stares up at the stars.

Madness all around him. He tilts his gaze past his nose

toward his feet—and there is Gwennie. *Ah, Gwennie.* He likes to think he helped her get off the Saranyu but, truth be told, she probably helped him even more.

Gwennie dances forward, knife in her hand, launching toward the poor, deluded, damaged girl. The one so broken she'd burn the house down to kill a lonely moth. But the gun goes up, and he gurgles a strangled cry—

Cicero.

Sweet, sweet Cicero.

The little catbird appears in a blur of blue-gray feathers, slamming himself into the face of Enyastasia Ormond. Wings beating. Talons scrabbling. The gun goes off, but it does so too late and in the wrong direction, and then Gwennie is right there, pistoning a knee into the girl's gut, and stabbing the knife down into her neck.

He thumps his head back again.

Once more, the stars. And a fingernail sliver moon.

Then a flutter of wings rippling the fabric of the night.

"Balastair!" chirps a voice.

At first he thinks it's Cicero, but it's not, not at all—Cicero is still in the air, still chirping and screeching in alarm.

"Erasmus," Balastair says with a small smile. "I've missed you."

THE HEARTLAND WAR

FOR A TIME, Esther Harrington thinks: *All is according to plan.*

War has erupted.

A hobo army from the south, hundreds of them with makeshift weapons: single-shot guns made from cans and gunpowder. Some of them gifted with the Blight—those, she thinks, will be hers soon enough. They will see that the path has opened for them and that it was she who opened it.

From the north: her people, her own glorious Blightborn. Marshaled by Edvard and Siobhan. Lashing vines and cracking roots.

All around them: their Empyrean enemies, once her people.

People who denied her.

They will all break.

They will snap like the stalks of Hiram's Golden Prolific.

Their machines will rust. The skull of every mechanical will

be a pot for a plant. The spines will form trellises on which will grow flowering clematis, or wisteria, or fat and luscious grapes. From their wires will hang baskets.

And the guardsmen themselves?

Their blood will fertilize the ground.

Esther Harrington stands in the midst of all of it. The war whirling on around her like the winds of a twister, she the mistress of its eye, the keeper of its funnel. She lets pollen cascade up into the sky—streamers of golden dust—and each grain of pollen is an eye from which she can see, a tiny mote like a fingertip so that she touches what the cloud touches.

Above her head, in the night sky, one flotilla—the Ilmatar. The other, more vicious one hovers close by, launching great sonic fusillades against the corn, taking out Empyrean as often as it takes out its enemies. A clumsy hammer held in the hand of a foolish child swatting roaches and smashing his own toes in the process. That flotilla—this *war-flotilla*—matters little to her.

What matters is the one far above her.

The Ilmatar.

Because there are her children.

Balastair, her true scion, but her other adopted children, too: Cael and Wanda. Soon with a child of their own.

It's during this moment of considering motherhood—hers and Wanda's—that something very delicate breaks. Like a hair holding a sword above her head. A hair that snaps. A sword that drops.

It feels like something is ripped out of her.

Some vital organ, a reproductive system—like an apple pulped in a crushing hand, like roots ripped out of dark earth.

Balastair is dead.

Her son's life force winks, and then it's gone. Gone in a sudden wave of panic and fear—and, for one small second, a kind of bliss.

But for her, that bliss is hollow: a crass facsimile, a signal ruined by transmission. All she feels is raw acid, sick bile, burning, stinking, corrosive *sap*.

My son is dead.

Rage fills her every space.

Her body begins to shift. The flesh warps. The bones crack. Her teeth become thorns, her hands become seeking roots—she rises off the ground, her cells multiplying at an exponential rate. The air around her a whirl of golden pollen and whipping seeds, a threshing tornado of corn-leaves slicing air.

The Maize Witch—the Blight Queen now—begins to scream.

UPROOTED

THE SOUND OF GUNFIRE. Rigo pats the side of his prosthetic leg nervously. *Tap tap tap tap.* Teeth gritted. Again to Kin: "We have to go."

"Sit tight. This is all . . . this is all normal. This has to happen."

"Gunfire? Gunfire is normal?"

Kin says nothing. Even Rigo can see the pensive look.

Nearby, off to the side of a building, a garden box hangs; from it dangles pink and purple flowers and some kind of berry drupes.

Those plants begin to shudder.

Rigo ducks, shushes Kin, then points at them.

They watch as the flowers whip about, twitching at first, but then thrashing—suddenly dismantling their own box. Then climbing down the building like some kind of nightmare monster.

And that's when, in the distance, the lights start going out.

"Hell with this," Rigo says.

The Dirae runs.

Or tries to.

She dropped the gun. Her foot is hobbled. Her neck is home to a short, stubby throwing knife—and blood bubbles up over her hand holding the knife in place. She knows not to remove the knife because then she is truly dead. Behind her, the girl— Shawcatch, the Lottery winner—kneels over the dead Empyrean man. Her grief has stopped her pursuit of Enyastasia. Good. Maybe the Dirae will fight another day.

But then, while looking behind her, Enyastasia's good foot catches on a root coming up out of the cobbled street. A root that has no place here, but she has no time to consider the proper placement of roots. All she can do is hold her hands out—palms that sting as they barely catch her fall. She cries out in rage and frustration. She looks for the remaining guards, but all she sees are dead shapes bound in tightening vines.

The air shakes and shudders around her.

A shadow descends upon her.

Leaves drift through the air. Scraping as the wind moves them about.

She looks up.

Propped up on its roots: a massive tree. Earth hanging, bits of broken stone nestled in the crooks of those roots.

Its bark splits like a monstrous mouth—splintered teeth, tongue of leaf and branch. It bellows: *You killed my son!*

Then it bows toward her. She feels branches cracking over her. Stabbing into her. Something winds around her neck. Another in her mouth, down her throat. Flowers bloom inside her heart, her lungs, her stomach.

She erupts.

A garden blooms in her pieces.

The flotilla comes alive. It is a green flotilla—vineyards, trees, flowers, greenhouses. Then the greenhouses shatter. The trees become hands pulling themselves out of the ground. Vines pull bricks from bricks. Flowers twist and spit, coughing poisonous pollen.

Cael can sense it all.

Wanda must be able to as well.

Because her head lolls back on her neck.

The look on her face is one of bliss.

A horrible thought reaches him: *Maybe she's doing this all on her own.*

No—can't be. He can sense the Maize Witch's shoots and tendrils. But Wanda is in there, too. She's part of it somehow. Helping her do all this.

Pop is next to him, firing the rifle at the advancing guardsmen—

Cael has a moment. One moment to get this right.

He picks up the crate. Hauls it over to the other end of the bridge, where Gwennie is kneeling by Balastair, where Boyland has joined her and is trying to get her to come away—"Come on, Gwennie," Boyland is saying, "we have to go, we have to get out of here—"

Cael drops in front of her. Next to Balastair—who lies still, his empty eyes looking heavenward. *Don't think about him right now, there's no time.*

"Gwennie," Cael says. He yells her name, shakes her: "Gwennie!"

"Cael," she says. "Oh, gods, Cael. What's happening?"

"This," he says, thrusting the crate toward her. "Take it. Get out of here. Get to the skiff—get it down to the Heartland and as far away as you can."

"Where?"

"I don't know! Somewhere. Anywhere."

"The factory," she says. "The old processing facility."

"East of Boxelder, south of Bremerton. Yeah. There you go." That's where they first really came to know each other, saving her little brother from a misguided adventure in that old rat-trap. It's way outta the way.

And then, as if on perfect cue, the hum of a skiff's engines. Rigo pilots the skiff into the canyon between Empyrean buildings, setting it down on the far side of the bridge.

"C'mon, c'mon, c'mon!" Boyland shouts.

He and Cael help Gwennie up.

They afford one last look at Balastair.

Cicero the bird trails after them, whistling a mournful dirge.

Boyland and Gwennie head back over the bridge, hauling the crate. Cael trails after—Pop is waving them on, hobbling toward the skiff as Rigo shouts.

Cael turns, stops, grabs Wanda, shakes her: "Wanda, we have to go. I don't know what's gonna happen to this place, but it's time—"

She catches both of his wrists. Her gaze flits all over him, worry crossing her face, then bewildered rage.

"Where is the crate?" she asks.

"Don't worry about that," he says. "We have to fly!"

Her hands close tighter around his wrists. Pain shoots up his arms. Her mouth opens. He sees a throat spiraling with thorns, each red as fresh blood. The words that come out are not spoken so much as they are a song sung by all her cells—she a flower that is opening, petals blooming, a horrible thing awakening. *"We. Need. That. Crate."*

His gaze betrays him, and he knows it, but he's not sure what else to do—he looks to the skiff, to the others watching this scene unfold on the bridge. He rips a hand away from Wanda's grip, waving them on:

"Go! *Go, godsdamnit, go!*"

She takes her free hand and points it at the skiff.

No, no, no—

Her arm ripples, becomes bark, then glistening cellulose, then a tangle of roots and vines—it extends outward, a botanical geyser of plant-flesh, reaching toward the skiff even as it rises in the air—

"Wanda, stop! *Stop!*"

But she doesn't stop.

He knows what happens next. She'll tear the skiff down out of the air.

She'll have the crate. The *colonies.*

And he doesn't know what happens then.

"I'm sorry," he says. He says it softly, knowing that the words cannot be heard over the din by human ears, knowing, too, that despite that, Wanda will hear his words anyway—the apology there inside her mind, pleading as if it were a living dream.

Her eyes flick toward him, verdant, inhuman, enraged.

Cael tackles her off the bridge.

45

THE CEILING OF HEAVEN

THE SKIFF ROCKETS through the darkening streets
of the flotilla. Gwennie knows she should be frightened—Rigo is
pushing the craft to its limit, and though he's turning out to be
a far more capable pilot than she would've expected, she knows
that at any moment they could crash: hit a bridge, clip a building, go spinning off the edge of this thing like a top. And even
then, once Rigo takes it over the edge—can he pilot this thing
through the sky? Back down to the ground? Can he handle the
buffeting winds, the swift descent? Are they all dead and they
just don't know it yet?

These things should terrify her, but right now, all she feels
is raw. Shocked. Emptied of everything. The images flit through
her head like blackbirds: Balastair, shot dead. Lane, dead back in
Pegasus City. And Cael, once again high in the sky and then suddenly lost to her, plunging down to gods-know-where—crushed

by the engines in the Engine Layer, or gone through to the unyielding ground below. He survived it once. Maybe he could survive it again.

But she's not an idiot. The chances of surviving that kind of fall twice—?

A deep cold settles into her. All around her in the skiff, they're packed like sardines: the suffering and those similarly shocked. Boyland with bloody arms and haunted eyes. Pop weeping into his hands over the son he just lost anew. Rigo piloting the ship with wide eyes and white knuckles, shell-shocked into frightening competence.

And in the middle of them: a crate.

A weapon. *Her* weapon. In their hands.

Beneath them, in the city, ants already crawl. Soon they'll bring the city crashing down, killing the people who remain here. And enough will probably survive to breed more in the Heartland. Spreading out. Killing the technology they already have.

A triumph, however small, for the Maize Witch.

Back there, Pop said: *They'll wipe out the Empyrean and the Heartland. No visidexes. No motorvators. No corn to run the engines, but no engines, either.*

Rigo rockets them toward the edge of the flotilla. On her shoulder, the catbird, Cicero, trills and tra-la-las. The ghost of Balastair watching over her.

That's when something hits her. Something else said back there.

What was it Balastair told them?

About killing the ants. *Extreme heat. Or cold, maybe.*

She shivers.

Or cold.

She reaches up, grabs Rigo's shoulder, and yells:

"We need to turn around! We need to head to the control tower!"

THE BLIGHT QUEEN

CAEL GASPS.

He sits up. Everything aches.

It's morning. Everything is quiet but for the sound of wind through the corn. Hissing and crackling. The susurrus of the field.

The wind has teeth, he thinks—an absurd, old thought.

He stands up and almost gags.

Empyrean soldiers hang impaled on cornstalks, stalks that shouldn't be able to support that weight but . . . so goes the powers of the Maize Witch. The ground beneath them is red with gore. Flies hum about. Whatever battle happened here, it's now over. This is the aftermath. Which leaves the question: How did he get here?

It strikes him, then, the memory—

Falling. He and Wanda tumbling through the air. His old nightmare of falling from such a great height played out again,

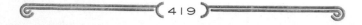

as if it was always his destiny to fall. As they plunged through cold, open air, Wanda changed. She became something else in those final moments of descent, as the hungry corn rushed up to greet them—her body ruptured in all directions, and she became some thrashing, horrible thing. Limbs and whip-cord vines and spiraling thorns. A hundred mouths, a thousand eyes. Even now he can smell the too-sweet stink of rotten flowers and ruptured fruit.

Wanda enveloping him—this time, not Esther saving him, but his Obligated. They fell hard, but she swaddled him, and they rolled—all his world gone topsy-turvy, ass-over-eyeballs, until his head struck the ground and:

Darkness.

Behind him, the whisper of something else. Not corn. Softer leaves. And the moistened squirming that comes with it.

"Cael," Wanda says.

He turns, and she's there—once more looking like Wanda except for her leaf-tipped fingers and iridescent eyes. She's not alone.

Cael's blood goes to cold sap.

"You . . . what . . ." He can barely find words. "Esther."

Esther Harrington is like a spider caught in a web of her own design—her naked human form seems small in the massive nest of plant matter surrounding her. Vines like snakes hold her up. Flowers bloom and die and rebloom. Flytrap mouths snap at the air. The gunshot crack of roots breaking as they knot together. Fruits swell, ripen, then pop.

He is small in her shadow.

"You may call me the *Blight Queen*," she says. Her voice comes not just from her mouth but from all around him—as if the corn echoes it.

"The war is over, Cael," Wanda says.

"It was short," the Blight Queen says, her voice resonating with a buzzy sound, as if her body was home to a hive of hornets. "Our time is now."

Cael wants to ask *who won the war*, but he knows: *nobody did*. Nobody but her.

"Where is my weapon?" the Queen asks him.

"I don't know what you mean," he lies.

"The crate. My *son's* legacy." Her voice thrums with anger. "You know."

"I sent it away. We can't use it. We use that, everything changes— "

"We can. We must. The corn must die."

"It's not just the corn. You know that. It'll doom all the Heartland. Those ants will kill all the progress we've made." He shakes his head, grimly resolute. "Don't lie to me. You coulda killed the Golden Prolific any time. Right? *Right?*"

All she does is smile.

He goes on: "How much of this has been you all along? You invented the damn corn. What about the piss-blizzards?"

"My eyes and ears. And how else would I spread my Gift?" She drifts closer to him. "Where. Are. My. Colonies."

"I told you, I sent them away— "

A cracking branch hits him across the face, cutting his brow and knocking him to the ground. A vine snakes along the blasted, flattened corn and then around his ankle. He tries to crabwalk away, but it yanks him forward again, toward her.

"We have an opportunity here. My son is dead, but I think of you like my son. A scion. An offshoot. All your life, you lived in poverty. Hardscrabble and dust-caked. That can change. Your sister. Your father. Wanda. Your *daughter*. We can all be a family. We can all have whatever we want. Our Gift grants us that, but only in a world we control. Can you imagine what that would be?"

Wanda smiles sadly. "We can finally have a taste of a good life. Not just for us. But for our daughter. Don't you want that?"

"Is this what you want?" he asks Wanda. "To be some kind of . . . monster, some murdering freak of nat-*aaaaaaaar*—" The vine tightens and yanks, snapping the bone inside his ankle. The pain is white-hot, like staring into the sun. "Please. Please. Stop."

Wanda flinches at his cry. She looks to Esther. Her voice, a grief-struck plea. "Don't hurt him."

"He stands in the way of our future," the Blight Queen says. Then, to Cael: "Do you want to limp like your father?"

The vine coils farther up his leg, to his knee, to his thigh.

It tightens.

"I can make that happen for you," the corn whisper-screams.

"Wait—" Wanda says.

But the Blight Queen hisses at her, and Wanda grows quiet.

"We can have a different world," Cael says, growling through the pain. "We can do it our way. A world where we all work toward something bigger than us. Where we try to figure it all out together. Pop was right, Wanda. This is about power.

We can't just trade one monster for another, can't go from the Empyrean to—"

The vine twists again. His shinbone cracks.

He weeps, head slamming back into the corn. He presses his fists against his eyes. "Please. Lord and Lady, don't do this. . . ."

The Blight Queen hovers closer. Other vines tickle the ground and slide up alongside him, tracing lines up his arms, his sides. "I should have made you like I made Wanda. I put more of myself inside her. She's more like me than anyone else in this world." She chuckles. "She practically *is* me. My wishes made manifest. My flesh, my blooms, my fragrance. We share it. You are a rogue shoot. Proving yourself an invasive, a mutation I cannot abide. I will give you one last chance, Cael, my son. I saved you so many times, but I will end you if I must. You won't make me do that, will you? If you make me hunt down my prize, I will do so with great cruelty. I will take your precious Gwennie and I will tear her to pieces. The earth will digest your father. Young Rodrigo—a plump little dumpling. Him I'll keep alive. My thorns can drink from him for endless nights, that fat little tick."

"Wanda," Cael says. "Please."

The vine breaks his knee. He bites through the tip of his tongue.

The Blight Queen sighs. When she sighs, all the corn sighs. A shudder of stalks, leaves, tassels.

"Then I will do this the hard way."

He suddenly can't breathe. Vines coil around his neck, tightening. He holds his arm up—his own Blight-vine grows again, but it's nothing against her. She catches it, braids her own matter into it, then rips it out at the root, unmooring the whole thing from his arm and chest. Wanda screams, but the sound of her cries are lost under the thrumming drum of his blood trapped in his ears—head like a bucket under a rainstorm, like a blister about to pop—

Darkness—

At the edges—

Wanda clawing at the Blight Queen—

His heart stops.

Pulses. Like light flashing underwater.

Something inside of him.

Blood-slick vines.

Wanda standing over him. Tear-shiny face.

Screaming. Soundlessly.

The breath he takes feels infinite. A great heaving, sucking gulp—air rushing in, in, in, so much air that he feels like he must have a hole in him where the air is leaking right back out—

But then he can't take in any more breaths and—

The air rushes out in a hot, ragged exhale.

He tastes blood.

Above him, movement. The darkness of unconsciousness—maybe even of death—recedes, and when it does, he sees Wanda and Esther the Blight Queen. They smash together, rising up on roots like stilts, hundreds of vines twisting together, braiding, merging. *No.* Not merging—battling.

He tries to stand—but again his breath leaves him, and worse, he's reminded that his one leg is now nothing more than a shattered broomstick held together by the barest splinters. Cael drops back to one knee, screaming.

From the tangle of roots and vines above his head, he sees Wanda's face emerge—she looks upon him in horror.

And the Blight Queen tears Wanda apart.

Wanda knows she's dying.

And even now, a part of her thinks: *I deserve this.* She has gone against the woman who created her. Esther. Her new mother, who took the frail thing that Wanda once was and changed her. Made her strong. Took her differences and made them meaningful. But then Esther—the Blight Queen now—was going to hurt Cael.

And Cael said things. Things that made sense.

He spoke of a world that was better. Where they worked together. And where the power wasn't just in the hands of one group. That, Wanda realized, was what the Blight Queen wanted. She didn't want freedom. She didn't care about the Heartland. She only wanted power. The same thing everyone wanted.

Except Wanda. Wanda didn't want power. She just wanted Cael.

And then the Blight Queen killed him. Stopped his heart dead.

Wanda leaped upon him, plunged herself into him—all her threads and shoots and runners. She found his heart, squeezed it and gave it life anew, and once it began to beat again, she threw herself against the one she once thought of as *Mother.*

A betrayal. She knows that.

Then she heard Cael awaken in pain—and Esther seized the opportunity. Now Wanda's the one who's dying. Esther is rending her apart. Prying branches and serpentine vines punch through her, hook her by the ribs, curl around her hip bones, all of them pulling in different directions.

Then, suddenly, a shriek. A familiar sound. She feels Esther hesitate—and again Wanda can see. Through the maze of roots and the mesh of leaves she sees a surprising face: Mole, the boy, once one of Boyland's Butchers, lately of Esther's entourage. He's shrieking, clambering up Esther's body and smacking her limbs and tendrils with a nail-stuck board. Wanda can feel Esther's pain and surprise.

"Told you not to hurt her!" Mole whoops.

It's a small moment, but valuable.

A vine curls around his middle, flings him into the corn.

For one moment, Esther's face is exposed again—her true face, her human face.

Wanda feels Cael's awareness flare anew.

And a ball bearing flies straight and pocks Esther right in the temple. An arc of amber blood squirts from the wound. Wanda sees Cael on the ground—the slingshot in his hand, the sling's pocket dangling free as his eyes roll back in his head—

Esther screams, mouth wide.

Wanda puts everything she has into it.

She plunges herself in through that opening.

And she tears the Blight Queen asunder.

Cael awakens once more.

Wanda holds him close.

"It worked," she says, kissing his cheek, kissing his mouth. Spit connecting them—she laughs, giggles nervously, wipes it away.

"Wh . . ." It feels like he's talking through a throat lined with rusty razor blades. "What . . . did you . . . do?"

"I opened up your chest and made your heart beat again."

"Oh . . . Okay."

He passes out again.

The sun is high in the sky when he awakens.

This time, it's like waking from a fever dream. Sweat-slick and terrified.

His head rests in Wanda's lap. He looks up and she smiles down at him.

She helps him sit up. And that's when he sees Esther Harrington.

Dead. Or presumably so. Her nude human form mounded atop a hillock of dead vines and arthritic roots. Her eyes stare out, empty. Her hair lies draped over the desiccated plants like a waterfall.

"I had to kill her," Wanda says. "Because she killed you. I'm sorry about everything. She was in my head. I really thought . . .

I really thought she was my mother, in a way. But I broke her tender neck and pulped her brain. I think maybe her consciousness fled into the corn. But don't worry, I think I can kill that, too." She smiles sweetly and kisses his cheek. "I love you, Cael McAvoy."

"I . . . love you, too, Wanda Mecklin." He doesn't say: *I don't know who we are or who we're gonna become or if we can even be together.* But he does love her.

"Whatever," Mole says, standing there, his cheeks smudged with dirt. He flings down the board he was holding and, shaking his head, stomps off into the corn.

EPILOGUE

LONG WAY
FROM BOXELDER

THUNDER RUMBLES across the Heartland. In the distance, rain falls from gray clouds—like pulling insulation down through a ruined ceiling.

Amaranth McAvoy hawks up a loogey and spits it in the limestone gravel of the driveway—*splat*. She bites on a fingernail, chomps it down to the cuticle, and flicks away what she chews. Her feet tap. Her fingers snap.

"You are so gross," comes a voice from behind her.

"Well, howdy, Ginger," Amaranth says, cocking an eyebrow. "And whatever. I spit like a boy, so what? Boys do it and nobody says boo to them about it."

Ginger Zinger—tall, lean, wispy as wheatgrass, pretty as a pink rose—shakes her red hair and pouts. "So. Gross." She pulls out a small brown bottle from her leather satchel. "Nip of gin?"

Amaranth rolls her eyes. "I ain't drinking now. Today's too important." Fancy little Empyrean girl, that Ginger. Whatever.

Amaranth casts her eye back toward the house and the barn. No sign of Pop. Good. She drops to her knee like she's about to tie her shoe, but instead, she rolls one of the logs marking the lines of their driveway back by a couple feet, exposing a dug trench. "Besides, gin? Ick."

Inside: a few bags of fruit, vegetables, goat jerky. Plus a visidex and a long lever-action rifle with the picture of a fox engraved into each side.

"Holy hell-wang, a rifle." Ginger whistles. "And how old is that visidex?"

"Does it matter?" Amaranth shrugs. "Got all the maps we need."

Another voice calls to them. A boy.

"I don't think we should do this!"

It's Ernie Cozido.

"Ernie, shush," Amaranth says. "You don't have to come. Nobody's twisting your nipple."

Ginger arches an eyebrow, then sighs—a common sound, as if All The Things exasperate her. Amaranth swears: that girl is like an old woman.

"Ernie *is too* going with us," Ginger says, and then to Ernie: "And don't think you're getting out of this. This is important to Am, so it's important to us. Are we copacetic on that point, little dumpling?"

Ernie—gawky, with a bright white set of overbitten chompers—nods. "I know, I know, I'm coming. It's just—I'm scared. I've never been out of the Heartland before. It's . . . scary." He sighs. "And I hate the rain. And the jungle. They have bugs down there big enough to suck your eyeballs clean. They do that. Suck all the juice out of your eyeballs and then plant eggs in there and then you're all bug-eyes after that."

"You are so dang dramatic, sheesh." Amaranth rolls her eyes. "It isn't scary. It's just . . . new. New things are awesome, old things are dumb." She wets her lips and picks up one of the bags. "Guys, I just . . . I just wanna find her. Okay? We won't go far. I promise."

That is a promise she's gonna have to break. She feels bad about it now, dragging them along like this, but it is what it is. She needs them and figures it's better to ask forgiveness than to ask permission.

A few drops of rain patter against the tin barn roof, like little stones thrown. Ginger says: "Your pop's gone, right? He won't know we left right away? I'm presuming we have some lead time."

"He's off at Mader-Atcha City, selling a couple goats."

Ginger grins. "Then shall we?"

"I'm ready," Ernie says.

"Me, too," Amaranth says, puffing out her chest and her chin, trying to make it look like she isn't scared, too. "Let's go find my mama."

From the knothole in the barn door, Cael peers out.

He watches his daughter and her two friends hoist their packs. Amaranth picks up the rifle—his rifle, or, more properly, Pop-Pop's rifle—and then they wander out down the long drive-way to the plasto-sheen road.

He sighs. "They're headed into the River Glades through Bleakmarsh."

"And you want me to go after them."

He hasn't seen Gwennie in a handful of months, but she hasn't changed much. A little ropier. Leaner and meaner. Her hair is longer, too, bound up into tails on each side of her head in the Moon Coast way—can't see it under her rumpled leathers, but her one arm is inked from wrist to shoulder. All the various sigils and signs of the places she's been, the people she's seen.

"No," Cael says. "I just . . . want you to follow along. Make sure they're okay. Things ain't easy out there."

It was fifteen years or so ago, when the walls came down, when the world opened up. The Empyrean had to park their flotillas after the day the Blight Queen died. Together, and only together, he and Wanda reached out and killed all the corn in the amount of time it takes to snap your fingers, the reign of Hiram's Golden Prolific brought to a jarring halt—and that was a rough transition all its own, turning the floating cities into terrestrial ones (modeled in fact after what Lane had accomplished with Pegasus City) and helping merge all the worlds: the Heartlanders, the Empyrean, the Blighted, the hobos. At first, chaos reigned. Things still aren't quite right. Fights rise up— folks get hurt, killed. But a relative peace has been ongoing in this part of the world. It's not the same everywhere else. Pockets of the old Empyrean civilization still exist. Not flotillas, but in mountaintop fortresses, jungle camps, undersea bases.

And turns out that not everyone in the world gets along with everyone *else* in the world, too. The fisher-folk of the Braided Glades, for instance, got something they call a "blood debt" against the River Glade nomads, and that means Amaranth and the other two kids are heading right toward bad mojo.

Rigo groans behind them and gets up off the barrel he's sitting on. He scratches his big beard, then tucks a bit of his long hair behind his ears. "I still think we just should've told them we knew their plan. That would've stopped them."

"Uh-uh." Gwennie shakes her head. "Cael's right on this one."

"A rare moment," Cael says.

"A rare moment, indeed, McAvoy." She smirks. On her shoulder, Cicero the catbird shuffles on his feet, trilling and warbling. "What I mean, Rigo, is that those kids are gonna do what they're gonna do either way. Remember us at that age? Going off half-cocked at everything."

Cael chuckled. "Merelda was the worst."

"Pssh. You just *think* she was the worst. We were always charging into dead towns or corn processing facilities. Sticking our noses where they had no business being stuck. Blight rats and hobo traps and . . . well. Point is, they'll find a way to jump whatever fence we build. Might as well let them do it."

"Fine, fine," Rigo says, nodding reluctantly. "You know, Ernie's not going to be good out there. This isn't . . . his thing."

"I'll make sure he's all right," Gwennie says. "Maybe this'll put a little hair on his knuckles. It did for you."

"Hair on my knuckles and a leg chopped off." Rigo laughs, shrugs. But Cael can see all the old ghosts flitting about behind his eyes. Memories. Good ones, sure. But all the bad ones, too.

"We'd go, but—" Cael hobbles over to the middle of the room. "Rigo's got six other kids to worry about, and I turned into my father."

"How is Pop?" she asks.

"He's good. Tired, you know."

"And your mama?"

"Well, she's doing all right," he says, sucking air through his teeth. "Making improvements every day." After the Empyrean came down to the Heartland and became a part of it, things changed. Education opened up again. Technology, too. And part of that meant medicine. New procedures, new techniques. They got her on some kind of gene therapy; took a few years, but all the tumors went away. Still, though, she had to relearn what it was to be . . . human. To walk around and to talk. She remembered things—but she processed most of it like it was a dream (or, sometimes, a nightmare). "Pop helps her around. They have each other now, and Merelda when she's not off on some half-assed adventure, and they have Amaranth, too."

"All the more reason to keep her safe."

"Yep. How's Scooter and Squirrel?"

"Still married."

He laughs. "Marriage. Them. Who'da thunk it?"

She reaches across, holds his hands. "Could've been us, once."

A few moments of quiet stretch into an awkward silence. Rigo grumbles and mumbles: "I think that's my cue. Gwennie, it has been a pleasure, and I appreciate what you're doing." He grunts as he lifts up on his one good foot and plants a scratchy-beard kiss on her cheek. "Thank you, my dear."

He heads out the front.

"You hear about Boyland?" Cael asks Gwennie.

"Mayor now, so I hear."

"Lieutenant mayor or something of Mader-Atcha City."

She laughs. "Long way from Boxelder."

"Jeezum Crow, you ain't wrong about that." Cael pauses. "He

saved the Heartland in a way. Both of you did." The Ilmatar had been taken over by the ants—enough where if that damn thing landed, it would've been a plague on all of them. Boyland and Gwennie went to the control room of that flotilla and put themselves at great risk to save the day. It was Gwennie's idea—fly the flotilla high enough so that the cold kills the ants.

It worked, miracle of miracles. They were able to fly it high enough to kill the colony, keep the city from falling apart, and then land it—if very, very roughly—down in the corn. The Ilmatar is still out there now. Like Pegasus City was meant to be—it's out there now, home to some of the old Empyrean remnants and Heartlanders, too.

"Forget the old days." Gwennie squeezes his hands. "How're you holding up?"

"Ah. Eh. Fine."

"C'mon. Spit it out."

"It's good, it's good, everything's good." He can see her lean in, her smile growing bigger—it's the look she used to get when she was gonna tickle little Amaranth. "Fine, fine, it's hard. Pop's old. I feel old—gods, my leg sometimes feels like it's burning up. But it's more than that. It's something . . . bigger. Deeper." At that, his Blight-vine twitches around his arm.

She arches an eyebrow.

"Can't you feel it?" he asks. "Everything's changing. Life goes on. World gets older. Things are good. Amaranth is good. But she . . . you know, she doesn't know her mother. That's what this is all about. Used to be Wanda would come around, but she's . . ." He sighs. "The Blight took a harder hold of her than it did most others. She's just like Esther was. Lot of power, and I think it messes with her head. I've heard she's doing good things in the Glades, though. Helping people farm the banks of the river. Irrigate and all that. But . . ."

Gwennie raises an eyebrow. "But?"

"But you know, she's still out there . . . killing the old Empyrean. Hunting them down like they're war criminals. And maybe they are, I dunno. But that's gonna be hard for Amaranth to deal with. Wanda isn't really human anymore. I think I still am, but her—she's too far gone." The two of them were together for a while—long enough to have the baby and raise it a few years—and for a time Wanda did a good job at masquerading. Pretending to be something she wasn't. But it was a force like wind, or gravity, or age—she was what she was, and one night she just left. Cael loved her, but he was scared of her, too. And Wanda's absence struck Amaranth hard—it was a hole that grew year after year. "How'll that be for Amaranth? She's expecting . . . I don't know what. For her *mother* to be there. Not some *monster*."

"Everything's gonna be hard for her to deal with, Cael. Maybe easier for her than it was for us. That's something, at least."

"That is something, I guess."

He wonders if they had a part in that, in changing the world, making it better. Sometimes his ego lets him believe it. Other times, he's not so sure.

Gwennie leans in, gives him a hug, a kiss on the cheek. She smells like soap still. Clean, fresh. But there's a little grit there, too. An earthiness. Under her fingernails. Behind her ears. In the leather of her coat.

"I miss you," she says.

"I miss you, too. But you ain't ever gonna settle down, and as for me"—he spreads out his arms—"that's all I can do these days. Settle down deeper."

"Maybe one day I can convince you to come on another adventure."

"I doubt that."

She winks. "At least you didn't say no. That's a change."

"I guess it is. I guess it is." He nods. "All right, she's got a bit of a lead on you now. Thanks for keeping her safe, Gwen."

"Anything for you, Captain."

And then she's gone.

And he misses her like he misses his youth.

ABOUT THE AUTHOR

Michelle Wendig

CHUCK WENDIG is the author of The Heartland Trilogy and the Atlanta Burns series for young adults, as well as numerous novels for adults, including the upcoming *Star Wars: Aftermath*. He is also a game designer and screenwriter. He cowrote the short film *Pandemic*, the feature film *HiM*, and the Emmy-nominated digital narrative *Collapsus*. Chuck lives in "Pennsyltucky" with his family.

He blogs at www.terribleminds.com.